Local Author Dies in
Tragic Household Accident

Well-known crime fiction author, Annie Morrissey (55),
died tragically on Tuesday evening (3 July) after falling
from a ladder in the garden of her home in the rural
hamlet of Buckstone, South Shropshire.

According to the West Mercia police, the author's body
was discovered by a neighbour on Wednesday morning.

Annie Morrissey's agent, Caro Canto of the Canto
Literary Agency, paid tribute to a 'wonderful writer and
treasured client', and said, 'It's such a tragic loss, and it
breaks my heart that she won't be here to launch
Overlooked, her latest, action-packed thriller, which will hit
the shelves in October.' Ms Canto added, 'It's currently
available for pre-order from all good book sites.'

Local residents also expressed shock at the author's
death. Lady Sheila Ripley (92) said, 'Annie hadn't lived in
the hamlet for long, but she will be missed. Unlike some
people I could mention, she was a conscientious
neighbour.' Elaine Baxter (85), a volunteer at the
Buckstone Community Shoppe said, 'She'd pop in here for
a cheese scone and a natter most weeks. Shocking way to
go as well. She didn't seem the type to be up and down
ladders and that.'

Ms Morrissey is survived by a daughter, Niamh, and a
son, Brian. Neither were available for comment.

From the *Salop Advertiser Online*.

1

How *to* **Kill** *a* Crime Writer

Sarah Lotz is a screenwriter and award-winning novelist whose previous work has been translated into over twenty languages. Her last novel, *Impossible*, was shortlisted for the Bollinger Everyman Wodehouse Prize for Comic Fiction & the Comedy Women in Print Prize. She lives on the Welsh borders in a suspiciously uneventful hamlet with her family and far too many rescue dogs.

Also by Sarah Lotz

Impossible

How to Kill a Crime Writer

SARAH LOTZ

HarperCollins*Publishers*

HarperCollins*Publishers* Ltd
1 London Bridge Street,
London SE1 9GF

www.harpercollins.co.uk

HarperCollins*Publishers*
Macken House,
39/40 Mayor Street Upper,
Dublin 1, D01 C9W8
Ireland

First published by HarperCollins*Publishers* Ltd 2026

1

A catalogue record for this book is available from the British Library.

ISBN: 978-0-00-846405-9 (HB)
ISBN: 978-0-00-846406-6 (TPB)

This novel is entirely a work of fiction.
The names, characters and incidents portrayed in it are
the work of the author's imagination. Any resemblance to
actual persons, living or dead, events or localities is
entirely coincidental.

Typeset in Sabon LT Pro by
Palimpsest Book Production Ltd, Falkirk, Stirlingshire

Printed and Bound in the UK using 100% Renewable Electricity
at CPI Group (UK) Ltd

For Charlie Martins, Tadeusz Bradecki and Joe Vaz.
And for everyone who loved them.

A PROLOGUE AND A HALF

Play dead. Play dead. Play dead.

The wound at the back of her head is still leaking blood, but Leah Rebecca Overton blocks out the pain and cracks open her eyes. The light is dying, and far above her, leaves tremble in the wind. Other than the scrape of a shovel digging into earth, and the grunts of exertion from the man intent on burying her alive, it's deathly quiet. This woodland is in the depths of a vast, privately owned country estate, miles from the nearest road.

Another shovelful of dirt lands on her chest, and it takes everything she has not to flinch. *Not yet*, she tells herself. *Play dead.* She has to bide her time. Gather her strength before she acts.

No one will be coming to her aid. The cops aren't an option. Not in this rural county, where sheep and shotguns outnumber the residents, and secrets usually stay buried. And 'usually' is the keyword here because pressing into her back are the skeletal remains of the poor soul she'd unearthed from this makeshift grave just seconds before she heard the roar of the gamekeepers' quad bikes. She could've run. Didn't. Knows what Jed, her mentor, would've said about her decision to stay and fight: 'Why take unnecessary risks, girl?'

The answer's simple: *Because it's who she is. It's who she's always been.*

The odds had been against her but that was nowt new, and the shovel she'd brought along had come in handy. Took one of the men out with a blow to the throat. Side-swiped the second, enjoying the crunch of cartilage as his nose imploded beneath his balaclava. Would've dispatched the ringleader too if he hadn't snuck up behind her and slammed his shotgun into the back of her head, rendering her temporarily unconscious.

More dirt peppers her body, and she hears her assailant muttering, 'Bye-bye, bitch.'

Rage gives her the strength she needs, and she curls her fingers around the femur belonging to his previous victim. The time for playing dead is over.

Not finishing her off was his first mistake. Calling her a bitch will be his last.

That's how my mother began *Overlooked*, the sixth – and final – novel in her bestselling 'Private Investigator Leah Rebecca Overton' thriller series.

It's quite hard-hitting, isn't it? And no wonder, because 'always begin a book with a bang' had been Mum's motto, and she'd followed this to a tee. For example, Book Three kicks off with a passenger plane crashing into Ilkley Moor, and in Book Four's prologue, Leah Rebecca Overton heroically slides her motorbike under the wheels of a malfunctioning self-drive to stop it from smashing into a Tesco Express.

For my mother's sake, I wish I could do that too (begin this book with a bang, I mean, not crash a Ducati into a runaway Tesla). But seeing as what happened to me was far more implausible, it's probably best if I stick to the truth.

LITTLE SHOP(PE) OF HORRORS

It all kicked off on an otherwise typical Monday morning in early autumn, four months after I'd made the fateful – and ultimately near-fatal – decision to move into my dead mother's cottage in rural Shropshire.

I'm not great at recalling specific dates and times, but I know for a fact that it began on a Monday because that was the day that Glenn-from-next-door always set off to do his big weekly shop. This meant that Brian and I were rudely awoken that morning by a cacophony of slamming doors, parping car horns, and Glenn and his wife Janet having needlessly shouty exchanges ('I can't find the bags-for-life again, Jan!' 'Have you checked the boot, Glenn?' 'Course I have, pet – oh, hang on,' etcetera).

As I did every Monday, I thought, *you're just driving to the Aldi to get some peas, Glenn, not plotting an insurgence against Putin,* followed by the more melancholic, *had this weekly kerfuffle bothered Mum too?*

If it had, she'd never said so – not to me, anyway. One of the most painful aspects about living in my mother's cottage was discovering how little I'd known about her day-to-day life in the hamlet, and it didn't help that this was partly my fault.

After all, I hadn't exactly been enthusiastic about her

decision to move to rural Shropshire in the first place. In fact, back when she'd broken the news that she was swapping her Sheffield townhouse for a country cottage in the Midlands, I genuinely thought she was winding me up.

'Don't be daft, Niamh,' she'd said. 'Why would I joke about a thing like that?'

'Because you're a hardcore townie, aren't you?' She was forever striding along pavements in designer coats, mainlining artisanal espressos, and popping into independent bookstores. 'I mean, you've never even been glamping, Mum.'

'I fancy a change of lifestyle, and it'll do me good to get in touch with nature.'

'Why that part of the country, though?' I'd always assumed she was a hardcore northerner. She'd spent her whole life in Sheffield, and most of her novels were set in Yorkshire. 'It's hours away from everyone you know.' *Including me*, I didn't say.

She dodged the question, which wasn't like her, and said instead: 'Tell you what, why don't I take you to see the cottage next weekend?'

We spent the four-hour journey there singing along to the Abba Gold CD that was permanently jammed in her Mini's ancient sound system, which lightened the mood and gave us an excuse to avoid discussing my latest run-in with the bailiffs. 'Just wait till you see the place, Niamh,' Mum kept saying as we neared our destination, 'you're not going to believe it.'

She was right about that. As we drove along country lanes that were eerily devoid of traffic, and through villages that were pleasantly devoid of people, all I could think was: *which is it, Mum – midlife crisis or nervous breakdown?* I should stress that this wasn't because of the area itself. If anything, the landscape around Buckstone is almost *too* beautiful – all soft rolling hills, swathes of ancient woodland, and single lane tracks that go nowhere – and because hardly anyone knows that Shropshire exists, the local wildlife hasn't yet been decimated (there are even some hedgehogs and insects left in the county). No. The issue was that although the hamlet had the charming, timeless vibe of a folk horror film, it consisted of little more than a row of terraced cottages, a twee village hall, a tiny church, and an eccentric volunteer-run shoppe (the shop's spelling, not mine), and I was struggling to picture my urbanite mother sipping tea with a vicar, joining the Nimby brigade and trying her hand at cosy crime mysteries instead of hard-boiled thrillers.

But if nature was what she was after, she'd come to the right place, because the lane we took to reach her new home – half a mile from the hamlet – was so defiantly rural that it petered out into woodland (which, in turn, petered out into Wales). And I could see why she'd been taken with the cottage itself. With its higgledy-piggledy, white-washed stone walls, quirky lattice windows, and quirkier porch, it couldn't have been more chocolate-boxy, and its front garden was blooming with daffodils and some other attractive plants that were probably weeds.

'Well?' she asked. 'What do you think?'

'I really like it.' I did. I would've liked it a lot more if it weren't for the proximity of the neighbouring properties. Directly opposite lurked a sullen barn conversion that resembled an apocalypse bunker, and the cottage was sandwiched between two architectural opposites: a bleak manor-style house that could've been drawn by an evil child, and an aggressively well-maintained new build that looked as if it had been accidentally beamed out of suburbia. I remember thinking that there was something tragically self-conscious about the newer house – perhaps it knew it was supposed to be on an executive housing estate. In its gravelled frontage, two depressed gnomes fished in vain for a garden, and even its wheelie bin gleamed. Of course, I didn't know then that its lack of greenery was down to Glenn's unhealthy addiction to his hedge strimmer; nor could I have known that in eighteen months' time, those gnomes would end up being clues in an incredibly odd murder investigation.

But it was the sinister manor that took up most of my attention. Its front garden was a riot of rose buses, but the house itself was sepia toned, as if it existed in an era before technicolour was invented. 'That place looks intriguing.'

'Isn't it fabulous?' my mother said without any sarcasm. 'Apparently, it was the country seat of an aristocratic family which used to own all the surrounding land and properties.' Curiously, despite being a socialist, she seemed to fancy the prospect of living in the cap-doffing shadow of a mini version of Downton Abbey. 'According to the estate agent, the elderly "lady of the manor" still lives there.'

Although it was a bright spring day, the manor's curtains were all drawn. 'Perhaps she's a vampire,' I said, unaware that my future self would go to great lengths to avoid being emotionally drained by Lady Sheila Ripley.

The quirkiness extended to the cottage's interior, and in the farmhouse-style kitchen, there was an ancient range cooker that even I found charming, mainly because I assumed that I'd never have to use it. The place clearly hadn't been lived in for a long time and reeked of neglect, but it came across as cosy rather than ominous.

'It needs some remedial work, of course,' said my mother, massively understating things.

It couldn't have been more of a contrast to her usual minimalistic aesthetic. There were only two bedrooms – one of which was little more than a box room – and instead of a lounge, there was a 'snug', which did what it said on the tin. 'Where will you put all your books?'

'The attic's fairly spacious, so I'm thinking of converting that into a writing room and library.'

Behind the kitchen was a tiny cloakroom, and a utilitarian area my mother insisted on calling a 'boot room'.

'Isn't that discriminatory against coats and hats?' (This made her smile.)

The back door opened out onto a covered patio, beyond which stretched an extensive, tree-strewn garden, which would've been lovely too if it hadn't been hemmed in by the manor's crumbling boundary wall and the suburban interloper's creosoted fence.

'It was the garden that sold me on it.' More oddness – she'd never met a houseplant she couldn't murder. 'Just look at that chestnut tree, Niamh. Isn't it magnificent? And listen to the bird song. You don't get that in Sheffield, do you?'

You did, but not at that volume. 'Are you sure about this, Mum? They've only just accepted your offer, so it's not too late to back out.'

A sigh. 'Oh, here we go.'

'I'm just worried you'll get lonely out here.'

'I've got work to keep me busy. And I can always get a cat.'

I still wasn't convinced. She wasn't an impulsive person, and this move smacked of impulsivity. But as far as I know, my mother hadn't regretted escaping to the countryside, which is all that matters. And after I did the same, I also gradually began to adjust to rural living.

Well, very gradually. I'm not usually fussy about where I live, but I'd be lying if I said it was easy coming to terms with the area's lack of diversity and Deliveroo and its abundance of unusually large spiders and local gossip, and never having lived in anything but a flat before, acclimatising to the elderly cottage's anthropomorphic creaks and groans took some doing too.

Far thornier to navigate was living in the shadow of my mother's death, but it helped that I put in place several grief-avoidance strategies, such as gaming and binge-watching whenever I was awake, and steering clear of the attic and the Death Zone outside. All the same, if it hadn't been for Brian, I'm not sure I would've coped. He was the main reason I'd decided to live there in the first place – it wasn't as if he could've moved in with me, seeing as at the time, I was technically homeless – and it was a welcome relief to discover that we were both undemanding creatures of habit. My days usually involved grief-distracting, snacking, and hiding from the neighbours; Brian's consisted of napping, snacking, and psychologically torturing Lady Sheila's Bedlington Terrier. As long as I remembered to feed him, and he remembered not to sleep on my keyboard, we got along swimmingly (in all the ways that matter, my relationship with my mother's cat was the most successful one I'd ever had).

I knew from experience that if you lose yourself in other worlds, and do the same thing every day, time tends to pass in a blur. And as the weeks blurred into months, I stupidly allowed myself to fall into a false sense of security.

Which brings me back to that Monday morning.

Unaware that the blurring would shortly be coming to an abrupt and shocking end, after Glenn had parped off to the supermarket, I dug through my floordrobe for some clothes that weren't *too* covered in cat hair, and slunk downstairs to give Brian his breakfast.

It's strange to think that the worst thing I expected to deal with that day was a bit of local gossip. Well, that and the dread I always felt whenever I was forced to walk into the hamlet for supplies, but that was my own fault for: a) forgetting to place the online grocery order again; and b) doing absolutely nothing to address my worsening social isolation and anxiety issues. Still, at least I wouldn't have to worry about running into Glenn because it would be hours before he returned from his epic journey to the nearest hub (an upmarket town fifteen miles away that was predominantly populated by spaniels and men in burgundy trousers). To be fair, other than his intrusively noisy shopping and gardening habits, and a suspicion that he didn't believe in the climate crisis, I didn't have anything particularly personal against him, but I preferred to avoid him because he'd found my mother's body. Janet wasn't much of a threat because she rarely ventured out into the wild, and the owner of the barn bunker opposite – aka the Weekend Wanker – wasn't an issue today because he only pitched up on Fridays or whenever his alarm went off. In any case, I'd never actually spoken to him, and according to Glenn, Pam and Elaine from the shoppe, the postie, and the man who delivered the heating oil, the Wanker only ever communicated via abusive messages on the community WhatsApp.

So that just left Lady Sheila.

Fishy gunk inhaled, Brian sashayed off to pursue his greatest passion – lolling in the maple tree that overlooked the manor's walled garden, waiting for poor old Petticoat the terrier to emerge. I grabbed my backpack and headed out too, albeit with less enthusiasm.

Fortunately, apart from a couple of squirrels who were having a domestic in the barn bunker's driveway, the coast was clear, and hoody up, I made a break for it, keeping my head down in case Janet was glaring out of her kitchen window again.

It was the sort of crisp, cloud-free day that the locals would describe as 'beautiful for autumn, isn't it?' before launching into a forensic analysis of the potholes in the neighbouring village, and other than a trio of highly strung pheasants, I had the lane to myself. The problem with walking is that it stimulates thought, but I distracted myself by swishing through crisp piles of fallen leaves, listening to a murder podcast, keeping an eye out for Sheila, and dodging the postal van, which had the tendency to cruise around the hamlet like the shark out of *Jaws*. At the end of the lane, I crossed over and hurried past the row of terraced cottages, which would've been lovely if they hadn't been parasitised by PVC conservatories; the tiny church with its enormous, out-of-proportion graveyard; and the village hall, with its noticeboard advertising activities like *Tea and Me!* and *Chair Yoga!*

When I reached the shoppe, I surreptitiously glanced through the window to see what I'd be up against. Today's volunteers were doppelganger shoppe stalwarts, Pam and Elaine, both of whom had coronas of white hair tinged with yellow as if they'd been dipped in nicotine at birth (I knew for a fact that they weren't related, because they were always saying 'everyone thinks we're sisters but we're not'). By anyone's measure they were pleasant people, but like everyone in the hamlet, they enjoyed talking about my mother, and I'd learned the hard way that death could be a particularly gruelling conversational subgenre. People either backed away from it, eyes glassy with existential dread, shared their own Death Stories, or – if I was particularly unlucky – fished for minutiae about my mother's accident.

I took out my phone, and as I shouldered my way in, breathing in the familiar waft of mouldy veg, I pretended to be on an important work call. '. . . can I call you back? . . . Oh. Well, if it's *urgent* . . .' I shot Pam and Elaine an apologetic, *wish I could chat, but my hands are tied* smile (it wasn't the first time I'd used this ruse), and as I filled my basket with scones, a bloated white loaf, and cheese with unidentifiable fruity bits in it, I blabbered on about *blue sky thinking* and *getting the reports in asap.*

The real danger would come when I was paying, but fortunately, by the time I made it to the counter, still 'mmhmming' into the phone, another hamletee had wandered in for a cake and a chinwag, and they were all having too much fun dissing the council to pay me much mind.

Embarrassingly, halfway out the door, I received a real call from Daphne, my stepmother. I'd stupidly forgotten to reply to her last email, so I had no choice but to take it.

'Oh, thank the Lord,' she said when I answered. 'I've been worrying about you, honey.'

'Sorry I didn't message you back yesterday.' I deployed a lie that I knew would lessen her anxiety about me: 'I had a friend over.'

'You did?' I could practically hear the relief hissing out of her: *Hallelujah! The weirdo finally has a friend!* 'I'm so *happy* for you. Who was it?'

'Just someone from work.' A lie on top of a lie. I'd quit my last job – writing terrible SEO content for an online interiors site – the second the bank had released some pre-probate cash.

'Did you do something nice together?'

'Watched a movie.' Which was partly true because Brian and I had rewatched *Get Out* the night before.

'That's nice. Are you eating well?'

'I've just bought some stuff for lunch.'

'Something green, I hope?'

There was absolutely nothing green in my backpack (it was mostly beige). 'A spinach and pine-nut salad.' Because that was ridiculously implausible, I added: 'Ready-made. In one of those tub things.'

'That sounds good, honey. And remember that if you're not coping, you're always welcome to come back here and stay with me and your father.'

This choked me up a bit because I knew that she meant it. I could hardly tell Daphne that I would rather get stuck in a lift with a clown than return to the glamping business she ran in Cornwall. Mainly because I'd been staying in one of her pods when I heard the awful news about my mother, but also because the wifi there was shite. 'That's kind of you,' I said instead. 'But Brian and I are trundling along okay.'

'Uh-huh.' I steeled myself for what I knew was coming next, which was: 'And how *is* your grief journey going, honey?'

Daphne meant well, but grief wasn't a journey, and even if it was, it would be an objectively terrible one, like a never-ending coach trip around Gatwick Airport. That said, despite her propensity for spirituality, wellness and crystals, I was fond of Daphne, and my mother had liked her too. Originally from Texas, she'd met my father online and had relocated to the UK to be with him. She was fifteen years his senior, relentlessly upbeat, and had no side to her (the only mystery about Daphne was what she saw in my father).

I changed the subject. 'How's Dad?'

'Hard at work in the studio. He sends his love.' I was pretty sure that was stretching the truth.

As I neared the end of the lane, Daphne had to ring off to deal with a truculent glamper and I paused to send Meera, my mother's best friend, a proof-of-life message because she also panicked if she didn't hear from me once a week. My smugness at remembering to do this life admin was eradicated when the postie's van came creeping past and braked like a cop car blocking a getaway driver.

'Morning my lovely!' the postie called, resting her elbow on her open window and settling in for the long haul. She too was an objectively pleasant person, but it was difficult not to resent her because she only ever brought bad tidings or spam for retirement villages. Just two days ago, like the world's most cheerful drive-by shooter, she'd dropped off a package containing an advance copy of *Overlooked,* my mother's final novel, which was about to be published posthumously and was therefore grief-avoidance kryptonite. As soon as I'd realised what it was, I'd chucked it into the cupboard under the stairs.

'Don't often see you out and about,' she said without an edge. 'Still, the fresh air will do you good, I'll bet. The first few months can be difficult, can't they? I remember when we lost my nan. The thing about it was . . .' But before she could really get going (I'd heard all three of her Death Stories before, anyway), she was interrupted by the *clang-creak* of Sheila's front gate.

We shared a brief *oh shit* glance, then the postie muttered, 'best get on', hurriedly handed me a brown envelope, and reversed like a racing driver, leaving me alone in the lane with the large tweedy woman fiddling with her wheelie bin.

I should say here that Sheila wasn't *all* bad. Despite her la-di-da accent, she wasn't snooty (she was always saying, 'one doesn't need to bother with titles these days, my dear'). Plus, she was the only person in a ten-mile radius who never mentioned my mother, which, in retrospect, I should've considered odd. On the downside, she only ever talked *at* me rather than *with* me, and was an indefatigable complainer, and the last time she'd cornered me, I'd been forced to endure a forty-five-minute diatribe about a hamletee who'd dumped grass-cuttings on a footpath, and a lengthy gripe about various residents' (admittedly complain-worthy) gardening misdemeanours.

But unless I wanted to chuck myself over the cottage's hedge (not an option, I was too unfit), I had no choice but to face the onslaught. 'Morning, Sheila.'

No response. Not even a glance in my direction. 'Good morning, Sheila!' I tried again. Still no acknowledgment. Then she shuffled back through her gate. *That's odd*. More than odd – unprecedented. But instead of relief, in came guilt. Had I offended her in some way? Unlikely, because I never managed to get a word in, and curiously, she seemed to approve of my gardening habits (or lack thereof – during my tenure in the cottage, an army of brambles and thistles had staged a hostile lawn takeover). But seeing as the last two times she'd knocked on the door I'd deployed my 'work call' ruse, and the time before that I'd pretended to be out, perhaps it had finally dawned that I was avoiding her.

Then again, perhaps she'd just forgotten to put her hearing aids in.

It was then that I made the mistake of opening the envelope the postie had all but chucked at me. Ironically, I wouldn't have minded being talked at for once, because even a whinge about Glenn's non-stop leaf-blowing activities would've been a welcome distraction from the fact that it contained the dreaded 'three weeks' notice' letter confirming the date of the inquest into my mother's death. Meera and Daphne seemed to think that I'd 'feel better about things' once the inquest was over, which I wouldn't, because that wasn't how denial worked, and just the thought of sitting in a courtroom while a coroner interrogated every detail of my mother's fatal accident was enough to bring on an anxiety attack.

I was so shell-shocked that when I zombie-shuffled into the kitchen, I didn't notice the intruder until after I'd dumped the mail-bomb and the groceries on the butcher's block. Actually, that's not true. I smelled her first – a whiff of tobacco smoke – which should've bothered me more than it did because I hadn't smoked anything for weeks. It was only when I felt that prickly sensation you get when you're being watched that I looked up and clocked what was in the room. And instead of going *nope!* and fleeing like a sensible person, I froze.

It's a cliché to say that 'time slowed down', but it really did. I became hyper-aware of my surroundings: the tower of tomato-sauce-crusted plates, waiting in vain for their turn in the dishwasher; the dusty draining-board, colonised by empty ramen tubs; the elderly stove's hotplate lids, which were also covered in dust because I still hadn't figured out how to use them. And most of all, the woman leaning against the fridge. Not just any woman. An impossible one.

The most disturbing thing of all was that I knew *exactly* who she was because she looked *exactly* like my mother had described her, and how I'd always pictured her in my head. To the extent that along with the shock, I'd felt an initial jolt of recognition – unbelievably, I came very close to saying *oh hiiii* as if she were an acquaintance I'd failed to dodge in a supermarket. I took in the trademark black tailored suit. The vegan leather combat boots that were the implausible triumvirate of comfortable, hard-wearing and stylish. The cap of cropped hair that she trimmed herself because she was too busy uncovering high-stakes malfeasance to indulge in fripperies like head massages in salons. The partially smoked gold-tipped cigarette held elegantly in her left hand.

The only rational explanation was that I was having some sort of creative mental health episode brought on by the shock arrival of the inquest letter. But if my brain was going rogue again, why on earth would it delude itself with her? Because other than small talk, death talk, and late-stage capitalism, there was nothing I disliked more than Leah Rebecca Overton.

THE GRUDGE

I should pause here to say that I haven't always loathed her. In fact, there was a time when Mum and I used to joke about how ridiculously capable Leah was. 'Should've got *Leah* to do it,' we'd say, whenever one of us, usually me, forgot to do something important; '*Leah* wouldn't have fucked that up.' And if either of us were facing a tricky life decision or obstacle (again, usually me), our go-to phrase was: *WWLD? What Would Leah Do?*

Not only that, but I'd helped my mother bring her into the world.

Mum had broken the news that she was 'thinking about writing a crime novel' eight years ago, when I was staying with her for the university Christmas break. She'd dropped this bombshell with uncharacteristic hesitancy, and had caveated it with: 'Unless you think that's a stupid idea?'

'Why would I?'

'Well, because you're the writer in the family.'

'There's not a family quota, Mum. Anyway, screenwriting's different, and I've only just started studying it.' I didn't dare tell her that I was finding the clamour of university life far more challenging than I'd expected.

'So you really don't mind if I give it a bash then?'

'Course not. I think it's a grand idea.' I did. My parents' divorce had recently been finalised, and because my mother no longer had to micro-manage my father's ego and sock drawer, she had time to do stuff she enjoyed, and reading thrillers was by far her favourite pastime (she was constantly exceeding her Kindle's storage capacity). Plus, she was working as a probate solicitor at the time, and quite a lot of lawyers decide to become authors, probably because after years of witnessing their clients getting screwed over by the system, they have to do something to preserve the illusion that justice exists. And because she was an obsessive fixer, I knew she'd enjoy having full control over an outcome for once.

I spent the next week acting as my mother's literary midwife. She'd already nixed the idea of making her protagonist a practising lawyer ('not enough violence – usually'), and Leah was never going to be Detective Inspector Overton because my mother's lefty sensibility wasn't conducive to writing about an organisation that admitted to being systemically racist. In the end, she decided to make Leah an ex-lawyer-turned-private detective, 'you know, Neevy, like V. I. Warshawski' (I didn't – despite being unhealthily addicted to true crime content, horror was more my thing). But that profession made sense too because my mother's job involved a fair amount of investigative work, like tracking down dead people's relatives and foiling greed-driven inheritance malfeasance. And it was a no-brainer to make Leah's heritage mirror her own – Yorkshire born and bred, with some Irish ancestry thrown in. 'There should be a strong element of wish-fulfilment to her character too, Neevy. You know, like a female Jack Reacher' (him I did know – I'd watched the series). So Leah was given the added edge of being a tragic orphan who'd learned how to fight surprisingly expertly to survive the horrors of the underfunded care system.

In case the story ever became a long-running series, she also decided that her PI should begin life in her mid-twenties – that way, by Book Thirty or whatever, Leah wouldn't be forced to fight crime from a Stannah stairlift. Which was where I came in as my mother's Millennial Consultant and Character Sounding Board. In fact, I came up with Leah's name. From the age of eleven to thirteen, I'd been bullied by a girl named Leah Maddox, who despite being effortlessly cruel, was also effortlessly cool (I realise now that she was probably a sociopath).

Overall, and ironically considering how things turned out, I'd enjoyed being my mother's literary sidekick. And continued to enjoy it as she completed the first draft, sent it out to agents, got a response from one improbably named Caro Canto, did a year of redrafting, and secured a modest publishing deal. And when the book came out, I acted as her handbag carrier at the launch – which I didn't enjoy, but that's only because I have a low tolerance for wine and crowds.

In the first novel, Leah was less of a threat than she eventually became, mainly because at that stage, she was scrappier and a bit *too* stereotypically northern, and it was difficult to resent someone who 'owt'-ed and 'nowt'-ed every three pages. I only began to take against her when my mother was finalising Book Two, which was around the time that I embarked on what my mother termed my 'Troubles', as if my decisions to drop out of university and opt out of 'normal life' were akin to sectarian violence. The more shambolic I became, the more capable and perfect she seemed to make Leah – often in detailed and specific ways that directly counteracted my character flaws – as if

21

she were trying to fictionally Munchausen-by-proxy-but-in-a-good-way her fucked-up daughter. And as the Leah books became more popular and my mother was able to give up probating and write full-time, Leah took up more and more space in her head, and I took up less. I know that sounds childish, and clearly, it's stupid to envy and compare yourself to a fictional character, but as Leah would say, *these are just the facts of the case.*

For context, here's an excerpt from Leah's Wiki/character page:

> Leah Rebecca Overton is a hot-shot private investigator and former lawyer who specialises in going undercover to expose high-stakes corporate and political corruption. Leah is described as chic, tall and athletic, a woman of few words and a lone-wolf character who runs at least ten miles a day. Adept at self-defence, she never shies away from confrontation, and is known for being no-nonsense, blunt to the point of rudeness, and driven.

And here's what mine would be if I were a fictional character:

> Niamh Morrissey is an unproductive member of society and university dropout who is currently living off the proceeds of her dead mother's estate. She was once described by a former housemate as 'what would happen if Wednesday Addams and a hobbit shat out a baby' and doesn't do any exercise apart from gaming, which doesn't count. Adept at denial, she avoids confrontation at all costs.

I'm not saying that my mother created Leah because she

secretly wished she had a daughter who was an ex-lawyer-slash-PI, although that would come in handy in certain situations. But what she had wanted, without a doubt, because it stained her every word, look and gesture, was a daughter who saw the point of being ambitious. A daughter who was resilient, brave, and proactive. A daughter she wouldn't have to worry about.

NOPE

In the books, Leah was always flicking her Zippo lighter, cocking an eyebrow, cracking her knuckles, smouldering (not literally, unfortunately), 'looking inwards' and on the rare occasions she smiled, she always did so with an adverb attached (usually wryly or dryly, but sometimes enigmatically). And as I stared at her – still in a serious state of shock – she smiled enigmatically, cocked an eyebrow, and flipped her Zippo's lid. I'm quite sensitive to sounds that aren't music, and it was the lighter's CLICK that snapped me out of my fugue. I dragged in a lungful of smoky air, and then let out a burp of dismay.

Leah made a moue of distaste, and said: **Right charmer, you, aren't you?**

It speaks! I reached for the closest thing to hand – a wooden spoon I'd used a few days earlier because I'd run out of clean normal ones – and threw it at her head. She didn't attempt to deflect it because she didn't need to. It went right through her and bounced off the fridge door onto the floor.

She looked down at it derisively, then glared at me. **What's your problem?**

I almost laughed at this. *How long you got?* This didn't stop me flailing for something else to chuck at her, but all that came to hand were the scones, so I didn't bother because baked goods make crap weapons in any circumstances. With considerable effort, I made myself speak, the shock making my voice sound like I'd been huffing helium: 'Am I *really* seeing you?' Along with, *am I really standing in the kitchen having a conversation with my dead Mum's protagonist?*

She gave me a long, unreadable look, then: **You what?**

'Because you're not real. You *can't* be real.' The main problem was, she looked real. Well, not *real* exactly, but more detailed and convincing than you'd expect for a delusion, which was why I'd felt compelled to chuck stuff at her. I'd even given her the scar under her left eye that she'd received courtesy of a scalpel-wielding serial killer in Book Two. And I hadn't missed that her voice sounded exactly like my mother had described it: 'smoky toned' and 'laced with the burr of her South Yorkshire roots'.

I tried to swallow, but my mouth had turned to cotton-wool. *Okay. Think. You're imagining her for a reason.* I pointed at the inquest letter: 'Did that make me summon you?'

Eh?

'The inquest letter. Did it summon you somehow?'

What do you mean by 'summon'?

'Um. It means call or—'

I know what the bloody word means.

'Oh . . . right. Sorry. Did it, though?'

Keeping her gaze fixed to mine, she killed the cigarette under her heel, then slid the imaginary butt back into its delusional packet – somehow managing to make this responsible task look cool.

That wasn't an answer, though. Even in the best of circumstances, my mind tends to operate like a wonky-wheeled shopping trolley, but I did my best to come up with a semi-logical follow-up. 'Why am I imagining you then? Because you absolutely can't be what you appear to be.'

Can't I?

'Well no. Fictional characters only come to life in . . . fiction.' As film was my medium of choice, I dredged up some examples: Nicolas Cage in *Adaptation*, Will Ferrell in that film with Emma Thompson, Ryan Reynolds in *Free Guy*, and most of the characters in *Deconstructing Harry*, which had been on the curriculum of my film literacy module until there'd been a protest about it (I found loads of other examples later). 'There must be a reason why I've dreamt you up.'

She lost the caginess and huffed in exasperation, which reminded me of Mum to such an extent that I blurted: 'Are you the spirit of my dead mother?'

She baulked at this (I didn't blame her).

If Brian hadn't sashayed in then, this bonkers non-conversation might've gone on for a while. Without pausing to glance at me, he padded straight over to Leah. Even if she *were* real, this behaviour would've been out of character because he wasn't a fan of strangers. So much so, that shortly after Mum's death, he'd buggered off for three days because Daphne, my father, and Meera had been in and out of the cottage helping with the sadmin (he'd returned home fatter though, so at least someone had enjoyed their grief journey).

Saying, *Ey up, kitty-cat*, Leah crouched down to stroke him. And then – horror of horrors – he began to purr and arch his back as if she were the cat version of reiki. Cats are supposed to be capable of seeing ghosts and spirits, which is why they feature in so many horror films and relatively fewer romcoms, but whatever Leah was, she wasn't a ghost – that would have entailed her being alive at some point – and unless the laws of physics had changed since I'd thrown the spoon at her head, she wasn't made of solid matter. Which meant that *I was sharing a hallucination with my dead mother's cat.*

That was a *nope!* too far, and I fled into the adjoining boot room. I made for the back door, but then instinct kicked in and I threw myself into the downstairs cloakroom instead (I'm not an outdoorsy person). I locked the door, sat on the lavatory seat and tried and failed not to hyperventilate. I'd left my phone in the kitchen, so even if I'd wanted to ring the emergency services and then wait two years for a mental health appointment, I couldn't.

Clearly there are countless metaphors for grief and loss, but I preferred the obvious ones, and imagined my pain, sorrow and guilt (there was a lot of guilt) about my mother's death as a bogeyman lurking in a basement. So far, I'd managed to keep the basement door shut and had even avoided the jump scares that were the compulsory precursor to all horror film finales. Until now. Because the bogeywoman hadn't just broken out of the basement, she was lurking in the fucking kitchen. The obvious explanation – that my brain had masochistically conjured her up to bully me into dealing with months of repressed emotions – would've been reasonable if it weren't for the inconvenient fact that Brian could see her too.

A minute passed. Then another. I held my breath, then opened the door a crack. I'd half expected her to be skulking outside it, but apart from the usual mountain of used cat-food pods, the boot room was empty. 'Hello?'

Nothing. *Phew.* Then, from the kitchen, came a muted CLICK.

Slam. I locked the door again and resumed my position on the toilet seat.

Now what?

I didn't have anyone to talk to about this, which was my own fault. I'd let all my friendships lapse, and if I reached out to Daphne or Meera, I'd be involuntarily sectioned, and then what would Brian do? Leah didn't have any friends either, although that wasn't because she suffered from executive dysfunction and kept putting off responding to their messages, but because my mother had to keep killing them off to preserve her lone-wolf status.

Crushingly, this confounding situation was another reminder that the one person I really wanted to confide in was no longer available and never would be again, and into my chest came a weighty rush of sorrow – a sensation that always made me feel like I was incubating one of those xenomorph parasites from the *Alien* franchise.

A lone tear leaked out and trickled down my cheek.

Quick – think about something else! Unfortunately, I'd chosen the worst place possible for brain-distraction purposes. The only décor consisted of one of my father's oil paintings, which he'd given to my mother shortly after they'd split up (as if divorce wasn't punishment enough). It depicted two women dressed in Amish-style garb, standing on a cliff top and gazing at an out-of-proportion ship that was sinking into the ocean. Knowing my father, the women were probably supposed to be watching the family patriarch heroically going down with his vessel, but if so, they didn't look that bothered about it. He was okay-ish at doing water, but terrible at capturing light – the rays coming down from the clouds looked like scaffolding planks. Nor was he great at figurative work, because the older of the two women had a bun at the back of her head that resembled a huge wart, and the younger one appeared to have an extra arm. The painting was probably meant to be a howl of self-pity, but whatever its meaning, it seemed that I'd inherited my penchant for literal imagery from my dad's gene pool. And his lack of ambition, because he'd given up working as an accountant shortly after he'd met Daphne and her money. What I hadn't inherited from him was his single-minded belief in himself, because even though his art was shite – and I'm not being unkind, it really, objectively was – he didn't care, and devoted every waking moment to it.

When I'd stared at the painting for long enough to figure out that the younger woman's extra arm was probably meant to be one of those handheld telescopes (two hours), I crept back into the kitchen, praying that Leah was gone.

She wasn't. She was sitting nonchalantly on the butcher's block, and next to her, insouciantly cleaning himself on the bread board as if it was just a normal day, sat Brian. As I entered the room, they both turned to look at me like a pair of gaslighting collaborators. CLICK went that annoying Zippo, which had been given to Leah by Jed, her PI mentor and father figure. I could even make out the engraving on it: 'Love Life', which my mother hadn't nicked off one of those 'Live, Love, Laugh!' wall slogan things, but had borrowed from Maya Angelou (Leah, of course, had impeccable taste in literature).

I stared at her. She glared back. Then she smiled wryly and cocked an eyebrow, as if to ask, *now what?*

It was a good question, and *maybe if I just ignore you, you'll go away* was my unspoken answer. After all, that had worked semi-successfully with bailiffs, course tutors, and the one person with whom I'd had a brief and disastrous relationship, so why not with delusions-slash-possibly-supernatural occurrences too?

IT FOLLOWS

It didn't work. If anything, her presence seemed to solidify. Unlike pretty much every challenge I'd faced in life so far, avoidance wasn't going to cut it, because wherever I went, so did she.

In case my brain was acting like its own green screen and projecting her, over the course of the next twenty-four hours, I did the following in the hopes of rebooting it and ousting her:

1. Not thinking about her, which failed because it's impossible not to think about something when it's continually in your face (she even followed me into the upstairs bathroom, which meant that I had to keep my underwear on when I showered).

2. Doing another play-through of *Resident Evil: Village*, but it's impossible to survive a boss fight against a gigantic mutant woman with knives instead of fingernails when something far more implausible is sitting on your bed and judging your every move.

3. Blasting Eurovision tunes at full volume because Leah was a music snob who only listened to Northern soul

31

(Northern soul was the only music genre that my mother and I could find that hadn't already been taken by another fictional detective at least once). Result? An increase in the 'looks of contempt' quotient.

4. Going outside to get complained at (or snubbed) by Sheila, and into the back garden to get patronised over a fence by Glenn (nothing and no one would be able to put up with that), but for once, neither were around. What this did do, however, was confirm that Leah's presence wasn't limited to the cottage.

5. Getting stoned on my last bit of weed and extremely drunk on the only alcohol in the house – half a bottle of Glenfiddich that my father had left behind after Sadmin Week – but this only resulted in Leah glaring at me in disgust while I projectile vomited into the kitchen sink.

It was during my bout of alcohol poisoning that I confirmed that the only place she didn't – or couldn't – haunt me like the embodiment of a migraine was the cloakroom. At the time, I didn't question the non-logic of *why* she didn't follow me in there – I was far too busy feeling grateful for the respite (I'd only get to the bottom of that mystery later). Clearly, I would've preferred to spend every waking and sleeping moment in there, but I had to venture out every so often to eat, caffeinate, charge my phone, feed Brian and replenish my mother's bird feeders in the back garden. (I couldn't *not* do that – my mother had begun over-feeding the county's wild bird population when she'd first moved in, and I didn't want to be responsible for causing a blue tit famine.) Whenever I did so, I found myself avoiding looking Leah in the eye, like prey avoiding the gaze of a predator. Being under constant, judgemental surveillance had the effect of curtailing my usual slobbish impulses, and I even emptied the dishwasher, repacked it, and switched it on again. I didn't attempt to talk to her again in case this cemented her presence even more, and she didn't speak to me either – well, not verbally, anyway, because Leah could say a lot with just her eyes, none of it complimentary.

During my stint in my sanctuary, I also did some research for 'know thy enemy' purposes. According to Reddit, although there were several conditions that caused delusional thinking and auditory, olfactory, and visual hallucinations, there were no reported cases of human–feline *folie à deux*, so psychosis was unlikely, unless my condition also involved me hallucinating Brian hallucinating Leah, which seemed unnecessarily complex, and equally as unlikely, as I was fairly sure that my unconscious mind was as lazy as my conscious one.

'Fictional characters coming to life' was indeed a popular trope in all literature and movie genres, but the key point here is that every example I found was fictional and not biographical.

When that well ran dry, I did a deep dive into muses, because although the most likely explanation was that she was a by-product of a nervous breakdown, she'd been knocking about for nearly forty-eight hours by that point, and my mind wasn't usually that consistent. I confirmed that most muses are women, which is unsurprising because the work is unpaid, involves a shit-ton of emotional labour, and they never get any credit for it, although apparently, they have to be 'invoked', which I hadn't done (not consciously, anyway). But even if Leah was a muse who also moonlighted as a protagonist, she'd been my *mother's* muse, not mine; and again, that didn't explain Brian's response to her or why she was haunting me. It was doubtful that she was a succubus who fed off creative energy because I had very little of that, and Brian had even less.

As a last, desperate resort, I decided to revisit the source material – the Leah books themselves – on the off-chance that the key to banishing my stalker was hidden within their pages. I knew the first five pretty well, mainly because I'd reread them for self-flagellation purposes, but also because whenever my mother began a new Leah adventure, I'd help her remember which of the recurring supporting characters she'd already killed off. The only one I hadn't read was *Overlooked*, although she'd emailed me the first draft, like she always did, for my feedback. At the time, I was being no-fault evicted from my studio flat in Bradford, and because pretending that wasn't happening had taken up all my energy, I'd put off reading it until it was too late.

There wasn't enough battery life left on my phone to download the manuscript, so I had no choice but to read the actual advance copy of the book, which was still in the cupboard under the stairs with the Henry Hoover. As I tiptoed towards enemy territory, the sound of yapping floated in from outside – it seemed that Brian the traitor had tired of acting like Leah's familiar and resumed his terrier-torturing activities, which pepped me up a bit.

Instead of lounging unhygienically on the butcher's block, Leah was leaning against it, and as I edged past her, trying (and failing) to look nonchalant, she treated me to a suspicious side-eye.

You're up to something, she said, making me jump.

'No, I'm not,' I lied. *Oh, hang on . . . did she just read my mind?* Which shouldn't have come as a surprise because she *was* my mind. *Wasn't she?* The problem was, my brain kept insisting that she was an autonomous entity, mainly because she looked, acted, and sneered like one.

But whatever she was, one thing was for sure: I couldn't spend the rest of my life in a windowless cloakroom staring at my father's mansplain of a painting. I'd made a nest in there with a sleeping-bag, and although I'm only five foot one, my back was killing me from napping curled around a toilet pedestal. I took a deep breath, and said: 'Please don't take this the wrong way, but are you planning to hang around for much longer?'

A Death Stare, which, thinking about it, was more in my lexicon than my mother's.

The seconds ticked by as I waited in vain for an answer – a verbal one anyway. 'Are you not answering because you can't or won't?'

I'm not answering because it's a stupid question.

The lure of the cloakroom beckoned. *Don't give up.* Perhaps it would help if I treated this situation like a non-logical puzzle game and fished for info until I stumbled across a clue (I could play those for hours). 'Can I ask you another question, then?'

Depends how stupid it is.

The one I really wanted to ask was: *What do I have to do to get rid of you, and will it involve a brain scan, a psychiatrist, or an exorcist?* but in the end I decided to go with a Brian-related query because I knew for a fact that she was a cat person. 'You and Brian seem to know each other well. Does that mean you used to hang around Mum all the time too?'

A shadow – or something like a shadow – clouded her gaze, which gave me hope that there was more to her than sociopathy. Then: **Not *always*.**

At last! Some sort of answer! 'Just when she was writing you?'

What do you think?

'I don't know. That's why I'm asking.'

Another Death Stare.

Keep going. 'So, if you didn't hang around Mum all the time, then why won't you leave *me* alone?' I didn't say: *Also, I used to fantasise about you tripping over a bathmat in your industrial loft apartment and falling out of the window.*

Unfinished business, course.

'Right. And that means?'

She rolled her eyes, which was another new piece of choreography. **What do you think it means?**

In the books, Leah was always answering a question with another question (it was never not annoying). 'Are you talking about the crap way I've been dealing with my mother's death and all the stuff to do with her accident? Because if so, then I promise I'll try and do better and . . .' I trailed off: she was glaring at me with even more disgust than usual, which was quite a feat.

You know as well as I do that it wasn't an accident. The silence stretched – Leah was adept at maintaining suspense. Then: **She was murdered.**

WHEN A STRANGER CALLS

Leah's murder pronouncement should've been another *nope!* moment, but there's only so much absurdity a person can take before they just roll with it. Nor should it have come as that much of a shock, because accidental deaths were never accidental in Leah Overton's world – my mother was always making her solve murders made to look like misadventures and suicides.

'That's insane,' I said, when I could speak.

Is it. Said just like that, without a question mark.

'Well yes. Because it *was* an accident. Mum fell off a ladder while she was trying to fix the guttering at the side of the cottage and—'

She held up a hand to cut me off. ***Quiet. We've got company.***

A second later, someone knocked on the front door, which, true to form, made me jump. Several tense seconds ticked by, then whoever it was knocked again. 'Should I see who it is?'

Course. Could be our first lead.

Oh dear. Because no one except for the neighbours, lost ramblers, or Jehovah's Witnesses pitched up unexpectedly, I usually hid until they got fed up and left. But after almost three days of delusional interaction, for once I was desperate for human contact, and I ran to the door and yanked it open.

On the doorstep, smiling expectantly, was a middle-aged, pink-cheeked woman dressed in a flowery jumpsuit and Crocs. *Not a rambler then.* She was soft-looking, like a hug personified, and even though I assumed she had to be a member of a religious cult, if she hadn't spoken first, I might've said, *I need help.*

'Sorry to bother you, bab. I'm Tracey, Sheila's niece. From next door?' Then her gaze slid past my shoulder, and her smile faltered, as if she'd spotted something odious or unexpected – both of which would describe Leah Overton. Shaking this off, she focused her attention on me again.

Her confusion had been momentary, but . . . *what if she'd seen the PI in the room?* I glanced over my shoulder to check. Leah was indeed lurking behind me, but the source of Tracey's befuddlement could equally have been the giant stain on the kitchen wall, caused when I'd thrown a full mug of coffee at a spider (I hadn't intended to hurt it – it was a knee-jerk fear reaction).

But instead of saying something like, 'I'm sorry, I didn't realise you had company' or 'Fuck me, that wall needs a bit of a clean, doesn't it?' she said, 'You *are* Annie Morrissey's daughter, right?' and gave me a funny look, undoubtedly because I hadn't yet spoken and didn't exactly look my best, seeing as I'd spent the last two nights sleeping fitfully in a toilet.

'Yes! That's me!' I said, overcompensating for being weird. '*Hi.* Hi! It's so nice to meet you. I didn't even know Sheila had a niece. She's never mentioned you, and . . .' I cut myself off in case that came across as insensitive. Also, some part of my brain noted that Tracey had a Brummie accent, which was at odds with Sheila's la-di-da tweediness, although she did share her aunt's substantial height and florid complexion.

'Did I catch you at a bad time?' she asked.

'Yes, I mean, no. I'm . . . things here are . . . I was busy doing stuff . . .' I trailed off.

Behind me, Leah muttered, *hopeless*, to which Tracey didn't react.

'Auntie said you're always working. Mind you, it's a good idea to keep busy at a time like this, isn't it?' She scrunched up her face. 'I'm so sorry for your loss. I only met your mother once or twice, but she seemed like a lovely person.'

So she knew the victim, did she? Ask her where she was at the time of the murder.

'It wasn't a murder,' I blurted.

'I'm sorry?' frowned Tracey.

'Um. I meant to say . . . my mother's death. It was an accident.'

Pah.

'I know, bab. It must've been a shock for you, losing her like that.' I steeled myself for a bout of prying or a Death Story recitation, but instead, Tracey got to the point of her visit. 'Reason I've popped over is I was wondering if I could get Auntie's cake tin back from you. She's been going on about it all morning, can't shut her up. "It's just a tin, Auntie," I keep saying to her. "I'll buy you another one on eBay." But she gets things stuck in her mind, you see, and . . .'

Shite. Weeks ago, Sheila *had* kindly left a bereavement cake on the front porch, but because I don't like fruit cake, I hadn't eaten it, and because it was me, instead of giving it to the birds, I'd just left it in the tin and forgotten about it. And also because it was me, I'd forgotten to thank her for it, which probably explained why she'd ignored me the other day. By now, the cake had probably metastasised into a new life form, and I could hardly return the container without decontaminating it first. 'I'm right in the middle of . . . something. Is it okay if I drop it round tomorrow?'

'Course it is. I'm staying with her for a bit, just till she's back on her feet. As you probably know, she's been having a few health issues.'

I didn't know that. Could that have contributed to her atypical behaviour too? Mind you, she hadn't looked ill – physically anyway. I tended to think of Sheila as the human equivalent of a sturdy old sofa, and she hadn't appeared to be losing any of her stuffing. 'I hope she feels better soon.'

'Me too,' said Tracey, with feeling.

A few seconds of awkward silence followed. Not inviting Tracey in for a cup of tea was an unforgivable countryside code lapse, but I gave myself a break. (Also, I didn't have any milk. Or sugar. Or tea for that matter.)

'Well, I'd best get back to it,' she said eventually. 'Thanks for being so understanding.'

I shut the door and rested my forehead on it. I'd sweated right through my hoody, and although interacting with anyone usually drained my battery, I was still too adrenalised to feel knackered.

From behind me came, *Call that an interrogation?*

It was time to confront the figment in the room again.

This cake lead – we should follow it up. Could be appeasement confectionery.

'Um. What?'

Sign of a guilty conscience.

'That's . . .' *Was* there a word for what this was? I settled on 'crazy'.

***I'll tell you what's crazy. Burying your head in the sand.
If there's one thing I hate, it's cowardice.***

'That's not true. You also hate guns, refined sugar, and
Instagram.' I might've been proud of this unusually sharp
come-back if she hadn't then smirked and said:

***You know what I also hate? People getting away with
murder.***

'Okay, fine. Why are *you* so sure that she was . . . that
it wasn't an accident, then?'

Gut says it's murder. In fairness, Leah's gut instinct was
always right – so much so that to prevent every mystery
getting solved in the first ten pages, my mother had been
forced to make her ignore it. Then she glared at me, and
said: ***So does yours.***

'No, it doesn't.'

Her gaze morphed from smouldering to accusatory, and
I felt myself wither inside as the last remnants of the basement door crumbled into dust.

When I'd first clocked her in the kitchen, had I known,
deep down, that this was where things were destined to
end up? Yes. No. Maybe. Because shamefully, there *were*
a few aspects about my mother's accident that I'd found
troubling right from the start, but I hadn't foregrounded
them at the time because: a) they hadn't seemed to bother
anyone else; b) I'd been so banjaxed by shock that it had
been enough of a challenge to accept that my mother was
gone at all; c) once the shock had worn off, I'd shoved all
the bothering things into the basement along with all the
other inconvenient truths.

The first bothering thing was that although my mother
had been obsessive about keeping things in good nick, she
was unlikely to use a ladder because she had an intense
fear of heights. So much so that when she'd converted the

attic into her writing room, she wouldn't go up the stairs until they'd been boxed in, even though they weren't that steep. Secondly, her shoulder had been bothering her, which I knew for a fact because the one and only time I'd stayed with her in the cottage – two weeks before her accident – she'd asked me to do the vacuuming, because dragging the Henry Hoover around had been too much for her. Vacuuming was the only chore I didn't hate, although I hadn't taken Henry for a spin since she'd died because Mum and I used to joke that it was like being stalked around a room by a leering, red-faced disembodied man. (Also – why put a face on a vacuum?)

And then there was this: I knew for certain that she'd died after eight p.m. because she'd sent me a voice message at 19.59 that I still hadn't found the courage to listen to. In fact, there were three unopened voice notes lurking on my phone. And although it doesn't get dark at that time of year till nine p.m. or so, who fixes the guttering at night?

See?

'I don't see anything,' I lied. Also: *Had she just read my mind again?*

Yes, you bloody well do. There are questions that need answering, and we need to answer them.

Don't want to. 'Look. I'm not saying there wasn't anything *off* about Mum's accident, but I never thought she was . . .' – *oh God* – '. . . *murdered.*'

No? Why not?

'Um . . . because who'd want to do that to Mum? She was a writer, not a whistleblower, and she wasn't in a relationship. And the police would've done something if they'd suspected foul play.'

A sneer. ***Because they always get it right, don't they.***
Naturally Leah had inherited my mum's distrust of the
authorities.

I really didn't want to verbalise the next bit, but my
desperation to kibosh the insanity trumped the cowardice.
'Also, she died from a single head injury that was consistent
with a fall, and there were no other injuries or defensive
wounds or whatever.' I hadn't been able to face dealing
with the Coroner's Liaison Officer (Meera and Daphne had
done that), but I knew this for a fact because thinking she
was being helpful, Daphne had told me the preliminary
autopsy findings in detail ('she would have been knocked
out immediately, honey'). Obviously, I was relieved that
my mother hadn't suffered, but I'd rather not have been
told the specifics of her death (to me, the second most
mentally scarring phrase in the English language will always
be 'non-penetrating traumatic brain injury').

Ever since I'd left the safety of the cloakroom, I'd been
incubating a grief parasite, but the shock of Leah's
pronouncement and a desperate desire not to look weak
in front of her had kept it at bay. Until now. But just as
the pressure in my chest became unbearable, Leah distracted
me with another irritating Zippo CLICK.

Deep breath, deep breath. 'Look, I know you always
think everything is murder' – and fair enough, because in
Leah's world, it always was – 'but this is real life, not a
crime novel.'

A shrug. ***Life can be stranger than fiction.***

'No, it can't. Anyway, how would you know? You don't
actually exist. You're basically a wish-fulfilment character
who dresses like John Wick and does unrealistic things like
confronting corrupt cops in deserted parking lots and going

running alone at night in dodgy areas without taking a phone or telling anyone where you're going. *No one* does that.' I was practically shouting at this point, which was so unlike me that I wasn't sure if I should apologise or burst into tears.

Instead of lashing back, Leah remained as calm as a suited and booted cucumber, then smiled dryly. ***About time you showed a bit of backbone.***

Despite myself, this backhanded compliment brought on a wave of shameful warmth. Then something else struck me. Was this actually a warped grief quest, like a crime-themed version of the *John Wick* franchise, *P.S. I Love You*, or *The Babadook*? Having spent over seven hundred hours playing *Baldur's Gate 3*, I wasn't averse to a quest, although trying to solve an unlikely murder with a delusion I shared with a cat seemed like an objectively pointless one. Then again, it would probably be less tedious than working through the five stages of grief like a sensible person, and I couldn't put that off forever, because so far, getting stuck at denial + avoidance = mental health crisis. And if it resulted in my brain and/or the universe ditching my nemesis, then: win-win.

Also, as much as I hated to admit it, Leah was correct. There was something dodgy and mysterious about my mother's accident; being forced to confront all the oddities surrounding it in one go had brought *that* home.

And then there was this: my mother had spent years trying to get me to take an interest in something other than gaming, true-crime podcasts and horror films, and was always saying, 'For God's sake, Niamh, at least get off your bloody arse for a bit.' It was fitting, in the most tragic way possible, that I was being bullied into doing that by the one thing in her life that had never let her down.

I turned back to Leah. 'If I – or we – prove that Mum was . . . unlawfully killed, or confirm that she did in fact die in an unfortunate household accident, do you promise to get out of my life?'

Once the unfinished business is finished, you bloody well try and stop me.

So, I thought, *fuck it*. It wasn't as if I had anything else on.

APT PUPIL

'So.'

So.

'Where do we start?'

Leah began to pace, which she tended to do in the books whenever she needed to 'chew over some facts', and always did 'like a cat' (one of the exotics, not a ginger tub like Brian).

Seeing as you're a newbie, we'll kick off with the basics: Method, motive, and opportunity. First, let's run through the method.

'Well, like I said, she fell off a ladder. But how would that even work? As a pre-planned method, I mean. I know you're not a fan of the police, but I watch and listen to loads of true-crime stuff, and in real life, cops can always tell whenever a crime scene's been staged.'

They don't if the perp knows what they're doing.

Perp. Ouch. That had been one of Jed the Mentor's terms and my mother had over-used it in the first draft with unintentionally hilarious results – so much so that back when we'd been on bantering terms it had been one of our silly, long-running jokes: *Do you think the killer did that on perp-pose, Neevy?*

And it could've been a crime of opportunity.

46

'I don't think that's very likely, do you? I mean, look where we are. You're lucky if you get a passing squirrel, never mind a passing murderer.'

A Death Stare. *Nowt gets solved with a closed mind.*

'Right. Of course.'

A curt nod, then she resumed pacing. Fortunately, the kitchen-slash-dining area took up most of the cottage's ground floor, so I didn't have to worry about accidentally brushing shoulders with her. Was she this intimidating and mardy in the books? No. She was bolshy, humourless and blunt, but she didn't come across as unlikeable (to her readers, anyway). But then again, her supporting characters tended to be more active than me, and if they weren't, they were usually murdered by Mum's editor before they made it to print.

Let's move onto motive. What are *the main motives for murder?*

This was said in a patronising, *bet-you-don't-know* tone of voice, but like all true-crime addicts, I did know what they were. This didn't stop me from taking out my phone to double-check though.

What are you playing at?

'I'm just Googling.'

A guff of distaste. *Of course.* Another of Leah's quirks was being pathologically tech-averse, which was a wildly impractical trait for a PI to possess, but as my mother had pointed out, it was a canny way of keeping the mystery and action going without the need to set the books pre-smartphone. (So, for instance, whenever Leah got bonked on the head and zip-tied to a warehouse radiator by a balaclava-ed assailant, instead of just dropping Jed a pin, she was forced to use her wiles to escape.) Fortunately, there was always a disposable nerdy contact on hand to trawl through a perp's social media history if necessary, and because Leah was paranoid about being tracked, my mother had given her an inexhaustible supply of untraceable burner dumbphones, even though it was incredibly bad for the environment to keep lobbing handsets into strangers' bins every few chapters.

To prove that I wasn't a complete pushover, I asked ChatGPT instead, turning the phone to face Leah as it tongue-popped and crooned: 'The main motives for murder are anger, concealment, jealousy, revenge, love, and gain.'

A dry smile. *Let's start with* **gain**. *Who had the most to* **gain** *from her death?*

Oof. I'd walked right into that one.

Well?

'Me,' I croaked. Despite my mother's increasingly desperate attempts to get me to 'opt back into society', by making me the beneficiary of her estate, she'd inadvertently given me the means to continue opting out of it. But thinking about it, if this were a Leah Overton thriller, the murderer *would* probably be me. Mum had loved smuggling the answer to the mystery into the first third of a novel, and then circling back to it via a sea of red herrings. Not that any author worth her salt would choose me as an antagonist, seeing as I was unusually passive, and until recently, my life had been relatively free of high-stakes drama. I couldn't even blame the Troubles on anything particularly traumatic because they'd begun incrementally after I'd failed socially and creatively during my second year at Birmingham University, and seeing as their main tenets were anxiety, arrested development, fear of failure, and existential dread, they were the opposite of explosive.

'But it couldn't have been me' I said, a bit too defensively. 'I mean, I know I'm delusional because . . . well, *you*, but I was staying in one of my stepmother's glamping pods in Cornwall when Mum died, and I'd remember if I drove two-hundred-and-fifty miles to Shropshire to fake a murder. Well, not *drove*, because I don't own a car, but—'

***You were staying in a* what?**

'A glamping pod.'

Which is?

I knew what glamping pods were, so why didn't she? 'Glamping's a bit like normal camping, only posher.'

Seems pointless.

It was, a bit. '*Do* you suspect me?'

Don't be daft. Course I don't.

'Thanks.' I almost smiled at her.

Not a compliment. You clearly don't have the nous to plan owt, never mind a murder.

That was unnecessarily harsh, even if it was true.

So, money's not a motive. What about anger?

Me again. Another burp escaped, and for a second, I was worried I was going to be sick – the nausea exacerbated by the memory of the last words I'd said to my mother. 'She never fell out with anyone.' *Only . . . that's not true, is it?* A shadowy memory surfaced: During my disastrous two-day visit with Mum, hadn't she muttered something about Caro, her agent, and called her 'that bloody woman'? Mind you, that would have been around the time that she was due to deliver the follow-up to *Overlooked*, and she always became extra spiky whenever she was hitting a deadline.

Leah lit a cigarette, and I opened the kitchen window to dispel what should've been an imaginary stench. At some point I'd have to ask her to stop smoking indoors in case illusory second-hand smoke was harmful to delusional cats.

What about feuds?

'*Feuds?*' That was oddly specific. 'Is there something you know that I don't?'

Just asking the question. That's how investigations work.

'Right. Of course. But . . . can I ask *you* a quick question?'

You just did.

'Another one, then. Even if you only hung around Mum when she was writing you, you must've spent a lot of time with her here.'

That isn't a question.

'Here's one, then. Where were you when Mum died?'

She flinched. *What?*

'I said—'

I know what you said. You think I'd be doing this if I knew who did it?

Did I? I wasn't sure – the question had just popped out – but it had rattled her. *Good. See how* you *like it, Leah bloody Overton.*

Back to feuds.

'But—'

I said, back to feuds.

She gave me another Death Stare, and my backbone, which was fragile anyway, crumbled. 'Well, she refused to go on social media – which is where most people do their daily feuding – even though this annoyed her publishers.'

A raised eyebrow at this.

'Not wanting to self-promote on Instagram isn't enough of a motive for *murder*. Anyway, even if Mum's publishers decided to kill off one of their authors for some reason, they're literary people, not weapon-toting mercenaries.'

Appearances can be deceiving.

Another cliché, which wasn't like her. She was clichéd in a lot of ways, but rarely verbally – in the books, at any rate.

What about closer to home?

'The neighbours, you mean?'

A curt nod.

You tell me, Leah Overton. 'Well . . . I don't remember Mum saying much about Lady Sheila – that's the aunt of the woman who popped round – other than she thought she was "a bit of a character", which, by the way, is a massive understatement. I'm pretty sure she found Glenn and Janet's obsession with garden neatness baffling because it is. I mean, why live in the countryside if you don't like mess? And I don't remember her saying anything at all about the Weekend Wanker – that's the bloke who owns the naff barn conversion opposite. But even if she was feuding with him for some reason, he only rocks up on Fridays or when his alarm goes off, and Mum died on a Tuesday. Which doesn't completely rule him out, but still. Honestly, there's not enough going on round here for a chapter of a cosy crime novel, never mind your genre.'

You're just not paying attention. There's always something going on under the surface of any small town. She looked off into the distance. *The fewer the people, the bigger the secrets. And in places like this? Secrets usually stay buried.*

Right. Thanks for that, Captain Portentous. I didn't bother saying that I knew for a fact that secrets never stayed buried in Buckstone because even I was aware that Elaine from the shoppe had conned an extra wheelie bin out of the council. Unfortunately, I also neglected to do the obvious and question why a thriller protagonist who predominantly solved injustices in urban environments suddenly appeared to be an expert on rural secret-keeping.

What about revenge?

'No one would want to get revenge on Mum. Everyone liked her.'

What about the victim, then? Did she have any axes to grind or personal grievances?

Ugh: *Victim*. I thought about asking her not to use such a cold and impersonal term, but then again, being less specific, it was less likely to bring on a grief ambush. 'Not that I know of. As *you* should know, Mum used you and the books to vent about any real-life issues and injustices that were bugging her.'

Hmmm. She resumed her pacing, but I didn't miss that her body language had tensed up. Were the books and her previous cases also sore spots for her? It seemed so. *Interesting.* As she strode towards the adjoining snug, I mentally ran through the main plots of the first five novels:

Book One: *Oversight* (aka Leah's 'origin story'). In which trainee solicitor Leah Overton discovers that the law firm at which she's doing her articles is facilitating dodgy NDAs for an abusive local tech bro. Shortly after becoming a whistleblower, Leah jacks in her law career and joins forces with her future PI mentor Jed Angel, whose agency, 'Angel and Associates', has been looking into the tech millionaire's malfeasance (basically, Leah and Jed take down a West Yorkshire version of a Silicon Valley broligarch).

Book Two: *Overkill.* In which freshly minted PI Leah goes undercover in Wakefield General Hospital to track down a Dr Shipman-esque serial killer. Impressively, and despite the enormous body count, my mother had managed to seed in a message about the dangers of privatising the National Health Service.

Book Three: *Over and Above.* In which Leah goes undercover in an airline manufacturing company in Sheffield that's been putting profits before safety concerns and human life, and almost loses her own life when she gets involved with a fake NTSB air-crash investigator named Zane.

(Zane! My mother had been *terrible* at coming up with masculine names, and this had been another one of our shared jokes before things turned frosty between us.)

Book Four: *Overboard*. In which Leah ditches the niche north in favour of a more international flavour – Caro had suggested that this might improve the chances of foreign rights sales – and goes undercover as a cabin steward on a cruise ship that's registered in the Bahamas to avoid being investigated for ignoring anti-pollution legislation and covering up some suspicious passenger deaths. Naturally, it ends with Leah having a violent showdown with some corrupt cruise-line shareholders in the engine room.

Book Five: *Over the Odds*. In which Leah returns to her roots and infiltrates a gang of right-wing conspiracy-mongers suspected of murdering an activist who was spearheading an anti-fracking campaign in the Dales. This one ends with Leah going head-to-head with a billionaire oil baron who in looks and personality is an unholy mix of ex-Shell CEO Ben van Beurden, and a Henry Hoover.

If any real-life technocrats or private health fund, airline, cruise ship, and oil company bigwigs had taken offence at my mother's (thinly veiled) portrayals of them, I hadn't heard about it. Which reminded me that I still hadn't read *Overlooked*, and nor did I know anything about the book my mother had been working on at the time of her death. She'd been a stickler for research – *was* it possible that she'd stumbled upon some unexposed malfeasance and had been taken out in a murder made to look like an unfortunate household accident? (Unlikely, because she'd been a writer of escapist fiction, not a crusading journalist digging up secrets on the Saudi or British royals.) 'What was the follow-up to *Overlooked* about?' I asked Leah anyway.

Her back to me, Leah stopped pacing.

'You must know that, seeing as you were her mouthpiece – or facepiece.'

Face*piece?*

'You know what I mean. Mum must've almost finished it. What's it about?'

Love.

'You mean like a dating scam or something?'

She spun around to face me. *No. **The next motive. Love.***

Christ on a bike. But I stored her reluctance about the new book to pick over later. 'Like I said earlier, she wasn't in a relationship or dating anyone.'

And you're sure about that?

'Well, fairly sure.' After my mother's last relationship had fizzled out – she'd had a brief fling with an aviation lawyer she'd consulted when she was researching *Over and Above* – I remembered her saying that she was 'done with all that shite', but to be *absolutely* sure, I'd have to check her devices for dating apps. Which—

'Oh *shite.*'

What?

'Mum's phone.'

What about it?

'We couldn't find it.'

I also began pacing. Which helped, even though I wasn't looking where I was going and tripped over Brian's kibble bowl.

The week after my mother's death mostly had the hazy, fragmented aspect of an arthouse-movie flashback, but I clearly recalled Meera and Daphne, who by then had formed an unlikely sadmin task force, asking me if I knew where Mum's iPhone was (they wanted to check her contacts in case they'd left out anyone who needed to be informed about her death). They'd turned the place upside down looking for it, and I'd suggested using the 'find my phone' app, but that was a no-go because Mum hadn't enabled her device's 'Find My' features. They'd presumably checked the Death Zone too, in case the phone had tumbled out of my mother's pocket when she'd fallen off the ladder, but what if they hadn't and it was still there, possibly subsumed by the weed army?

CLICK, then: *We need to investigate the crime scene.*
Oh crap. Also: 'Did you just read my mind again?'
An excruciating pause, then: *Don't flatter yourself.*

THE BIRDS

I couldn't indefinitely postpone a visit to the gravelly area between the side of the cottage and Glenn and Janet's boundary fence because that was where the recycling bin was stored, and at some point, I'd have to dispose of the infestation of empty cat food cans in the boot room if I wanted to fit in there. But it had been an unusually busy day already, and although it was only getting on for four p.m., I didn't fancy doing that right then.

Unfortunately, before I managed to come up with a convincing excuse, a blue tit I'd dubbed Augustus Gloop tapped his beak on the kitchen window and glared at me. Having lived in loads of flat shares over the years, I was an old hand at being on the wrong side of passive aggression, but none of my former housemates held a candle to the way the birds behaved if I didn't constantly replenish their suet balls. Fortunately for Augustus, who was so overfed that it was a miracle he could fly at all, my mother had been a doomsday prepper when it came to tubs of wild bird food, and there were still stacks left in the garage (she'd also hoarded cat food, toilet paper, and those green and yellow washing-up sponges).

Prevaricating with Leah was one thing, but ignoring the birds' demands was quite another. But at least I could use the finicky act of refilling the feeding tubes as a delaying tactic. 'Come on, then.'

I grabbed the tub of suet balls from the boot room and made for the back door. For some reason, Leah seemed to expect me to open it for her, which was difficult to do without coming uncomfortably close to her, and also odd because when she'd shadowed me around the cottage, doors hadn't been an obstacle to her stalking activities. I was also worried that I reeked of nervous sweat, but if so, Leah didn't mention it (mind you, being both a figment and a smoker, her sense of smell probably wasn't that great anyway).

On the upside, all was quiet from behind Glenn's fence. On the downside, the suet balls didn't need replenishing – I'd just been summoned as muscle to repel a squirrel hanging defiantly off one of the feeding stands.

Stomach a knot of dread, I walked the three metres to the Death Zone. After months of avoiding it, my imagination had recast it as an ominous alleyway, all chiaroscuro shadows and blood-stained stones, but of course it was far more benign. It was the one area that the weed army hadn't colonised – perhaps they also found it triggering – and the neglected recycling bin, placed at the far end next to the side-gate, seemed to gaze at me in relief: *Finally! I was getting worried.* The only thing that came close to my noir-esque imaginings was the broken section of guttering, which was far higher up than I remembered and dangled down like a PVC hangnail.

'It's pretty high up, isn't it?' I said eventually, my voice coming out thick. I bit the inside of my cheek to stop the fledgling chest-burster from expanding. *Not working.* Then Leah CLICKed her lighter, and once again, the sound was enough of a distraction to tamp down the sorrow.

Visiting the site of her author's death didn't seem to be having an adverse effect on her. If anything, she looked mildly bored. To be fair, compared to a plane crash site, or a tech-bro's sex dungeon, it lacked the drama of the crime scenes she was used to frequenting. Also, my mother had given Leah a 'carapace' to shield her from the inconvenience of having emotions, which came in handy whenever she was called upon to investigate the murders of people she knew (Jed, for one). Leah was supposed to be vulnerable underneath it, but she rarely was, and seeing as I had the resilience of a slug living in a salt pan, this protective shell was one of the many aspects of her character that I envied.

All the same, I decided it wouldn't hurt to ask: 'Are *you* okay?'

Why wouldn't I be?

'Well, this is the place where your author . . . you know . . .'

Thoughts?

'About Mum being your creator, you mean?'

A sigh. *About the bloody crime scene.*

Clearly the carapace was in full working order, and I felt a bit foolish for giving a shite. 'Well, like I didn't say out loud earlier, Mum was scared of heights, and if her shoulder was still bothering her, the last thing she'd do is drag out a ladder to fix the guttering.'

Hmmm. Leah lit up yet another cigarette.

'You're not supposed to do that.'

She cocked an eyebrow.

'I don't mean smoking,' – it wasn't as if she could get cancer in her condition – 'but you're only supposed to have one ciggie a day, or three per book. And you're only supposed to take three drags of each one.'

Am I? For once, this was said non-confrontationally, which was actually quite disconcerting.

'Well, that's what you usually do, isn't it?'

A shrug.

Despite the rising cost of tobacco, my mother *had* only allowed Leah to take three puffs before making her dispose of her cancer-sticks in a responsible manner. In the first draft, Leah was in danger of coming across as too perfect, so I'd suggested that she should have at least one bad habit, flaw or weakness. And because my mother's only vice was pasta (which isn't actually a vice unless you sprinkle it with cocaine instead of parmesan), after spotting a pouch of tobacco in my bag, she'd given Leah one of mine. It had also kicked off a long lecture about emphysema, which was fair enough, seeing as smoking had sent two of my grandparents to an early grave. (I hadn't told my mother that I only used tobacco for spliff purposes because she would have thought that was worse.)

It was then that a robin flew down to perch on the recycling bin – the first time I'd seen one in the garden. I'd read somewhere that robins were supposed to signify that the soul of a dead loved one was knocking about, and as if to back this up, it cocked its head and gazed at me with such a familiar expression of resigned disappointment that I half expected it to chirp: *For fuck's sake, Niamh, I've been gone for four months, and you* still *haven't taken the bins out?*

Before I could whisper, 'Help me out here, Mum,' it shook itself and made a bird-line for Leah. Despite knowing that the chances it was harbouring my mother's soul were slim, as Leah crouched down and held out a hand to it, I was hit with such a powerful wave of that old familiar envy, I had to look away.

As a distraction, I cast around for the bright pink protective iPhone case that I'd given to my mother a couple of Christmases ago because she was always dropping her phone in the bath. Realising that a cursory search wouldn't cut it, I got down on my hands and knees to root through the mulch and fallen leaves along the fence line, but all I unearthed was an admittedly fascinating ecosystem of slugs, worms, and silver beetles.

I stood up and brushed dirt from my jeans. Thankfully, the Mum-robin had moved on.

Well?

'No phone.' Just then, a gust of wind pushed a flurry of leaves against the recycling bin. *Oh, hang on . . .* 'Why would she have bothered about the guttering anyway? It wouldn't have been clogged with leaves at that time of year.' It was now, though. My mother's favourite chestnut tree, beneath which she used to sit with her morning coffee, was shedding at a rapid rate, as was Brian's beloved torturing post. 'Plus, she wasn't skint, so why didn't she hire someone to fix it for her?'

After a blip of surprise that I wasn't being an idiot as usual, Leah said, **good thinking**, which again made me feel disproportionately warm inside.

'Shall we do a recap? You're always doing those in the books.'

Go ahead.

'So, we know that the guttering did need sorting because it still does. Which implies that Mum had been attempting to fix it.'

Or *the perp ripped it off to stage the scene.*

'Or like you said before, it was an opportunistic crime.'

Or *the ladder was tampered with beforehand.*

'Or . . .' I'd run out of 'ors'. But I rallied and volleyed back with, 'But how would someone go about tampering with a ladder without it being obvious? I mean, if the perp had sawn through one of the rungs, even the police would have spotted that. That seems a bit unrealistic.' *Even by your standards*, I didn't add.

Where is it?

'Where's what?'

The ladder, of course.

Good question. 'Maybe the police took it away.'

Why would they? According to them there was nowt suspicious about the scene. Where else could it be?

'Well, I suppose Meera, Dad, or Daphne might've put it in the garage. That's where Mum stored all her gardening equipment and stuff.' I didn't recall seeing it whenever I collected a fresh supply of Brian or bird food, but that could be because the spiders had turned the garage into an arachnid Tokyo, and I always darted in and out of there as fast as possible.

Let's go.

ARACHNOPHOBIA

Once again, Leah waited impatiently for me to open the back door for her and did the same with the one in the boot room that led into the garage.

'Can't you just float through doors like a ghost?'

In answer, she cracked her knuckles for the first time. The sound of popping cartilage set my teeth on edge, which was probably her intention.

Naturally, after I'd switched on the light, a particularly large house spider came skittering towards me, and I instinctively yelped (I'd inherited this irrational fear from my father, who was such a chronic arachnophobe that on his post-divorce dating profile he'd probably stipulated, *Seeking someone with fuck-tons of money and a spider catcher*). But instead of deriding me, Leah dropped to her haunches, and mirroring her action with the Mum-robin, held out a hand to it. The spider hesitated, and then scuttled beneath one of the shelves. It was probably planning to do that anyway, because as far as I know, spiders don't respond to hand signals like dogs, and that was more likely than adding 'spider whisperer' to Leah's already extensive résumé. Mind you, after I'd pointed out that Leah exhibited some dark triad psychopathic traits, instead of making her more vulnerable, my mother had decided to 'make animals like her' – the implication being that underneath Leah's carapace was a 'heart of gold'. That said, although this was an objectively unscientific explanation for the way Brian and the robin reacted to her presence, it probably wouldn't account for the spider's behaviour.

They can't hurt you. House spiders are the Labradors of the insect world.

Her words hit me right in my solar plexus. 'What made you say that?' I said, when I could breathe again.

She stood up and shrugged. ***It just came to me.***

'Mum used to say that to me.' She'd done so to dilute my irrational fear, which had backfired because Labradors tend to be excessively friendly and greedy – basically the last attributes you'd want in a large arachnid.

So?

'Did she ever say that to you? Or did you overhear it?' Then something else struck me. 'Did you two ever have normal conversations? About . . . I don't know, stuff that wasn't related to the books?' It was far too easy to imagine Mum up in her attic, lolling in her chair and saying, *I just don't understand it, Leah. If only Niamh had your drive and determination. And self-confidence, and bravery, and dress-sense, and integrity, and and and.*

Her body language had tensed up again, but to steer myself away from pathetic territory, I decided to press her. 'How *did* it work, anyway? You and Mum? Did you appear to her like this, in a very literal way, and then the pair of you brainstormed plots together?' *A bit like Mum and I used to do.* 'Or did she come up with the ideas and you acted them out in your version of the world like a puppet?' And then I had yet another nauseating thought. Leah had also been born out of my mother (albeit from a different part of her anatomy), which meant that she was the closest thing I had to a sister. Like most only children, I'd gone through a stage of wishing I had a sibling. *Not anymore.* 'Well? How did it work?'

Not relevant. She paced towards the garage door. *It's not here.*

'Eh?'

The bloody ladder, of course.

'Oh right.' The spider and sibling traumas had pushed that out of my mind.

Who else might've taken it?

'Well . . . some of the locals came over to drop off condolence cards and stuff. But it would be weird to do something kind like that and then help yourself to the garden equipment. And the neighbours wouldn't have nicked it, because Sheila's in her nineties and I know for a fact that Glenn's got his own ladder because he's always up on it trimming things. That's how come he saw Mum . . . lying there that morning and called the ambulance.' *Only it had been too late for an ambulance, hadn't it?*

You what? If he found the body, then he's our primary witness, **and** *a suspect. We need to interrogate him.* **Now.**

'The perp isn't always the person who finds the body,' I said, even though it often was in *Cold Case Files* and *Nightmare Neighbours from Hell*. A look of steely determination had come into Leah's eyes, so I decided to try and deflect her with something less awful. 'Shouldn't I message Daphne and Dad first? They might have done something with it.' I owed Daphne a proof-of-life email anyway.

We should speak to them in person.

'Can't. They live in Cornwall.'

Interrogation's best done face-to-face. You can tell a lot from body language.

'Right. So you want me – or us – to travel two-hundred-and-fifty miles, which would take at least six hours, just to ask about a ladder?'

A curt nod.

'Can't I just call them instead?'

Fine. Then a smirk. *Oh, hang on.* Had I just been tricked into making a phone call? *Shite.*

I made for the door, but instead of following me, she paused to stare intently at one of the shelves.

'What is it?' *Please don't let it be another spider.*

She didn't respond, so I tracked her gaze to a bundle of zip-ties. To be fair, in the books they were the baddies' PI-restraining tool of choice, so seeing them was probably quite triggering for her. They also gave me a pang, albeit not for the same reason. Because Leah was constantly getting waylaid by balaclava-ed henchpeople, all of whom came equipped with endless supplies of plastic restraining equipment, she needed to be able to break free of her bonds relatively easily and plausibly, and to this end, my mother and I had spent ages researching the various ways this could be achieved, and had even practised doing it.

She snapped out of her trance, and barked: *Get a shift on,* as if I'd been the one holding things up.

Back in the kitchen, I scrolled to Daphne's number. Then again, my father was the most likely candidate for ladder disposal. Not because ladders are particularly masculine items, but I seemed to remember that during Sadmin Week, he'd spent a lot of time doing fuck-all in the garden while Meera and Daphne dealt with all the difficult shite. And a call with my father wouldn't involve a discussion about grief journeys, which I could do without seeing as I was currently undertaking one, and it wasn't going well.

'What should I say? My father isn't the sharpest tool in the box, but even he'll think it's weird that I've suddenly developed an interest in the ladder.'

Play it by ear.

'Great. Clichés are always helpful. Next, you'll be telling me to "just be myself."'

A derisive huff. *No, I bloody won't.*

It had been weeks since I'd last spoken to my father, which suited both of us. I should say here that our mutual reticence wasn't because we disliked each other, but because we shared some unflattering traits. Along with a fear of spiders and a penchant for literal imagery, I'd inherited his emotional cowardice, which meant that our interactions tended to be stilted, as if our communication styles cancelled each other out.

When he answered, his voice was drowned out by the blare of terrible rock music he always played whenever he was abusing one of his canvases.

'Can you turn that down, Dad?'

'Hang on,' he shouted.

I pictured him stomping over to the studio's state-of-the-art sound system, dressed in his paint-splattered jeans and T-shirt combo, his scraggly hair tied at the nape of his neck. The father of my childhood had worn grey suits to work, and in his free time had done conventional middle-class things like watching cricket and playing golf. It had been a bit of a shock when he'd grown his hair long and taken up midlife-crisis painting. I couldn't decide if under his small-c conservative exterior he'd always been a free spirit, or if he was still an accountant at heart, but enjoyed dressing up in bohemian drag.

'What's happened?' were his first words when he returned.

'Nothing's happened.' Which was the understatement of the decade, but anyway.

'You don't usually call.' Not true. I never called. Neither did he. 'Did you try phoning Daph? She's out looking at hot tubs.'

Hot tubs always made me think of human soup. 'That's nice. For the business?'

'Might get one for the studio, too. My back's been bothering me, and Daph thinks it'll help me relax after a day's work.'

'That's kind of her.' Too kind in my opinion.

'Shall I get her to call you when she gets back?'

'Actually, I wanted to talk to you.'

'Right. I see.' He harrumphed. 'Um . . .'

I'd have to ease him into it. 'How's the painting going?'

'Good, good. I'm experimenting with abstraction, which is invigorating.'

Probably wise, considering the state of his figurative work. 'That sounds interesting.'

'It is.'

'Great,' I said, drying up. Leah rolled her eyes impatiently. It was all right for her. Being fictional, she could avoid the drudgery of laying conversational groundwork, and she never did boring small talk in the books – her two speeds were gruff interrogation and kickboxing.

A few seconds of awkward dead air, then he said, 'Aren't you supposed to be at work?'

'I work from home, remember?'

Leah raised a judgemental eyebrow at this blatant lie, which was a bit rich seeing as she was constantly going undercover and pretending to be someone she wasn't.

'How's the car running?'

'It seems fine,' I lied again. I hadn't yet dared drive my mother's Mini in case it still smelled like her, and it was currently shrouded in four months' worth of grime like an abandoned vehicle in a layby.

'Chap did a good job on it.'

'What?'

'Chap who fixed it.'

'What are you talking about, Dad?'

Alerted by the change in my tone, Leah eyed me shrewdly.

'The Mini. Don't you remember? Garage phoned the landline a couple of days after Annie . . . you know. Wondering why she hadn't come to fetch it. Did a good job on the bodywork.'

'She'd had a *crash*?'

'Just a dent. Fender bender, apparently.'

'Hang on . . . so you're saying the Mini wasn't there when we arrived at the cottage?'

'You don't remember that?'

'No.' I couldn't remember anything about the car journey from Dad and Daphne's pad in Cornwall to Mum's cottage – Daphne had given me a couple of her benzos, and I'm not great with Class A drugs.

'Mind you, Daph and I didn't notice it was missing at first. We assumed it was in the garage.'

'Mum never parked it in the garage.'

'Didn't you see the invoice? I left it in the console. You can pay us back when you're ready. Reckon your mother decided it wasn't worth troubling the insurance about.'

Ladder.

Still thrown by the car bombshell, I gave up attempting to segue into the subject: 'Did you take Mum's ladder away?'

'Why would I do that?'

'I don't know. Maybe you thought seeing it would upset me.'

Silence. Clearly, that hadn't occurred to him, which was fair enough, because it had only occurred to me a second earlier.

'Might Daphne or Meera have done something with it?'

'Doubtful. It'll be around there somewhere. What do you need it for?'

According to my delusion, it's a major clue in your ex-wife's murder enquiry. 'Um . . . the guttering still needs fixing.'

'I don't want you going up there, Niamh. Best get a specialist in.'

'Yeah. Did you think it was weird that she was even up there? Because of her fear of heights, I mean.'

'Come to think of it, I did.' A pause, then: 'Remember when you were a kid, and we did that zipline at Snowdonia?'

'Yeah. To get to the start of it, we had to go up a rickety tower thing, and she wouldn't go near it.'

'And then she interrogated the bloke who was running it about the safety harnesses. She didn't want you to go on it, but you insisted.' His voice thickened. 'You screamed all the way down.'

'So did you.'

'I still can't believe she's gone.' He sniffed.

I sniffed too. 'Me neither.'

Then we cleared our throats in unison – the closest we'd ever come to revealing our vulnerabilities to each other.

He harrumphed again. 'Shall I get Daph to call you back?'

'No need. Just give her my love.'

'Wilco . . . I . . . Call anytime.' Then, as if to make up for revealing his softer side, he hung up abruptly.

Leah was gazing at me intently. **What was that about a crash?**

'Give me a sec.' I shook out my hands to dispel the after-effects of the call, which had been the emotional equivalent of a zipline ride. I knew that Mum's death must've upset him – despite the divorce they'd remained on good-ish terms – but he'd never expressed it before. I'd assumed that he too had hidden his feelings behind a basement door, or that his repressed emotions leaked out via his artwork. Poor Dad. Either way, Operation Murder Quest was turning out to have some unexpected – and not entirely negative – side effects.

CLICK. Which, as usual, snapped me out of my reverie. It occurred to me that perhaps Leah used the lighter on me in the same way that dog trainers used those clicker things.

Well?

I filled her in.

Interesting. We could have a case of road rage revenge on our hands.

'You think? According to Dad, it *was* just a fender bender.' All the same, my wonky-wheeled mind detoured into the 'Running Over the Plot' trope, as seen in *I Know What You Did Last Summer* and several other horror films, which involved someone driving along a deserted road at night, running over a stranger, assuming the stranger was dead without bothering to do any form of CPR, doing a runner and pretending it never happened, and then getting stalked/psychologically tortured/murdered by said vengeful stranger who might or might not have come back from the dead. Ridiculous, even by my standards (for a start, my mother had been an overly cautious driver), so I decided not to mention it. Although . . . something else my father had said was niggling at me. 'What about the fact that the Mini wasn't in the driveway?'

Go on.

Encouraged by this response and the treacherous part of my psyche that wanted to please her, I said, 'Well, anyone who knew her habits might've assumed she wasn't at home. What if someone had been casing the joint, tried to break in, and Mum had caught them in the act?'

A sneer: **Casing** *the joint?*

'What's wrong with that? I was just using your sort of private-eye language.'

I've never said that in my life. That was probably true. *But let's run with this.* Was *anything stolen at the time of the murder?*

'Well, Mum's phone is still unaccounted for.'

You sure nowt else was taken? Might be difficult to tell, the bloody state of the place.

'As *you* should know, the cottage wasn't as messy when Mum lived here.'

Hmmm. Leah paced over to the fridge and leaned against it. *We're missing something.*

It was then that I clocked my mother's magnetised notepad, which was stuck to the fridge door. I must have seen it so often, in fact, that it had become invisible.

What is it?

'Move away from the fridge and I'll show you.'

She eyed me suspiciously, then stepped away from it.

I ripped the notepad off the door, scanned it, and then waggled it at her. Beneath the numbers for the plumber, electrician, and emergency vet, were contact details for 'Ivan Morris (builder/handyman)'.

'Mum did have a handyman after all! So why didn't she call him to fix the guttering for her?'

71

Maybe she did and he didn't turn up.

'Or . . . What if he *had* turned up, they'd had a fight over . . . something, he did her in and then staged the scene? I mean, maybe he's some sort of handyperson serial killer or whatever.'

A scornful huff. *And then what? He returned at a later date to collect the ladder?*

'Yeah. Why not? Maybe it wasn't Mum's ladder after all, but his, and he collected it after the dust had settled because . . . it was his favourite.' Hang on . . . what was I doing? I was supposed to be shutting this down, not coming up with more batshit theories. 'Look, you're the one who insists it was murder, not me. So maybe we should just forget about the whole thing.'

No. You're right.

'I am?'

Perp or not, he could have valuable ladder intel.

Valuable ladder intel. Christ.

We need to interrogate him. In person.

'By "we" you mean me, and I've only got a landline number, not an address.' I didn't mention that I could easily reverse Google it. 'It's calling him or *nowt*.'

A stand-off. I looked away first, but because Leah then sighed and said *Fine*, it was a draw.

I was tempted to ask Leah for one of her smokes: calling strangers was well out of my comfort zone – talking to my own father had been a stretch – but for some reason, the anxiety wasn't as pernicious as usual. Was her fearlessness contagious? Or was I becoming addicted to this shite? Either way, I tapped in the number, and it was answered on the third ring, by a gruff, low voice.

'Hi. Is this Ivan?'

'It is.'

'Hi! I believe you did some work for my mother. Annie Morrissey?'

A pause. 'Oh aye. I read about what happened to her in the *Salop Advertiser*. Very sorry about it I was, too. Very sorry. Gave me a shock.'

Gave me one too. 'I was wondering . . . did my mother ever phone you about fixing her guttering? Before she died, I mean.'

A snort from Leah. *As if she could've done it afterwards.* I turned my back on her.

'Let's see . . . oh aye. She did.'

I whirled back around. 'She did call him!' I mouthed at Leah.

'. . . but I told her I couldn't do it on account of being away,' Ivan finished.

I was hit by a burst of unreasonable anger. *Oh, away, were you? If you hadn't been selfishly holidaying, then it's possible she wouldn't have been up a bloody ladder in the first place.* 'Somewhere nice?' I mumbled, trying not to sound bitter.

'Hospital. The cancer came back, see.'

Oops. 'I'm sorry to hear that.'

'What doesn't kill you makes you stronger.'

'That's true.' *It absolutely fucking isn't.* My palms were sweating – so much for being fearless. What to ask next? Then inspiration struck. 'Is it something that would cause an issue if you left it for too long?'

'Oh aye. That's why I had to have the op, see.'

'No, I meant the guttering.'

Another snort from the sidelines.

'Could do, yes. If the water seeps in, it could cause structural damage. Best sort that out before winter.'

Ladder.

'Can I ask you one more question? I don't want to keep you. Not with your . . .'

'Go on.'

'When you worked on the cottage, did you bring your own tools, or did you use my mother's? I'm only asking because I can't find her ladder. It's not in the garage.'

'Let's see . . . oh aye, I remember her ladder. Brand new, it was. One of those fancy foldaway ones. Not in the shed, is it?'

'There's a *shed*? In the garden, you mean?' Both he and Leah huffed with amusement at the same time, which was a bit like being mocked in surround sound.

'That's where they usually are, aye,' he chuckled. 'It's in the corner, up by the boundary fence.'

I couldn't believe I hadn't noticed it before (in fairness, the weeds, trees, and shrubs were so overgrown that they'd hide the existence of an aircraft hangar). Buzzing with a mixture of shame and excitement at this new intel, I thanked him for his time, and then hung up.

'There's a shed,' I said to Leah, needlessly, seeing as she'd been kibitzing on the call. 'Dad said that he hadn't done anything with the ladder, but what if Daphne, Meera, or even the police put it in there without his knowledge?'

Only one way to find out.

THE INVITATION

If this were a Leah book, it wouldn't be a forgotten shed, but a fusty bonded warehouse on an industrial estate, guarded by balaclava-ed men and a token woman to dilute the threat of sexual violence when Leah was inevitably captured and zip-tied to a radiator. Which was something I approved of (avoiding using sexual assault as a plot device, I mean, not constantly having tense encounters with hostile henchfolk).

But even if there had been a shed, Leah wouldn't have tripped over a bramble on the way there, landed on a dried-up thistle, spent five minutes picking spines out of her palms, discovered that the shed was padlocked, spent another ten minutes rummaging through kitchen drawers for the key, and then realised that it had to be the 'mysterious' one that was hanging on a key-rack next to the back door.

Anyway, back at the shed, I unlocked it and . . . no ladder. Not much of anything apart from a tower of seedling pots, and a spider cadaver. Talk about an anticlimax. 'Looks like this case might be shed and buried after all.'

Not even a smile.

I decided to have another stab at thawing the atmosphere. 'I'm not surprised you're a bit mardy. By this point in the plot, you'd usually be on the cusp of uncovering some sort of high-stakes corporate corruption. "The Case of the Missing Ladder" must feel like a proper *step* down for you.'

She remained stone-faced. To be fair, both puns were crap, and the Leah in the books was also a humourless jobsworth, which I'd always thought was a missed opportunity, because people from Yorkshire are renowned for their dry sense of humour.

'So what now?'

What do you mean, 'what now'?

'Should I report the missing ladder to the police?'

Like they're going to bother opening a case for that. She shook her head and sighed.

That was it. I'd had enough, and my exasperation at her bad attitude was so intense that it overrode my default conflict avoidance mode. 'Do you have to be such a patronising bitch *all* the time?'

Don't use that word. I hate that word.

'Fine. Do you have to be such a *massive* bitch all the time?'

Leah narrowed her eyes and stepped towards me. Instinctively, I backed away, and of course stumbled over another bramble and almost fell into the remains of the compost heap. 'Look . . . I won't use that word if you at least try not to be so horrible.'

Use that word again, and it will be the last mistake you ever make.

'That's a bit harsh, isn't it?

Not from where I'm standing,

Not wishing to escalate things further, I turned away and bent down to pick bramble teeth off my jeans. The Leah in the books definitely wasn't this dour and unpleasant

– not even to right-wing psychopaths, or greenwashing oil company CEOs, or serial-killing doctors. Perhaps her bad attitude stemmed from the fact that I was interacting with my version of her, and seeing as I loathed her, she was being loathsome back. Or perhaps she still held a grudge against me for throwing a wooden spoon at her head.

By now, the afternoon was morphing into dusk, and the light was taking on a pleasant blueish haze. If it hadn't been for Leah, I might've enjoyed being outdoors for once.

Ey up. We've got company.

A second later, Glenn's head and shoulders levitated over the top of Mum's overgrown hedgerow, and he batted away foliage like a suburban jungle explorer.

'How did you know he was going to do that?' I whispered at Leah.

A smug shrug.

'You all right there, Nina?' Glenn called (Glenn, like loads of people, always got my name wrong, and I'd left it too late to correct him).

'Hi Glenn!' I said, in the overly bright tone I'd used with Tracey. 'Yes, thanks! Everything's great!'

'Thought I heard voices.' *Voices*, not voice. A sickening thought rolled in: *what if* the delusion extended to me 'acting' the part of Leah, and having conversations with myself like Edward Norton in *Fight Club*? *No.* I was certain I hadn't done that with Tracey. Using 'voices' instead of the singular was probably just a turn of phrase.

'I was on the phone. Lovely evening, isn't it?'

'It is, pet.' Leah scowled at this, but I didn't consider the term 'pet' patronising because Glenn was originally from Newcastle. He held up a pair of secateurs. 'Hope you don't mind, but your leylandii was creeping over – thought I'd give it a trim. And if you want me to pop over and do the lawn, just let me know. Once the brambles set in, they'll run riot if you let 'em.' Said with an undercurrent of *too late*. But why shouldn't they also get a chance at life?

'Thanks. But I'll get round to it at some stage.'

A likely story, Leah muttered. On the plus side, Glenn didn't react to this snipe, which meant that I wasn't doing a *Fight Club* after all.

'I've got time on my hands,' he said. 'You just let me know.'

'I will, thanks, Glenn.'

Ladder. Now.

'Can I ask you a question, Glenn?'

'Fire away, pet.'

'You know the ladder that my mother was using when she . . . you know. Fell. Did you take it away by any chance? I don't mean nicked it or anything . . . just . . .'

Glenn took pity on me. 'I didn't, no. Gone missing, has it? Bit of that going around, like.'

Leah's ears pricked up (not literally), and my pulse rate increased. *Maybe my 'casing the joint' theory wasn't bollocks after all.* 'Have you had anything stolen?'

'I have, as it happens. Two of Janet's gnomes and half a hose pipe. And come to think of it, Graham from Warren Cottage said he was missing a flamingo.'

'Did you report it?'

'Not worth the bother. It'll be kids most likely.'

Except . . . there weren't any kids in the hamlet. Apart from me, the Wanker, and Sheila, who was Buckstone's sole long-term resident, it was exclusively populated by pensioners like Glenn and Janet who'd downsized to the area because they'd voted for Brexit and therefore couldn't retire to Malaga anymore. 'You really think it's kids?' I said dubiously. Although, to be fair, that was more likely than the existence of a garden-ornament-nicking organised crime gang.

Glenn tapped his nose, which was impressive considering that he was balancing on a ladder and had a sharp object in his other hand. 'I should know. I wasn't a bobby on the beat for thirty years for nothing.'

Predictably, Leah was now eyeing Glenn with exaggerated suspicion.

'You were a police officer?' My mother *definitely* hadn't mentioned Glenn's former profession to me, which, considering her virulent dislike of anything cop-related, was more than a little bit odd. 'That's . . .' I searched for the right word. **Suspicious.**

'. . . impressive,' I managed.

Glenn shrugged. 'I did my bit, pet, that's all I can say. If you need a ladder, I've got one here you can borrow.'

'That's okay, thanks. I was just . . .'

Ask him about the morning he found the victim.

Petticoat started yapping then. At some point in the drama, Brian had clearly slipped outside in order to psychically transmit insults to his hapless victim, probably in much the same way that Leah was psychologically torturing me.

'That bloody dog,' Glenn said, 'Goes right through your head, doesn't it?'

I nodded, even though, despite my misophonia, it didn't bother me, mainly because Brian was the one causing it. I was in the habit of automatically tuning it out and pretending that it wasn't my problem.

Ask him.

'Glenn . . . about my mother . . . Would it be okay if I asked you some questions about the morning you found her? Only if you're comfortable with it. I don't want to retraumatise you or anything.' *Please say no.*

'Thought you might want to do that at some point. It's natural. 'Specially now they've confirmed the date for the inquest.'

I took a shuddery breath. 'You know about that?'

'Course I do, pet. They'll need me there as a witness, won't they? I'd offer to do it now, but Jan will be wanting me to get the cod out of the freezer. Tell you what, why don't you pop over in the morning? Ten-ish all right for you? Or will you be on one of your work calls then?'

Leah snorted at this.

'My diary's pretty empty for tomorrow, so that'd be great, thanks.'

Another snort.

'Grand. It'll be nice to have you over.' He chuckled. 'Jan and me were beginning to think you were avoiding us. See you then, pet.' He reverse-levitated.

Shite.

I turned to my nemesis. 'Happy now?'

Leah didn't look happy – she never did – but she did look smug. *'Bout time we moved things on.*

'You can't think that Glenn had anything to do with it. What possible motive would he have? And if he is our perp, he'd hardly invite me over to chit-chat about it, would he?'

What part of 'nowt gets solved with a closed mind' didn't you understand?

I ignored this. 'And not all cops are dodgy, are they?' I hesitated and then said, 'I mean, before he set up his agency, Jed was a DCI in the South Yorkshire Police, wasn't he?'

She flinched as if this genuinely stung – the most overt sign of humanity so far. 'Sorry,' I muttered, which she ignored.

Jed had been slaughtered in *Over and Above* in a murder made to look like an auto-erotic asphyxiation accident

(he'd been on the verge of uncovering the aircraft manufacturer's malfeasance, and had been silenced by a
charismatic assassin). My mother had offed him at the
behest of her new editor, who'd thought it would be 'cool'
if Leah inherited his loft apartment, but before she did so,
Mum had consulted me, and we'd had a heated argument
about it. I'd been against her murdering Jed, partly because
I was fond of him (I'd been his sort-of literary midwife
too), partly because Jed was gay, and killing off LGBTQI+
characters for plot purposes is a tired and offensive trope,
and I was worried that she'd cop a lot of flak for it (which
she had, but nowhere near as much as when she'd broken
another cardinal rule in Book Five). Thanks to the carapace,
Leah had spent less than two pages mourning Jed before
throwing herself into her undercover role as a cleaner in
the dodgy airline manufacturer's HQ.

I changed the subject. 'And what are your thoughts on
the phantom child thieves? Mum didn't have any gnomes
or flamingos, but do you reckon they could've nicked the
phone and the ladder? I mean, what if she *had* caught
them snooping around, and . . .' Then something else struck
me. 'Concealment! When we were going through the
motives, we left that one out, which is weird if you think
about it, isn't it?'

How so?

'In the books, it's usually one of the main motives. In
fact, it features in all your storylines in some form. For
example, in *Oversight*, the reason the evil solicitors tried
to bump you off in a murder made to look like a suicide
was because they were trying to conceal their malfeasance
from Jed. And then that clerk of chambers tried to stab
you with a letter opener because you were going to do
some whistleblowing on the barristers.'

I'm rubbish at charm offensives, but maybe this was a good opportunity to try and lighten the mood again. I had to do something before the oppressive atmosphere plunged me, Brian, the birds, and the weed army into a depression. 'You were great in that book, by the way. I really liked it when you set the barristers' wigs on fire as a distraction while you stole their incriminating files.' This was true – my mother had done an amazing job describing the scent of burning horsehair. Not that it mattered either way because all I received in response was a dismissive CLICK.

'Is that all I'm getting? A click?'

Another CLICK. Only she somehow managed to make this one sound sarcastic.

WHAT WE DO IN THE SHADOWS

Back at Bullshit HQ (the kitchen), Leah resumed her pacing activities, and I hunted for something to snack on. The shoppe's supplies had run out, and the remaining human food in the house – my mother's hoard of tinned Italian plum tomatoes and dried pasta – required cooking. My only choice was a tin of fancy handmade chocolate truffles that were left over from the bereavement hamper Caro had sent to the cottage four months ago, and which I'd stashed under the sink because they were a guilt-inducing reminder that I hadn't yet thanked her for her kindness. The truffles were so far past their sell-by date that when I opened the tin, it let out a soft *gaaah* like a cursed sarcophagus, but I decided to eat them anyway.

Unsurprisingly, Leah shot me a look of unfiltered disgust as I crammed one into my mouth. Unlike me, Leah never ate anything resembling junk food. Not even a cheeky Twix while conducting an all-night stake-out on a corrupt CEO. Whatever hour she got in, and however physically demanding her day had been, she always whipped up a meal from scratch – invariably pasta. Leah was also vegan, which my mother had made her become in Book Three, coincidentally around the time that I'd become one after accidentally watching *Babe: The Sheep-Pig* again. And unlike me, Leah hadn't been undone by a McMuffin two weeks later.

'I'd offer you one, but you don't have a sweet tooth. Or a digestive system.'

A judgemental CLICK.

If anything, the burst of sugar made me feel even more knackered. 'Well, I suppose that's it for today.'

This job never stops.

'It's getting dark outside.'

So?

'Everyone goes to bed early round here. Don't you want to chill out for a bit, and watch Netflix or something?'

She was eyeing me as if I'd just spoken to her in Dothraki. Which was fair enough because she didn't own a screen of any sort and even her down-time activities tended to be 'high-octane' (e.g., kickboxing, running at night in dangerous urban areas, and in Book Five, a bout of MMA cage-fighting).

'And there's no urgency, is there?'

Course there bloody is. She nodded at the inquest letter, which was still on the butcher's block next to the wooden spoon that at some point, I must've retrieved from the floor.

There was always a ticking time clock in a Leah book, and seeing as we had less than three weeks before Mum's death was officially designated an accident, it seemed there was one in this story too. Which again gave credence to the theory that the letter's shock arrival was the catalyst for my brain's masochistic decision to manifest her. And on the off-chance that she wasn't a delusion, its arrival might also explain why she'd chosen that particular moment to break the fourth wall and pitch up in the kitchen, instead of doing the logical thing and showing up immediately after my mother had been found dead. But even so, I needed to divert her from suggesting that we 'gather more ladder intel'.

'Shall I do some research?'

What kind of research?

'Well, I could always have a look at the hamlet's WhatsApp group to see if anyone else is missing a garden ornament.' Or . . . *not*. Leah would never know if I played *Diablo Immortal* on my phone instead. 'I know you hate tech, but in real-life, most crimes get solved by going through perps' phones, or checking ring camera footage or . . .' It was then that something so blindingly obvious occurred to me that I blurted: 'I'm *such* an idiot.'

No arguments from me.

I ignored that. 'CCTV!' *God*, this lapse was more unforgivable than the shed blunder. The cottage didn't have a ring camera, but the Weekend Wanker's barn bunker was equipped with a prison-grade security system. And because his ginormous cameras were situated opposite the side-gate leading into the cottage's garden, the footage would reveal the identity of the perp or prove that no one had pitched up on that fateful night. But either way, a definitive answer could be forty-eight hours and a horrible neighbour away, the unfinished business would be finished, Leah would return to protagonist-purgatory or wherever, and I'd be free to go back to living like a human cat-slash-slug.

Explain.

By now, I should've known better than to share intel with her, but my people-pleasing side won out again, and I spilled the beans.

Hmmm. He won't show us owt if he's the perp.

'Yeah, but that would confirm that he's got something to hide, wouldn't it?'

True, followed by a nod of approval, which was so dopamine-inducing that I almost purred.

'I'd call him now, but I don't have his number.' I didn't even know his real name (it was unlikely to be Wanker). And contacting him on the community WhatsApp group wasn't an option because I hadn't actually bothered to join it (according to Glenn, it was just a stray sheep, wheelie bin, and pothole discussion forum anyway). 'It's a pity that it's Wednesday, and we'll have to wait till Friday.'

Not necessarily. You said he also pitches up when his alarm goes off.

Oh shite. 'Are you suggesting that we go over there and set it off? What if the cameras are linked to his phone and he calls the cops?'

Come up with a reason for being there, course. A cover story.

'Like what?'

It was then that the cover story came strolling in for his supper.

THE NIGHT HOUSE

By the time we got going, it was fully dark, and after I'd acted as Leah's doorperson once again, I hung back in the porch to steel myself. Despite being naturally nocturnal, I'd never actually dared to venture outside at night, mainly because other than the occasional glare of the Wanker's motion sensors, there was zero ambient light, which was brilliant for stargazing, but terrible for someone who'd seen too many folk horror films. It didn't help that the moon was hidden behind a shroud of cloud cover, and at the end of the lane, the usually benign-looking woodland had morphed into a pitch-black amorphous mass. It was far too easy to imagine something dangerous lurking in there, waiting to spring.

Nor did I fancy running into the Wanker at night. I'd only seen him from a distance, but he gave the impression of someone who made manspreading his life's work, and I knew he had a violent streak because the postie had told me that he never slowed down to let rabbits cross the lane, and I'd overheard Pam saying that she'd seen him deliberately run over a squirrel.

What are you waiting for?

'I'm just . . . preparing myself.'

Give over. This is a simple operation. An idiot could do it. She didn't say, *an idiot is doing it*, but the implication was there.

Using my phone as a torch, I crossed the lane, pausing at the edge of the Wanker's driveway to look over my shoulder. It was odd seeing the cottage from this vantage point, and I felt an unexpected pang of fondness for it. It had, after all, done its best to look after me (it wasn't its fault I didn't know how elderly buildings worked). The lights were all on in Glenn and Janet's, and framed in a top window, Janet was standing motionless, as if she was deliberately trying to be a horror trope. I knew she couldn't see me – the glow from my phone was too meagre – but I felt the need to wave all the same. After a beat or two, as if she sensed that I was spying on her, she jerked into life and aggressively drew her curtains.

I jerked into life too, and made for the Wanker's front yard, which, like Glenn's, was a gravelled wasteland, although the Wanker wasn't quite as pernickety about clearing away stray leaves. Amplified by the stillness, my footsteps sounded as if they were being transmitted by loudspeaker, and it was difficult to shrug off the sensation of being watched. A second later, the motion sensor lights flared on, which paradoxically made the atmosphere even more ominous because everything outside the pool of brightness disappeared into impenetrable blackness. I waited for my eyes to adjust, then took stock. Now that I was up close to it, the Wanker's abode looked even more like an apocalypse bunker – so much so, I half expected to see a Geiger counter next to the front door. It was clad in black slatted wood, and the only windows were narrow, oblong slits. Once upon a time, it had probably housed horses instead of Wankers, and I couldn't help but pity it: the poor thing couldn't help what had been done to it.

'How do you think the alarm works? Shall I just walk around for a bit?' Sheila had complained about it loads of times – 'a falling leaf seems to set the dreadful thing off' – but during my tenure, I'd only heard it go off once or twice, probably because I was usually wearing my head-phones.

Why are you whispering?

'Not sure,' I whispered. I did, after all, have a cover story. *Yes, I'm afraid my cat's gone missing, Mr Wanker. Don't suppose you've seen him?* The lights blinked off again, and I half expected Leah's eyes to gleam in the dark, but they didn't.

Let's go round the back. I'll take point.

'Great,' I said with relief, momentarily forgetting that she didn't actually exist, and would therefore be a useless human shield against a vengeful crop god, possessed scare-crow, or any of the other rural horrors my imagination was currently bombarding me with.

Leah glided and I crunched towards a paved pathway that ran between a patch of woodland and the side of the bunker. The second I rounded the corner, another phalanx of motion sensors flared into life. As if to make up for the frontage, the entire back wall was made of glass and bifold doors, but garden-wise, it was more of the same. The only plants were spiky succulents that looked as if they'd be more at home in Nevada than rural Shropshire, and most of it was smothered by decking, which housed a hot tub, and a stainless-steel barbecue.

Leah flinched as an owl – or owls – twit-twoo-ed, but I didn't, which surprised both of us. Especially me, because it had taken me weeks to acclimatise to the array of nocturnal animal noises. For example, I hadn't known that when countryside foxes yelled at each other, they sounded exactly like women screaming. (Urban foxes didn't do this. Or perhaps they did, but everyone ignored them because they assumed it was just women getting attacked as usual.)

'Now what?'

No answer. Come to think of it, she'd lost some of her edgy confidence. This wouldn't be because we were sneaking around in the dark doing something semi-illegal because she did that at least once a chapter. Perhaps she was confused because someone wearing a balaclava hadn't yet jumped out of the hedgerow to attack us.

'Did you hear what I just said?' To be fair, I was still whispering.

I heard you. Go up to the windows.

Bracing for the blare of the alarm, I did as she instructed, stepping up onto the deck and doing my best to look like someone who was worried about the welfare of their cat. The interior appeared to be just as grim as the exterior – all I could make out furniture-wise was the ghostly outline of one of those sectional sofas.

Try the door.

'What? If he's got me on camera, how would I explain that?'

No risk, no reward. Do you want to solve this case or not?

Yes *and* no was the answer to that, but because she'd no doubt bully me into doing it anyway, I grabbed the bifold's door nub and pretended to pull it.

'It's locked.'

Pick it, then.

'With what?'

A lock-pick, of course.

90

'Are you serious? Even if I had one, I wouldn't know how to use it.'

Hopeless. She stepped back and gazed up at the house's façade. Something else appeared to be confusing her.

'What is it?'

There are no open windows.

Of course. Whenever Leah needed to break into a building, if a lock wasn't pickable, there was always a dangerously high open window to squirrel through.

'I suppose that's it, then. What a pity.' I was about to suggest we give the whole thing up as a bad job, when she did her psychic thing again.

We've got company.

A second later, the faint crunch-crunch of footsteps came floating in from the front of the house. It wouldn't be the Wanker, because I hadn't heard his car arrive. Whoever the footsteps belonged to sounded large-ish – heavier than a phantom child thief, at any rate. My heart rate sped up. *Don't panic.* 'It's probably just a deer,' I whispered, more to myself than Leah.

What if it isn't?

Good question. Should I hide? Where though? I doubted I'd fit into the barbecue, and the hot tub wasn't an option because it was full of water and skin cells. I scurried over to it anyway, almost losing my balance when I skidded on a patch of wet leaves. The deck dropped off behind it, so I could always jump down there and crouch in the shadows.

What are you doing?

'Hiding of course,' I whispered as I inched my way to the edge.

You've got an excuse to be here, remember?

True. I kept forgetting that. But the fear was by now so potent, I could taste it.

The footsteps retreated.

Come on. Let's tail them.

'Um – no.'

What do you mean, **no?**

'What if they're dangerous?'

Thought you said it was a deer?

'They can be dangerous too.' Probably.

She took a threatening step forward. *Move! Now.*

Despite knowing that even if she was within kickboxing distance, she couldn't actually harm me (physically, anyway), I panicked and stumble-fell off the deck, which was when I heard – and felt – something crack beneath my heel.

Whatever I'd stepped on was buried beneath a mantle of fallen leaves, and I bent down to brush them away. 'Oh *shit.*'

What are you bloody well playing at?

'I've found something.'

A potentially big something too, because lying directly below the hot tub, the shards of its shattered screen glinting in the light of the motion sensors, was an iPhone.

THE BLACK PHONE

Back in the safety of the kitchen, I was still so wobbly from adrenaline that it took three tries before I managed to insert Mum's charger into the iPhone.

Leah sighed. *Get a bloody move on.*

'This probably won't work anyway.' An understatement seeing as the phone's screen was beyond repair and its charging port was clogged with moss. 'I'd better try and dry it out first.' You were supposed to put damp phones in rice, but because I didn't have any, I shoved it into a jar of macaroni instead.

A muttered *unbelievable*. Unfortunately, my discovery had done nothing to dilute her fury at my earlier cowardice. If anything, it had made it worse, no doubt because my lucky find had delayed her tailing activities, and by the time we'd made it back to the Wanker's driveway, the mysterious interloper had been long gone.

Of course, I didn't know for certain that it even was my mother's iPhone. It appeared to be the same model, but millions of people had iPhones. And it hadn't been slotted into its distinctive fuchsia case, but that might not mean anything either because Mum could've jettisoned my thoughtful but crap gift at any point (it was only after I'd given it to her that I remembered she hated the colour pink). Then again, the phone had clearly been lying there for a long time, and there was something a bit too co-incidental about stumbling across an iPhone in a neighbour's garden when my mother's device was missing.

'If it is Mum's phone, how do you think it got there?'

You tell me.

'Well, if he'd nicked it, then hiding it in his own garden would be pretty stupid. But I suppose it's possible that Mum went over to the Wanker's place for some reason and dropped her phone when she was there. The one thing we do know for certain is that she had it with her on the night she died, so—'

We do? How?

Oops. I'd forgotten that I hadn't told her about the voice message Mum had sent to me that night. *Oh, hang on . . .* did the fact that she hadn't brought this up mean that she *couldn't* read my mind? I bloody well hoped so, because I'd rather sneak around twenty horrible neighbours' gardens in the dark than get grief-bombed by my dead mother's voice. I dredged up a plausible sounding and tech-related lie. 'Um . . . from her phone records.'

A brief nod of acceptance.

Phew.

Why would she have gone over there?

'Um . . . to complain about the alarm, maybe? Which is possible, I suppose, because she died on a Tuesday, and he only usually pitches up on a weekday if something sets it off. But then why would she have confronted him in the back garden and not in the driveway? Unless he was in the hot tub at the time or something.'

Hmmm. Leah let a few seconds tick by, then said, *or they both were.*

'Both were what?'

In the hot tub. Together.

'*What*? You can't be serious!'

We need to consider every possibility.

Ugh, no ta. Although . . . people only usually went in those things with other people they knew very well indeed, and the phone *had* been lying directly beneath the hot tub. And my mother's taste in men had never been great – my father had cultivated a serious case of learned helplessness when it came to anything domestic or mental-load related, and the aviation lawyer she'd briefly dated when she was researching *Over and Above* had turned out to be an anti-vaxxer. And 'love' *was* on the motive list.

But no. 'Mum would *never* go for someone like him. I mean, his house is hideous, and he doesn't give a shit about bunnies and squirrels. And in any case, even if Mum and the Wanker were . . . you know, and they'd had some sort of hot-tub tiff that ended tragically, there's no way he could've carried Mum's body across the lane to stage the scene without being seen because Janet is always spying on everyone.'

Nowt gets solved with a closed mind.

Whatever. Needing some comfort, I automatically ate the last chocolate in the tin, which wasn't wise because it only added to the nausea, then dug the phone out of its macaroni nest and pretended to fiddle with it.

Well?

'It's totally banjaxed. And like I said, it probably isn't Mum's phone anyway. It's much more likely that the Wanker dropped it at some point.' *Please don't let it be her phone.*

She cracked her knuckles and nodded at the door. *Let's go.*

'Eh? Go where?'

Back over there, of course. Whoever was snooping around could still be in the vicinity.

'Like I said, it was probably just a deer or one of the neighbours checking to see why the Wanker's lights had come on. They'll be long gone by now.'

A Death Stare. *We haven't completed the operation yet.*

'The alarm isn't going to go off, and before you ask, no, I'm not going to throw a brick through the bifold doors. Who'll feed Brian if I go to prison?'

An even more vituperative Death Stare – she clearly had a bottomless pit of disdain to dip into.

We were less than one day into Operation Murder Quest, and it was astonishing what I'd been bullied into doing so far. And unless I managed to oust Leah, tomorrow would be even worse. I eyed the cupboard under the stairs, where my only (faint) hope of getting rid of her was languishing in the dark with a red-faced mechanical pervert. There had to be a reason why she shut down whenever the books were mentioned, and if this was some kind of grief-quest, then perhaps reading *Overlooked* was what I was *supposed* to do. At the very least, it would distract me from the horrible image of my mother sharing a hot tub with a squirrel murderer. And if I was going to bite the bullet and read it, it would be wiser to do it in my cloakroom sanctuary.

I darted over to the cupboard, retrieved the package and shoved it under my hoody.

What are you doing?

'I was just double-checking that the Henry Hoover was still in there. The place could probably do with a vacuum.'

Probably? It's a bloody disgrace. But she appeared to have bought the lie, no doubt because there was some truth to it (helpfully, there was a dust-bunny the size of a baby's head right next to her left boot).

'I'm just popping to the bathroom.' I fake-grimaced and touched my stomach. 'I might be a while. Cramps. Not from the chocolates. My period.'

A glance of distrust and possibly, disgust, and then she turned away. *Had* Leah ever menstruated in the books? Thinking about it, she hadn't. I would've remembered if she'd had to slip away from a stake-out to pick up some emergency tampons or beg one of her assailants for an ibuprofen. Perhaps she had one of those implant things.

'Why don't you go out for a run while I'm in there? If you can, I mean.'

CLICK.

I backed out of the kitchen, fled into my sanctuary, and locked the door.

'Me again,' I whispered to Three Arm and her mother Wart Head.

Okay. Let's do this.

I sat on the toilet seat and tipped the book out of its padded envelope. Paperclipped to the cover was a note from Caro:

Niamh! Here it is. I think Annie would have loved it, no? Call me. <u>*We need to discuss your mother's legacy.*</u> *Caro X*

I didn't know Caro that well, but I'd met her a few times at the book events I'd attended as my mother's handbag carrier. On the surface, she looked like the sort of grandmotherly stereotype you see in adverts designed to coerce elderly people into buying funeral plans – all twinkly eyes and cuddly knitwear. But according to Mum, that was just a cannily curated front: Caro was actually a wolf in Nana's clothing, and loved nothing more than 'eating commissioning editors for breakfast'. But because I wasn't a commissioning editor and my mother had made her a reasonable amount of money, Caro had always been extremely nice to me.

In came a sliver of shame. Well, not a sliver, a blast. After dodging Caro's emails for months, and neglecting to thank her for the bereavement hamper, the least I could do was thank her for sending the book. The beguiling spectre of avoidance whispered, *do it tomorrow*, but no. For once, I wasn't going to give into its temptations. But as a concession, I decided to send an email instead, and, as if I was being rewarded by the non-avoidance goddesses, I immediately received an 'out of office' response. This said that Caro wouldn't be available for the next two weeks, because she was attending a book fair in Qatar, and then a crime writing festival in Wales. Warmed by the glow of achievement and my lucky break in a delay, I felt strong enough to tackle *Overlooked*.

As per, the cover displayed a Leah Overton avatar peering moodily through her fringe, which, as I now knew to my detriment, only vaguely resembled the 'real one'. But instead of the usual cityscape scene, she was backgrounded by the outline of a rural hamlet and a posher version of Sheila's crumbling pile. My mother had begun writing it shortly after she'd escaped to the countryside, and bizarrely, it seemed that she'd been inspired by her new surroundings.

More than a little gobsmacked, I flipped it over to scan the blurb:

A case involving the suspicious death of a minor royal isn't exactly in Leah Overton's wheelhouse, but when

Henry Wentworth III asks her to investigate the fluke hunting accident that supposedly killed his uncle, she's intrigued. Lord Wentworth died just days after changing his will in favour of his mysterious manservant, and unless Leah proves that 'the butler did it', the family's ancestral home in the picturesque village of Buckworth will be lost forever.

But as Leah discovers, the butler isn't the only local with a skeleton in the closet. The villagers are harbouring a dark and deadly secret too – one that's been *overlooked* for years – and they're prepared to go to any lengths, including murder, to make sure it stays that way . . .

It wasn't clear from the blurb which real-life pressing social issue my mother had chosen to vent about in *Overlooked* (it was unlikely to be the plight of disinherited aristocrats). Nor was it likely that my mother had based the novel on some unexposed hamlet malfeasance, unless Pam and Elaine were running a county-lines drug operation out of the shoppe and were using retirees instead of kids to smuggle fentanyl across the Welsh border. Plus, the only aristocrat-adjacent hamletee was Sheila, and as far as I knew she didn't have a butler. Nor did she have a vast country estate, seeing as the original property had been broken up years ago, and all that was left of it was the rapidly decaying house.

Preparing myself for the usual bout of Leah Overton bravery and over-achievement, I turned to the prologue.

Considering how she'd been treating me all day, the fact that it involved her being buried alive in a shallow woodland grave might've cheered me up. But unfortunately, it did the opposite. I'd barely begun it when it hit me that the reason why Leah had suddenly appeared to be an expert in rural secret-keeping was because, in *Overlooked*, she'd become one.

Which, if she were just 'all in my head', would've been unlikely because *I'd never read that book* and had no idea that my mother had used the hamlet as its inspiration. Was this definitive proof that Leah *was* an autonomous entity after all?

Yes. No. Maybe. It was possible, after all, that Mum could've mentioned something about the plot in a voice-mail and I'd blocked it out, or when she'd emailed the first draft of the novel all those months ago, I'd glanced at the prologue and forgotten about it (consciously, anyway).

My brain cramped then, and I buried my head in my hands. 'Oh, fuck this,' I said out loud, then automatically apologised to Wart Head and Three Arm. Not that they gave a shite, seeing as they'd shortly have to organise a wake, root through bits of washed-up shipwreck for personal effects, and do the nineteenth-century version of sadmin. All tasks that I would much rather do than face what was currently in the kitchen.

I was tempted to give into the exhaustion and collapse on the floor, but no. I was buggered if I was going to spend another night curled around a toilet pedestal because of Leah bloody Overton.

Leaving *Overlooked* on top of the cistern, I sloped back to enemy territory.

Leah was leaning against the fridge, and judging by the smell, she'd been smoking again. As expected, I was greeted with a black look. ***You took your time.***

I thought about asking her if *Overlooked* had been inspired by more than just the hamlet's setting, but what would be the point?

'I'm going up to bed. You can sleep in Mum's room if you like. *If* you sleep.' She rarely did in the books.

Then, without waiting for a response, I slogged upstairs to my box room. I was vaguely aware that she'd followed me in there, but I flumped down on my bed and passed out anyway.

HOST

CLICK!

I woke up abruptly, and almost screamed when I saw Leah perched on the end of my bed.

Bout time you bloody well woke up, Leah said, keeping her voice unusually low, presumably so that she wouldn't disturb Brian, who was still snoozing on my floordrobe.

I fumbled for my phone to check the time: 8.54 a.m. One hour before Operation Glenn was due to commence.

Having slept in my clothes, I was desperate for a shower. And because I'd rather do that without Leah lurking in the bathroom as if I were a prisoner on suicide watch, I decided to ask her if she'd leave me to it.

Why wouldn't I?

'Well, when you pitched up you followed me round the cottage like a dog for days. It was weird.'

She raised an eyebrow. *As weird as throwing spoons at people's heads?*

Fair point.

But I hadn't requested she stay out of my cloakroom sanctuary, so why hadn't she stalked me in there? While I showered, dressed, and caffeinated, I tried to logic my way to an answer to that mystery. But the only one I could come up with was anything but logical: my father's painting.

If Leah had been my mother's muse, *what if* she was repelled by my father's artwork? And then . . . if something happened to my father, *what if* I was then haunted by his muse? Knowing my luck, she'd take the form of my three-armed avatar.

This ridiculous train of thought was typical of my brain, but it distracted me from the worst of the Glenn dread, and I was able to leave the cottage without ruining yet another hoodie with anxiety-sweat.

As we made our way towards Glenn and Janet's front door, Leah paused to eye their wheelie bin as if she suspected it might be packing heat. Mind you, it was padlocked shut – presumably to stop foxes foraging in it for shoppe scraps. Other than the bin, and Glenn's equally shiny SUV, the driveway was as desolate as the poor old barn bunker's, although, thinking about it, there did used to be two gnomes outside the front door – presumably they were the ones that had been kidnapped. And although the house couldn't have been more of an architectural fuck-you to the bucolic surroundings, now that I was within touching distance of it, I couldn't help but pity it too. The pair of wide featureless windows either side of the door seemed to gaze at me mournfully: *Get me outta here, kid, I don't belong here.*

It struck me then that I could do with some interrogation tips. 'How should I play this?'

By ear.

Great.

Judging by her smacked arse of an expression, she was still festering about the failure of Operation Night Wanker. Interrogating Glenn about that awful morning while a vitriolic PI lurked over my shoulder would be one horror too many, so I thought *sod it*, and had a last-ditch attempt at improving the vibe. 'So. You know when you went undercover as a hospital porter in *Overkill*, and you had to do emergency CPR on one of the evil private consultant's victims because there was a staffing crisis and, just as you brought the victim back to life, the murderer appeared and stabbed you with a scalpel?'

As expected, mentioning one of her past exploits resulted in the usual caginess. *So?*

'So, this is probably going to be worse than that.'

An eye-roll followed by what looked like a suppressed smile. *Hurrah! Progress!* This pepped me up to such an extent that my palms were only slightly clammy when I rang the doorbell.

As if he'd been lurking behind it, Glenn came to the door within seconds. 'Morning, morning. Would you mind taking your shoes off, pet?'

I did mind – my socks didn't match – but I did so anyway and was about to gesture at Leah to do the same before remembering that she was a figment. From upstairs came the sound of a reality show which, judging by the yelling, was one of the *Real Housewives* iterations.

'Who's that, Glenn?' Janet's voice floated down the stairs.

'I told you, pet,' Glenn shouted back, 'Nina's popped over. Annie from next door's daughter.'

A pause. 'Shall I come down?'

'No, no. You're all right.' To me he said, 'Janet's got one of her headaches again.'

Blasting the telly at full volume didn't seem like a wise way to deal with a headache, but I wasn't complaining – I could do without running into the woman who'd been glaring out of her window last night. 'Shall we do this another time?'

'No, no. Come on through.'

The scent of furniture polish was so intense that I could practically feel it buffing my nostrils, and unsurprisingly, the interior was as pristine as the wheelie bin. The hallway's white tiles shone like a glacier, and the only adornments were two photographs propped on a side-table, which Leah paused to eye with distaste. They depicted a much younger Glenn and Janet wearing police uniforms – the old-fashioned kind too: Glenn was in one of those pointy helmets.

'Janet was in the police force, too?' The photos weren't particularly flattering. Young Glenn was sporting a thick, blocky moustache, like the kind you only ever see on cops or sex offenders, and Janet's fixed smile was borderline-aggressive.

'Dispatch,' Glenn said. 'That's how we met.'

'Oh. That's . . .'

Doubly suspicious, Leah piped in.

'. . . cool,' I finished.

'You could say that she was my handler.' He chuckled. 'And still is.'

I genuinely thought Leah was going to gag at this, but I did my best to laugh politely. It had the weak tang of an overused joke: no doubt he said it to everyone.

He ushered me into the kitchen, and the pong of furniture polish was smothered by the eye-watering hum of bleach. Leah prowled around, no doubt looking for clues that Glenn and Janet were our perps. It didn't take her long. There was no clutter, and almost everything was white, albeit not in a chic, minimalist way. There was something off about the cabinet doors and the leather breakfast bar stools, as if the nineteen-eighties and the early two-thousands were locked in an interior décor wrestling match.

Glenn gestured for me to take a seat at the breakfast

bar, which was tricky because the stools weren't built for someone of my stature, and I had to grip the counter to stop myself from sliding off. Leah stalked over to the fridge, leaned against it, and folded her arms. As if I were a guest at a hotel, Glenn brought over a tray containing a teapot, a tiny jug of milk, and a plate of misshapen oat biscuits that I recognised as originating from the shoppe. My stomach grumbled at the sight of them.

'Shall I be mother?' he asked.

I recoiled at this, but he didn't seem to notice. The tea was so over-stewed it came out black, and I added milk even though I never drank it.

'Your home is lovely, Glenn.' It wasn't, of course, but I could play the small talk game if I had to. 'Did you design and build it?' *And if so, why?*

He chuckled. 'No, pet. Previous owners but one did that. We bought the place . . . let's see . . . year or so before your mother moved into the cottage. We've had a grand time here, but we're thinking about moving back to the north-east. Bit too isolated for Janet. And we've been having issues with the satellite dish signal and that.'

'Oh right. I'm sorry to hear that.' Why didn't they just use wifi like normal people? Surprisingly, the hamlet's broadband was pretty reliable and had only dropped once or twice during my pre-Leah all night gaming sessions.

'Your mam was a canny woman, pet. Very neighbourly. Offered to water the plants when Janet and I were on our cruise.'

I couldn't see any plants. Maybe he meant outside, although I couldn't see any out there either, seeing as the garden was basically a paved gulag. The only greenery was the mass of foliage poking up from my mother's garden, and the hedgerow that bordered the field on the other side.

From above, Glenn's home probably looked as if it'd been hit by a meteor made of weedkiller. It was no wonder that Sheila had felt the need to whinge about Glenn and the Wanker's 'disrespect' for the area's natural beauty and wildlife – after witnessing their efforts firsthand, I was tempted to do that myself.

'Now. What is it you want to know, pet?' Glenn said, softening his voice.

'Um . . .' *Oh God*. In came the grief-weight again. Fortunately, keeping my balance on the stool was killing my back, so I concentrated on that. 'Um . . . anything you can remember would be helpful.'

Glenn cleared his throat. 'What I can tell you for sure is that she didn't suffer. She looked very peaceful when I found her.'

The weight increased, and I took a gulp of tea in the hope that the bitter taste would keep it at bay. Other than adding a sliver of nausea to the proceedings, it didn't, so in desperation, I glanced at Leah. She was busy glaring at the back of Glenn's head, but just as the pressure became unbearable, she took out her lighter: CLICK. (I was now certain that she was using her lighter to dog-train my emotions.) 'That's . . . reassuring,' I said to Glenn, when I could speak.

'And I should know, pet. I've seen my share of accidents over the years, and the inquest will bear that out, you'll see. I said all that to your dad and Daphne when they were here, like. Didn't they pass it on?'

'They might've. I wasn't doing great around that time.'

'Don't blame you. Losing your mam so young.'

Leah sighed. ***Get on with it.***

'The thing is, Glenn . . . I'm struggling to make sense of why my mother was up there in the first place. I mean,

I know it was summer, so it wasn't dark, but it seemed like a crazy time to fix the guttering.'

Glenn sighed. 'I blame myself for that.'

For a second, I assumed I must've misheard him. 'Um . . . what?'

'It was me who pointed it out to her, see. Week or so before. I offered to fix it for her, but she said she'd get a handyman in. You won't want to leave it too long, I said. Happened to my brother's bungalow. Rotted his fascia boards, and the next thing you know he had to . . .'

The stressful nature of the situation notwithstanding, I sensed a drift into monologue territory and automatically tuned out, only snapping back to attention when Leah clicked her lighter again.

'. . . but it was fine in the end because he decided to move to Northampton.' Glenn took a sip of his tea.

Ask him if he heard or saw owt suspicious that night.

I came very close to blurting, *how?* Fortunately, Glenn picked up the slack.

'Might not have seen her at all that morning if it wasn't for that cat of hers. Heard it crying, so I took out the ladder and looked over the fence in case it had got itself stuck somewhere.'

Leah and I exchanged glances. *If only cats could talk.*

'I just wish I'd found her sooner,' Glenn continued, 'but Janet and I were out that night.'

Leah narrowed her eyes. So did I. 'Somewhere nice?' I asked, in the same strangled tone I'd used with Ivan.

'We'd been at the rep. *Starlight Express.* Fair drive, but it was worth it. Janet loves a good musical.'

'Oh, that sounds nice,' I lied.

Don't take his word for it. Get proof.

'Seriously?' I accidentally said out loud.

'What was that, pet?'

'Nothing. Sorry.' This was probably how newsreaders felt when they were interviewing someone, and a producer kept talking in their ear.

Do it.

I took another sip of teeth-staining tea to stall while I thought of a non-obvious way of doing that. In the books, Leah always had a plausible reason to ask: *and do you have proof of that*? But this was real life, and I wasn't a PI – undercover or otherwise. Then inspiration struck: 'Did you get a programme, by any chance? I'd love to see who was in it because . . .' *Christ,* this type of lying was hard. I had zero interest in musicals (people singing when they should be talking is never not disturbing), but I was *fairly* sure that *Starlight Express* was about trains of all the fucking things. '. . . because I like acting. And trains.'

Despite the statement's objective stupidity, Leah gave me a nod of approval, which again gave me a much-needed hit of dopamine. Glenn didn't seem to think the request was odd either, which made me feel sorry for any crime victims he'd dealt with in the past. 'Hang on, pet. Let me go and ask Janet.'

'I don't want to put you to any bother.'

'It's no bother.' Off he toddled, leaving me and Leah to listen to:

'Janet!'

'What?'

'Did we get a programme for *Starlight Express*?'

'A what?'

'A programme! Did we get a programme. Nina wants to see it.'

'It's in the drawer!'

'Which one?'

'The one where we keep the warranties!'

Etcetera.

I took the opportunity to squirrel three biscuits into my pocket and cram one into my mouth. 'This is exciting, isn't it?' I whispered to Leah, scattering crumbs. I tried to brush them up, but there was nowhere to put them other than in my pocket or my mouth, so I did a combination of both, and almost slid off the stool in the process.

Hmmm. If they were out, then that puts the Wanker back in the frame.

Oh God. I hadn't thought of that. 'No, it doesn't. Because from what Glenn said, the guttering did need fixing, so Mum was probably up there trying to—'

Quiet. He's coming back.

It was the fourth time she'd done this disturbing trick. Perhaps her hearing was sharper than mine.

Glenn returned brandishing a glossy programme. 'Here you go, pet. The main actor had eaten a bad prawn sandwich, so the understudy had to play Rusty, but he did a grand job.'

It didn't have a specific date on its cover, so it proved nothing other than Janet was into fucked-up musical theatre (and judging by the photographs, the show had been more disturbing than *Cannibal Holocaust* or even *Cats*). It was obvious that Glenn wasn't an investigative genius, but even he'd suspect I was up to something if I asked to see the tickets.

Now what? I side-eyed Leah for guidance, and she snapped, *Wanker.* For an instant, I thought she was dissing our current interviewee, then she rolled her eyes. *The* other *Wanker.*

'I was wondering, Glenn . . . do you know anything about the man who owns the barn conversion opposite?'

Glenn baulked at this. I didn't blame him. It was an abrupt change of subject. 'What made you ask that, pet?'

'Just curious. He seems to be a bit standoffish, and I was wondering if there's anything I should . . . be aware of.' Did that sound reasonable? It seemed to because Glenn had stopped acting nonplussed.

'He's a right miserable bastard, 'scuse my French. That bloody alarm going off at all hours. The music he blasts out when he's having his shindigs. Driving like a lunatic through the hamlet, thinking he owns the bloody place. And don't get me started on all that malarkey with the planning.'

'What malarkey?'

'Didn't your mam tell you about it?'

'No.' There seemed to be an ever-expanding list of things she hadn't told me, including the bombshell that she'd been harbouring a volatile muse.

'He wanted to build another house on that patch of woodland next to his place, even uglier than the one what's already there, if you can believe that. That's why he bought the place, see. We all objected, and your mam wrote to the MP about it too – said it would disrupt the wildlife.'

Wow. It sounded like my mother had turned into a 'Not in My Back Yard' person after all. And did we actually have a semi-plausible motive for once? And one that – thankfully – didn't involve hot tubs. 'When was this? Was it recent?'

'No, pet. Not long after she moved here.'

Which probably lessened the planning-dispute-as-revenge motivation, unless the Wanker had bided his time for some reason. 'Do you know what his name is, Glenn?'

'The MP you mean, pet?'

'No. Mr Malarkey opposite.'

'Let's see . . . Ray somebody . . . Ray Fiddle. That's it.'

111

'Ray *Fiddle*? He sounds like he should be a children's TV presenter.'

Glenn chucked. 'He does at that.'

Or a pervert, Leah said, deadpan, which made *me* laugh, even though she probably meant it literally.

'Did he know that my mother had objected to the planning stuff? I mean . . . could he have been harbouring a grudge against her?'

'Like I said, pet, we all objected, and he steers clear of us lot round here. Not that I blame him for avoiding her ladyship, course. Don't you worry about him. All mouth and no trousers, that one. And if he causes you any hassle, you come and tell me.' Glenn bristled paternalistically, which caught Leah's attention, and she went back to scowling at him.

'Thanks.'

Ask him if he was out and about last night.

'Speaking of Mr Fiddle,' – despite the tenseness of the situation, it was almost impossible to say his name out loud without laughing – 'I saw his motion sensor lights going off last night. Did you?'

'Can't say I did, pet. Used to the bloody things by now, mind.'

Leah sighed and shot me a 'told-you-so' look.

'Are you planning on staying on, pet? In the cottage, like?'

'Not sure yet.'

'No point rushing a decision. You see how you feel when the time is right, is my advice. Can't be much fun living all the way out here. Not much life around here, is there? You'll want to be around people your own age, I bet.'

I didn't comment on this because I was currently spending rather a lot of time with someone – or something – my own age, and fun it was not. I hoped he wasn't going to ask me if I was in a relationship or – worst of all – wanted kids, which the hamletees tended to do out of reflex, probably because in their day it was the norm, and back then even working-class people like my mother could afford to breed. Thinking about it, one of the few things Leah and I had in common was a desire to remain child-free, albeit not for the same reasons. (Leah: Lone Wolf + too busy overachieving and going undercover; me: Aromantic + even if I did want kids, I wouldn't have them because the world is so utterly, irrevocably fucked, and I'd be consigning them to a future of eating rats in an apocalyptic wasteland.)

'Now, is there anything else you want to know, pet?'

'I think that's it, thanks, Glenn.'

No, it bloody isn't. Car crash.

For a second, I got it wrong again and assumed she was critiquing my interrogative skills. Then I remembered that 'The Case of the Missing Ladder' did indeed have a car-crash element. 'There is one more thing if you don't mind, Glenn.'

He chuckled. 'You sound just like Columbo, pet.'

Who? Leah barked at the same time I thought it (I Googled it later). 'Did my mother mention anything about getting into an accident?' He recoiled at this. *Not that kind of accident, Glenn – she wasn't psychic.* 'In her car, I mean. Apparently, she had a fender bender just before she died, and the reason I'm asking is because . . . there are some issues with the insurance company.'

'Not as far as I know. Always seemed like a careful driver to me.'

'Right. Thought so.'

'Good on your mam for putting her foot down about the planning and all that,' Glenn continued. 'She seemed

113

like someone who was very . . . what's the word I'm looking for, pet?'

'Um . . . principled? Tenacious?'

'That's the one! You'd know that word, what with you being a writer too.'

'Eh? I'm not a writer.'

Glenn shook his head and chuckled. 'No need to be modest. Your mam said you were very talented.'

Oh Mum . . . For shame reasons, she'd clearly been lying to the neighbours about me. It wasn't as if she could've told the truth: *Yes, my daughter* has *fulfilled her ambition of dropping out of university, and we're proud of the enormous amount of student debt she's accrued over the years.*

'I told your dad I'd keep an eye on you, pet, but I didn't want to interfere, and he and Daphne said you were very capable and independent.'

It seemed that my father and Daphne had felt the need to lie about me, too.

'Anything else I can help you with, pet?'

Was there anything else? I side-eyed Leah for guidance, but for some reason she'd ditched the Glenn aggression and was currently 'looking inwards', which was something she tended to do before an inner monologue. 'No. You've been great, thanks Glenn.' I slid ungracefully off the stool.

'You call on me whenever you need, Nina. I meant it about the garden, like. I've got time on my hands.'

ONE MISSED CALL

Back in the cottage, Leah began to pace as per, but as with her weird 'inward-looking' behaviour at Glenn's, there was something subdued about it.

'Everything okay?'

Why did you lie to Glenn about not being a writer?

'Eh? I didn't. I'm not a writer.'

A distrustful glare. *Yes, you bloody well are.*

'Well, I used to be. Sort of.' The content I'd cobbled together for my last job didn't really count, seeing as I'd mostly just nicked it off TikTok (an open-source AI was no doubt doing that job right now).

Hmmm, she said enigmatically.

Oh shite. Was it possible that my mother had also been lying about me to the muse-slash-protagonist who she'd basically created to guilt-trip me into 'fulfilling my potential'? No. Leah probably assumed I was a writer because I spent most of my time dressed in PJs and sitting on my arse in front of a laptop.

'So that's Glenn and Janet off the list, then,' I said. 'Probably.'

No reaction.

'Did you hear me?'

I heard you.

'And what do you think about the Wanker intel? He must have been pissed off with Mum about the planning stuff, but why would he wait so long before he did anything about it?'

Revenge is a dish best served cold, she said, but I could tell that her heart wasn't in it.

Perhaps she'd concluded that life wasn't stranger than fiction after all. Or perhaps she was frustrated because the only way she could do the interrogating was via me, her malfunctioning ventriloquist's dummy.

But I decided to leave her to her inner-monologuing and get on with some Ray Fiddle research. I had no trouble finding a matching profile on Facebook, which, fortunately, wasn't set to private. I'd expected it to be an anti-immigrant, culture-war diatribe, but it was horrible in a different way, consisting mostly of pics of the Wanker wearing aviator sunglasses, leaning against sports cars, and misusing emojis. There were also several photographs of him with a glamorous woman with hard eyes, tagged 'Madelaine Fiddle'. I definitely hadn't seen her piling out of his fuck-the-planet SUV before, but then again, pre-Leah, it wasn't as if I'd been a curtain-twitcher like Janet, and entire weekends had gone by without me registering his presence at all. In fact, I hadn't even been disturbed by the 'shindigs' Glenn had mentioned.

On the bright side, the fact that he was married confirmed that my mother and the Wanker definitely weren't having some sort of horrible hot-tub-based affair. She'd loathed cheaters with a passion – apparently my grandad had been 'having it away' with half the women in South Yorkshire when Mum was kid – so even if the Wanker had been Idris Elba, she wouldn't have gone near him. But this didn't change the fact that he was still the most likely recipient of footage that could clear all of this up, and I now had a laundry list of discomfiting questions to put to him.

With the Wanker off the slate till tomorrow – I didn't fancy sending him a friend request and asking for his number – all that was left on the task list was: a) interviewing a poorly nonagenarian; b) listening to my mother's voice messages; c) braving the attic to examine her laptop; d) calling Meera, who might or might not know what had happened to the ladder, but seeing as she was way sharper than my father, I'd have to come up with a convincing backstory first. And because I'd rather be vampired than go anywhere near b) and c), I decided it was time to unearth the cake tin. I had, after all, promised Tracey that I'd drop it round.

The one good thing about never getting round to doing the recycling was that I knew for certain I hadn't thrown it out.

What are you doing? Leah grumped as I rooted through the once orderly kitchen cupboards.

'Looking for Sheila's cake tin. If we're going to interrogate her about appeasement confectionery, then I need to find it first.'

I eventually found it buried beneath a Jenga tower of empty Sheba containers. I shoved them into bin bags and dumped them in the garage for later disposal. The Death Zone hadn't been as bad as I feared, but I didn't fancy visiting it right then (I'd regret putting off this chore). The cake tin, which was decorated with kittens gambolling with dandelions, felt heavier than it should, as if it had a severed head inside it instead of a neglected cake.

Leah took out a cigarette and absent-mindedly tapped it on her palm.

'Would you mind smoking that outdoors? I don't want Brian to get cancer. Apart from my dad and Daphne, he's the only family I've got left.'

A sigh. *Fine.*

'Really?' *Who* was *this non-person?* 'Shall I let you out now?'

I'm not a bloody dog.

'I know that. Dogs don't usually smoke, do they?'

The faintest of faint smiles. *More progress!*

'I should probably open the tin on the back porch, anyway.'

Why?

'In case it explodes.'

Somehow, I managed to not drop it as I opened the back door for Leah. She lit up immediately and took three quick drags (perhaps she was trying to make a point). Thankfully, the birds ignored her. After witnessing Brian, the Mum-robin, and the spider's reactions to her, I'd half-expected them to alight on her shoulders like she was some sort of assassin-themed Disney Princess.

I placed the tin on the overgrown patio area, prised open the lid and stood back. Inside it was . . . a perfectly ordinary fruit cake. No mould. No sign that it had been left to fester for weeks. Stunned, I upended the tin, and the cake plonked out whole. I nudged it with my sneaker. 'Wow. Maybe Sheila used concrete instead of flour. Should I leave it out here for the birds? Or do you think it'll kill them?'

This seemed to perk her up. *Are you saying it could be poisoned?*

'No! Because it's rock solid. Why would Sheila want to poison me?'

She gave me a look that probably meant, *why wouldn't she?* and then crouched down to examine the cake the same way the cops in *Law & Order: SVU* do whenever they come across the body of a murdered woman. I half expected her to snap on a pair of surgical gloves and poke it with a biro. She looked up and cocked her head. ***What's that sound?***

From inside, I caught the faint ominous chords of 'Ave Satani' from *The Omen*. I must've left my phone in the kitchen.

'My phone's ringing. I'd better go in and get it. Tell you what, why don't you stay out here and finish your ciggie? I won't be long.'

I'd expected her to insist on tailing me, but she merely shrugged and continued to forensically investigate the cake.

By the time I reached the kitchen, the call had died. Worryingly, the missed call was from Meera, who usually messaged me. But as she was my mother's executor, it was probably to do with the probate. I was relishing being alone in the kitchen for the first time in four days, when Meera rang again. It was tempting to let my voicemail do the heavy lifting, but if I didn't answer it, she'd probably get the police to do a welfare check.

'Hi Meera,' I said, in my overly bright voice.

'What's going on, Niamh? Daphne messaged me. She said you've been asking your dad some peculiar questions about your mother.' *Shite* – I'd forgotten she and Daphne had a 'Fix the Dead Woman's Millennial No-Hoper' WhatsApp group.

'Nothing's going on.' I flailed for a plausible explanation that wasn't delusion-based, eventually landing on, 'I'm seeing a therapist. She suggested I try to come to terms with Mum's death by . . . exploring stuff about it.' As lies went, that one wasn't bad, and I almost regretted that Leah wasn't around to hear it.

'This person *is* a registered mental health professional, right?'

'Mmhmm.'

'What's her name?'

'Funnily enough she's called Leah. Leah . . . Maddox. Dr Leah Maddox. She's a grief counsellor.'

'Is it helping?'

'Mmhmm.'

'Well, I'm happy to hear it.' A pause. 'Daphne mentioned that you were looking for Annie's ladder?'

Phew. *Safer ground.* And this was the perfect opening for gathering valuable ladder intel. 'Glenn from next door thinks some kids might've nicked it.'

'That doesn't seem likely.'

'That's what I thought. Did you see it when you were here?'

'Yes,' she said tightly.

'Was it still in the . . . still by the side of the cottage?'

'Yes. Bloody thing. I gave it a right kicking as well.'

I wished I'd thought of taking out my grief-induced rage on a piece of garden equipment instead of bottling it up until it metastasised into a PI with a mood disorder. 'Did it help?'

'For about five minutes. Then I folded it up and leaned it against the wall. I meant to ask Declan to get rid of it so that it wouldn't upset you.'

That choked me up a bit. *Good old Meera.* 'That was really thoughtful of you.'

'It would've been if I'd asked him to do it. Are you sure your dad didn't put it in the shed?'

'You know about the *shed*?'

'You can't miss it, Neevy. It's a shed.' Meera sighed. 'Are you *sure* you're coping? You know my thoughts on your decision to live there.'

'Someone had to look after Brian.' *And – I didn't have anywhere else to go.* 'Really Meera, I'm fine. And I'm sorry I missed your call. I was out in the garden. Um . . . feeding the birds.' *And diffusing a cake bomb.*

'Annie would've approved of you doing that,' she said with a smile in her voice. 'She loved those birds, didn't she? You know, I'd be lying if I said I wasn't shocked when she told me she was moving to the shires, but she threw herself into fixing that place up, didn't she? I remember when she told me she was taking you to see it for the first time. God, she was nervous.'

Mum hadn't seemed that nervous to me. 'She was? Why?'

A longer pause. Meera was a straight shooter, and it wasn't like her to be hesitant. 'Look. Don't take this the wrong way, Neevy, but she was worried that you'd think she was leaving Yorkshire so that it'd be trickier for you to move back home.'

Ouch. That motivation *hadn't* occurred to me, although it should've done, seeing as my mother was always saying that she was suffering from 'the opposite of empty nest syndrome.'

'. . . but I told her not to be so daft and that you'd sort yourself out eventually. Now. While I've got you, do you think you're up to having a word with Caro? She said she's emailed you several times.'

'I sent her a message yesterday.'

'You *did*? I have to say, maybe the therapy is working, Neevy, which is wonderful to hear. Well. I suppose I'd better get back to the grindstone.'

But instead of sagging with relief and hanging up, I heard my quest-self saying, 'Sorry, Meera, before you go . . . Do you know if Mum was having any issues with the neighbours?'

A pause. 'Why are you asking that? Are you having problems with them?'

'No! Course not. They've all been . . . It's nothing like that. It's just . . . I don't know much about her life here, and Leah – Dr Maddox – thought it would be a good idea to work through my feelings about that.' I cringed.

Another pause, during which I could practically hear Meera weighing up whether to let me get away with this obvious bullshit or not. 'Well . . . I remember her saying something about an ongoing issue with some mardy bloke, but there's always one in every neighbourhood, isn't there?' *That must be the Wanker.* 'And not long after she moved in, there was some malarkey going on with Lady Wotsit.'

That word again. 'What malarkey?'

'Annie wouldn't tell me the details, but I got the impression that she was worried she might have offended her.'

'Oh right.' Everyone offended Sheila at some point. Mum had probably planted some begonias in the wrong place or something.

A sigh. 'Okay, what's really brought this on?'

'Nothing. I was just . . . I suppose I was wondering if anything was bothering her just before she was – just before she had her accident. Apart from me, I mean,' I let out a feeble half-laugh. Had Mum told Meera about our fight? Well, not *fight*, exactly. She'd said some things to me, and I'd said some things to her, and I would do anything to take them back.

'Oh, *Niamh*,' Meera said, softening her tone. 'You're not trying to blame yourself for the accident, are you?'

'No. Course not.' Except, that wasn't strictly true. Because if my mother and I hadn't fallen out, and I hadn't run away to Cornwall to sulk in one of Daphne's glamping pods, then Mum wouldn't have been alone that night. A grief parasite began to flex inside my chest, and without my CLICK defence to keep it at bay, I was forced to bite the inside of my cheek hard enough for it to bleed. Before I managed to blink it away, one of those lonely tears escaped and plopped onto the inquest letter, smudging the 'M' in Morrissey.

Meera sighed. 'Look . . . the fact is, we hadn't spoken for a few weeks. Maybe longer.' There was a tinge of guilt in her voice now too, along with an undercurrent of sorrow. A sobering reminder that I wasn't the only one who had an Annie Morrissey-shaped hole in their life. 'She always pulled back when she was working on a book. And around that time . . . well, she knew I had a lot on my plate, so she wouldn't have wanted to add to that.' That was true. Meera was juggling ailing parents and in-laws, her own probate law practice, and a thirteen-year-old stepson who was almost as fucked-up as I was. Yet, when Mum had died, she'd found the time to drop everything, travel down from Bridlington, and help me navigate the sadmin bureaucracy. More than help, because all I had to do was sign stuff. 'But Neevy, what happened to Annie, it was an accident. A quirk of fate. There wasn't anything you or anyone else could have done to stop it.'

'I know.' I swallowed. 'And thank you for everything you're doing to help me.' Shamefully, I realised I hadn't said that to her before.

'She would have done the same for me. And . . . look. We all know you've had your ups and downs, but she loved you. You know that, right?'

'I know. She loved you too.'

After we said our goodbyes, I crammed the last of the stolen biscuits into my mouth to take away the taste of blood and then hurried outside to join Leah before the thing in my chest burst through my rib cage. The irony of voluntarily seeking out Leah's company didn't escape me.

Leah had moved on from investigating the cake and was now standing stock-still, her back to me, head tilted in the direction of my mother's favourite chestnut tree. I couldn't help but wonder if she'd ever sat beneath it with Mum, perhaps with her hands cupped around a metaphysical coffee mug, the pair of them listening in companionable silence to the dawn chorus. Fortunately, Leah turned to face me before the envy had a chance to roll in.

'Um. Hi.'

You took your time. Who was the caller?

'Meera. Mum's best friend.'

And? Any new intel?

'Not really. Nothing to do with the case, anyway,' (I was wrong about that as it happens). I wasn't about to tell Leah that the reason my mother had moved four hours away from everything and everyone she knew was to prevent me from becoming a basement dweller. Although . . . perhaps she already knew about it. Perhaps it was one of the topics she and Mum had chit-chatted about over early morning coffee. *No. You're just being paranoid.* So far, Leah hadn't shown any signs that she and Mum had been particularly close. If anything, it was the opposite – she still hadn't used Mum's first name, or, come to think of it, mine – but this could be because she was a consummate professional with a carapace.

Did you ask her about the crash?

I was always forgetting about that. 'She didn't know anything about it.' Which was probably true.

Augustus had just spied the cake, and fluffed his wings, as if he were an overloaded Boeing preparing for take-off, then flumped down onto it. He pecked at it, cocking his head in confusion when that failed to yield any crumbs, and then his eyes seemed to fix lovingly on Leah. *Don't you dare, Augustus – remember who feeds you.* Fortunately, a siskin rocked up and despite being half his size, bullied him away from the spoils.

'I should probably put that in the compost in case it's harmful to birds.'

Nah. Let them have their cake and eat it.

I blinked at her in shock, and then laughed exaggeratedly. This attempt at humour, although objectively shite, was such an improvement on her usual terseness that I felt the need to encourage her. I was reaching for a cake-related follow-up pun, and had gotten as far as 'batter late than never', when she remembered that she was supposed to be a curmudgeon. **Let's make a move.**

The cake had come out clean, so when we went back inside, instead of rinsing out the tin, I just wiped it with a tea-towel, which wasn't just lazy but also unhygienic.

INTERVIEW WITH THE VAMPIRE

I opened Sheila's gate for Leah – wincing as its Pavlovian-in-a-bad-way *clang-creak* kicked in – and gazed up at the house.

Seeing Glenn and the Wankers' abodes close-up had changed my view of them – emotionally anyway – but this wasn't the case with Sheila's. It was simple in design, almost a perfect square with large sash windows, but the brickwork was covered with the husks of several long-dead climbing plants, which made the façade look as if it were being embraced by skinny skeletal fingers. The front garden really was lovely though, mainly because the rose bushes had been left to do their own thing, and because there were several rather beautiful stone statues of dogs in it. As we made our way up the overgrown path, I nodded at one that looked a bit like Petticoat. 'Look. A garden ornament that hasn't been nicked.' Mind you, the statues looked heavy – the phantom child thieves would probably need to hire a crane to shift them.

Once again, I hesitated before I rang the bell, even though my heart wasn't in it. 'So. Remember when you were on the cruise ship and everyone except you got ill because there was a massive storm and just after that you broke into one of the evil shareholder's cabins but two of their

126

bodyguards snuck up behind you and then tried to throw you over the side and you only got away because one of them slipped in some sick?'

So?

'So, this is going to be worse than that. And I mean it this time.' I did.

I rang Sheila's doorbell.

No answer.

Try again.

Still no answer. 'Talk about an anticlimax,' I said, unable to keep the relief out of my voice. 'Oh well. Looks like we'll have to—'

A second later, the door flew open, and Tracey peered out, bristling with irritation, which was a bit of a shocker, seeing as she'd been so friendly the day before. But before I could apologise for disturbing her, she smiled, and said: 'Oh, it's *you*, bab. Sorry about that. Did I keep you waiting long?'

I brandished the tin. 'We brought this back.'

She blinked in confusion and looked past me. 'We?'

Oops. 'Me, I mean. I did. Sorry . . . I'm not very good at speaking sometimes.'

Hopeless, Leah muttered, clearly back to her factory setting after her brief period of being almost human.

But Tracey didn't appear to be fazed by my word salad. 'Well, it's not always easy, is it?'

No, it isn't. Especially when you're being haunted round the clock. 'How is Sheila today? I was wondering if I could have a word with her. Um . . . to thank her for the cake in person.'

'She's not up to having visitors at the minute, bab. She's just had her lunch, and she always has a nap after that.'

Pressure her. Don't take no for an answer.

But it turned out that I didn't need to, because then Tracey said: 'Have you eaten by the way? I've got loads left. It's nothing special, only chicken soup, but you'd be more than welcome.'

'I wouldn't want to put you to any trouble.' I *really* wouldn't – eating in other people's houses was a recipe for anxiety and potential embarrassment.

'It's no trouble. You'd be doing me a favour. I always make too much – think I'm still cooking for a family.'

She stood back and trapped between a rock (social convention) and a hard case (Leah), I had no choice but to enter. 'Go on through to the kitchen. It's just at the end there.'

There was a faint undercurrent of dog in the hallway, but as I moved further in, that was smothered by the rich odour of baking and a lower note of something savoury and comforting. Then there was the sheer amount of stuff everywhere. The house gave the impression that at some point, it had been shaken like a snow globe, and the furnishings had just been left where they fell. The rooms that led off from the hallway were crammed full of knick-knacks, books, paintings, and stacks of randomly placed furniture.

The kitchen, which was three times the size of my mother's, was just as chaotic, but had more charm. I took in a grumbling old stove, a pot of soup simmering away on it. A dog basket with a grubby blanket. A large wooden table, heaving with cookery books, egg boxes and unopened mail. Every bit of wall space was covered with artwork, mostly beautifully rendered water-colours of birds (including several robins), and at the far end of the room, a large, impressionistic oil painting of a woman sleeping on a bed next to a dog, her arm draped over her face. And, on the kitchen counter, an enormous Victoria sponge cake, a tower of scones, and what looked to be a freshly baked loaf of bread.

Unbelievable, Leah muttered, aghast at this overt display of homeliness. She was even more of a pathological minimalist than my mother had been, and every surface and appliance in her loft's kitchen was clad in stainless steel (I'd always pictured it as looking like a morgue).

Tracey flapped a hand at the table. 'Make yourself at home. I won't be a minute.' She bustled over to the stove and removed the pot's lid, releasing yet another waft of deliciousness into the room. My stomach grumbled.

Nothing in the room was particularly clean, which made me feel less insecure about the wall stain in the cottage and my life choices. My gaze drifted greedily to the cakes again. 'Are you a baker, Tracey?'

She chuckled. 'I wish. Used to be a nurse. Paediatrics mainly, but then I retrained in mental health.'

Leah, who'd made it halfway across the room, paused to give Tracey a Death Stare. Perhaps she was worried that I'd inadvertently get some psychiatric help, and she'd be relegated back to protagonist purgatory.

'That must've been quite a demanding job.'

'Could be. Baking's how I destress.'

Judging by the array of baked goods, she must be under a fuck-ton of that. She ladled some soup into a bowl, and brought it over to me, along with a thick slice of the loaf and a block of butter.

'Thank you. It looks delicious.' It did. So delicious in fact that it overrode the self-consciousness. It was also packed full of barley, celery and carrots (I couldn't remember the last time I'd eaten a vegetable), and as I tucked in, my body practically wept with relief.

129

'I miss cooking for other people,' Tracey said, pottering over to the sink. 'My three have all moved out now. My youngest is probably around your age.'

I decided not to ask about her kids, in case they were massive over-achievers. Fortunately, I had an excuse because my mouth was crammed with bread.

'Now, how are you finding the cottage, bab? From what Auntie's said, your mother did it up lovely. That place needed a new lease of life. When it came up, I thought about putting an offer on it myself.'

'You did?' *You* wanted *to live next door to Sheila?*

'Wasn't the right time. I was still married then, and only retired last year.'

Leah, who was currently glaring at a serving dish shaped like a chicken, looked over her shoulder. ***Remember why we're here?***

Seduced by the food, I'd forgotten that I was supposed to be conducting an interrogation. I decided to start with the topic closest to Leah's heart. 'Can I ask you a question, Tracey?' I was getting sick of saying that.

'Course, bab.'

'Do the motion sensor lights from the barn conversion ever bother you? They went on last night, and they gave me a fright.'

'They don't, no. Auntie prefers to keep the curtains permanently closed in the front of the house so that the paintings don't fade. It can get spooky out here if you're a city person, but it'll only be a fox or a deer.'

'I thought that too,' I said pointedly, pretending not to hear Leah's indignant CLICK. 'But all the same, I was wondering . . . has anything gone missing out of Sheila's garden?'

Tracey turned to look at me, bemused. 'I don't think

so. Mind you, it'd be hard to tell. Why do you ask?'

'It's just . . . I can't seem to find my mother's ladder, and I'm worried it's been stolen. Glenn says that a few other things have gone missing from gardens in the hamlet.'

'Did he now,' Tracey scoffed. 'There's never been any crime round here. Nothing serious anyway.'

Until now, Leah said darkly.

'But if you need a ladder, there must be one around here somewhere you can borrow.'

'No. It's . . .' how to word it? 'The ladder . . . it's the one that my mother fell off.'

Tracey shot me a look rich with empathy. 'I'm sorry to hear that. Like I said, I only met your mother a couple of times, but Auntie spoke very highly of her. Said your mum even offered to water the roses when she was having trouble with her hip, and that's quite a job.' If Mum had offended Sheila in some way, then this had clearly mended the rift. 'Pity I can't say the same for everyone round here.' For a guilty second, I assumed she meant me because the only thing I'd ever done for Sheila was avoid her, but she didn't seem to be holding any grudges because she brought over an enormous slice of the Victoria sponge. 'Here you go, bab. You could do with putting on a few pounds. Can't eat it all myself.'

Leah rolled her eyes. **Great, more carbs.**

My brain trickled off into one of its stupid tangents: If Tracey was a cake, she'd be a Victoria sponge. If Leah were a piece of confectionery, she'd be one of those health bars that tastes like work. I'd be a box of cake mix that no one's bothered to make yet (or a fruitcake). I took a bite. Tracey had been generous with the jam and cream, and as it splurged out, Leah muttered, **un-bloody-believable**, and turned away.

'This is the best cake I've ever eaten.' It was.

Tracey beamed. 'Funnily enough, it was Auntie who got me interested in baking.'

'Really?' That didn't seem likely. The sponge I was stuffing into my cakehole was as light as a cloud, and the one on the patio . . . wasn't.

'That's how she came to be here, you see. She was working as a cook and a housekeeper.'

'Really?' I said again. 'I assumed Sheila had always been here. She sounds so . . . um . . .'

'Posh, you mean? Puts that voice on. Has done for years. She was born, bred and buttered in the Black Country, bab. She's a funny old one, Auntie is. Between the two of us, she wasn't much of a cook, but His Nibs seemed to like what she fed him. Wouldn't have married her otherwise.'

'His Nibs?'

Tracey put on a la-di-da voice: 'Sir Bernard Ripley, don't you know. Between the two of us, she only married him for the house. Well, and the garden. You're not supposed to speak ill of the dead, but he had a right bob on himself. Gambler, he was. Almost ran this place into the ground. That's why the estate had to be split up and sold off. I shouldn't say this, but if he hadn't passed on when he did the house would've been sold too, and that would've broken Auntie's heart.'

Something kindled. 'Um. If you don't mind me asking, how did he die?' *God, talk about a hypocrite.*

'Hunting accident. Gun misfired.'

I almost spat out my cake. *Coincidence? I think not.* Had Mum based *Overlooked* on Sheila's backstory? *Maybe Sheila was the inspiration for the murderous butler!* And: *what if Mum had suspected that Sheila might've murdered*

His Nibs and made it look like an accident? Could this have been the malarkey she'd mentioned to Meera? I tried to catch Leah's eye, but she was too busy staring at a fish-shaped jelly mould as if it were a dismembered foot. *We might have an actual unsolved murder here!*

'Poor Sheila,' I managed. 'That must've been awful for her.'

'Well, like I said, he wasn't what you'd call a pleasant person. Not that I remember much about him. I was just a kid at the time.'

'Do you know if Sheila ever told my mother about it?'

'She might've done. Why do you ask?'

'No reason. It's just . . . it's quite an interesting and tragic story, and neither Mum nor Sheila ever mentioned it to me.'

Another sympathetic smile. 'Well, Auntie wouldn't have wanted to bring that up after what happened to your mother.'

That hadn't stopped the rest of the hamletees sharing their Death Stories – I even knew the causes of death of the postie's last two Labradors (hip dysplasia and Cushing's disease) – and somewhat ironically, this made me feel warmer towards Sheila.

From outside came the familiar sound of yapping. There was a plant and junk-filled conservatory carbuncled onto the kitchen, so I was unable to see much of the garden from my vantage point, but no doubt Brian was up to his usual tricks.

'There he goes again,' she sighed. 'Once he starts barking, he won't stop. Must be the squirrels.' She wiped her hands on a tea towel. 'I'd better bring him in. Are you all right with dogs, bab?'

'I love dogs.' In fact, although I was extremely fond of

Brian – his recent treachery aside – I've always suspected that I might be more of a dog person, probably because dogs tend to be less judgemental than cats.

'I'm more of a cat person myself,' Tracey said, as if she'd just read my mind. 'But he's a lovely old boy, other than that racket.' She headed into the conservatory.

I turned to Leah, who I knew for a fact was also a cat person. 'Did you hear that about Sheila's husband? I mean, that's basically the plot of *Overlooked*!'

A flicker of the usual book-related caginess, followed by: *So?*

'What do you mean, *so*? If Sheila murdered her husband, then isn't she our most likely suspect? I mean, how many murderers can there be in the hamlet? And if she *is* a murderer, then she's got form when it comes to making murders look like accidents.'

A raised eyebrow. ***How does that connect to our case?***

'Well . . . what if Mum heard about His Nibs's accident, and decided to look into it because she thought it would make a good plot and while she was doing that, stumbled across something that proved that it wasn't an accident after all?'

Leah looked as if she was stifling a yawn. ***Motive?***

'Concealment again. Probably. Because *what if* Sheila discovered that Mum was intending to write about His Nibs's death and was worried that it would expose her as a murderer in some way?' No. That was stupid, even by my standards. For a start, Mum wrote fiction, not true crime, and even if she had been intending to write an exposé, then surely Sheila would've offed Mum *before* the book had been sent to the publishers. Unless she didn't know how publishing worked.

A scrabble of claws on wood, and Petticoat bounded

in. I steeled myself for another bout of Leah worship, but he came straight up to me, sat, and raised a paw. Up close, he was all woolly white fur, and soulful eyes (he did smell a bit, but that wasn't his fault). I stroked his head, and he rolled on his back, showing no sign that he was aware of Leah. As I tickled his belly, I couldn't resist shooting her a triumphant look. *See? Animals like me too.* Perhaps dogs were better judges of character than cats, birds, and spiders.

'He's taken to you, hasn't he?' Tracey said. 'Poor old thing is missing his morning walk, but Auntie isn't up to it at the minute, and I don't dare leave her alone at the mo.'

'I could take him tomorrow if you like.' It felt right to offer, and it was the least I could do after mentally pegging her aunt as a homicidal maniac. And because I still hadn't ordered any groceries, at some point I'd have to walk to the shoppe anyway.

We don't have time for bloody errands.

'Bless you, bab,' Tracey said. 'I can see you take after your mother. But won't it interfere with your work?'

'I'm taking a sabbatical.' I got up from the table. 'I'd better get out of your hair.'

Tracey popped the rest of the Victoria sponge into the kitten tin and handed it to me. 'Take this with you, bab. Can't eat it all myself.'

'Thank you.' *Shite.* I should've cleaned it properly after all. I glanced at Leah, curious as to why she hadn't made a snarky comment about the cake gift. But it seemed that all her attention was focused on the door at the far end of the room.

A second later, it creaked open and Sheila came shuffling in.

'Auntie!' Tracey rushed towards her. 'What are you doing up?'

135

Petticoat got up to greet his mistress, and Sheila bent down to pat him absent-mindedly.

'Hi Sheila,' I said, trying to hide my shock at her appearance. She was dressed in a long white nightie like a wraith out of a dodgy old horror movie, back when directors could get away with ageism and misogyny, and instead of her usual straight-backed demeanour, she was hunched in on herself. But it was the haunted look in her eyes that really threw me. *Could* someone go downhill this fast?

Sheila squinted in my direction, let out a slow, shaky breath, and then appeared to look over at Leah, who was lurking to my right. 'Oh, it's *you*, Annie. Did you do what I said?'

Oof.

Sorry, Tracey mouthed at me, and hurriedly whispered, 'Urinary tract infection. It can cause delirium in elderly people.' In a louder voice she said, 'That's not Annie, Auntie, it's . . .' she paused. 'Your name's gone out of my head, bab.'

'Niamh,' I squeaked.

'That's Niamh, Auntie. Annie's daughter. Niamh brought your cake tin back.'

'My what?'

'Your cake tin. The one you were asking about the other day?'

Sheila's eyes went completely blank.

'Come on. Let's get you into bed.' Tracey turned back to me. 'Are you okay to see yourself out, bab?'

All I could do was nod.

THE RITUAL

We were both subdued when we returned home. Me because I was still shaken by Sheila's 'Annie' pronouncement; Leah because who knows? Sheila's blindside hadn't seemed to affect her, so perhaps she'd had enough of the low-key everyday-ness of our witnesses-slash-suspects, none of whom had needed to be placated with a round-house kick.

The disturbing thing was, Sheila couldn't have mistaken me for my mother – Mum had been five inches taller than me, and blonde (basically the opposite of a Wednesday Addams/hobbit hybrid). Apparently, I was 'the spit' of my Irish gran, who'd been a tiny, square woman with a pugilistic face. And even if it were possible that Sheila *had* seen Leah, she didn't resemble her creator either (physically, anyway – they were both bossy and confident). But was it possible that Sheila had sensed my mother's 'spirit' in her? After all, Leah had been my mother's creation and presumably had some metaphysical version of her DNA running through her impossible veins (this, of course, reminded me again of my horrific sibling thought).

But that was just the tip of the discombobulation, because then there was Sheila's 'did you do what I said, Annie?' question too. There had been something almost accusatory in the way that she'd said it.

'So. Any thoughts on what happened back there?'
No one's that nice.

I'd actually been referring to Sheila's unsettling Annie pronouncement, so it took me a second to recalibrate. 'Tracey, you mean?'

Course. She's hiding something.

'What could she be hiding? She's a former nurse who's put her life on hold to care for her sick aunt, and she destresses by baking delicious cakes.' I felt quite defensive of Tracey. I hadn't felt that comfortable around a stranger for years. Admittedly, the decline in Sheila's physical and mental health was shocking, but on balance I thought it unlikely that Tracey was killing her off to get her hands on the huge array of weirdly shaped crockery. 'Is this your gut speaking again? Or are you suspicious of her because of what happened in *Overkill*? I mean, before you and Jed discovered that the murderer was a consultant with shares in an American private health company, your main suspect was that nursing assistant on the paediatric ward.'

She turned away.

I was tempted to let her get away with this book-related evasiveness again, but my unexpected and wholesome meal had given me a fresh burst of energy. 'Do you have amnesia or something?' Thinking about it, the number of concussions Leah had sustained during her (non)lifetime must be well into the double figures – if she were a person, she'd be a prime candidate for CTE. 'Because whenever I mention the books, you act like a murderous husband in a crime podcast – all sleazy denial and answer avoidance. Don't you remember *anything* about your old cases?'

Of course I remember. I just don't dwell on them.

More progress. 'Why not? Because they're traumatising for you?'

No point dwelling on the past. The present and future are more important.

Despite this being one of those self-help clichés, she said it as if she believed it, which made sense because my mother had ensured that each of the Leah books could be read as a standalone as well as part of a series.

I jumped back to the quest. 'But what motive would Tracey have to off Mum? She said she'd only met her once or twice, and she doesn't even live in the hamlet. Mind you, she did say that she'd considered making an offer on the cottage. Could Mum have gazumped her, do you think, and she was out for revenge?'

Gazumped?

'Right. Um, that's what you call it when you make an offer on a property, and someone swoops in and outbids you. Didn't you study it in the conveyancing part of your law degree?'

Leah shrugged.

To be fair, that part of her backstory had been very thinly sketched out. 'But even if gazumping is a plausible motive, which it probably isn't, why would Tracey wait so long before she took her revenge? I mean, Mum had been living here over a year before she died.'

I waited for her to say, 'revenge is a dish best served cold' again, but she didn't bother.

'Now what? Shall we do another recap?'

Fine.

'So. The ladder is still missing – probably nicked by the phantom child thieves. If any of the neighbours are our perps, then the most likely suspect is the Weekend Wanker, and we can clear that up tomorrow.' Hopefully. 'Then there's the fender-bender mystery. Oh, and Mum's phone. It's hard to keep track of all this.'

Not that bloody hard.

Then I had an idea: 'Shall I make a murder wall?'

A what?

'A detective-investigation-board thing. So that we can keep track of our potential suspects and theories.' I nodded at the coffee stain. 'I could stick it up there.'

Bad idea. If someone's got eyes on us, it'll give the game away.

'Oh right. How about if I do it in code then, and use symbols instead of pics of the possible perps, and witnesses?' It wasn't as if I could use photographs anyway – I hadn't yet dared look at any of my mother, and it would've been weird if I had any of the neighbours.

Fine.

I didn't have a white board, so I used printer paper instead. I had stacks in my room because my mother had used it as an extended office space (yet more evidence that she'd downsized to prevent me from becoming a literal basement kid). And in the drawer in the boot room, I found a stash of Blu Tack, some Post-it notes, and several felt-tipped pens.

'So, I'm thinking, PP could stand for 'potential perp", W for "witnesses", M for motive—'

I get the picture.

Undaunted, I sketched out a clock for 'time of death', a ladder, a car, a phone and a gnome, all with question marks next to them. Sadly, I'd inherited my father's artistic ability, but it was relaxing and absorbing all the same.

I moved onto our suspects and witnesses, choosing a cake for Tracey, some vampire teeth for Sheila, and a vengeful squirrel for the Wanker.

'What symbol shall I use for Glenn? One of those pointy police officer helmet things?'

A truncheon. Then she side-eyed me and said, *just don't make it look like a penis.*

Was that another joke? It wasn't clear because it had come out deadpan, but I laughed exaggeratedly again all the same. 'I'll try.' But of course, it did look exactly like a penis, so I put a moustache on it, which somehow made it look even more like one. And seeing as Janet also used to be a cop, I drew a walkie-talkie as her avatar. I even drew a sketch of Brian, who, according to Glenn's account, was also a witness.

Using a Pinterest image as a guide, I stuck the pages up and stood back. It looked less like a murder wall and more like an abstract art installation collated by a deranged toddler.

'What do you think?'

The stain was better.

'Yeah.' Although what it did do was underline how slow-moving 'The Case of the Missing Ladder' was turning out to be. By this stage in a book, my mother would have introduced at least three sub-plots. Which reminded me that I still hadn't finished *Overlooked*. And as much as I'd prefer to distract myself from the dread of facing the Wanker tomorrow with another play-through of *Resident Evil: Biohazard*, I was curious to see how closely the plot mirrored Sheila's backstory, even though I'd (mostly) put that tenuous motive to bed.

'I'm just popping to the bathroom. Cramps again.'

A sardonic look that clearly meant, *if you're going to lie, at least do it well.*

WHAT LIES BENEATH

'Me again,' I whispered to my possible future muses Three Arm and Wart Head. *Please don't haunt me.*

Because I'd been in the habit of leaving everything to the last minute – essays, anything work-related, life – I was quite good at speed-reading, and it didn't take me long to get the gist of the plot. Far thornier to navigate was the queasy, surreal experience of reading about Leah while her doppelganger lurked in an adjoining room. However, I confirmed that my Leah was indeed far mardier than Mum's version, who, despite also being forthright and a pathological risk-taker, didn't feel the need to treat her supporting characters with eloquent distain or auditorily harass them with her lighter.

As for the setting, the fictional village of Buckworth had a pub in it that was owned by a Michelin-starred chef, a library that hadn't been closed by the council, zero potholes, and the local shoppe was an upscale 7/11 that stocked things like fresh pasta and artichoke hearts (clearly my mother had been engaging in wishful thinking). And because Leah was going undercover in the village as a historical romance writer who'd escaped to the countryside to finish her latest bestseller, for once she was able to wear her favourite black suit attire 24/7 instead of slumming it in undercover high-viz, even though bespoke tailoring wasn't the ideal get-up for doing things like hiding in hedgerows or chasing quad biking perps across muddy fields on a Ducati.

Nor was my mother doing a spin on 'the butler did it' trope, because by page fifty, Leah had wrapped that plot strand up. Not only did the butler have an alibi, but it turned out that he'd been Lord Wentworth's long-term significant other, and in the end it was the Lord's nephew who'd engineered the murder-made-to-look-like-an-accident. So even if my mother had been doing a take on Sheila's past, she'd masked it well.

As for the villagers' dirty secret, that centred around a nearby industrial-sized blueberry farm that exploited and abused its workforce, most of whom were undocumented migrants. But instead of being ardent gossipers, the local villagers in *Overlooked* happily turned a blind eye to the multiple abuses occurring on their doorstep – a bit like characters in a Lars von Trier movie or real-life Reform and MAGA voters. It was more melancholic in tone than its predecessors and was basically a treatise on 'evil thrives when good people do nothing', which was difficult not to take personally, as my mother had always been on at me to do more than just whinge about the multiple issues that fed my various malaises.

But I was proud of myself for finally reading it, and proud of my mother for writing it. I glanced up at Wart Head, who my father may or may not have thought of as my mother's proxy, and whispered, 'nice one, Mum'.

And then I turned to the acknowledgements and saw this: 'And to my daughter Niamh, who made it all possible.' Which, seeing as I'd done less than fuck all to help her with *Overlooked*, was so blatantly untrue that for a second,

I assumed it must be sarcasm. Then I read it again, realised she was referring to her writing career as a whole, and all hell broke loose.

Well, not hell; this was worse. This time, the weight in my chest was so heavy and immediate that I was unable to breathe. Out exploded a *kark!*, which sounded more like a seal bark than anything human, the blockage cleared, and then I ugly-cried with the exaggerated abandon of a character actor in an independent film. It wasn't the first time I'd cried for my mother, but those had been surface-level tears, like the run-off from a leaky pipe, and what was pouring out now was deeper and darker. Expelling it didn't just involve my eyes and heart, but my entire body.

And just as it seemed to ebb, my brain latched onto something that set if off again – like picturing my mother up in her attic, typing out those words, oblivious to the fact that in less than a year, she'd be dead (or, possibly, in a robin), and her real disappointment of a grown-up child would one day read them while sitting on a toilet, just metres away from the spectre of her over-achieving fantasy daughter.

But what really struck me as I sobbed and snotted and howled and karked was how *lonely* this all was, and how different *being* alone and *feeling* alone were. *There was no one to knock on the door and ask me if I was okay.* Even though our relationship had been under strain for years, I'd assumed that my mother would always be there to catch me, like one of those nets they put under jungle gyms to stop kids plummeting to their deaths. *This wasn't supposed to happen. She wasn't supposed to die.* In some part of my brain, I'd assumed I'd go first – my grasp on life had always been more tenuous than Mum's.

It was this that made me take out my phone and scroll to her voice messages. She'd got into the habit of sending them to me during the writing of *Over and Above*, after suffering from a bout of carpal tunnel syndrome. They'd usually start with, 'Hiya, hope you're doing okay,' but would inevitably drift into ruminations about Leah-related stuff ('so I've been thinking . . . do you think Leah should suspect that Zane is a stooge for the airline so early on?' etcetera). Sometimes I listened to them at double speed. If I was having a bad week, month or year, I didn't listen to them at all.

The earliest of the three had been left a few hours after our final fight, when I was travelling down to Daphne's place in Truro. In movies, grieving characters were always replaying dead loved ones' voice messages over and over (it was an effective way of doing exposition), and maybe people enjoyed doing that in real-life, too. If so, I wasn't one of them, because I only got as far as: 'Hiya, Neevy—' before the *Nope!* kicked in. It was the 'Neevy' that did it – she hadn't used that diminutive for years.

I looked up at Three Arm and Wart Head. At least when they got around to mourning the patriarch on the doomed vessel, they'd have each other to lean on (if that scenario had even been my father's intention – for all I knew, they could be shipwreck rubberneckers). It was then that it hit home that I was living in the biggest movie trope of them all – the child–parent connection conundrum: daughters attempting to bond with estranged/and or dead mothers, sons with distant and/or dead fathers, and less often, the other way around. Death, after all, is the number one *inciting incident*. And if this was a film, then my explosive crying jag would be the climax: *after months of emotional cowardice and denial, she'd finally accepted her mother's death, and could move onto the next chapter of her life . . .*

Physically and emotionally, I felt like I'd been hollowed out with a wooden spoon, which sounds horrific, but curiously, wasn't entirely unpleasant. I crept out of my sanctuary, hoping against hope that Leah was out of my life. It was now dark outside *and* inside, because even if my previously repressed emotions weren't the mythical unfinished business, Leah was physically incapable of flicking on a light. And if she was lurking in the kitchen, I couldn't see or sense her. 'Hello?' I whispered, fumbling for the light switch.

A CLICK from behind me.

Out blipped the hope. This was why fiction was fiction. I whirled around. She was leaning against the fridge again, toying with her lighter. 'I thought you'd gone.'

A frown. ***Why would you think that?***

I didn't have the energy to be evasive. 'Because I had a big cry.' Leah rarely cried, but when she did, it never lasted longer than three sentences, and she always did it in the shower where no one could witness it, like a repressed man from the nineteen-fifties. 'Don't worry, I'm not expecting you to be sympathetic or anything. Unless you want to be, that is.' Any sort of comfort, however meagre or sarcastic, would've been welcome right then.

A blank stare.

No hope of that then.

'It was your last-but-one adventure that set me off. I was reading it in the cloakroom. You know, the one where you saved a butler from being framed by a Viscount, narrowly avoided getting buried alive, attacked a game-keeper with a femur, fought off some traffickers in a pub kitchen with a spatula, and helped some exploited farm workers burn a static caravan and nick a Land Rover Discovery.'

Case, *not adventure.*

Whatever. 'In case you're wondering, it wasn't the plot that upset me, although that was pretty hard-hitting, but the acknowledgements.'

This resulted in an eye-roll, a gesture which I now knew for a fact wasn't in Book Leah's repertoire. 'You're not going to leave me alone, are you?'

Like I said. Unfinished business.

Great.

I fed Brian, and then took my hollowed-out insides and the cake up to bed.

GRAVE ENCOUNTERS

The following morning, instead of being CLICKed into consciousness, Brian woke me up by batting at my face like he used to do in the good old pre-quest days. Nor was Leah sitting at the end of my bed like a sociopathic Mary Poppins, but crouching on her haunches, forensically investigating my floordrobe.

'Morning,' I said. 'How did you not-sleep?' The possibility that the unfinished business could be finished today made me feel warmer towards her – a bit like how you can feel charitable towards a vile housemate on the day they're moving out.

She stood, then gestured at the bundle of hoodies and jeans at her feet. *You should sort that out. It's a bloody disgrace.*

'You can talk. There's cigarette ash all down your suit.' There was. Her shirt was creased as well, which, if she *was* a by-product of my brain would be apt, because I've never ironed anything in my life. Come to think of it, nor had Leah. In fact, she rarely dropped her six identical black suits off at the dry cleaners (my mother hadn't been a fan of quotidian detail).

She blinked in surprise, then peered down at her lapel with something approximating horror. Also, I noticed that

148

her usually slick hair needed a wash and a trim. Perhaps my natural scruffiness was infectious. 'Maybe you should pop back to your fancy loft apartment for a shower and a change of clothes. If you can, that is.'

What's that supposed to mean?

'Well, you've hardly been very clear about how any of this works. Where *do* you go when you're not here?' My brain latched onto an image of a metaphysical muse/protagonist holding cell, packed full of fictional characters from long-running crime series waiting for their authors to post their metaphorical bail. ('Oi, Reacher, say your goodbyes, you've been reimagined again . . .' etcetera.)

In answer, I was treated to a more aggressive CLICK than usual.

But I had to admit she was right about the floordrobe. I wasn't quite ready to be stalked by the Henry Hoover, but I had time to do some washing before my Petticoat chore (Brian would just have to sleep on my bed from now on). And, although I wasn't exactly looking forward to a shoppe excursion, it could hardly be more onerous than the previous day's catalogue of emotional gut-punches or my upcoming Wanker interrogation, so I almost felt blasé about it. In fact, my main worry was that Brian would venture into the front garden and witness my canine adultery.

My nervous energy translated into action, and I managed to do not one but two loads of washing before Leah and I sneaked out the house.

This time Tracey came to the door straight away, and Petticoat acted as if he was overjoyed to see me, which was a lovely experience, and completely ignored Leah again, which was an even lovelier one.

We set off. Fortunately, Brian hadn't intuited that I was cheating on him, but as we rambled along the lane, instead of walking next to me and Petticoat, Leah lurked behind us, like an autonomous shadow or a homicidal bodyguard.

'You can walk next to us, you know. We're not in *The Handmaid's Tale*.'

What?

'Never mind.' I'd forgotten that she didn't do pop culture.

On the bright side, I discovered that dogs are brilliant for self-consciousness – there was something contagious about Petticoat's joyful fascination with absolutely everything: *Look! A leaf! A feather! A bit of squashed dung!* And, because I wasn't scurrying along, head down like a fugitive, for the first time, I really took in the details of my surroundings: an interesting tree in a field that had whorls on it like a face (it actually looked a bit like Pam and/or Elaine); a bird of prey darting and swooping above us; a tiny rodent sprinting across the lane and then back again as if it had suddenly remembered it had left the oven on.

At the end of the lane, we paused to let the postal van zip safely past, and then turned towards the shoppe. The front gardens of the cottages were empty of potential chit-chattees – Friday was *Chair Yoga!* day – although in one I spied a lonely, plastic flamingo. Poor thing – presumably its mate had been kidnapped along with Glenn's gnomes.

'Look. Another crime scene.'

Hilarious.

'I bet you'll be glad when all this is over. You must be bored shitless.'

A blip of surprise. **I *never* get bored.**

'Never? Not even when you're on a stake out?'

No.

A *ziiiip* as several cyclists whipped past us like a flock of unflatteringly dressed birds, before alighting next to the shoppe. They were already inside when we reached it, and bolstered by my canine anxiety sponge, I didn't bother doing a window recce before I went in. Dogs were allowed in the store, so I didn't have to tie Petticoat outside and then worry about someone nicking him – which they wouldn't anyway, because he wasn't a garden ornament. I held the door open for Leah, but fortunately, whoever was behind the counter was too busy dealing with the cyclists to witness this odd behaviour.

Once inside, Leah's body language tensed up, and her eyes betrayed a flicker of that rare uncertainty. Why, though? The shoppe must be the least dramatic and dangerous setting she'd ever been in – it would only pose a threat to a coeliac sufferer.

'Didn't you come here with Mum?' I whispered.

A shrug that had more of a 'no' feel to it than a 'yes', and therefore implied that she *hadn't* followed my mother around like a judgemental sentient shadow, which didn't seem fair.

Petticoat dragged me towards a shelf displaying a meagre selection of sliced meat. Ignoring Leah's glare, I slipped a packet of cooked chicken slices into my basket for him and then made for the scones.

No.

'What do you mean, "no"?' I whispered.

She nodded at the paltry vegetable section.

'I can't cook.'

Won't, you mean. It's not rocket science.

To appease her, I randomly picked out an onion, a bulb

of garlic, and a depressed-looking courgette, and then hurriedly piled some edible things into my basket while she wasn't looking.

The woman behind the counter looked familiar, but it took me a few seconds to clock that it was Janet. She gave no sign that she recognised me, and seemed to be going out of her way to avoid any eye contact. And she definitely knew who I was because although we'd never chit-chatted, she was in the habit of judging my crisp choices through her kitchen window whenever I received a grocery delivery.

'Hi Janet,' I said. 'Lovely day, isn't it?'

But instead of following the rural chit-chat code, she merely nodded and said: 'Is that Sheila's dog?'

'Yes. She's not feeling very well.'

'I'll bet,' she muttered, then busied herself with ringing up my goods.

Okay . . . 'And how are *you* today? I hope you're feeling better.'

'Better?'

'When I was over at your place yesterday, Glenn said you had a headache.'

'I'm fine,' she said tonelessly. (If Janet were a piece of confectionery, she'd be a slightly stale digestive biscuit.)

Being on the other side of chit-chat avoidance was disconcerting, but perhaps she was a fellow introvert. Or maybe she was being stand-offish because Glenn had told her that I'd nicked all their biscuits. 'I didn't know you volunteered here.'

'I don't usually. Glenn had to get the MOT done.'

'Oh right.'

She didn't say another word as I stuffed the groceries into my backpack, but as I was on my way out, she muttered, 'Word of advice? Watch your bins.'

What was *it with the hamletees' bin obsession?* But presumably, Janet meant this as a cryptic warning about foraging foxes. 'Oh right. Thanks.'

It was a relief to be outside. 'That was weird, wasn't it?'

She's hiding something.

'Yeah. By the way, is there anyone who isn't?'

Brian.

'Hilarious.'

Petticoat steered me towards a footpath that wove through the cemetery, the entrance of which was partially blocked by a decaying pile of grass-cuttings. (I could also see why Sheila had felt the need to vent about the villager responsible – it really was a selfish thing to do.)

The graveyard was far larger than it had any right to be, seeing as there couldn't be more than fifty people living in the hamlet, but perhaps in the olden days it had been the death version of one of those carbon-capture outsourcing schemes. It was dotted with shaggy trees, and the gravestones were so ancient and worn that I could barely make out the names and dates on them. Petticoat pulled me towards a bench under a large yew – a pit stop was clearly part of his morning routine – and it was then that a particular stone caught my eye. It wasn't as well-worn as the others, and the inscription simply read: 'Thelma. She was a free spirit.' It was the only one adorned with flowers, although they'd clearly been there for a while.

I found myself welling up. It could've been because it was a reminder that unlike Thelma, my mother didn't have a gravestone, or even one of those plaque things. She'd stipulated in her will that she didn't want a funeral and wished to be cremated – which had been a surprise, seeing as she'd been quite a sociable and eco-minded person. So all I had was a plastic tub of ashes, which were still on her bedside table, because the one thing she hadn't been clear about was what to do with them. I had a vague idea of mixing them with Brian's when he eventually died, but that was as far as I'd got.

Leah, who was lurking next to a mossy Celtic cross, was looking inwards again and hadn't noticed that I was leaking, but for once, I managed to get myself under control without the help of her lighter. It seemed that last night's grief explosion had dislodged the equivalent of that plug bears use when they hibernate so that they don't shit themselves all winter, and from now on, I'd be experiencing random bouts of emotional incontinence.

I sat and gave Petticoat his sliced chicken, which he took delicately before flopping down at my feet.

Leah shrugged off her own introspection and lit up a ciggie.

'What will you do when you run out of smokes? Will you just magic some more? Or is there a protagonist corner shop or online outlet you can visit?'

Eye-roll. Sigh. CLICK.

'Where *do* you go when you're not here?' If we did finish the unfinished business today, then this might be my last chance to get an answer. 'I know you never leave me alone, but do or *can* you go somewhere else? Like . . . to another world or multiverse or whatever?' And then I told her about my protagonist holding-cell theory.

Stupidest bloody thing I've ever heard.

Fuck it. I leaned back and gazed up at the yew tree. I was used to doing nothing, but not nothing like this (my nothing usually involved at least one screen and some crisps). Trees, it turned out, were wonderful, and I could see why people liked them.

Come on. We've got business to attend to.

On the way back I made a mental note to bring Thelma some more flowers, although being a free spirit, she'd probably prefer gin.

RESIDENT EVIL

It turned out that the 'business we had to attend to' had thoughtfully arrived earlier than usual, because when we returned from our ramble, the Wanker's fuck-the-planet-mobile was parked selfishly in the lane.

But despite being on the verge of gathering valuable intel that might bring the quest to an end, as I packed away the groceries, my innate anxiety at the prospect of talking to a stranger came trickling back, along with a hefty dose of self-consciousness.

Leah, of course, had never suffered from any type of dysmorphia because even when she'd been left for dead on the floor of a cruise-ship engine room, she still managed to look 'arresting' (also, being tech averse, she'd never trawled through Instagram and felt her soul slowly dying). There was no way I was going to reveal this insecurity to her, but needing some sort of reassurance, however meagre and unlikely, I said in what I hoped was a nonchalant tone, 'Do you think I should get changed before I interview the Wanker? I mean . . . do I look professional enough?'

Leah looked me up and down, assessing my usual hoody and baggy jeans combo, which were clean for once. **No. Stay like that.**

'Really? Okay. Good. Thanks.'

Your total lack of style will take him off guard.

Nice.

Let's go.

She was crackling with energy again. And no wonder. Antagonising odious men was basically her reason for being.

My stomach switched to spin cycle as we crossed the lane (considering the task ahead, it had been a bad idea to eat cake for breakfast). I decided not to recite one of Leah's previous exploits this time – I wasn't in the mood for silliness – and in any case, I was too busy grappling with the sobering reality of what I was about to do. Getting the CCTV footage was the main objective, and I'd need to come up with a plausible excuse to ask for that. And then there was the phone conundrum. I couldn't decide if I should bring it up right away or leave it till last in case it spooked him. And if it *was* his, I'd have to say I'd found it in the lane or something, or he'd do me for trespassing. Of course, I should've thought all this through *before* we were on the Wanker's doorstep.

'How should I play this?' I whispered to Leah.

By ear, course.

Fuck's sake.

After doing a quick burp to ease the stomach pressure, I rang the bell.

A woman wearing bubble-gum pink workout gear answered the door, which took me completely off guard. She was around my – and Leah's – age, and was outrageously glamorous, with bushels of hair, and long fingernails with little pictures on them (if she were a cake, she'd be a gluten-free petit four). Perhaps she was the Wanker's daughter.

'Help you?' she said without betraying a hint of curiosity.

'Hi. Sorry to bother you. Is . . . Mr Fiddle in?' I bit back the hysterical burble.

'Hang on.' Without fully closing the door, she whirled round and padded back into the house, and a couple of seconds later I heard her calling, 'Babe? *Babe?* Someone's at the door!'

Not his daughter, then. 'That's not his wife,' I whispered over my shoulder to Leah.

Good. We can use that as leverage.

I peered through the gap in the door, jumping back as the Wanker, who was dressed unseasonably and unflatter-ingly in teeny white shorts and a sports shirt came barrelling towards me (he was clearly a hot cross bun with bacon in it).

He greeted me with a semi-aggressive: 'Yeah?'

I swallowed. 'Hi. Um. I live just over there, and—'

'Come to complain about the alarm, have you?' He nodded in the direction of Glenn and Janet's place. 'I told that twat it wasn't my problem, but the company's. I can't help it if they can't get their fucking act together.'

Wow. Despite all the evidence to the contrary, I'd assumed he'd at least put on a pretence of being civil (even billionaires bothered to do that occasionally). 'It's not the alarm. It's . . . um . . .' His aggression had put me even more on the back foot and my brain had gone blank.

'It's *what?* Spit it out, I can't hang around all day. The bloody hot tub's on the blink again.'

'Oh right. Sorry to hear that. But . . . um. This is going to sound . . . Things have been going missing from people's gardens, and—'

He narrowed his eyes. 'I haven't bloody well been taking them.'

'I'm not accusing you of anything.' A flash of movement in my peripheral vision – Leah had moved up next to me. Other than when I was acting as her doorperson, I'd never been in such close proximity to her before, and it really brought home how tall she was – not that this was a new experience, because I often only came up to people's waists. But for once, I was glad of her presence.

'Who are you, anyway?'

'I'm Annie Morrissey's daughter. Like I said, I live in the cottage opposite.'

'Oh right. Her. With the Mini. And the attitude. Haven't seen her around for a while.'

I glanced at Leah. If this had also thrown her, she didn't show it – she was too busy Death Staring at the Wanker's veiny forehead.

I swallowed again. 'Don't you know?'

'Know what?'

'She . . .' – a pause as I fought off a kark – '. . . died.'

'She what?' The Wanker appeared to be genuinely surprised by this news, but for all I knew he could be a good actor.

'Didn't anyone tell you?'

'What, round here? They don't tell me anything.' Not even the topic of death was able to soften him up.

'Wasn't it on the community WhatsApp?'

He snorted. 'Left that ages ago. Bunch of Nimby fuck-tards. When did it happen?'

'Four months ago.' *Four months and nine days, to be exact.*

'What was it, car crash?'

I side-eyed Leah. 'Why would you say that?'

'Backed straight into me, didn't she?'

Oh. That's one mystery solved. And, having witnessed his lane-blocking parking habits, it was something I should've thought of earlier.

'She was lucky I'd just had a bull bar fitted,' he continued. 'Would've cost her a fortune if she'd caused any damage. Terrible fucking driver.'

Even Leah gasped at this callousness.

I did more than gasp. Much more. The only explanation for what I did next was that I was standing shoulder-to-shoulder with a 'strong female character' and had absorbed some of her fearlessness via osmosis. A cold calmness came over me, time did that clichéd slowing-down thing again, and I heard myself saying, 'That's rich coming from you. You can't even park your fucking wank-mobile properly. A driveway's called a driveway for a reason, dickhead.'

He reared back as if I'd slapped him. Before he could collect himself, I barrelled on: 'Not only that, when someone tells you that their mother has died, the least you can do is say, "I'm sorry for your loss," even if you don't mean it, and the fact that you didn't do that is even more proof that you're an objectively shitty person. Worse. You're basically the human equivalent of a condom stuffed with ham,' – Leah snorted at this – 'or that putrid gunk that leaks out of a fridge when you don't defrost it often enough. And you know something else? I'm glad you didn't get planning permission because your taste in architecture is . . . crap.' (I ran out of steam at the end there.)

His face turned the colour of a Henry Hoover, then he went to slam the door. I don't know what made me do it – well, I do, because Leah had done it three times in six books – but I stuck my foot in the gap to prevent it from closing fully. But because I was wearing a Converse sneaker, and not a vegan leather combat boot, it *really* bloody hurt. Out of the corner of my eye, I saw Leah nodding approvingly, which as usual was paradoxically gratifying.

If he attacks, go for the throat.

'What do you think you're playing at?' he blustered, flinging the door open again. 'Who the *fuck* do you think you are? You can't just—'

'Babe!' the petit four called from within the house, stealing his thunder. 'The water's still cold!'

He muttered, 'Christ,' under his breath. 'I'll be there in a minute,' he yelled over his shoulder.

Ask him if that's his wife.

'Is that your wife?'

He recoiled. 'What business is that of yours?'

Tell him, none. But it could *be.*

'None.' By now, the adrenaline and foot pain were making me feel nauseous. 'But it *could* be.' Unfortunately, because I'm not Leah Rebecca Overton, this came out sounding less than convincing.

'That supposed to be a threat?' Back to his bully-boy persona, he leaned towards me.

Tell him, no, it's a bloody promise.

It was this cliché that brought me back to my senses. What the hell did I think I was doing? If the confrontation escalated, it wouldn't be Leah who'd end up as collateral damage. 'Sorry. Sorry. I . . . look. I didn't come here to piss you off.' Not that doing that would be difficult, since it was clearly his default setting. 'It's the grief. It makes me a bit, you know.'

What are you playing at?

'Not *helping*,' I hissed.

161

He'd moved into *uh-oh, I'm dealing with a nutter here* territory, and eyed me dubiously.

'I really am sorry,' I said. 'But . . . do your cameras work?'

'*What?*'

'Your CCTV cameras.'

'Course they fucking work.'

'Can I see the footage?'

'What the fuck are you on about?'

Leah cracked her knuckles again. 'The thing is . . . my mother's car insurance company are fighting the claim, and it might be helpful if I could send them some footage of her accident.'

'Thought you were here about a theft?'

Shite. 'Yeah. That too.'

Bloody hopeless, Leah said, stepping back as if, like Mum, she was washing her hands of me.

'Couldn't give it to you even if I wanted to.' He sneered triumphantly. 'Memory only stores three weeks' worth.'

'Doesn't it go up into the Cloud?'

'They're high-res, not your cheap rubbish. You know how much memory you'd need for that? Now do me a favour and fuck the fuck off.' And then he heaved the door shut again, and I jumped back just in time to avoid my foot being severed.

In came the prick of post-confrontation tears, and I stared at the door, blinking until they receded. Also, I'd completely forgotten about the phone. But after his reaction, it seemed doubtful that it was Mum's after all. The Wanker had probably dropped it back when the hot tub had been in working order.

When I turned around, Leah was smoking again, and after taking a deep furious drag flicked the butt in my direction. Not being real, it didn't hit me, or if it did, I didn't feel it, but I felt the sting of her contempt all the same.

I hobbled past her and crossed the lane, so wobbly from adrenaline that I could barely open the front door. I was tempted to slam it behind me before she could glide in, even though that would have been a pointless gesture. I limped to the sink and drank water straight from the tap.

Why didn't you bloody well threaten him?

'I *did* threaten him. I called him a meat condom and fridge gunk, what more do you want?'

Those weren't threats, they were insults.

'What good would it have done anyway? You heard him, he didn't have the footage.'

Could've been lying. You didn't even ask him for his bloody alibi.

'How would I have done that? For the last time, this isn't one of your cases. In real life, people don't just tell you stuff when it's convenient.'

They do when you blackmail them. You didn't even bloody try. You had the upper hand.

'No, I *didn't*. You saw him. He was getting really aggressive.'

He wouldn't have done owt. No muscle.

'You don't know that. Anyway, it's all right for you. You don't have to worry about getting hurt. Look at me. Do I look like someone who does kickboxing for fun and can handle themselves in a fight?'

You don't look like you can handle owt.

'And that's the other thing – not everyone who's from Yorkshire says "owt" and "nowt" all the time. I'm surprised Mum didn't give you a fucking flat cap and a pint of Theakston's.'

Least she gave me a backbone.

163

I came very close to punching her then. Not that it would have achieved anything (although the following day, I did try to punch her, and it didn't end well). I limped into my cloakroom instead, locked the door, and waited to see if the fury would result in a kark-fest. Fortunately, it subsided into a low throb of anger instead.

I sat on the lavatory seat, gingerly removed my sneaker and sock and inspected my poor injured foot. I'd expected to see a giant purple bruise, but the skin was unblemished, which was disappointing because it meant that I couldn't even use it to try and make Leah feel bad about goading me. Not that she *would* feel guilty about that, because a) sociopathy; b) despite constantly getting punched, knocked out and scalpel-ed, Leah always carried on as if any injury she sustained was barely an inconvenience. Because that was yet another unfair and unrealistic thing about her. Being a wish-fulfilment character, she could move round the world with relative freedom, and therefore hadn't been forced to cultivate an inner warning radar, or come up with complex de-escalation strategies to diffuse unwanted and potentially dangerous interactions with strangers on public transport, etcetera. There was no need for Leah to avoid dark alleyways or deserted streets at night or to run through a brief, panicky risk assessment every time she climbed into an Uber, went on a date, or worked late with a colleague. My mother and I had discussed this aspect of the novels at length, and by discussed, I mean 'had a screaming fight'.

I wasn't ready to face Leah yet, so to kill time, I did a deeper dive into the Wanker's wife's background. It transpired that she was the CEO and founder of a hugely successful property investment company, and because the Wanker only featured at the bottom of its website as a 'business liaison manager', I suspected that he was sucker-fishing off his wife's cash and success. But seeing as she was also a high-profile member of the Countryside Alliance, which, despite its name, seemed to hate the countryside because its members were all about ripping foxes to pieces and shooting badgers for fun, they clearly deserved each other.

Next, I researched 'domestic CCTV storage capabilities' and confirmed that the Wanker had been telling the truth about that. *So much for tech saving the day.* In came a fresh wave of anger at him, both for kiboshing my hopes that his intel would finish the unfinished business, and for being so callous about my mother's death.

After fantasising about punching him in the throat for a bit, the anger transferred to Leah for putting me in that situation in the first place. I'd been manipulated by her more than once, and I was sick of being called hopeless even if it was one of my defining traits.

It was this that made me decide to do what I'd been putting off for four months. She'd put me in the line of fire. I was going to do the same to her.

Whispering 'wish me luck' to Three Arm and Wart Head, I returned to the kitchen.

Leah was once again sitting on the butcher's block, and, back at her side, as if paying me back for taking his nemesis out for a walk, was Brian.

Stopped sulking?

'I wasn't sulking. I've been thinking.'

Oh good. About what?

'Our next steps. Seeing as all this investigation has thrown up is dead end after dead end, we've only got two choices left.' I waited for her to ask what they were. She didn't. 'Option one. Give up and accept that it was an accident after all. Because let's face it, pretty much everything's pointing that way.' I paused for dramatic effect. '*Or* option two. Embark on the only course of action left to us, although you're not going to like it.'

She cocked an eyebrow.

'I'm afraid,' I said, with a smile that I hoped was both *wry* and *dry*, 'that we're going to have to go full tech.'

CAT PEOPLE

The final grief frontier. Well, not the *final* one – I'd only managed to listen to less than two seconds of my mother's voice messages before being hijacked by a kark-fest – but it was the one I'd been dreading the most. And, predictably, by the time I reached the bottom of the attic stairs, my vengeance-fuelled motivation had sputtered out (I could see why revenge was a dish best served cold).

But I could hardly turn back without looking weak. Then I remembered that my foot was still sore, so I stood on it with the other one, and the excruciating pain gave me enough of a distraction to climb the stairs.

I opened the door, took a deep breath, and then . . .

. . . not much. At least not at first, because as with the Death Zone, the anticipation and dread had been far more insidious. The air was fusty and warm, and aware that Leah was lurking somewhere behind me, I took a moment to acclimatise.

It was dusty, but free of spiders – perhaps the 'Labradors of the insect world' also thought of it as a no-go mausoleum. My mother had kept most of her books up here, and because there was very little horizontal wall space before the slanted ceiling began, they were placed in double-thick piles around the perimeter. Her author copies of the

Leah books were tightly stacked in the area next to her desk, their spines displaying multiple thumbnail illustrations of the fringe-peering avatar. I thought about asking Leah if seeing them was like looking into one of those endlessly reflecting funhouse mirrors, but didn't because I was still pissed off with her.

I moved further in. On the desk sat my mother's MacBook, which was still attached to the power outlet, along with a framed photo of me aged around fifteen, chubby but not cherubic, and untroubled by the Troubles. Me at that age was probably the sweet spot for Mum. Stalling before I opened the computer, and on the off-chance that Meera and Daphne had overlooked it, I rooted around for Mum's phone. It wasn't on the floor or in the filing cabinet, which was tightly packed with colour coordinated files labelled 'house', 'insurance', 'tax', and – horribly – 'will'. There was also a worryingly bulky one marked, 'Niamh'. I peeked inside it, clocked that it contained a printout of the last screenplay I'd ever written, then slammed the drawer shut. *Nope! Nothing to see here.*

CLICK, which, for once, wasn't for my benefit because I could smell smoke again. I was about to ask Leah to douse her cigarette – my mother would have hated anyone, even her fantasy daughter, smoking in her sanctuary – but kept schtum when I took in her body language. Her shoulders were slumped like mine usually were, and she was gazing through the skylight, although the view wasn't much to write home about seeing as all it consisted of was Glenn's roof and his enormous, outdated satellite dish.

I didn't want to feel sorry for her – after all, the main reason we were even up here was because she'd chucked an imaginary cigarette butt at my head – but I couldn't help it. 'Are you okay?'

Without turning around, she snapped: ***Why wouldn't I be?***

'Well, because this was where Mum did her writing, and coming up here must be triggering for you.'

I hate that word.

'Triggering, you mean?'

A nod.

Fair enough. She'd never been a fan of firearms, or emotions.

Then she looked over her shoulder. ***Are* you *okay?***

It took me over a minute to get over the shock. 'I think so. I'd expected it to be more upsetting, but . . . Thank you for asking, though. I mean . . . that was . . .'

Another nod and then she went back to looking outwards.

But I'd spoken too soon about the upsetting part, because when I opened the desk drawer, inside it was a grief-bomb in the shape of a Zippo lighter engraved with 'LOVE LIFE!', which I'd given to my mother shortly after her first book deal, and which set off a series of dangerous thoughts, such as *I'll never be able to give her a stupid but also thoughtful novelty present again* etcetera. To stop the emotional incontinence, I was again forced to stomp on my poor injured foot, which had done absolutely nothing to deserve this treatment.

I slipped the lighter into my pocket and took a deep breath.

Okay. Now for the hard part.

I sat in my mother's faux leather office chair, the material worn and cracked and still holding the imprint of her body – which, curiously, was comforting instead of kark-inducing – and opened the laptop.

I couldn't use my mother's fingerprint to unlock it for obvious reasons, and I wasn't a competent hacker, so I had no choice but to play password roulette.

I tapped in my name. *Nope.*

Then I tried 'Brian'. Then 'Brian the Cat'. Then, reluctantly, 'Leah Rebecca Overton'. *Nope. Ha!*

After ten minutes of winging it with variations on names and dates, I gave up and just typed in PASSWORD. Which worked. FFS.

I'd expected the laptop to be frozen in time – it had been months since it had last been updated – but the tech goddesses were on my side, and my mother's email account came straight up. But because it was the most likely repository of secrets I'd rather not know about, I decided to leave it till last. I wasn't sure what *kind* of secrets, because being a woman, and not in a relationship, it was unlikely that she'd been harbouring a second family (a double domestic load for a start, and how would she have hidden the pregnancies?) But also, there was something deeply melancholic and lonely about seeing it still open, blithely going about its business, which made me think about all the other orphaned accounts that must be out there, living on after their owners had died. A digital graveyard, only unlike free spirit Thelma's neighbourhood, this virtual world of the dead wasn't restful, seeing as it was kept alive by relentless spambots and desperate scammers.

I delved into the documents and folders, none of which were password-protected, and mirroring the analogue stuff, were all neatly labelled. The MacBook was fairly new, and because my mother had been crap at backing anything up (she'd distrusted the Cloud in a very Leah-esque way), the contents were relatively sparse.

I clicked on one entitled, NEW LEAH. At least I'd now get to see what she – and presumably, Leah – had been working on.

Up came the title page, *Over It: A PI Leah Rebecca Overton Thriller*, which made me smile, because 'Over It' was exactly how I felt about pretty much everything except for Brian and cake, and perfectly encapsulated my thoughts about 'The Case of the Missing Ladder'. Then, as I scrolled down, I stopped smiling because this was all it consisted of:

CHAPTER ONE

It's three a.m. and the night and the city belong to Leah Rebecca Overton. She prefers to run when the world is sleeping; thinks of the city's shadowy alleyways as her playground. Feels an affinity with their darkened windows and blackened brickwork. Like her, they hold their history and secrets close.

It's a short one tonight – only fifteen miles. Has to take it easy. Doctor's orders. She's just had the stitches removed. Seventeen this time. Machetes will do that. *No big deal. It's just another scar.* Another close call. *Goes with the territory.* She adjusts the headphones attached to her portable CD player, her light footfalls keeping time with the beat of Gloria Jones's 'Tainted Love', which never gets old. Not for her the practicality of an iPhone. No one's going to be scraping *her* data anytime soon. *Or anything else LOL.* Analogue is how she rolls. Untraceable. Old school. Smarter that way. If you ever need to get hold of her – and you'd better pray you don't – you've got to play by her rules.

She ups her pace as she crosses *blah* street – *don't forget to check map.* Feels no regret as she passes the Stanley & Fitch law chambers, the brick-and-mortar symbol of her previous life. She's someone who exists on the fringes, unbound by *blah.* Up she runs towards *blah* and *blah,* before ducking down another back alley, this one lined with less salubrious offices *also do a google earth in case the area's been gentrified.*

Lost in her thoughts and the music, the crunch of broken glass beneath her feet comes as a surprise. To her right, the black mouth of a building, the shattered remains of a display window spiking around it like broken teeth.

What do we have here, then? A robbery? Or something else?

She takes her penlight out of her bumbag and shines it over the brass name plate: 'Zelda Raven Literary Agent'. Carefully, she climbs into a dingy office space, books scattered everywhere.

Not just books: A body too. A woman with short red hair who's dressed in a fluffy cardigan, a fussy blouse and elasticated trousers. No. Not red hair. Grey. It looks red because it's clumped with blood.

Why would someone break into a book agency? *Good question* ☺. But they have. For some reason. She's left her burner phone behind. Not that the cops will appreciate a call from her. She and the boys and girls of the South Yorkshire constabulary don't play well together. Never have. Never will.

The blow on the back of her head comes at the same time she senses someone behind her. She doesn't black out, but it's close. Hears a man's voice saying: 'Gonna kill you, bitch!'

Her head clears. Thinks, *I hate that word* and *I'd like to see you try.* She flicks blood out of an eye *or eyes depending on where the head wound is* and says

Don't forget cat food!!!!!!!!!
Milk
Flour
Olives
Potatoes

https://www.ecohub.co.uk/WUXYTXOZ-Kitchen-Cleaning-Sponges-Non-Scratch/

Bloody hell. Deeply discombobulated by the lack of a word count and the fact that my mother appeared to have been taking the piss out of her own writing, I sat back in the chair and watched the cursor blinking for a bit. Also – the scene featured the murder of a book agent who, like Caro, appeared to favour cuddly clothing, so clearly Mum *had* been harbouring a grudge against her. A serious one as well, because my mother reserved her fictional revenge scenarios for the categories of people who were actively making things worse for the rest of us.

In case there was another document hidden somewhere, I double-checked the folders, and even delved into the trash. Schedule-wise, she should have been on the home stretch of Book Seven. The document had last been modified six weeks before her death, so what had she been doing instead?

And did this lack of a work in progress explain Leah's caginess? After all, answering a question with a question was something people also did when they didn't know *how* to answer.

I swung around to face her. She'd moved from the window and was now standing with her back to the door. Her shoulders were still slumped, and her eyes were guarded. 'From what I've discovered so far, it doesn't look like Mum had been working on much of anything. Is that why you've been so cagey about the new book?'

She became very still – almost too still, as if she'd literally put herself on pause. Then she sighed and gave me a curt nod.

'You could've just told me that.'

Wasn't relevant.

'Course it's relevant! Mum's state of mind around the time of her death is vital intel. Did she have writer's block or something?'

A shrug.

'But you were her muse, weren't you?' No response. '*Weren't* you?'

Maybe she was a malfunctioning muse. Or perhaps she really was nothing more than a grief-induced delusion. After all, the evidence to the contrary wouldn't exactly stand up in court, seeing as my only witnesses were me, a cat, a robin, *possibly* a spider, and a disorientated woman suffering from a debilitating UTI. 'When my mother was writing you, did you have autonomy? I mean, were you able to make your own decisions, or did she just move you around like a piece on a chess board?'

Course I have autonomy.

Have, not had. Which was unsettling, but also implied that she was more than just the product of my harried mind.

I decided to leave her be – for now. I had other odious tasks to get on with.

Next, I checked my mother's browsing history: *The*

Guardian. The Guardian. The Guardian. Tons and tons of links to articles about birds. A couple of menopause websites. An advice column: 'My grown-up son has no friends; how can I help?' *Nope.* And then I came across something unexpected: it seemed that she'd been visiting Netflix daily, which was odd because unlike me, she'd been more of a reader than a watcher. Her account wasn't live – the monthly direct debit would've been frozen – so if I wanted to check her viewing list, I'd have to revive it.

I glanced over my shoulder. Leah was now staring into space, which was subtly different from 'looking inwards'.

Okay. Email time.

I scrolled back to the date of my mother's death. By the looks of it, she'd been in the habit of deleting her emails and clearing out her trash once a week or so – probably not because she had something to hide, but because it was part of being hyper-organised. There wasn't much there, but discounting a couple of requests for book blurbs, and a Trump meme from Meera with the subject line 'LOL', there were five of note, none of which my mother had responded to:

Two messages from Caro, sent two days before Mum's death, both of which read, *Call me. URGENT.*

The urgency was no doubt related to the lack of a manuscript delivery, which might also explain why Mum and Caro had fallen out so spectacularly, but I wouldn't be able to confirm this until Caro returned from her weird geographical mix of literary events.

The next email was from a publicist outlining arrangements for my mother's attendance at a crime-writing festival, at which she'd apparently intended to soft-launch *Overlooked.*

And then there were three identical messages, sent on consecutive days, from someone called GinnyRebel757, which simply said, *Rebel says hi*. Attached to each one was a photo of a black cat's face looming aggressively into shot like a feline mugshot.

Even without the murder context, this would've been creepy enough, because Rebel had been the name of Jed's cat, who Leah had inherited along with the real estate. Rebel had been inordinately fond of Leah, which, to a certain type of reader (and okay, yes, to me), *had* made her come across as more relatable – until my mother had made the fatal error of murdering Rebel too.

My mother had loved Brian, and Brian had loved her, but she hadn't been Rebel's greatest fan – albeit for practical, not personal reasons. 'That bloody cat,' she'd griped in numerous voicemails, 'I spend more time coming up with side-characters who can cat-sit than figuring out plot lines.' Which was true, because it's incredibly difficult to be a lone wolf and go undercover for long stretches of time if you have to keep going back to your industrial loft to feed the cat and clean out the litter tray (which, thinking about it, I didn't recall Leah ever doing). This had become a particularly tedious bugbear in *Overboard*, seeing as Leah had spent two-thirds of the novel pretending to be a cabin steward on a cruise ship. Which was why my mother had decided to dispatch poor old Rebel in the prologue of Book Five (he'd been humanely, albeit involuntarily euthanised by a sub-plot baddie as a warning).

I swung the swivel chair around again. 'Rebel was the name of your cat, wasn't it?' I'd expected a snappish response to this rhetorical question, but instead, she flinched and said: *You don't have to rub it in.*

'Sorry. I begged Mum not to kill him off.'

That was true. Admittedly, by the time I'd got around to responding to the voice note in which she'd outlined her plans for committing literary felicide, my mother had already written the scene, but even if she hadn't, I suspected she would've ignored my advice anyway. (Which was, 'please don't fucking do it, just rehome him or something.') And, despite my mother taking pains to ensure that Rebel's death was quick and painless – to the extent that she'd made the cat-murderer a former veterinary assistant who'd conveniently just stolen a consignment of pentobarbital – unsurprisingly, Rebel's demise hadn't gone down well with her readership. Fortunately, she hadn't been on social media, but the hate had filtered through via emails, a couple of hand-written letters, and several one-star reviews. (I WILL NEVER READ THIS AUTHOR AGAIN!!!) By then, my mother had slaughtered a vast number of innocent people, including children, the deaths of which had passed uncriticised, and although some readers had taken umbrage at Jed's murder, that was nothing compared to the tsunami of Dead-Rebel outrage. My mother had been thick-skinned by nature, but it had shaken her, and we'd traded voicemails about it for weeks afterwards. Curiously – or not – supporting her through it had temporarily hauled me out of my own malaise.

Why are you asking about Rebel?

I did my best to fill her in, which wasn't easy seeing as Brian had more technical nous than she did. 'Do you think the messages were meant as threats of some kind? I mean, Mum got tons of hate when she offed Rebel, and there isn't a friendly exclamation mark after the "hi". And the attached pics all feature a black cat, just like Rebel.'

Rebel had one white paw.

'I'm not saying they're *actual* photographs of Rebel because that would be even weirder and creepier than you, and they *are* just of the cat's face anyway, but—'

Were any sent after the murder?

Good point. I turned back to the screen. 'No. The last one was sent the day before – I mean, night before – Mum died. Which *is* creepy, right? I mean, news of her death wouldn't have filtered out for at least a couple of days, and this GinnyRebel person was clearly in the habit of sending a message a day. Bit of a coincidence.'

There's no such thing as a coincidence.

'One for the murder wall?'

She nodded.

I closed the MacBook with relief and a conflicting sense of sorrow. My brain was often its own worst enemy (it had, after all, begun to equate people with baked goods), but it was sharp enough to clock that avoidance was also an effective way of delaying the dreaded F-word ('finality' – not 'fuck'). But counterintuitively, my low-grade excitement at this new lead appeared to be taking the edge off that. 'Let's get out of here.'

Clearly relieved, Leah seemed to shake off her melancholy like a wet dog after a bath.

I paused at the door. Something else about Rebel's death had been niggling at me. 'Can I ask you a question?'

You just did.

'Do you have to keep doing that? It's getting annoying.' Arrested development was supposed to be my thing, not hers. 'Were you *really* sad about Rebel?'

Course I bloody was.

'How come you let Mum murder him then? Because if you do have agency and autonomy, surely you would have stopped her doing it?' *Gotcha.*

She narrowed her eyes. Then: CLICKCLICKCLICK.

In retaliation, I took out the Zippo I'd given Mum and flipped the lid back. But instead of a CLICK, it made a tinny twock. Which was disappointing.

SIGNS

After a brief pit stop in the cloakroom, I put together a plate of carbs, did a sketch of a cat for the murder wall – differentiating it from Brian by putting devil horns on its head – and settled at the kitchen table for Operation Dead Cat Avenger. Going down online rabbit holes was *my* comfort zone, and for the first time since this whole nightmare began, I felt like I was taking the lead. Apeing Leah, I cracked my knuckles, put on my headphones, and fired up one of my gaming playlists.

Most people tend to use the same moniker across social media, and fortunately GinnyRebel757 was no different, although they seemed to prefer vintage platforms, like Tumblr, Facebook, and Goodreads. There was a suspicious lack of personal info or pics, but they were a prolific crime-fiction reviewer and had given the first four Leah books detailed five-star reviews. Interestingly, they hadn't posted anything about *Over the Odds* – not even a 'DNF' followed by a sad cat emoji.

Hmmm.

Next, I turned to their Tumblr account, which was topped with a meme of Leatherface from *The Texas Chainsaw Massacre* revving his chainsaw, along with the text: ME WHEN AUTHORS KILL CATS IN BOOKS.

179

Okaaay. Moving on . . .

It was then that I discovered something that would change everything: as well as being a prolific reviewer, GinnyRebel was a prolific writer of fan fiction, and topping their character list was a link to 'Leah Rebecca Overton'. After seeing the chainsaw meme, I clicked on it with trepidation, but what I encountered was the opposite of disturbing – unless you consider cats gambolling in industrial lofts disturbing – because most of the content just depicted Leah hanging out in her morgue of a kitchen with Rebel and not doing much of anything (although Rebel did do a lot of chirruping). The writing was pretty good, even if the characterisation was way off, seeing as GinnyRebel's Leah had clearly had some hardcore grump management therapy and did stacks of smiling without any adverbs. They were so divorced from the threatening messages and the blatantly on-the-nose chainsaw meme that I began to question if I had the right GinnyRebel757.

And then I came to a scene that wasn't just Leah and Rebel chirruping at each other. This one featured Amara, a side character and plot armour tech person who'd made her first, brief appearance mid-way through Book Three, and who'd only escaped being slaughtered in later books because she was half-Syrian and a wheelchair user, and by then my mother had learned her lesson about the pitfalls of needlessly killing off non-dominant culture characters.

I took off my headphones. 'Um . . . GinnyRebel's been writing about you.'

She narrowed her eyes. *You **what?***

'Shall I read it out?'

Another glimmer of that rare uncertainty.

'You'll like it, I promise.'

*

'Leah!' Amara said urgently. 'You have to see this. Your gut was right about Jax. He is trying to hack into the database.'

Leah leaned over Amara's shoulder to look closer at the screen, and she could smell the scent of Amara's hair, which was apples. They both held their breath. The air felt weighty with possibility. Then Leah reached out a hand, and delicately touched Amara's shoulder.

'Do I have your consent for this?' Leah breathed.

'Yes,' Amara said. 'I've been waiting for this for so long.'

And then Amara pushed her chair back from the desk and then their lips touched and—

Enough.

Leah's face didn't betray much of anything except irritation, but there was a new aspect to her body language that I was *fairly* sure was embarrassment.

I smirked. *'Do you have a thing for Amara?'*

She rolled her eyes, then resumed her pacing, but that wasn't a *no*, was it?

Then, as if my mind was punishing me for enjoying Leah's discomfort, it dug up an aspect of the Leah books which, over the years, I'd worked very hard not to dwell on.

My mother hadn't been a fan of romance – fictionally, anyway – but the first three novels had included some cringe-inducing sex scenes (cringe-inducing for me, I mean – they were tastefully written). Leah went about her sex life in much the same way she did her career – dangerously and dispassionately. Being tech-averse, she obviously didn't use the apps, but to be fair, she didn't need to, because there was always a convenient shag-interest knocking around in a side plot. In the first few novels, Leah's choice of partner tended to be ex-military and capable of killing

181

a baddie with their bare hands if necessary (it was usually necessary), but a couple had also been adept at making ravioli from scratch, which they'd inevitably do late at night in their underpants (while *wearing* their underpants, I mean). Leah had stopped having sex with burly men in *Overboard* when she'd had a fling with Lucretia, who was a really, *really* good-looking Brazilian cruise ship entertainer. Coincidentally, my mother had decided to queer Leah up after I'd mentioned that I was casually dating a woman I'd met on Discord. But *of course,* unlike my disastrous two-week fling, which had ended in mutual ghosting, Leah's far more successful relationship only came to an end when Lucretia was forced to go into witness protection.

A few months after that, I realised that I was aromantic/ asexual, which I'd always been but had to figure out because no one comes with a detailed manual, and also because it had taken me a great deal of time and thought to comprehend why I'd always felt like I was living in a country that didn't take my personal currency, seeing as so much social interaction was predicated on sexual attraction. I was so giddy with relief at this revelation, that instead of keeping it to myself, I made the mistake of telling my mother, who listened to me without interrupting, and then said: 'Do you think that's what Leah is too?' She'd apologised for that, but the damage had been done, and although she'd never explicitly described Leah as ace, from Book Five onwards Leah hadn't shagged anyone of any gender (also: after that, I stopped telling my mother anything about my life).

Shoving this back into the basement, which was futile because it no longer had a door, I dove back into Operation Dead Cat Avenger. Although most of the fanfic was Leah + Rebel + Amara based, GinnyRebel had also written pieces about other characters too, including one called Carrie Ng, who rang a distant bell for some reason. According to Wiki, 'Dr Carrie Ng is a fictional forensic pathologist, and the protagonist of a series of detective novels written by British author Rose Parkinson. Carrie, who is of Korean and British heritage, is known for being forthright, outspoken, and a champion of the underdog.'

She sounded like another Leah, but that wasn't why her name had caught my eye. *Hang on . . .* I seemed to recall Mum mentioning something about Carrie's author at some point. I clicked on the 'Rose Parkinson' link, and . . .

'Oh wow.'

What is it?

'So . . . GinnyRebel has also written fanfic about this other character called Carrie Ng' – *know her?* I almost said – 'And guess what?'

Get on with it.

'Carrie's author, Rose Parkinson, also died relatively young.'

Cause of death?

'Hang on.'

I came across a short article in *The Guardian*, as well as a link to an obit, but the details were patchy. 'All it says is that the police don't believe the death to be suspicious, which is usually code for "took her own life."'

Suicide?

'I think so. I mean, I don't know for sure, obviously.'

Hmmm. When did she die?

'Um . . . eighteen months ago. Shall I do a deep dive?'

Go for it.

Six searches down, there was a link to a podcast interview, dated a few weeks before Rose's death, entitled 'Author Rose Parkinson talks cancel culture, criticism & cats.'

'I think we'd better listen to this.'

I unplugged my headphone jack so that Leah could hear the interview too.

The interviewer, who was one of those *it's all about ME!* people, blethered on about their own 'process' for a while, then introduced Rose and allowed her to speak. Despite having an accent as posh as Sheila's fake one, there was a tinge of desperation in Rose's voice that came through most strongly whenever she laughed, which I recognised as the hallmark of anxiety and/or low self-esteem. I immediately felt sorry for her, and uncomfortable – Leah and I were, after all, listening to an author's voice from beyond the grave.

The first few novels in the series had been bestsellers, but then Rose had started receiving criticism for creating a protagonist whose background and ethnicity were different to her own – mainly because she'd made some pretty dire culturally inappropriate errors. This had clearly burned her badly, but oblivious to this, the interviewer then asked her to talk about 'her relationship with her main character'. For obvious reasons this caught my attention, especially when Rose said: 'It's a cliché to say this, but I often felt that Carrie was leading the way, and I was just acting as her ventriloquist or translator.' A pause. 'I don't mean that in a literal or patronising way . . .'

As my mother's book event handbag-carrier, over the years I'd heard loads of authors banging on about how their characters 'had a mind of their own' or 'just wrote themselves', but thinking about it, I didn't recall my mother ever saying this about Leah. And judging by Leah's responses to the subject of her autonomy, it seemed that my mother had been the one who'd controlled the narrative (which, considering that she'd been a control freak in other areas, wasn't that surprising).

The interviewer bolloxed on about some other unrelated bollocks, and I tuned out for a bit and ate what remained of Tracey's cake. A CLICK snapped me back just in time to hear Rose saying, '. . . but that was nothing compared to when Mr Paws – the stray kitten that Carrie and her pathology assistants had adopted – died after eating a poisoned sausage roll in *Knife Edge*. After that I stayed off social media.'

I wasn't sure a mortuary should have a cat knocking about, strictly speaking – that didn't seem very hygienic for a hospital setting even if the patients were all cadavers – but the point was, the similarities were a bit too close for comfort. 'Bloody hell.'

You got that right.

I paused the podcast, and stood up, tingling with nervous energy.

'Recap?'

Recap.

Brian, who'd been driven inside by the rain, didn't know who to look at as Leah and I paced back and forth – it was a wonder he didn't get whiplash.

'Okay . . . Two authors. Both aged fifty-something. Both deceased. Both with semi-unclear causes of death. Both UK-based writers of thriller fiction. Both of whom murdered cats in their novels. Both of whom wrote fiction featuring unrealistically competent protagonists,' – an indignant CLICK – 'protagonists who *both* featured in GinnyRebel's fanfic. Coincidence?'

Like I said before, there's no such thing as a coincidence.

'Yeah . . . but the idea of a book blogger who murders authors in creative ways as revenge for slaughtering fictional cats is a bit far-fetched, isn't it?' And if they *were* doing that, then pinning a very literal meme about it would be an extremely reckless thing to do.

A shrug. ***Stranger things have happened.*** (This was said without any irony.) ***We need to confirm the cause of death. See if there's owt suspicious about it.***

'How?' *Could* anyone just look up at a death certificate online? 'If only we could get Amara on the case.'

A muttered, ***Give over.***

I sat back down and was about to ask an AI bot my death certificate question, when I sensed something behind me. *Oh God.* Mirroring her fanfic version's actions with Amara, Leah was looking over my shoulder, which was squeam-inducing for a host of reasons – not least because if she *were* copying GinnyRebel's scenario, and we *were* metaphysically related, then she'd be straying into incest territory. Also – and I'm not being judgemental – she smelled a bit. Not just of tobacco smoke, but like someone who'd worn the same clothes for too long. Bizarrely, this new body odour detail was far more disturbing than the incest horror. Perhaps it was a race against time before she became an actual real-life person. I almost reached out to touch her to see if she was solidifying, but having just read the fanfic, changed my mind.

And curiously, she appeared to have magically shed her tech revulsion. 'I thought you hated the internet?'

Don't hate owt.

Mind you, my mother had given her that characteristic, so perhaps now she was 'free', she'd begin the brain-rot death march into algorithm land (it was surprisingly easy to imagine her leaving judgemental comments under pasta-influencers' accounts).

See who Rose is survived by.

I suspected I knew where this was heading, but I did as I was told, and clicked back to the obit, which stated that Rose was survived by a son, Jamie. 'What about GinnyRebel, though? Shouldn't we see if we can find out their real identity? I mean . . . I could get to know them online. Catfish them. Draw them out.' I'd never done that sort of thing before, although when I used to dabble in the multi-player gaming world, I sometimes let people assume I was male to avoid misogynist bullshit.

Can't let them know that we're on to them. If you mess up, they could go underground.

'They're a book blogger who writes stories about chirruping cats, not a Russian super-spy.'

You don't know that.

'Yeah, I do. I mean . . . the likelihood that they're some sort of author serial killer must be even less than Tracey being our perp. This is . . .' I searched for the right word, landing on: 'Paranoia.'

It's only paranoia when you're wrong. Look him up.

Unfortunately for me, Jamie was all over social media, and I knew for certain that he was the right Jamie because his accounts were littered with pics of him and his mother, along with messages saying, 'miss you mum' as well as stacks of links to grief blogs (including several mentioning the dreaded word 'journey'). He appeared to be in his early twenties and had a lot of expensive-looking tattoos. He also changed his hair pretty much every week, and wore glasses in some pics, and coloured contacts in others. If he were a confectionery item, he'd be an Instagram-friendly, deconstructed mille-feuille surrounded by rose petals.

We need to talk to him. In person.

'I *knew* you were going to say that. Can't I just send him a DM?'

You what?

'A direct message. I mean, I know you're always accosting strangers and bullying them for info, but it doesn't

187

work like that in real life. I mean, if I just show up and start bombarding him with intrusive questions about his dead mum, he'll just tell me to fuck off and then call the police.'

Scroll back up.

Scroll? That was *definitely* not a Book Leah word.

There.

At the top of Jamie's Instagram account was a link to something called the 'Better Together' group, which 'met every Saturday from 1–3 p.m. at the Luxton Church Hall.'

Jamie looked like he'd be more at home advertising veneers or saying, *it's giving dead mum realness* on a reality show than hanging around in church halls, but what did I know? The only spiritual person in my life was Daphne, and although I wasn't against religion on a micro level, I was very much against it on a macro level, seeing as all the organised ones had issues with LGBTQI+ people, which wasn't just massively cruel, but stupidly stupid.

I clicked on the link, which gave more info – none of it reassuring. Because it turned out that 'Better Together' was a 'grief café', of all fucking things. 'Oh, come *on*.'

Do you want to do this professionally or not?

'Not. Obviously. I don't even know where Luxton is. I mean, it could be in Scotland for all I know.' (It wasn't. Unfortunately.)

Then the unfinished business will remain unfinished. She let the moment hang before adding, sinisterly: *forever.*

Christ. But this tipped the scales in favour of this thing being a grief quest constructed by my broken brain in order to fulfil my mother's greatest wish that I'd get out of the bloody house for a bit. Even if there was no way that my broken brain could've known that the GinnyRebel stuff would lead to another deceased author whose son just happened to frequent grief cafés. But anyway. 'Fine. Whatever.'

Leah was eyeing me critically *and* cynically, which I know for a fact is impossible because I tried to do it later, and failed.

'What?'

Your clothes. You were right. They're bloody awful.

'I didn't say they were *awful*. I said they weren't professional.'

That too.

'I haven't got time to buy anything. It's tomorrow. And it isn't as if I can borrow your suit because even if it existed, it wouldn't fit because you're basically a human giraffe, and in any case, it smells like an ashtray.'

I did, however, know where there was an easily accessible supply of smart attire because I hadn't yet packed away my mother's clothes. But did I really want to end another traumatising day by rooting through my dead mother's wardrobe?

No. But nor did I want to spend the evening being sartorially judged by an emotionally volatile physics-defying private investigator, so without telling her where I was going, I limped back upstairs.

DEATH BECOMES HER

I hadn't categorised my mother's bedroom as a Trigger Zone because she hadn't got around to personalising it, and it basically resembled an Ikea advertorial with extra wooden beams. The only reason I hadn't moved into it was because I couldn't face hauling my stuff five yards along the landing.

But.

But.

I'd recently learned that without the shield of avoidance, the bereavement world was full of traps that were waiting to ambush you like an over-enthusiastic balaclava-ed hench-person. And it kept changing the rules, because the things I'd assumed would slay me hadn't, and the things that I hadn't been expecting – acknowledgements in a book; a stranger's gravestone; a novelty gift lighter – had. So far, the sight of the canister of ashes on my mother's bedside table, and the contents of her cupboards hadn't kicked off any karking, but just in case, I entered the room cautiously.

'Hi Mum,' I whispered to the ashes.

What?

I nodded at the plastic tub, which had been the crematorium's choice not mine, and was decorated with a floral scene, a bit like the cake tin, only without any gambolling

190

kittens. Leah was eyeing it with confusion – so much so that I half-expected her to ask, *how did she fit in there?* – and I thought I knew why. Although she'd seen loads of dead people, most of whom had been offed in gruesome and often creative ways, she probably lacked the context for what came after that because my mother had never specified how the various murder victims' relatives had chosen to deal with their remains. Thinking about it, nor had my mother stipulated what had happened to poor old Rebel's body (I hoped Leah hadn't just put him out with the bins; ditto Jed).

Gingerly, I opened the wardrobe's door. In films, grieving people are always burying their faces in their dead loved ones' knitwear, and although I'd never been tempted to do that, I held my breath in case I was hit by an olfactory trigger (being unfit, I couldn't hold it for long). Fortunately, the clothes didn't smell much like Mum – not that she'd smelled much of anything; she'd rarely worn perfume, and unlike me, she hadn't been particularly sweaty.

I picked out a pinstriped blazer and held it up.

Don't be daft.

I grabbed another one, which I quite liked because it was made of grey velvet and looked comfortable.

Leah shook her head in exaggerated disgust like a stylist with zero interpersonal skills.

'Why should I take fashion advice from someone who dresses like a funeral director?'

Is that supposed to be an insult?

'If you had your way, *would* you dress like that? I mean, I know you have to wear various outfits when you're undercover and cosplaying as an office cleaner or whatever, but don't you get bored of wearing the same thing when you're just being you?'

191

I literally don't care what I wear.

'*Literally*? You've never used that word before.'

My mother had literally hated the word literally.

She narrowed her eyes and pointed at the next item on the rack, which, surprise, surprise, was a black tailored jacket.

I slipped it on. My mother had been far taller than me, and I felt like I was playing dress-up. But I didn't *hate* wearing it. 'Well?'

That'll do.

My hair, which was the colour of Glenn's over-stewed tea, was kept in a boring short bob that often frizzed into a mushroom shape, and which, like Leah, I trimmed myself. Not because I was too busy head-butting tech-bros, but because I didn't like being touched by strangers. It was just long enough to scrape into a ponytail, which no one would find offensive. 'I'm not wearing make-up.'

Leah never did either, so she didn't comment on this.

I glanced in the mirror. Not bad. The fact that it was four sizes too big came across as an intentional stylistic choice. It was then that I realised I could see Leah lurking behind me, which was disquieting because I'd assumed that like a vampire, she wouldn't have a reflection. Seeing us together in our similar attire really brought home how different we were in height, demeanour, attitude, and conventional attractiveness. Opposites in every way, yet linked by someone who was somehow also in the room, albeit forever out of reach.

WE ARE STILL HERE

According to Google, Luxton was only an hour-and-a-half's drive away. Which would've been easily doable, if it weren't for the following:

a) It had been two years since I'd driven anywhere, and although I didn't mind driving, I was trepidatious about doing it with Leah in the car.

b) Unsurprisingly, the Mini's battery was completely flat. (On the plus side, I was able to slide into the driver's seat without karking – helped by the fact that other than the invoice for the repair, which my father had indeed left pointedly in the console, my mother had also been obsessive about her car's cleanliness.)

c) Because of swingeing council cuts, public transport wasn't an option, so I had no choice but to go next door and ask Glenn for a jump-start.

'Off anywhere interesting?' Glenn asked when I told him about my predicament, and then looked confused when I took too long to come up with a lie (which was, pathetically, 'going to Tesco for some pasta'). Fortunately, Glenn being Glenn, he had a mobile battery charger in his garage, so he didn't need to bring his own car over, and he acted as if I'd made his year by asking him for a favour.

He popped the Mini's bonnet and attached the cables. 'We'll let it charge up for a bit first, pet. Won't take long.'

Leah lit a cigarette and leaned against the gate, somehow managing to look bored, annoyed, and suspicious all at once. Because of course *she* had never needed to go through the tedium and embarrassment of asking a neighbour to give her a jumpstart – her vehicles were either in perfect nick or had recently exploded.

The state of the car's exterior was clearly causing Glenn some concern, which was fair enough because there was green moss growing in the rubber bits around the windows, and he was the sort of person who washed his vehicle whether it needed it or not. 'It'd be best to keep it in the garage if you're not going to clean it much, pet.'

'I would, but the door sticks.' This was both true and not. The door did stick, which was why my mother hadn't parked the Mini in there, especially since her shoulder had started giving her trouble, but even if it had opened automatically, I knew myself well enough to know that I wouldn't bother squeezing it in there.

'Probably nothing that a bit of WD40 wouldn't sort. I'll bring some over if you like.'

'I wouldn't want to bother you, Glenn.'

'It's no trouble.'

Leah yawned exaggeratedly, which I'd never seen her do before.

Glenn nodded at the barn bunker. 'Did I see you going over the road yesterday, pet?'

I fished for a suitable lie, and snagged a better one than the last. 'Oh. Yeah. Mum's cat disappeared for a bit, and I was checking to see if he was over there.'

Glenn sniffed as if he didn't quite buy this, but anyway.

'Mr Fiddle seemed surprised when I told him about Mum's death. He said he hadn't heard about it. Do you think that's possible? I mean, everyone in the area knows about it, don't they?'

'Like I said, no one around here can stand him. Nasty piece of work.' He sniffed again. 'Mind you. He would've seen the ambulance, course.'

'I'm sorry?'

'Driver had to ask him to move his car so that she could back it out of your mam's driveway. He'd parked right opposite, see. Beyond me why he can't park the bloody thing in his own driveway.'

'Hang on. Are you saying that Ray was in the hamlet on the night that Mum died?'

'Don't ask me, pet. Me and Janet were out that night, like I said. All I know is that he was there on the Wednesday morning. Give you a hard time when you went over there, did he? Want me to have a word?'

A *pah!* followed by an even more aggressive CLICK.

'No. It's fine. He wasn't that bad.' *Bad doesn't even begin to cut it.* And if this new intel was anything to go by, he was either a homicidal maniac and a world-class actor, or even more of a selfish bastard than I'd realised. 'I don't suppose you have a ring camera do you, Glenn? I'm thinking of getting one, you see, and I was wondering if it was worth it.'

'No pet. Never seen the need.' To be fair, he wouldn't need one with Janet. 'No through-traffic, see. Wouldn't get opportunistic crime here.'

'Except for the garden thefts.'

'Like I said. That'll just be kids messing about.' He nodded at the Mini. 'Try it now, pet.'

I slid into the driver's seat and inserted the ignition fob. The engine roared into life, but unfortunately, so did Abba, thanks to the CD that was permanently stuck in the car's antique music system. Fortunately, I was still too distracted by Glenn's Wanker bombshell for this to spark a kark.

Glenn tapped on the passenger window. 'Keep it running, pet.'

Shaken, I climbed out.

'When did you last check the tyre pressure?'

'Um . . .' – never, obviously – 'a while ago?'

'Hold your horses. I'll go and get my compressor.'

I waited until Glenn was out of earshot, then rounded on Leah. 'What Glenn said . . . does that put the Wanker back in the frame, do you think?'

He was never bloody out of it. No alibi, remember?

True. 'But what should we do about it? The Wanker will only tell me to fuck off if I go round there again. I suppose our only course of action is to wait until he leaves, and then see if we can find any more evidence that he is our perp. It'd probably be best to look around in daylight this time, though.'

A shrug, followed by *fine.*

Curiously, the prospect of future snooping didn't seem to excite her. Although perhaps this was because we were segueing from 'The Case of the Missing Ladder' into 'Operation Grief Café', and whenever my mother added a new side-plot, she tended to jump straight into it and leave any previous plot threads hanging until much later.

Glenn came bustling back with his compressor and

started fiddling with the tyres. 'Now, even though you've got run flats fitted, you should always check the pressure see, and watch them potholes because . . .'

I tuned out (who wouldn't?), but this time it wasn't a CLICK that brought me back but the *clang-creak* of Sheila's gate, the sound of which gave me that knee-jerk *erk* reaction, even though I knew she wasn't well enough to engage in any hardcore energy vampirism.

A few seconds later, Tracey and Petticoat appeared. Petticoat lunged towards me joyfully, and Tracey called, 'Hiya!', then recoiled when she spotted Glenn.

I was in the uncomfortable position of making introductions, but as I began, Tracey shut me down.

'We've met,' she said tonelessly. Glenn gave her a curt nod and went back to messing with the tyres.

Awkward.

'Um. How's Sheila today?' I asked.

'More like her old self, thanks, bab,' Tracey said, although it wasn't clear if she thought this was a good thing or not (probably not). 'Nice to see you. I'd best get on.' And then, with another black look at Glenn, she walked away.

When she was out of earshot, Glenn did his nose-tapping thing at me. 'Ran into her the other day when I went round to complain about that bloody dog again. That yapping was driving Janet barmy. Mardy cow that one, isn't she?'

I didn't know what to say to that – Tracey had been the opposite of mardy to me. But I also empathised with Janet's plight, because there were some sounds that I found unbearable too – the slurp and smack of people chewing; the scrape of a fork on a plate; any type of musical ballad.

But it hadn't even occurred to me that there might be other neighbourhood feuds going on that hadn't involved my mother, and into my mind slid a reel of a fist fight between Glenn and Sheila, with Sheila roundhouse kicking Glenn through the gate, which sent him spiralling backwards into Mum's ladder. (I don't know why I assumed Sheila would win the fight with violence – she could've achieved this just by talking at him.)

'All done,' Glenn stood. 'I'll pop over and sort that garage door out for you another time, pet.'

'Thanks again, Glenn. That's kind of you.'

'You're welcome. Drive safe now.' He gave me an awkward pat on the shoulder, then headed home. Leah watched him leave with an expression that was closer to hate than suspicion.

'Seeing as Glenn and Janet find Petticoat's barking so irritating, that probably explains why Janet was so grumpy with me when she saw me out with him. Or maybe she's just weird.'

A snort. ***You'd know all about being weird.***

Oh good. So we were back to this again, were we?

Let's go.

Embarrassingly, I automatically went to get into the passenger side, and judging by the resulting smirk, Leah wasn't fooled when I tried to pretend that I'd done it on purpose to open the door for her.

Things went steeply downhill from there.

ROSEMARY'S BABY

Thanks to our late start, we arrived in Luxton at ten past two, which gave us only fifty minutes before the grief café was due to shut its doors. Unfortunately, the church hall, which was situated on the outskirts of a bigger, posher hamlet, had been easy to find, and I parked outside it and then collapsed onto the steering wheel.

The journey had been so stressful that I'd sweated through my shirt. Not from the actual act of driving, because that had come back to me immediately, or even from the dread of the horrible task ahead, but because of Leah bloody Overton, who'd sniped and snarled at my poor Google Maps voice every time it had helpfully given me a direction, to the extent that I thought she was going to headbutt the phone. I'd felt like the mediator in a marriage that was destined to end up on a murder podcast (it seemed that she hadn't got over her tech aversion, after all). And when she wasn't abusing my phone, she'd abused me with an onslaught of sighing, staring, glaring, smoking, and CLICKing, and by repeatedly asking why the journey was taking *sooooo looooong*, like a toddler with exceptional stamina.

She hadn't specified *why* she was being more unpleasant

than usual, but I suspected it was because I was literally in the driver's seat for once. I'd tried to lighten the mood by asking her what type of cake she thought Glenn might be, but that hadn't gone down well.

Seemingly oblivious to my mental as well as physical exhaustion, she snapped: *Move it.*

'I need a minute.'

You don't have one. **Move.**

'*No.*'

The latent stress of the drive morphed into anxiety. Bereavement-crashing felt like a dirty and horrible thing to do, even though I had a perfect right to do it, seeing as I was bereaved.

'I can't do this. It's not as if I can tell Jamie the truth, and . . . it's *cruel*. How am I supposed to go about it?'

Just be yourself.

'Are you taking the piss?'

No. Now move it.

'*Fine*. But I'm doing it *my* way and not yours for once.'

A CLICK that clearly meant, *good luck with that.*

I did a sniff test to double-check that I didn't reek too badly of nervous sweat, left the safety of the Mini, and then, without opening Leah's door for her – an empty gesture because she was at my heels in seconds – headed towards the hall.

The words 'grief café' had conjured up a sepia-toned image of solemn people dressed in muted colours, drinking tea out of delicate cups, and weeping softly, but the only thing that matched my expectation was the hall's smell – a not unpleasant mix of dust, wood, and soup. The tables dotted around the room were draped in rainbow-coloured tablecloths, nobody except for me and Leah was dressed in black, and the atmosphere was anything but grim. In fact, several people were laughing, but I doubted this was because they'd hated their loved ones – if that were the case, they would've gone to a Starbucks instead.

I spotted Jamie immediately, which wasn't difficult because he was the only attendee with a bleached quiff and neck tattoos. He was perched on one of the tables, talking at a group of much older people, and although I couldn't hear what he was saying, his audience appeared to be rapt, as if he were a youthful cult leader.

I stood awkwardly in the doorway, unsure what to do next. At first no one noticed me, which to be fair, wasn't a new experience. Then, a couple of people looked in my direction, which set off an attention domino effect, and within seconds I was the beneficiary of smiles and warmth. I began to relax, but next to me, Leah did the opposite – being a crime thriller protagonist, she probably wasn't used to seeing the good side of people.

A woman who reminded me of Tracey in demeanour if not appearance (she was a jam roly-poly rather than a Victoria sponge) came over to greet me. 'Welcome,' she said, taking one of my hands in both of hers, which I pretended I didn't mind. 'I'm Pat, the group's coordinator. I haven't seen you here before, have I, my lovely?'

'No.'

Pat's eyes, body language and voice dripped with empathy, which sounds disgusting, but wasn't. 'You'll find that we're a friendly bunch. What's your name?'

I opened my mouth to say 'Niamh', but heard myself blurting 'Leah' instead, which must've stunned Leah as much as it did me, because there was a delay before the CLICK of outrage.

'What a lovely biblical name,' Pat said, without sounding creepy at all. 'How did you hear about us?'

'Um . . . I saw it online.' *When I was stalking one of your members as part of my grief-quest-slash-murder-mystery investigation.*

'Well, I'm glad you found us. The grief journey can be a long and difficult one, can't it?'

You literally *have no idea, Pat.* But there it was again: *journey.*

'I'm afraid we'll be wrapping up in thirty minutes or so, but you'll get an idea of what we're all about.' She nodded at a catering table containing two large thermoses and a tower of disposable cups. 'Go and get yourself a hot drink, Leah, and I'll introduce you.'

What are you playing at? Leah sniped, as I made my way over to the table. ***This isn't an undercover operation.***

'It is now,' I whispered back. Because of course going undercover was what I'd subconsciously felt the need to do: *I am Leah Rebecca Overton. Hotshot Private Investigator. Overachiever. Cool. Confident. No-nonsense. Adept at throat-punching.* Playing a persona was supposed to help with self-esteem issues – it was, after all, one of the reasons that drag kings and queens did it. Unfortunately, it had the opposite effect on me, probably because dragging up as a 'strong female character' was a persona too far, and the last time I'd tried it, I'd almost lost a foot.

So instead of strolling over to the drinks table, pouring myself a black coffee and nonchalantly checking out the scene, I couldn't figure out how to use the nozzle thing on the canister, and then I struggled to turn it off, and coffee dribbled onto the floor, and then I had to waste loads of paper napkins mopping it up. And I was on my knees, midway through this ad-hoc clean-up operation, when I heard Pat saying, 'Leah?' in that worried tone of voice people use when you haven't heard them the first time.

She means you, *idiot*.

Two minutes in, and I'd already forgotten I'd gone undercover for no reason. I scrambled to my feet and clocked that Pat wasn't alone: standing at a slight remove from her, and not looking charmed about being dragged away from his acolytes, was Jamie. If I *were* a PI, this would have been a lucky break, but because I wasn't, it wasn't.

'This is Jamie, Leah,' Pat said. 'As it's your first time, I thought you'd prefer to connect with someone your own age.'

'Hi,' Jamie said with zero enthusiasm.

'I'll leave you two to it,' Pat beamed, then winked at both of us as if she was some kind of death-related match-maker who'd just scored a win.

'I like your jacket,' Jamie said. 'Is it a Westwood?'

'Thanks, and mmhmm,' I said because I had no fucking idea what it was. 'And I like your tattoos,' which I imme-diately regretted saying because it made me sound like a desperate auntie trying to get down with the kids. 'I hope I didn't interrupt something.'

'I was just going out for a vape anyway.' He nodded at the door. 'Come with if you like.'

'Sure. Great. Thanks.'

Even though this outcome wasn't the result of anything I'd done, I turned to give Leah a triumphant glance, and received a glare in response.

As we headed out, people followed our progress with 'aw, bless' smiles on their faces, and a few of them called, 'You off, are you, Jamie? See you next week, love.'

I'd expected Jamie to lurk around outside the door like a normal vaper, but instead he walked briskly towards the neighbouring church without checking to see if I was

203

following. If this were a Leah book, he'd have a special skill that I needed at just the right time, and we'd become reluctant or not-so-reluctant allies. Then, inevitably, he'd be killed off three chapters later in a murder made to look like a suicide. Also: Had I met my opposite number? *By any chance, are you being stalked by your dead mother's protagonist, Jamie?* This seemed unlikely – he appeared to be far too together for that.

Just past the church, he paused and nodded at a gate. 'I usually go in there.'

'Great!' I said, a bit too enthusiastically, seeing as it led into a graveyard. Which I supposed was convenient – you could bury your loved one and then pop next door to the grief café.

Unlike free-spirited Thelma's, this cemetery was devoid of trees, and the pathways weaving through it were gravelled and free of greenery (Glenn would approve). Judging by the gravestones, the majority of which were polished black marble with gold writing on them, this was a far more upmarket affair than our hamlet's. I followed Jamie over to a bench midway along the path.

Once we were seated, he let out a stream of bubblegum-flavoured vapour and asked, 'Who did you lose?'

'My mum.'

'Me too.'

'I know.'

He looked at me sharply. 'Did Pat tell you that?'

Oops. Because I'm an idiot, instead of taking this easy way out, I found myself babbling: 'No . . . it's more because, well . . . Because your sadness seems more like it's from a mum dying rather than a dad. Not that death or grief or even parents have to be gendered or anything like that. Or that everyone even *has* to have a mum and a dad. You could have two mums or two dads or no parents at all, or you can adopt your own family or be adopted or . . .' Not only was I talking utter shite, but I'd also accidentally gone full woke. I *am* full woke, but it can be dangerous to do that out in the wild these days.

CLICK. Leah, who was standing diagonally opposite me in prime judgemental viewing territory, sighed and shook her head. Jamie looked like he was deeply regretting leaving the safety of his flock.

'Sorry,' I said. 'I babble when I get nervous. Which happens a lot. Or I say weird things. Which also happens a lot.' I let out a lame, desperate laugh. 'I've got chronic social anxiety you see, and um . . .'

It turned out that telling the truth was absolutely the right thing to babble, because he relaxed. 'Me too. It fucking sucks, right?' Then he took a baggie of weed out of his pocket and shook it. 'This helps. But it might not be your thing?'

'Yes please. It is very much my thing.'

I'd expected Leah to be horrified by the appearance of some drugs, but she just shrugged. Mind you, perhaps that was because I was undercover, and when you do that you have to go with the flow (when she'd infiltrated the alt-right gang, she'd been forced to eat a KFC Zinger burger in front of them because they distrusted vegans).

Because he was Gen Z, I'd expected him to have a special pipe, but instead he took out a tin of tobacco and skinned up with the practised ease of someone who did it multiple times a day. He lit up, took a deep drag, and passed it to me.

It was very good weed, and within a minute, I could feel it sanding the sharp edges off my anxiety. I took another drag for luck and handed it back. 'Do you live around here?'

'I've got a place in Hoxton. But after Mum . . . I come back here most weekends to be close to her, you know?'

Ouch. I did know. Sort of. Albeit in a different, more avoidance-related way. 'Is this where your mum is buried?'

A flicker of horror. 'No. She had an eco-burial. I meant the area.'

'Oh right. Course.'

'I don't actually like graveyards.'

'Me neither,' I lied, because I had to say something to keep the conversation going. I eyed the phalanx of stones in front of us, which, unlike Thelma's simple but poetic epitaph were engraved with just names and dates, and the category of family member they were related to. They also all had the word 'beloved' on them. Egged on by the dope's softening effect, I pointed this out to Jamie. 'I know you're not supposed to speak ill of the dead and all that, but do you think it's likely that all of them were beloved? I mean, statistically speaking, *some* of them must have been a bit annoying or whatever.' Which made me think of the Wanker, whose truthful epitaph would just be CUNT.

Jamie snorted. 'Yeah. I know what you mean.'

Encouraged, I continued. 'But I suppose you can't really put, "here lies Peter, he was a total shithead."'

Jamie blinked, and then he let out a high-pitched giggle. 'Oh my *God*. That's so dark. Um . . . "Derek, beloved father, son, and secret racist."'

I was giggling now too. Leah was shaking her head in derision, which made the whole thing funnier. 'Celia. She hated dogs.'

'Paul. Nosepicker.'

'Leah. She was an annoying bitch.'

Jamie sobered up. 'I thought *your* name was Leah?'

Oops. 'Yeah. It is. I was just being self-deprecating.'

Unbelievable.

The ice, which I'd inadvertently and successfully broken was beginning to crystallise again, and I fished for something grief-related to say. 'I can see why you come to the grief café thing, though. It's lonely, isn't it? Death and grief and . . . all that, I mean.'

'Yeah. *Yeah*, it is. And like everyone in there gets it. Sort of. Not in *totally* the same way as me because most of them are obviously *way* older, which is fine and I'm not being ageist, but . . . when I'm with them I don't feel like I have to hide what's going on inside.' He took another drag, and forgot to pass it back to me, which was probably a good thing, but also annoying. 'Not even my partners get what it's like.'

'At work, you mean?'

'No. My triad.'

Leah perked up – she probably assumed he was talking about the Chinese mafia.

'Everyone just wants you to be okay and to be over it,' he continued. 'My worst is when they don't know what to say, but instead of just being *honest* about that, which would be fine, they say empty shit instead.' This time he remembered to pass the J to me. I'd have to be careful, though. I couldn't risk a whitey or the paranoias – I'd blow my cover.

'Like clichés, you mean?'

'Yeah. Things like . . . I dunno. Time will heal. Which it *doesn't*.'

'My worst is when people bore on about their own death stories.' Leah shot me a Death Stare followed by a warning CLICK. *Oops*: I'd forgotten that the sole reason I was doing this was to encourage him to bore on about his own death story. 'Sorry. I didn't mean that. Sometimes they're helpful because grief is different for everyone, isn't it? I mean . . . I'd love to hear yours. Only if you want to tell me about it, that is.' Thank God I'd been honest about my verbal incontinence. 'So . . . um. What did your mum do for a living?'

A long, shuddery sigh. 'She was a writer.'

'Oh, that's cool. What kind?'

'Crime fiction mainly.'

'Really? I love crime. What was her name?'

'Rose Parkinson. She wrote a series about this forensic pathologist called Carrie Ng.'

'Oh wow. I love her stuff.' This came out sounding beyond false to my ears, and I hated myself a bit as I said it, but he didn't seem to pick up on it.

'You've read her books?'

'Yeah. They're great. Carrie's such a strong female character and I liked it when she . . . looked after that kitten.'

An absent-minded nod. Then, to Leah's absolute disgust, he chucked the joint's roach onto the path, even though there was a bin right next to us, and immediately began rolling another one. I wasn't sure this was a great idea because his eyes were already bloodshot, and I almost asked him if he was driving, which reminded me that I was, and shouldn't have any more.

'Did your mum like being a writer?' I asked.

'Yeah. But that changed when she got all that hate.'

'What hate?'

'Don't you know about that? I thought you were a fan?'

Fuck's sake. This undercover malarkey was harder than it looked. It was a bloody good job that I wasn't attempting to infiltrate an alt-right gang – I would've been head-butted and cable-tied to a warehouse radiator by now. 'I'm not on social media much. Um. For ethical reasons.'

Fortunately, this seemed to impress him. 'Anyway, as you know, Carrie is half Korean and half Scottish and because Mum wasn't, she got a lot of hate for that. She only came up with her because she wanted to be more representative, and because she liked dim sum.' A strangled sob. 'Even though I told her it was originally a Chinese delicacy.'

'I'm so sorry. That must have been awful.'

'Yeah. It was.'

'Did she . . . did she get the normal kind of general hate or was she targeted by anyone in particular?' This was stupid enough to penetrate his dope-induced brain fog and he gave me a WTF? look. 'What I mean by that is . . . sometimes fans can get toxic when they're pissed off, can't they?'

'Oh right. Yeah. Yeah, they can. And yeah, it was bad. Then she thought about giving up but didn't, and tried switching to the third person instead. But she never finished her last book. Her agent got a ghost to finish it.' He didn't mean a literal ghost, of course. Which, quite frankly, wouldn't have been weirder than my current situation. 'And that felt . . . complex?'

'Like a betrayal, you mean?'

'No. It was complex because that one was hyper-successful, like a *New York Times* bestseller? And now they want to do another one. And they're also going to do a Netflix series which will be . . .' He paused to light the second spliff, but his lighter had run out of gas.

CLICK went Leah's smugly.

He shook his again, then gave up. '*Fuck.* But anyway . . .' He shrugged. 'I don't usually talk like this.'

'I suppose the series carrying on . . . I suppose it's a way for your mum to . . . I mean . . . for her character to live on. That's what some writers say, isn't it? That their characters have a life of their own?' I glanced at Leah as I said this. She'd become very still again and was eyeing me guardedly. *Interesting.*

'Yeah. Yeah. Thanks. That's true, I guess. And also, the money from the option and royalties will help the start-up, and she would have liked that.'

'Start-up?'

'I run a sustainable fashion business?'

'Oh. That's great. Good for you.' Clearly, and despite being at least six years younger than me, Jamie wasn't using his horrible *The Monkey's Paw* life-twist inheritance to carry on doing 'nowt'.

Ask him how she died.

'*No*,' I accidentally said out loud.

Unsurprisingly, Jamie gave me a funny look.

Ask *him*.

Christ. 'Sorry. I was . . . Look. You don't have to answer this, I mean obviously you don't, because . . . But how did she . . .' I couldn't even say the word.

He sighed again. 'I'd rather not talk about it.'

'I totally get that, and you mustn't feel that you—'

'Because I get asked that all the time. Like, *all* the time? My therapist says it's because people intrinsically fear death and they want to know all the details so that they can avoid the same thing happening to them, and . . .'

I opened my mouth to say, I don't know what, when Leah snapped: **Wait. Let him talk.**

'They said it was an overdose, but . . . she wouldn't *do* that. And if it was, then it was accidental.'

Oh God. 'I'm so sorry. I shouldn't have asked.'

'It's okay. It gets easier every time I say it, you know?'

I absolutely did not know that – I felt the opposite whenever I was interrogated about Mum's accident – but I said I did anyway.

'What about yours?' he asked.

'Mine?'

'Your mum.'

Tell him the truth.

'Um . . .' *So the thing is, Jamie, everyone thought she'd died in an accident but according to this PI I know – don't ask – it might not have been an accident but possibly a murder, and if not a murder then possibly a manslaughter and – funny story – the reason I'm even here talking to you today is that my dead mum, who by the way was also a writer who probably met yours at some point, wrote a character who was a bit like Carrie and—*

Pull your bloody finger out and tell him.

'You don't have to go into it. It's . . .' Then his phone buzzed, and he frowned and checked the screen. 'Listen, I've got to go. But thanks for this. Message me, yeah? It'd be good to do this again.'

Which made me feel even worse.

I stayed where I was – trying very hard to ignore Leah's increasingly censorious glare – and watched him walk away. He was probably off to rejoin his triad, which I knew for a fact wasn't the Chinese mafia because that would be cultural appropriation, but a sensible consensual relationship with two other people, who I hoped made him feel less alone even if they were shite at death.

I picked up the discarded roach, popped it in the bin, and then faced the muse.

So much for doing it your way. That did nowt to further the investigation.

'I tried my best.'

That was your best?

'I don't think you *get* how hard that was for me. How hard *any* of this is. The only reason I even went along with this horrible thing was because I'm so bloody desperate to get you off my back.'

I stormed back to the Mini, but then I realised I needed to pee, so I had to U-turn and visit the hall's lavatory block. And while I was doing that it struck me that Leah hadn't shadowed me in there, nor had I asked her not to. It could've been out of choice (no one uses a public toilet for fun), but *what if* – as was the case with my cloakroom sanctuary – she *couldn't* go in there, like a demon unable to cross the threshold of a church?

And then I got it. *This was not her world.* Her stranger-in-a-strange-land behaviour in the shoppe probably stemmed from the fact that the stores she usually frequented were kiosks that sold tobacco and illegal burner dumb-phones. Thinking about it, that would also explain why I'd never seen her eat. She only tended to do that once per novel because there are only so many ways you can describe someone effortlessly making pasta from scratch (curiously, this rule didn't seem to apply to her smoking habit, though). Not only that – was this why she'd behaved like a toddler on the drive? Because although Leah was constantly going undercover in various locations, her journeys usually only took a sentence or were completed during a chapter break: she'd probably never spent that long in a car.

And the *other* thing she'd never done in any of the books was go to the lavatory, which was fair enough because no one wants to read about that (hence we never hear about Jack Reacher's prostate or Poirot's piles). She'd probably only been able to go into the upstairs bathroom because it had a shower in it, and showers were her occasional secret crying zones.

Another minor mystery solved. And as usual, it wasn't one that would speed up the plot.

CRASH

Unfortunately, driving can be as effective as walking when it comes to stimulating thought, and because I was sulking with Leah and she was sulking with me *and* the poor beleaguered Maps voice, I couldn't even use her appalling passenger etiquette as a distraction.

My meeting with Jamie had left a nasty aftertaste, and the further away from Luxton we drove, the stronger it grew. I felt dirty. Cruel. Manipulative.

I should never have gone along with that.

Because this was the real world and not a Leah Overton adventure-slash-case, my actions had real-world consequences, which had been fine until now because the only person who was in danger of getting hurt was me. And although our encounter hadn't resulted in Jamie getting psychologically bruised, finagling a meeting with someone whose mother's death had been so traumatising that eighteen months on he still felt the need to visit a support group, was an objectively shitty thing to do.

Exacerbating my self-loathing was another toxic emotion: envy. Because although Jamie was still wrestling with his grief, what he didn't appear to be shouldering was any *guilt* about his mother's death. And without the protection of the basement door, my stupid mind kept lunging towards a memory that wasn't just laced with guilt, it was sodden with it, and after battling it to the point of exhaustion, I gave in.

I don't remember exactly how the fight started, but I do know it was something petty, like my mother asking me not to leave dirty coffee mugs in the sink and to put them in the dishwasher instead, followed by me saying *I can't it's full* and her saying *well bloody well empty it then* and me saying *I will just not right now* and her saying *it's always just not right now with you isn't it* and me saying *whatever* and her saying *did you look at those links I sent you* and me saying *what links* even though I knew what she was talking about and her saying *the links to accommodation there are a couple of studio flats that look quite nice and you like Bradford don't you* and me saying *I can't afford the deposit* and her saying *I've told you I can help with that* and me saying *I don't want your help* and her saying *oh come on Niamh you have to meet me halfway here* and me saying *don't worry you've made it very clear that you don't want me here* and her saying *I just don't understand why you won't live up to your potential that's what I had to do* and me saying *yeah well that's great for you isn't it but when you were my age you didn't have overpopulation or the climate crisis or the housing crisis or pandemics or AI or billionaire fuckheads ruining everything for everyone and yeah I know you had impending nuclear war blah blah blah but guess what we've got that too on top of everything else and by the way while you and the boomers were being so fucking amazing and proactive and just getting on with things it would have been nice if you hadn't completely fucked up the planet while you were at it* and then her saying *oh god not this again the least you could do is try and change the world for the better and not just moan about it* and me saying *like Leah you mean* and her saying *that's not what I said* and me saying *I know you've created the perfect fucking millennial but I can't compete with that* and her saying *it's not a competition,* and then I'd said:

'I bet you wish she was your daughter instead of me.'

And then she'd said, 'At least she's *doing* something with her life.'

And then I'd said: 'Well, I hope you'll be very happy together because you'll never fucking see *me* again.'

I think, at least sometimes, that Leah was more real to my mother than I was.

I just wished Leah was less real to *me.*

We were edging closer to the outskirts of the hamlet, which brought me back to when Mum had first taken me to see the cottage, which led to *she wouldn't have moved here at all if you weren't so crap.*

Which led to *and if she hadn't moved here at all, then she wouldn't be—*

CLICK.

You're going to miss the turn-off.

I braked just in time and turned into the lane. 'Oh great. Now you're backseat-driving. Any other part of my life you want to take over?'

No ta.

'You really think you're better than me, don't you?'

No.

'Yeah, you do.'

I *don't* think I am.

Which was when I went to punch her, only you can't punch something that isn't there, so I crashed the car instead.

GET OUT

If this were a Leah book, the Mini wouldn't have been a Mini, but a Polestar or a Ducati, and the Polestar or Ducati would've spun, flipped and implausibly exploded the second Leah had managed to crawl far enough away, miraculously unhurt except for a bit of blood on her face that instead of looking gross and alarming would have *framed her unusually arresting features.*

But because it wasn't, and I was only going ten miles an hour, what actually happened was that when I lunged at her, I lost control of the steering wheel, we hit a pothole, the car veered up the bank and shuddered to a stop with its nose buried in a hedge – fortunately without enough force to deploy the airbags.

Tick, tick, tick went the engine, horribly in time with my pulse.

I thumped the steering wheel. *I can't even crash properly.*

The big crying jag hadn't ousted Leah. Going along with the murder quest hadn't softened her up – if anything, it was having the opposite effect. She was basically protagonist Long Covid. *Was this my life now? Forever?* I would've preferred to fling open the door and storm off histrionically, but I was trapped because my side was blocked by the hedge, so instead I collapsed onto the steering wheel and sobbed: '*Get out. Get out of my life.*' (Despair, I discovered, was related to chest-bursting and karking, neither better nor worse, just different.)

I didn't look at Leah while I did this, and she didn't CLICK at me. I don't know how long I despaired for, because even after the sobs subsided, I stayed where I was for quite a while. Which tells you everything you need to know about how quiet the hamlet was, because other than an imaginary PI and a curious sheep in a nearby field, I was able to do this without witnesses. Nor do I know how long I might've stayed like that if Leah hadn't said:

Bran muffin.

'What?'

That's what type of cake Glenn is. A bran muffin.

I raised my head from the steering wheel but didn't turn to look at her. 'And Janet?'

A tea biscuit.

I sniffed. 'I thought she was more of a digestive.'

That also tracks.

'How come you can name different species of biscuit? You never eat snacks.'

Jed did.

That was true. He was always snacking on cakes and steak bakes during stake outs (if my mother hadn't killed him off, he would probably have succumbed to high cholesterol at some point). 'Is that your way of saying sorry for making me crash the car?'

We didn't crash. We rolled to a stop in a hedge.

Without caring if Leah judged me for it, I pulled up the edge of my T-shirt and wiped my face on it. 'So, you *don't* think you're better than me, then?'

She let several seconds roll by, then:

I didn't say that.

I SAW THE TV GLOW

Other than a few scratches, the Mini (and the hedge) were unhurt. Which was a relief, even though we'd managed to not-crash less than half a mile from home.

Brian was waiting for us on the butcher's block, but instead of jumping down and padding to Leah first, he came straight over to me and wound his body around my legs as if he sensed that I needed comforting. 'Thanks Brian.'

If this irritated Leah, she didn't show it. Her almost-apology had thawed the atmosphere between us, but it was still chilly.

I fed Brian and then, before I lost my nerve, said: 'Look. We can't go on like this. In case you haven't noticed, I don't respond well to conflict.'

I've noticed. Deadpan. No sarcasm.

Didn't stop you doing it though, did it? 'And I'm sure you hate this situation as much as I do, so going forward—'

You what? I don't hate this situation.

'You act like you do.'

This seemed to surprise her.

'You have literally been treating me like shite and bullying the crap out of me since you got here. I didn't ask for this. And I know I can be crap sometimes' – I paused for the expected *only sometimes?* jibe, but it didn't come – 'but I've been doing my best to go along with this. And, if you want to know the truth, I've had it. Your attitude seriously sucks.' I waited for her to respond. She didn't. Nor did she look snarky or defensive. 'Aren't you going to say anything?'

You haven't finished.

True. 'So. Seeing as you've made it clear that you're not going to leave me alone until we finish the bloody *buggering* unfinished business, we need to lay some ground rules.'

Agreed.

'Really?'

What part of agreed *is unclear?*

I almost smiled: this was more like her usual behaviour. 'I'm not saying you have to be *nice*, because that would be impossible. But you've got to understand that there are some things *you* can do, but *I* can't. Like talking to random people without getting horribly anxious, or deliberately goading horrible men. Because in my world that usually ends badly for women, even though I wish it didn't.'

Fine.

She was taking this unusually well.

'Why are you treating me like shite, anyway? I mean, you weren't this vile to Zane McCabe in *Over and Above*, and he double-crossed you, got one of his friends to murder Jed, and then tried to get you killed.'

Ugh. Zane. She mimed vomiting, which was such a non-Leah thing to do that I laughed. It was also fair enough and an understatement, because shortly after joining forces with him (he was one of the pasta-making-after-sex men), Leah discovered that Zane wasn't the NTSB air crash investigator he purported to be, but a stooge for the aircraft manufacturer, and when he'd tied her to a radiator, he'd used two zip-ties instead of one. (It was only later that I realised she hadn't answered my question.)

And then something else occurred to me. Had she been so aggressive because she was trying to hide that she was scared and confused? Because if she hadn't experienced much of this world before, then shoppes and long car journeys and plots not tying up neatly and the necessity of doing dull small talk must be deeply disorientating. I came close to saying, 'I'm scared too,' but if that were the cause, I doubted she'd admit it.

'So. What I'm saying is that we need to work together instead of against each other.'

Agreed.

'And compromise.'

Agreed.

'And you have to stop calling me hopeless, even when I am being hopeless. Just think it instead.'

Fine.

'And if we ever have to go in the car again, you can't act like an evil toddler.'

Fine.

'Why are you going along with this?'

A shrug. *You're being proactive. And honest.*

She left out the 'for once' because as per, it was implicit *and* explicit in her expression and body-language.

But it was progress, and to reward myself for being proactive and honest, I reached for the cake tin.

No. You need to eat some proper food.

'Thanks, Mum.' Then I realised what I'd just said.

You're going to cook something.

'I told you. I can't—'

I'll help you.

Sarah Lotz

Leah Rebecca Overton's Napolitana Sauce

INGREDIENTS

5 *cloves of Garlic* ('That seems like a lot. Are you
sure?' **Yes**).

Three cans of Italian whole plum tomatoes ('Can't I
just use the ready-chopped ones?' **No, you
bloody well can't.**)

Olive oil ('How much?' **A glug.** 'What the fuck's a
glug?' CLICK.)

A pinch of sugar if necessary ('How do I know if it's
necessary?' **Never mind. Just leave it out.**)

Assorted herbs ('Can I use dried ones?' **Fine.**)

Salt and pepper to season.

METHOD

Heat the olive oil. Chop the garlic and cook quickly.
(**Not that bloody quickly, you're burning it.
Take it off the heat for a bit.**)

*Add the tomatoes, crushing them up with a wooden
spoon.* ('Remember when I threw this at your
head?')

*Stir in the herbs and seasoning and leave to simmer on
low heat for two hours.*

'Two hours?'
At least.
'That's a lot of time to kill.'
And then I remembered there was a possible way of
doing that which might further the quest *and* give me some
much-needed brain-numbing screen time. 'There's some-
thing I need to do.'
She moved to follow me.

'No. It's fine. I've got this.' I ran up to the attic and collected the MacBook without needing to stomp on my poor foot, although coming back down was worse because the scent of cooking took me back to the kitchen in my mother's old house.

When I returned, Leah eyed the laptop with suspicion. ***What are you doing with that? Research?***

'Kind of. You'll see.'

To swerve the risk of Leah peering over my shoulder again, instead of sitting at the kitchen table, I made for the snug. I rarely used this room, not because of any avoidance-related stuff, but because the coffee table was too low for gaming, and I preferred to binge-watch in bed. It was as sparsely furnished as the rest of the cottage, but still managed to be cosy. I thought about lighting the carcinogenic wood-burner but couldn't because I didn't have any matches or wood, so I turned on the normal heating instead.

I gestured at the couch. 'Sit.'

I sat as far away from her as possible and set about reviving my mother's Netflix account.

What are you doing?

'Trying to solve another minor mystery. We're about to find out what my mother was doing when she was supposed to be writing. Well, some of the time anyway.'

Brian sashayed in and jumped up to sit between us.

I successfully brought the account back to life, and checked out my mother's viewing history, which was . . . unexpected. It seemed that she'd been working her way through series after series of *Law & Order: Special Victims Unit*. It was doubtful that she'd been trawling for plot ideas as they were notoriously batshit, and although the Leah adventures often strained the boundaries of credibility,

223

they never used sexual assault as a jumping-off point for a storyline about cryogenics or baby farms.

I placed the laptop on the coffee table. 'Ready?'

I pressed play, and surreptitiously watched Leah's expression as the voice-over droned: 'In the criminal justice system, sexually based offences are considered especially heinous. In New York City, the dedicated detectives who investigate these vicious felonies are members of an elite squad known as the Special Victims Unit. These are their stories.'

Then the trademark double-percussive *DUN-DUN* intro.

I'd expected Leah to be dismissive – it was, after all, a very cop-heavy show – but five minutes in, I could tell by her fixed gaze that she was hooked.

And so my fictional detective and I sat on the sofa with a delusional cat and watched a bunch of fictional detectives crouching next to the body of a fictional victim and staring at it as if it were a non-fictional fruitcake.

The pasta sauce was delicious, by the way.

THE OMEN

DUN-DUN.

Instead of being bullied awake by the CLICK of a Zippo lighter or a cat's paw batting at my face, I was rudely awoken by the *Law & Order* soundtrack. I'd fallen asleep on the couch, and next to me, still glued to the laptop (not literally) was Leah.

I stood up and attempted to ease the crick in my neck. 'Have you been up all night watching *SVU*?'

Without taking her eyes from the screen, she nodded.

'I thought you distrusted cops?'

They're not all cops.

True. There were also some aggressively competent lawyers with whom Leah probably identified, and a fabulous forensic pathologist whose main role was delivering plot exposition, which she somehow managed to do without laughing.

'You don't find the plots a bit . . . far-fetched?'

She huffed as if I'd just said something offensive. **Don't be daft.**

Fair enough. She was, after all, a character who'd once held the CEO of an international oil conglomerate in a headlock until he'd passed out on his boardroom floor. And maybe she found the show comforting, seeing as perps were caught and appeared in court in less than an hour, red herrings were nixed within minutes, and none of the protagonists were forced to walk a poorly neighbour's dog or sit in a car for an hour-and-a-half. This world probably made more sense to her, even if at that very moment, Detective Olivia Benson was shoving drugged chocolate into the mouth of a stereotypical 'street person'.

I went through to the kitchen, which still smelled – not unpleasantly – of garlic, and because it looked like it was quite a nice day, I decided to drink my coffee on the porch, like Mum used to do.

The feeders were still half-full or half-empty, and the cake was where I'd left it – impervious as a patisserie statue, although it was now topped with a smattering of bird droppings. Perhaps Augustus had staged an inedible baked goods dirty protest.

I sat on the porch's rickety wooden bench. Something felt *off*. Then I got it: *Leah hadn't followed me outside without me asking her to leave me alone.* Which was wonderful and freeing, but also disconcerting – like that subconscious itch you get when you've forgotten to do something important.

I watched and listened to the birds for a while, but my mind kept straying back to the quest. So far, our most promising lead was so ridiculous that even the *SVU* producers would have binned it: *A fiendish serial killer, travelling across the country to wreak revenge against authors who'd murdered cats and kittens in their novels.*

I took out my phone to check on our main suspect anyway, who it turned out, had recently posted a message saying, 'can't wait for this' on a Goodreads group tagged 'CrimeTime', which wasn't a forum for potential criminals, but a discussion board for a crime-writing festival.

A festival that was due to take place in Wales in a few days' time.

A festival that Caro – who might or might not know why my mother had stopped writing, but who had definitely been having some kind of beef with my mother – would also be attending (it was unlikely there was another crime-writing festival going on in Wales that weekend – it was a very small country).

And.

And.

A festival at which – as I knew from reading her emails – my mother had been planning to launch *Overlooked*.

There's no such thing as a coincidence.

But of course there is. Coincidences happen all the time in real life, but if you make them happen in fiction, then people assume you're just being lazy. Although, to be fair, it wasn't *that* much of a coincidence seeing as GinnyRebel was a crime fiction fan who probably went to niche book festivals all the time, and Caro's agency specialised in representing thriller authors.

Daphne would no doubt consider the fact that all roads led to CrimeTime as a sign from the universe. *It's clear where you need to go to complete your grief journey, honey.*

But it didn't matter if it was a coincidence, or the progression of an incredibly odd murder mystery, or a metaphysical sign, or my subconscious knitting together a bunch of disparate clues to push me towards attending the book festival at which my mother would have launched *Overlooked*. A book festival that if I hadn't once said, *I would rather get trapped in a lift with fifty clowns than go to one of those things ever again*, my mother would've asked me to attend as her handbag carrier. And the reason it didn't matter was because there was a more pressing consideration: *Should I tell Leah or keep it to myself?*

Ladder thefts. Grief cafés. Regional book festivals. Christ, what's next? A bake sale?

Also, I couldn't decide if the irony of attending a book festival with my dead mother's protagonist was hilarious or horrifying, and it made me wonder if this was another reason why Leah had shown up when she had – the timing seemed a bit too convenient otherwise.

I sat where I was until Brian came out for his morning torture session (shamefully, I didn't attempt to stop him, even though I'd bonded with Petticoat).

Then I went back inside.

Leah was still absorbed by the far more exciting drama unfolding on my mother's laptop screen.

'Can I pause this for a sec?' I did so anyway, even though she wasn't happy about it. 'There's something I haven't told you. Well, two things. Look. Before she died . . . well, *obviously* before she died, Mum left three voice messages on my phone. And . . . I haven't had the courage to listen to them yet. Which I know is pathetic, but—'

It's not pathetic.

Was she being sarcastic? Bizarrely, it didn't seem so, because then she said:

You can do it when you're ready. You're not ready.

That had come out sounding borderline empathetic. So much so that I was tempted to see if there was a body-snatcher pod hidden behind the couch. 'Really? You're not going to call me a coward?'

A shrug. *I've lost people too.* This was said matter-of-factly, but just for an instant, I detected the shadow of pain in her eyes, as if a hairline crack had appeared in her carapace. **What's the second thing?**

If I told her, there would be no going back. But for once in my life, I decided not to take the easy option: we'd come too far for that. 'I know where GinnyRebel's going to be on Friday.'

So?

'What do you mean, *so*? I thought you'd like that. I mean, it's a solid lead.'

It'll probably come to nowt again. Her eyes strayed back to the fake cops on the laptop screen.

Whoa. 'But we've got to try, haven't we? You've never given up on anything.' *Unlike me*, I didn't add. 'And yes, I know that so far, the investigation's been a bit unexciting, and there have been loads of red herrings – probably more than you're used too – but we've got to see it through, right?'

No response.

'*Right?*'

A sigh, then: *Fine.*

Bloody hell. Not only had I magically turned into someone who gave quite a good pep talk, but it seemed that overnight, Leah had turned into someone who needed one.

KILL LIST

Curiously, when I'm gaming, I'm capable of doing mindless and/or complex tasks with a drive and dedication that I never exhibit elsewhere (my mother had found this aspect of my character particularly exasperating). So, instead of leaving everything until the last moment, I decided to reframe my brain and prepare for Operation Book Fest as if I was gearing up for a mythic raid. To this end, I wrote a to-do list on the notepad on the fridge:

Find cat sitter for Brian.
Research CrimeTime.
Book accommodation.
Message Daphne.
Come up with strategies instead of just winging it.
Pack.
Clean Mini.

In the pre-quest days, just the act of writing the list would have been enough to make me feel as if I'd achieved something, but for once, I got on with the tasks too, and even added an extra one to the list. Not only that, but I was able to do most of them in relative peace because Leah attacked binge-watching in the same way that she handled her cases – aggressively and obsessively. I now understood why harassed parents used screens as babysitters.

FIND CAT SITTER FOR BRIAN

It turned out that my mother had been correct about the cat-sitting conundrum – not that this excused her radical solution. I didn't like the idea of Brian being left alone, but it wasn't as if Leah and I were going undercover for three months or were at risk of being kidnapped – we'd only be away for two days, and I was fairly certain that book festivals in North Wales weren't kidnapping hotspots.

My choices of cat sitter were Tracey or Glenn, and although I felt guilty about adding more to Tracey's plate, she was my first choice, seeing as she'd mentioned that she was a cat person. In any case, if I left out extra food for him on Friday, and if we came home at a reasonable time on Sunday, she'd only have to feed him once on the Saturday morning. And when I asked her, she agreed without doing one of those forced smiles and offered to 'pop round now' to 'see where everything is'. Unfortunately, I'd completely forgotten about the murder wall in the kitchen:

'That's interesting, bab.'

'Yeah. My dad did it.'

Unlike Leah, Tracey was too polite to say, 'the stain was better.'

LOOK FOR MORE EVIDENCE IN THE WANKER'S GARDEN IN DAYLIGHT THIS TIME
(This was the extra task.)

Still unable to believe that I was driving this part of the

investigation, after waiting for Glenn to parp off to do his weekly shop (it was a Monday again), and bribing Leah away from her binge-watching marathon ('c'mon, it might be dangerous'), we set off across the lane.

Or we would've done if Janet hadn't been standing outside her gate, hosing down her recycling bin, and staring at me unsmilingly.

'Morning Janet. Um. I'm just off across the road to see if I can find my mum's cat. He's gone missing, you see.'

She sniffed. 'He's right behind you.'

I turned to see Brian sitting nonchalantly on the cottage's gate post, oblivious to the fact that he'd just stymied a surveillance op.

It was then that it began to rain, so I decided it was best to take a page out of one of my mother's books and leave that plot strand hanging for a few chapters.

RESEARCH CRIMETIME

According to its website, CrimeTime was a relatively new, niche festival that changed locations every year. Despite this, every event was sold out, even the tedious-sounding ones that didn't feature anyone famous.

The events were being held in various venues in an off-beat, colourful village called Portmeirion, which catered mainly to holidaymakers, and didn't have any permanent residents except for sculptures. Apparently, it had been built in the early-twentieth century by an eccentric man who'd been a fan of Italy and wanted to do a version of it in Wales, and it seemed apt that the next part of the fake murder mystery would take place in a fake village. It was frequently used as a filming location, and had been the main setting for an ancient spy-fi series called *The Prisoner*, which genre-wise was also apt, but not in a good way.

As a concession to Leah, instead of depending on the Maps voice, I wrote down step-by-step directions on several Post-it notes and stuck them to the Mini's dashboard. And to keep her (hopefully) entertained on the drive, I compiled a playlist of Northern soul tracks which I quite liked, although even my dad's rock choices would be preferable to Leah barking ***Don't you bloody well tell me to stick to the assigned route*** at my phone.

BOOK ACCOMMODATION

Because the area was a tourist hotspot even when there wasn't a low-key festival going on, my only options were a terrifying-looking Airbnb with scathing reviews, or the sole room left in one of the village's two main hotels. Which wasn't strictly a room, but a suite in what appeared to be a castle, which, after an hour of mental wrangling, I decided to book, even though two nights' accommodation cost more than I used to shell out on my monthly expenses.

MESSAGE DAPHNE

<Grief journey is going well & I also made some pasta. Hope all is well with you and Dad>
    <That's nice honey. Did you find the ladder?>
    <No. Glenn from next door says some kids nicked it>
    <That's worrying. Why would children steal a ladder?>
    <Dunno. They're also nicking gnomes, flamingos & hosing attachments>

This went on for a while.

COME UP WITH STRATEGIES INSTEAD OF JUST WINGING IT

I was determined not to leave this part till we were on the festival equivalent of the Wanker's doorstep, so once again I dragged Leah away from her round-the-clock binge-watching and made her help me.

'So.'

So.

'Our two main tasks are as follows. One: ask Caro if she knows why Mum stopped writing, and why she wanted to speak to her so urgently. Two: identify GinnyRebel, find out why they were sending those creepy repetitive messages, and confirm or disprove that they're an author slayer.'

Leah acted as if she was listening, but her eyes kept straying back to Mum's MacBook. I knew how she felt – I used to do that whenever anyone interrupted my own time-sucking activities, and being on the other side of it was incredibly irritating.

'But how are we going to identify GinnyRebel? I still can't find any personal info online. I suppose the obvious way is to befriend them on the CrimeTime group and arrange to meet in a safe location.'

Can't risk tipping them off.

'I wouldn't tip them off. I'd just chit-chat about cat and book stuff.'

No. Interrogation is always better in—

'—person. I know.'

GinnyRebel had helpfully listed which events they'd be attending, so our only other option was to hang around the venues and cross-reference attendees as if we were playing an elimination logic puzzle, which seemed like a needlessly convoluted way of going about things. But if all else failed, I could message them once we were there. I hated messaging people anyway, so I preferred this option.

I knew where Caro would be because she was taking part in a panel on Saturday afternoon called 'Ask the Agents', which considering the circumstances was also apt, but then what wasn't?

PACK

My mum's jacket could use a clean, but I reckoned it would pass muster – compared to Leah's suit, which was now also dusted with cat hair, it looked pristine. I was becoming quite fond of it, mainly because it was that rarest of things – a lady blazer that not only had two working pockets on the outside, but a large and therefore practical one in the inside.

I also packed my mother's advance copy of *Overlooked*. Seeing as she couldn't be there, it felt right to bring it along for the ride.

CLEAN CAR

This was the task I'd been dreading the most because the poor old Mini needed a lot of cleaning, and I'd suspected it would be a boring and exhausting chore (it was).

I was midway through doing it when Glenn appeared, making me jump. Then Leah showed up as well, which also made me jump because she'd spent the previous four days being a couch PI, and I hadn't been expecting her. Mind you, she'd also shadowed me when Tracey had popped over – her inner radar for neighbours was clearly capable of penetrating the *SVU* firewall.

'You're doing a grand job there, pet,' Glenn lied. 'I've got some upholstery cleaner if you want it.'

'Haven't got time for that, but thanks anyway.'

'Off out, are you pet?'

'I'm going away for a couple of days.'

'Somewhere nice?'

'A book festival. In Wales.'

'That does sound nice,' Glenn lied again. He held up a can of WD40. 'Shall I give this a go?'

As he was fiddling with the garage's hinges, he mentioned that Janet, his human ring camera, had noticed that the guttering was still unfixed, which made me wonder if she'd had been spying on me, and if so, if that might also explain her rude behaviour. From her perspective, it must look like I spent my free time decanting cakes onto porches and arguing with myself in the garden.

'I'll pop over and fix it when you're away, pet. I'd do it now, but we've got an estate agent coming in a bit.'

As usual, he wouldn't take 'no' for an answer, and in any case, we had to wrap it up because he'd successfully completed Operation Garage Door. The funny thing was, when he opened it, I found myself worrying about the spiders. After months of living in the dark with nothing but the occasional soft glow of artificial light, they probably felt like they were experiencing a solar flare event.

After the usual round of 'thank yous/it's no troubles' Glenn went back home, Leah went back to her new friends, and I went to close the garage door before too much generational spider trauma could be wrought. It was then that I spotted the bin bags full of Sheba cans that I'd meant to put into the recycling. I had no idea which day the recycling was collected, but I decided to take the bin out anyway – it might appreciate a change of scenery.

It took quite a lot of effort to drag it out – either I was weaker than I thought, or it was full. I flipped the lid and was assailed by the scent of stale alcohol. And no wonder: it was packed to the brim with empty sherry bottles, some of which were broken.

Weird. My mother hadn't been a drinker – like me, she'd had an unusually low tolerance for alcohol. Nor did I recall her ever seeming drunk when I'd stayed with her. And apart from the remains of my Dad's Glenfiddich, which I'd regurgitated shortly after Leah hijacked my life, I hadn't come across any booze in the cottage. Daphne didn't drink, and Meera drank only cider because she had coeliac disease.

But if Mum had become a drinker, that might explain why a) she'd fallen off the ladder; and b) why she'd decided to fix the guttering at that time of night. Also – could this be behind Janet's cryptic 'watch your bins' warning? I supposed it was possible that during her curtain-twitching activities, she'd seen Mum dumping bottle after bottle in the recycling bin and was giving me a Janet-style heads-up so that I didn't get a shock.

I decided to keep this discovery to myself for now. I hadn't lost *all* my avoidance skills, and deep down inside, I didn't want something so tragically mundane, and possibly avoidable, to be the reason my mother had lost her life.

VILLAGE OF THE DAMNED

Up until I had a panic attack, which happened when I was next to a human-sized chess board in the middle of the fake Italian village, Operation Book Fest had been going better than expected.

In contrast to the grief café hell trip, the drive had been quite pleasant. As promised, Leah had behaved herself, although the spectacular Welsh scenery we were driving through appeared to befuddle her (*where are all the bloody people?*).

The only journey-related blip was that I'd neglected to put 'fill car with petrol' on the to-do list. Fortunately, just before we ran out, we came across a garage nestled at the end of a mountain pass, and next to it, like a capitalist tumour feeding off the otherwise unspoilt countryside, was a Starbucks outlet (from which I bought a venti Americano, two croissants, a Twix in honour of Jed, and a cheese toastie).

And we made it to the hotel without needing to use the phone for directions, although we couldn't have missed it, seeing as it was, as advertised, a bloody big castle. Considering that Leah was a thriller and not a fantasy protagonist, I'd expected her to be more impressed and/or befuddled by it, but then I remembered that one of the dodgy airline bigwigs in *Over and Above* had bought a Scottish castle as a tax write-off, and she'd spent a chapter tailing him there. Admittedly, after I'd squeezed the hedge-bruised Mini between a Tesla and a Polestar, it had taken me longer than it should to get up the gumption to leave the safety of the car. (I'd pretended to Leah that I was waiting for a leg cramp to pass – not that she was fooled.)

Other than that, the only hotel-related blip came when I was checking in. I'd been steeling myself for a formal and judgemental welcome, but the receptionist greeted me warmly, and was laid-back and chatty-in-a-good-way (a jam doughnut rather than the expected Eton Mess). The issue came when he asked, 'Is your other party coming later?' Because it seemed I'd forgotten that Leah wasn't a person, and had accidentally booked for two.

'Um. No, she . . .'

Died, Leah piped in unhelpfully.

'. . . couldn't get a cat sitter.' Fortunately, the receptionist thought this was an acceptable excuse and kindly provided me with a map of the village, as well as detailed directions of how to get there, even though it was only a quarter of a mile away and the path that led down to it was very clearly signposted.

Although the room's size was intimidating, the décor wasn't – if anything it was too simple and practical for a castle – so I didn't need to worry about spilling coffee on priceless antiques. There was a separate lounge area with a couch for Leah to *SVU* on, a mini-kitchen, a bed that could comfortably accommodate a triad, and a bathroom sanctuary that was spacious enough to hide in for *days* before claustrophobia set in. So far so good. Apart from the fact that my mind kept nibbling at the bottles-in-the-bin discovery, I felt . . . okay. A *bit* like an imposter. But . . . *okay*.

We'd also arrived with time to spare before GinnyRebel's first event, so after I'd spent fifteen minutes figuring out how to use the coffee pod machine, and one minute drinking the tiny bit of coffee it produced, we set off on our first recce.

The path was sandwiched between a scrubby bit of woodland and a field that sloped towards the estuary in the distance. It had been years since I'd been anywhere near the sea, and the sight of it filled me with a childlike excitement – so much so that I had to remind myself that I wasn't here for a relaxing break, but to track down an improbable serial killer.

'If we have time, we could go to the beach.'

No ta.

'Why not?'

Don't like the ocean.

'Why? Because of *Overboard*?'

Course.

I didn't blame her. I wouldn't like it either if a pair of seasick henchpeople had tried to throw me into it.

We traversed the tiny village's ginormous parking lot, accidentally wound up at the service entrance, retraced our steps, and eventually located the front gates.

The man checking the tickets was as friendly as the receptionist, and thanks to my recent stint of small-talk immersion therapy, I was able to chit-chat about weather-related stuff with barely any inconvenience. There were a lot of people milling in and out, and within minutes I clocked that they fell into two camps: book event people and normal tourists. The festival tribe members exuded a sense of purpose and favoured smart but boring outfits; the normal tourists were clad in unseasonable holiday gear, and wandered around aimlessly, trailed by unhappy children.

Chit-chat gauntlet successfully navigated, Leah and I ventured further in. The first thing that hit me was how closely the village resembled its photographs, which shouldn't have surprised me – it wasn't as if architecture was capable of photoshopping itself. Cobbled streets wove through, up and around multilevelled, candy-coloured structures, all of which were turreted, domed, curlicued, and adorned with pointless balconies. I appreciated that it didn't try and hide what it was, which was a folly built by an eccentric man who'd clearly had a lot of time on his hands, and enjoyed putting sculptures of mythological beings under archways. I could see why people liked coming here on holiday – it encouraged you to step out of the boring real world for a bit, like a mini-Disneyland without any rides.

I took out my phone – I'd decided the best way to talk to Leah without looking odd was to pretend to be on it all the time. 'What do you think?'

About what?

'This place, obviously.' I nodded at a mermaid who was casually hanging out in an alcove. 'I mean, that's not something you see every day.'

A shrug. The aesthetics of a setting – however off-kilter – probably didn't matter to her. They were all just sites for possible clues, or the backdrop to a future violent showdown.

We made our way down to the main drag, passing more higgledy-piggledy candied buildings, some colonnaded structures that looked like they'd popped over from ancient Greece, and a tent selling tickets to the book events, which seemed pointless seeing as they were all sold out.

The village's main attraction was an impressive sunken forecourt, which was framed with aggressively manicured strips of lawn emblazoned with STAY OFF THE GRASS signs. Its highlights were a decorative but shallow pond, and the human-sized chess board, which was roped off to stop anyone having fun on it. GinnyRebel's first event – 'Fact vs Fiction: is true crime eclipsing the imagination?' (yes *and* no in my case) – was due to start in five minutes in the Hercules Hall, which was housed in a large, less crenellated building on the other side of the chess board. I was about to suggest that we make our way over there, when, with no warning, the full surreal impact of Operation Book Fest crashed in on me, my pulse rate picked up, and my scalp began to prickle. Suddenly, the buildings' pastel colours seemed too bright, their shapes too peculiar, the people around us too loud, the estuary below us too glittery, the air too briny.

'Can we just hold on a sec?'

Why?

'I think I'm having a panic attack.'

I'd expected Leah to roll her eyes and say, *give over, what's there to panic about?* But instead, she deployed her magical lighter:

CLICK.

'Not working.' I shook out my hands. My fingers were going numb, so much so I was in danger of dropping the phone.

CLICKCLICKCLICK, then:

Breathe.

And just like that, the tightness in my chest loosened, and perspective began to restore itself.

'Thanks,' I said when I could speak.

A curt nod.

By the time I'd recovered, people were already funnelling into the hall's stairwell. Because it was a book event, the majority were middle-aged or older, and none of them looked like they might be serial killers, book bloggers, or even fanfic writers, not that any of those occupations had a particular dress code.

'So, I suppose the best course of action is to hang around here and see if we can spot our possible perp going into the event.' God knows how, it wasn't as if GinnyRebel was going to be wielding a chainsaw or wearing a cat costume.

They might be inside already.

'Then we'll have to hang around until everyone leaves.'

No. Let's go in.

'Can't. Tickets are all sold out.'

Break in, then.

'It doesn't work like that in real life.'

Yes, it bloody does. It can't be harder than crashing a Davos event.

Which she had actually done when she was tailing the oil tycoon in *Over the Odds*, ironically by pretending to be a member of the maintenance staff and carrying a ladder under her arm. (It only struck me much later that this was the first time she'd referenced one of her previous adventures without me bringing it up first.) 'That's not going to work here. Why would I be taking a ladder into a book talk? Also, where would I get one?'

Just walk in like you belong, then.

Seeing as I'd *just* had a panic attack, I didn't fancy doing something that might kick off another one, but not wanting to appear cowardly trumped common sense. As expected, 'just walking in like you belonged' was impossible, because at the top of the stairs were a couple of women checking everyone's tickets. They appeared to be friendly and jolly – this was, after all, a book festival and not a World Economic Forum event – but they also looked like not much got past them. Which it didn't. Because when I pathetically attempted to sneak in behind a pair of book people, one of the women said: 'Sorry? Excuse me?'

'Hi. *Hi.* Um . . .'

'Do you have a ticket?'

'Um . . . a ticket?'

'For the event?'

'Um . . .'

'Isn't it on your phone? When you pre-booked?'

'Yes, but . . . oops. I must've deleted it.'

'Don't worry. Your name will be on the list.'

'Right. That's . . .'

'What is your name?'

'You know what? I'm causing you a ton of hassle.'

I slunk back down the stairs, burning with mortification.

Well bloody done.

'I told you it wouldn't work.'

The wind was picking up, and I was glad that I'd thought to wear a hoody under the oversized jacket. The place was now heaving with tribe members, but the self-consciousness that usually plagued me in busy settings wasn't as debilitating as usual. I wasn't sure if this was because I'd done the anxiety equivalent of pre-drinking by having already had a panic attack, or because I was accompanied by an imaginary frenemy, who wasn't being a complete nightmare for once.

'Let's explore for a bit.'

There was a bridge you could stand under that played a recording of someone speaking, which we didn't do for long because we both found it disturbing. Then we wandered down to the village's main hotel, but that made Leah antsy because it looked directly over the estuary, so we backtracked and hung around next to a domed building housing a giant gold Buddha instead. Then we went into a gift shop that sold paraphernalia related to the ancient spy-fi show, and I spent ages explaining the concept of science fiction to Leah, which was extremely difficult because her only two points of fictional context were *SVU* and Maya Angelou, whom she rarely referenced anyway. (Probably because getting copyright permissions for literary quotations was a nightmare.)

We sat on a bench that gave us a good sightline of the hall's exit and took it in turns to assign cakes to various passers-by, which we couldn't do for long because Leah's knowledge of confectionery was limited to Jed's snacking habits, and not everyone could be a Twix or a bran muffin or a Cornish pasty, even though there were quite a lot of Cornish pasties knocking about.

For the first time since she'd pitched up in my life, I realised that I was enjoying her company. 'Would you call this a stake out?'

Course.

'Even though we don't know what the person we're staking out looks like?'

It's still a stake out.

'I feel like we're camping a rare spawn.'

What?

'It's a gaming thing. It's . . .' Feeling like someone trying to explain the theory of relativity to an insect, I tried to think of a simple way to describe it. 'So. In certain games, which, if you think about it, are a bit like this quest, if you're lucky and you sit around for hours, a rare mob will spawn and the first person who tags – I mean – kills it will get a . . .' I stopped because Leah's eyes had glazed over – no doubt like mine did whenever I was being monologued at by Sheila. Then I realised that the attendees were exiting from the building, and she was staring intently at someone.

Shite.

Whoa. Apart from her trademark 'bloody', Leah only swore when something particularly life-threatening was about to happen (my mother had only allowed her to say two 'shites' and one 'fuck' per book). 'What is it?'

I've found our perp.

PET SEMATARY

'What do you mean, you've found our perp?' I eyed the crowd. The only book event person who connected even tenuously to our theme was a woman of around my age and height who was wearing a red anorak like the diminutive villain in *Don't Look Now*. But that wouldn't be the reason why Leah had singled her out – she wouldn't recognise a classic horror motif if it bit her on the arse – so it was presumably because Anorak was carrying an enormous bag emblazoned with the slogan NOT RIGHT MEOW I'M READING. Anorak also kept glancing at her phone and fiddling with her bag, which I recognised as the hallmarks of social anxiety. If I was going to pick anyone out of the crowd as a possible serial killer, she'd be at the bottom of the list (or maybe just above the small child in a wheelchair). 'Do you mean the woman in the red anorak?'

A nod.

'Because of the bag?'

What?

'Her bag. It's cat-themed. I mean, it's a bit of stretch, but . . .'

Leah gave me one of her long looks and then sighed. *No.*

'What is it then? Your gut?'

A shrug – albeit a more evasive-looking one than usual.

After glancing at her phone again, Anorak began walking away.

'If you think it's her, then shouldn't we follow her?'

Leah hesitated. *Fine.*

'What's up with you?'

Do you want to tail her or not?

She stalked off ahead of me. Maybe her gut radar really had pegged Anorak as our perp. But if so, why the hesitancy?

Anorak was drifting away from the village's forecourt, apparently making for a pathway that I knew from my research (and map) led up into a curated garden and woodland area, which was peppered with East Asian-style pagodas and bridges (presumably the Portmeirion guy had eventually got bored of doing Italy).

I caught up to Leah, and she slowed to match my pace. 'What was that about back there?'

Keep your bloody voice down.

'That's not an answer.'

I know. I'll tell you later.

I didn't push her on it. The path was getting steeper, and seeing as I basically had the muscle mass of a stick insect, I needed to preserve my stamina. Within minutes, we'd left the noise and vibrancy of the village behind us. Mirroring its creators' architectural free-for-all approach, the foliage was a mishmash of prehistoric-looking ferns, stately oaks, and several towering redwoods (I empathised with them; they, like me, were far from home and well out of their comfort zones). Keeping at a safe, hopefully unsuspicious distance, we trailed Anorak past a lily pond framed with more Jurassic-era plants, through a glade housing some randomly placed wooden carvings, including one of a poor teddy bear who'd lost his eyes to the ravages of the elements, and up a steep, narrow pathway, at the top of which I caught a glimpse of one of the fabled pagodas. Seeing as I'd recently discovered that I quite liked nature, it was a pity that most of my attention had to be focused elsewhere. Because it didn't take long to discover that it was extremely difficult to tail someone without making it look obvious – especially when they kept stopping to take pics. At one point Anorak paused to take a photo of a wooden signpost and took so long about it that I had to pretend I was tying my laces even though I was wearing my Ash trainers which only had a zip.

When we reached the sign, I realised where we were headed: to yet another graveyard, which was thematically in keeping, although seeing as this one was for dogs, wasn't as on the nose as usual. I'd read about the dog cemetery on the village's website, but I hadn't expected to end up here – at least, not this early on.

It was situated in a small woodland clearing, and taking pride of place was a large carving of a dog with sticks piled in front of it. He had a mournful look about him, which wasn't surprising considering that his mates were all dead.

Oblivious that she was the subject of a surveillance op, Anorak was taking photographs of the misshapen gravestones that were dotted around.

Leah eyed the dog statue. *Brian would love this.*

Taken by surprise, I laughed out loud, which naturally caught Anorak's attention.

'Sorry.' I said to her. 'I wasn't laughing at the dead dogs. Just . . .' I held up my phone. 'Someone just sent me a funny cat meme.'

'Oh. Okay.' She carried on doing what she was doing. On closer inspection, I realised she was (probably) slightly older than me and was wearing Leah-esque combat boots. She also had very pale blue eyes and stacks of ginger hair.

I fished for something else to say. 'Where do the cats go, do you think? It seems weird to have a cemetery for dogs and not cats.'

A slight smile. 'I thought that.'

'Maybe the people around here are dog people.' I nodded at her bag. 'I can see that you're not.'

'Oh. I like both.'

Leah had tensed up again and appeared to be staring fixedly at the empty air a couple of metres to Anorak's right.

Back off. She glanced at me and said, **Not you.**

Then she shivered. Although it was less of a shiver and more of a shudder – a bit like the full body lurch I did whenever I saw a spider. It was doubtful that she was sensing the spirits of the dead dogs – she was, after all, a cat person – and although she'd been distracted when we'd visited Thelma and Jamie's graveyards, she hadn't been this uneasy.

Should I carry on with the operation? If I did, I'd have to be quick about it because there weren't that many graves for Possible GinnyRebel to photograph. 'Are you here for the book festival?'

'Yes. You?'

'Yes. Been to any good events?'

'I've just been to the "Fact vs Fiction" one.'

'I really wanted to go to that.' I'd done my research, so I could engage in quite a good discussion about that for a few minutes without the need to lie. But although this conversational groundwork was less boring than usual, it wasn't what I was here for. Leah and I hadn't discussed if this was supposed to be a clandestine operation or not, but it struck me that if Anorak *was* GinnyRebel, then going undercover again might be a clever way of confirming her identity – even though that hadn't gone well last time.

When the chit-chat ran out of steam, I said: 'I'm Leah, by the way.'

I waited for her to tell me her name. She didn't, but she *did* say, 'I've always liked that name.'

'Thanks. Um. Any particular reason?'

'Do you know the Leah Overton series?'

Better than you might expect. 'Oh yeah. I'm a big fan. I actually knew the author a bit.' I swallowed. This was dangerous territory – and not just because I was in danger of tipping her off. If I wasn't careful, it could cause a karking episode. 'Did you hear what happened to her?'

She lost the eye contact and nodded. 'Yeah . . . that was awful.'

A couple of people arrived to check out the dead dogs, and I moved out of the way to give them room.

Anorak clearly wasn't much of a talker, so it was up to me to keep it going. Unfortunately, Leah was still being weird, which was distracting and annoying because I was doing some good undercover work here. 'Sorry, I didn't catch your name?'

'Gina.'

It was *close* to Ginny, but that wasn't a confirmation. 'That's a nice name too. What other events are you going to?'

I listened closely as she ran through them, my pulse rate picking up as each one correlated with the schedule I'd memorised (I probably knew it better than she did). The curious thing was, I quite liked this possible GinnyRebel, which was counterintuitive because even if she wasn't responsible for my mother's death, those emails had been sinister.

'. . . then the panel on ghostwriting, and the Fluffy Carrington launch event tonight.'

Hmmm. The name Fluffy Carrington was familiar, but that event hadn't been on GinnyRebel's list. 'Fluffy Carrington? Wow.'

'The . . . a reviewer I know scored us some invites at the last minute.' She didn't exactly say this smugly, but it was clearly a big deal.

'That's amazing.'

'I . . . we've got an extra one, if you want it?'

'I wouldn't want to intrude.' I *really* wouldn't – unless she *was* GinnyRebel, which I still didn't know for sure.

'No one else is using it.'

'Are you sure? That would be amazing.' *Amazing.* Why had I started using that word?

'I can pay you for it.'

'You don't need to. We got them for free.' She suggested we meet outside the venue, which happened to be the Hercules Hall – the site of my most recent embarrassment.

Then I had an idea. 'Sorry. Um . . . could you give me your email address? Just in case I get lost or something.'

Fortunately, she didn't question why I hadn't asked for her number instead. 'Sure. It's GinnyRebel757@gmail.com.'

Somehow, I managed to stop myself from doing a fist-pump, and although I couldn't resist shooting Leah a triumphant glance, I needn't have bothered because she wasn't paying attention. 'Is the Rebel bit after the cat in the Leah Overton books?'

A nod.

'He was great that cat, wasn't he?'

Ginny glanced anxiously at the path – it was, after all, almost time for her to attend her next event ('Cops vs

Lawyers' in the main hotel). 'Are you going back down?' she asked.

No! Let it go first.

Calling Ginny 'it' was a bit much, even if she was a murder suspect. 'Not just yet. I also want to take some pics of the graves.'

'Okay. See you later then.'

'Great. Thanks again. It was amazing to meet you.'

I waited until she was out of earshot and for the other people to leave before I rounded on Leah. 'What the *fuck*?'

I need a minute.

I was tempted to snap *MOVE*, like she'd done to me pre-Operation Grief Café, but I didn't because I knew what someone not letting you have a minute felt like.

So I looked at the inscriptions on the graves instead, which were more personal than most of the human ones I'd encountered. I put another stick next to the mournful dog statue, even though it had so many it could've opened an outlet. Its soulful eyes reminded me of Petticoat, which me made think about Brian. Which made me think about what Glenn had said about Brian crying that morning, which made me think about Mum lying in the Death Zone all night by herself, which made me think that maybe she hadn't been alone after all and that perhaps Brian had kept watch over her, which made me think how deeply painful that must have been for Brian, which made me think how fucking stupid I was for not considering this before, which made me think that Brian probably had a serious case of cat PTSD, which made me think that was maybe why he was taking everything out on poor Petticoat, because lashing out was what people and possibly cats did when they were traumatised. Like Leah had done to me during our trip to Luxton – and basically ever since she'd pitched up.

I glanced over at her – she was smoking furiously, but other than that, appeared to be calmer. 'Okay. Are you going to tell me what's going on? Because while you were being . . . odd, I had to do all the work. Successfully, by the way, because she *is* GinnyRebel.'

Not here.

We set off along a pathway which wove through more magnificent trees and spiralled down to a wider thorough-fare that was flanked by a pond. Up ahead I could make out the red curves of what was presumably one of the East Asian-inspired bridges. 'Well?'

She wasn't alone.

'Eh? What do you mean? Was someone spying on us or something?'

No. I'm saying, she had company.

'Not getting you. Who?'

A long-suffering sigh. *Me.*

'What?'

A version of me.

'Eh?' Then I got it – or almost got it. 'You mean like a *fanfic* version of you?'

A shrug.

Oh come on! *As if this case wasn't batshit enough.* I genuinely didn't know whether to scream or laugh, so I did a combination of both. 'That's . . .' Once again, there wasn't a word for what this was, because the fact that my hallucination now appeared to have an extended universe of her own made all the bonkerness that had come before it – including Leah's original and shocking appearance in the kitchen – seem banal in comparison.

Also, I wasn't sure what was more discombobulating: the fanfic plot-twist itself or seeing Leah so shaken by it. 'Could it see you?'

Yes, it bloody could. Bloody thing kept staring at me.

More hysteria was threatening to explode, but thankfully, it was easier to contain than karking. 'Are you sure it was supposed to be you?'

Yes. Mostly.

'What do you mean by, "mostly"? What did it look like?'

Black suit. Black boots. Enormous eyes. And . . . it was smiling.

A laugh did snort out then.

It's not bloody funny.

'No. You're right.' *It's fucking hilarious.* 'Um. That must have been weird.'

A miserable nod.

'Did it talk?'

No. Thank Christ.

The blasphemy was new too. 'How come I couldn't see it?'

How would I know? It wasn't there all the time. It kept coming and going.

Not fair was my gut reaction to that. 'Can you see other characters or muses too?'

No.

'So, you can't, like, have an intel chat with Carrie Ng or team up with her or whatever?'

Give over.

'Are you sure you saw it and weren't just hallucinating?'

Welcome to my world, Leah Overton.

Course I'm bloody sure. I've got eyes in my head, haven't I?

255

'So has your doppelganger by the sounds of it. Exactly how enormous were they? Did they look like anime eyes?'

What *eyes?*

'Never mind. What do you think it means? Because the fact that there's a version of you shadowing Ginny must mean *something*, right?'

Like what?

'Um . . . that you must live in her head a fair bit?' *Like you do in mine*, I didn't say.

A shrug.

'And surely that implies that she's a Leah Overton super-fan, and therefore the last thing she'd want to do is kill off Leah's – I mean – *your* author?'

I don't want to talk about it anymore.

'You should be flattered.'

I said, *I don't want to talk about it.*

'Yeah, but—'

CLICKCLICKCLICK.

'I bet GinnyRebel doesn't have to put up with that from her Leah.'

Enough!

I left her in peace as we wandered back to the hotel. The implications of fanfic Leah were a spiralling black hole that I was pretty sure would do that quasar thing to my brain if I fell into it. It also tipped us into another genre. Sci-fi. Or horror again, and I was just getting used to being in cosy crime-slash-very-low-key-noir. But. *But*. If Leah was able to 'see' the alternative version of herself, then surely this absolutely proved that she *wasn't* just a delusion? Because if she *wasn't*, how else could she have pegged that Gina was GinnyRebel? (Well, apart from the bag, of course.)

DEAD RINGERS

Back in the hotel room, I shelved the muse-within-a-muse philosophy because the more I thought about it, the more it broke my head, and decided to research Fluffy Carrington instead. Leah lit a cigarette and kept glancing at my laptop – no doubt equally desperate for a distraction.

In the end I gave in, settled her on the couch with her *SVU* comfort blanket, and used my phone instead.

According to Google, Fluffy Carrington was an amateur sleuth by day, a drag queen by night, and had appeared in eight 'cosy crime comic capers', known as the 'House of Carrington' books. Unlike lone wolves Carrie and Leah, Fluffy never worked alone – be that on stage or when she was solving showbiz-related crimes – because she relied on a gang of found family, whom she mothered under the mantle of the House of Carrington. The author, A. J. Tillman, was a former drag queen who now dragged up and performed as their main character, which pre-quest I would've thought was a fun idea, but now found too uncomfortably meta for my liking. GinnyRebel hadn't written any fanfic about Fluffy and her gang, but on the off-chance that there was a connection to the quest, I did a search for Fluffy Carrington + Animal + Death. All that came up was a link to the blurb on the seventh novel:

Someone is killing off contestants on UK Talent Quest, and the new top contenders for the prize, dog-trainer Melody and her performing Shih Tzu Devine, are next on the list . . . But according to a plot-breakdown in a detailed Goodreads review, there was no link to our case, seeing as Fluffy managed to save Devine by using a wig as a dog decoy.

I was fairly sure, no, *completely* sure, that GinnyRebel wasn't a serial killer. And not just because it was a fucking stupid theory anyway, but because I knew it in my gut, and if Leah could depend on hers for over 600,000+ words, I could depend on mine at least once. But I still wanted to know what – if anything – those 'Rebel says hi' messages meant. Plus, when I'd brought up the Leah books and the fact that I knew the author, most people would've responded with something braggy like, 'I knew her too – in fact, I used to constantly send her cat-related emails.' I also wanted to know what she saw in Leah that had inspired her to write so much affectionate fanfic. And I was *desperate* to know if she could see *her* Leah as clearly as I did mine. Although how I'd go about asking that was not yet clear.

I was too anxious to eat, but I made myself scoff some truffle-flavoured minibar peanuts that probably cost more than an actual Mini. The time went quickly, which it always did whenever I was dreading something, and, for once, it wasn't just me who was on edge. Not even an SVU episode about a sociopath who was stealing sperm from unconscious overachievers and selling it to people who didn't know how genetics worked was enough to distract Leah from the trepidation of running into her doppelganger again. And because Brian wasn't around and I hadn't asked her to smoke outside, she was blazing her way through cigarettes. I hoped the smoke wouldn't translate into the real world, because then I'd be in for a massive fine.

'You don't have to come along, you know. You can stay here.'

Don't be bloody daft.

'I'll be *fine*. Also . . . if the other Leah *is* with her, and you start acting weird again, you'll put me off my game.'

I said, *you're not going alone.*

I was secretly glad about that.

DON'T LOOK NOW

As was the case with the hamlet, the village had a far creepier vibe at night. The lack of people, low lighting, darkened windows, and relative silence gave it the feel of an abandoned film set. Leah and I were twenty minutes early for our assignation, and because both of us were harbouring varying degrees of anxiety about what was to come, instead of sitting on a bench and festering, we wandered around for a bit.

Because nervousness of any type was a new experience for Leah, I decided to have a stab at giving her another pep talk. 'It'll be okay, you know. Honestly. You should think of Nice Leah as the embodiment of a compliment.'

Nice? *Why the bloody hell do you think it's* **nice?**

'Well . . . because the Leah in the fanfic is nice, I suppose. She – or you – basically just hangs out in the kitchen watching Rebel chirrup and chase moths. While doing a *lot* of smiling.'

She fake-vomited at this, which made me laugh. 'It isn't as if it can hurt you, is it?'

Of course, it bloody can't. She lit up another cigarette.

'I get why it must be unsettling, though. It must be like seeing a ghost of yourself, only one that's been filtered through someone else's mind.'

Not helping.

'Sorry. But you should probably get used to it. I mean, GinnyRebel isn't your only reader, so there are probably more Leah Overton versions knocking about. Just think, if you could figure out how to communicate with them, you could have your own clone army.'

Eye-roll, sigh, CLICK.

That was more like it.

Ey up. Leah nodded to where GinnyRebel, who appeared to be with two other people, was making her way towards the hall's entrance.

'Is it there?'

No.

Leah's anxiety might have receded, but mine hadn't, although the fact that GinnyRebel greeted me with a genuine smile helped. Then she introduced me to her companions, who were around my age, and were both very warm and friendly and whose names I immediately forgot, but mentally dubbed a butterfly cupcake and a Hobnob. Apparently, they were a couple, and despite the disparity in their sugar levels, they seemed to complement each other. The cupcake was a Fluffy super-fan and was wearing a T-shirt with 'Team Carrington' on it, and her biscuit spouse was toting a bag filled with books for Fluffy to sign. I wondered if they had Fluffy fanfic avatars attached to them like balloons.

'I told them what you said about there not being a cat cemetery,' GinnyRebel said.

'Oh right.' People were streaming into the hall, so thankfully I didn't need to fish for a follow-up comment. I was dreading being recognised by the Gatekeepers of Book Hell, but it turned out that I could have just wandered in because no one was checking tickets. It was a mill-about-and-lean-on-tables event, and not a formal sit-down thing, which I preferred because it would be easier to slink off and hide in a corner. There were tables piled with Fluffy books and an enormous bar area laden with red and white wine and fruit juice. I bought a book, and then, instead of being sensible, I took a glass of red wine.

What are you playing at? You need to keep a clear head.

I couldn't answer Leah back, so I drank it instead, even though in my opinion wine tastes like it's already been drunk.

GinnyRebel and her mates seemed to expect me to join them, which was nice of them, and thinking *I am Leah Overton. I am cool and collected and I can do this*, I wandered over to their table. I asked them how they knew each other (they'd met online like normal people) and Ginny said they were staying in an Airbnb together to save cash.

'Did you come here by yourself?' Cupcake asked.

Nope! Funny story . . . 'Yes. I came here on a whim. A last-minute thing. I've always wanted to see this place anyway.'

'Where are you staying?'

'In the castle just outside the village,' I said without thinking, and which immediately made me feel insensitive – GinnyRebel had *literally* just told me that the only reason they could afford to come here was by pooling their resources. 'Um . . . I got lucky and managed to score a room for a major discount.'

'What do you do, Leah?' Ginny asked.

Seeing that I was with people who probably knew Leah Overton better than I did, I could hardly say, *oh me? I used to be a lawyer, but now I'm a hotshot private investigator*, and because I didn't want to tell them the truth (nowt + avoidance), I said: 'I'm a screenwriter. Well . . . trying to be one anyway.'

This seemed to impress them – a bit. 'What are you working on?' asked Hobnob, who, in keeping with her confectionery type, had been the quietest one so far.

'Um . . .' I knocked back some more wine as an excuse to stall, and because I couldn't think of anything else to say, regurgitated the logline of my final screenplay – the one I'd unexpectedly stumbled across in my mother's filing cabinet: 'It's a horror thriller about a woman who gradually starts turning into a giant spider.' But instead of saying *what a load of shite*, Ginny and the Hobnob appeared to find this interesting, and asked if it was an allegory about misogyny and identity, to which I said 'yes', even though it was just about a woman who turns into a giant spider and then eats all of her Tinder dates for no reason other than that's what female spiders tend to do.

This turned into a discussion about horror films, and then book-to-screen adaptations, which was so engaging that even Leah seemed interested. Then they told me what they did, which was less enjoyable. Cupcake was a medical student, Hobnob worked for a wildlife non-profit, and GinnyRebel, who – I don't know why – I'd assumed was a no-hoper like me, was doing a PhD on something to do with genetics. I had no clue how she managed to find the time to write fanfic, review novels, go to book festivals, study an incomprehensible STEM subject, and send possibly threatening emails to authors.

A stranger who knew the couple came up to say hi, and the vibe immediately changed. GinnyRebel fiddled self-consciously with the stem of her glass.

Bloody thing's back.

GinnyRebel was saying something to me, but I was finding it impossible to concentrate. I also had to restrain myself from staring intently at the area just behind her head.

'Sorry, Gina. Can you say that again?' Fortunately, the room was filling up and the chitter-chatter was quite loud, so I could use that as an excuse.

'I was asking if you've read the Fluffy novels.'

'Not all of them. I liked the talent show one the best, though.'

I'm worried it's going to start humping my leg.

There was no way I could multitask like this. I took out my phone. 'Will you excuse me a sec? I'm just going to check on my cat. The person who's looking after my cat, I mean.'

'Of course.'

I stalked into an adjoining corridor area and pretended to be on my phone again.

'Get it together. This is hard enough as is it. What is Nice Leah *doing*?'

Lurking.

'That's it?'

What more do you want? It's doing my bloody head in.

'Look, just stay out here. I can't do what I'm supposed to be doing with you acting like this.'

Give over. I'm not leaving you alone.

'We're at a book event. What's she going to do? Beat me over the head with a paperback?'

I'm not leaving.

'Just try not to look at it, then.'

On the way back to Ginny, I picked up another glass of wine to help dampen the nervous energy. I was chasing the sweet spot of inebriation where my sense of self seemed to align with the world, but although I can tell when I'm in danger of getting too stoned, that wasn't the case with alcohol. One minute it was loosening me up and the next it was coming out in technicolour.

'What's your cat's name?' GinnyRebel asked.

Before I could answer, in strode Fluffy. Who did deserve the adjective 'amazing', seeing as she was approximately twice my height, and was even more glamorous than Jamie. There were whoops and applause as Fluffy stepped up onto the podium to begin her routine. Judging by the reaction of the crowd, it must have been entertaining, but I barely caught a word of it. Muddied by the wine, I was too busy wondering if Fluffy the character-slash-muse was flattered or creeped out by the fact that her author was in the habit of dressing up like her, and if A. J. Tillman was able to 'see' their protagonist as clearly as I did Leah. So far, GinnyRebel didn't seem to be aware that she had a Leah ghosting around her like one of those wavy-armed balloon people, so perhaps it was just me. And then I moved on to thinking up ways I could possibly introduce 'Rebel says hi' and Leah into the conversation: *You know what I really hate, Gina? When cats die in books. How about you? So, Gina, have you ever sent anyone cat mugshots? Why do you like Leah Overton so much, to the extent that apparently you have your own weird version knocking about?*

A round of applause, and more whoops. Then someone announced that 'Fluffy will be more than happy to sign your books.' Cupcake and Hobnob dove into the crowd, but GinnyRebel stayed where she was.

It's gone, Leah said from behind me. ***About bloody time.***

'Aren't you going to get your book signed?' I asked GinnyRebel.

265

'I always wait till the end. I don't like crowds.' To be fair, the queue was very long. 'I'm just . . .' She signalled that she was heading to the bathroom.

Which gave both Leah and me a much-needed breather. It occurred to me then, that although this sort of event should've been a kark-trigger, once again the quest was acting as a distraction.

'Are you okay?' I said to Leah out of the corner of my mouth.

She nodded.

'If it comes back, just turn your back on it and pretend it doesn't exist.' Possibly the weirdest thing about this situation was that I was teaching Leah Overton avoidance skills. 'Or you could—'

'Niamh?'

Uh-oh. Heading towards me in a flurry of knitwear and faux-granny warmth was Caro (if Caro were a cake she'd be an iced bun with a razor blade inside it). 'I *thought* it was you.' Air kiss, air kiss. 'How *brave* of you to be here. It's so wonderful to see you, my darling. How are you?'

'Um . . .'

'I'm so sorry I haven't responded to your email. It's on my radar. As you can imagine, it's been a bit of a whirl-wind. My flight was delayed, and it was *literal* hell on earth as you can imagine, so I arrived late and I'm just popping in to show my face. And then I have an event tomorrow so it's all go, go, go.'

Still flummoxed by her arrival, I reached for something to say. This wasn't the right time or place to ask Caro what I'd come to Wales to ask her. 'I'm really sorry that I haven't thanked you for the hamper you sent me. Especially because it was such a kind and thoughtful thing to do. I feel really terrible about it.'

'My darling, *please* don't give it another thought. My intern deals with the gifting side of things, and he's impossible to offend. Skin like a rhinoceros.'

Right. Moving on. 'I really wanted to go to your event, by the way, but there were no tickets left.'

'How sweet. Leave it with me, my darling, I'll put you on the list.'

'Thanks.'

'You're more than welcome. I must say, you're looking *so* well. Annie would be *so* proud of you, my darling.'

Oof. There was a kark on the horizon, but thanks to the combination of a CLICK and another slug of wine, I managed to hold it at bay.

'Now. One doesn't want to broach the subject because it is a very sensitive time, but at some stage we must talk about your mother's intellectual property. I do feel that there's still life to be had in the Leah franchise.' I looked over at Leah – she'd become very still and was watching Caro intently. 'I've had some success with ghosts, you see, or established writers taking on another author's mantle. And of course, with *Overlooked* coming out next week, and it being dearest Annie's final book, there will be a fresh surge of interest.'

Ouch. Talk about ruthless. I was beginning to understand why my mother had felt the need to bump her off (fictionally, that is).

Someone had come up beside me – but it took me a second to realise that it wasn't Leah, but GinnyRebel.

'Sorry, Caro. This is Gina.'

Caro's eyes glazed over as the social-cachet AI in her mind calculated whether Ginny was someone important or not. *Nope! Moving on.*

Thinking, *fuck you, Caro,* I said: 'Gina's a brilliant reviewer and fanfic writer.'

'Wonderful. So good to meet you, Gina.' Straight back to me. 'I must dash. If you don't show up, they think you don't care. Come and see me after tomorrow's panel, my darling, and we'll chat.'

Caro bustled away, and I was thinking, *Phew, narrow escape – didn't blow my cover*, when GinnyRebel said:

'How do you know that I write fanfic?'

Shite. My only choice was to come clean. 'It's a long story, but I should probably start by saying that my name isn't Leah, it's Niamh, and Annie Morrissey was my mother.'

GinnyRebel wasn't sure where to look – not out of guilt, but confusion. Which brought on a surge of panic from *my* Leah, because it seemed that GinnyRebel's version only pitched up when she was feeling uncomfortable. 'I'm so sorry for your loss.'

'Thanks. And . . . the reason I'm here is because my mother was going to be here and . . .' Someone had left a glass of wine on the table – white this time – and I picked it up and knocked it back even though it had a lipstick smear on the rim. 'And the reason I know you write fanfic is because I was hoping to run into you. The thing is . . . when I was going through my mum's emails, I saw several from you, and . . . I suppose I wanted to know what you meant by them.'

'Why didn't you just message me and ask?'

Saying, *because at that stage we thought you might be a serial killer* probably wouldn't go down well. 'Um. I was coming here anyway and . . . I prefer talking to people in person.'

'That makes sense.'

'It *does*?'

'You said something about emails?'

'Oh right. You sent three to my mother just before she

died. They all said the same thing, "Rebel says hi" without an exclamation point.'

GinnyRebel frowned. 'Oh. *Oh*. Yeah. I sent them a few times because I assumed they'd got spammed. My email does that sometimes. And I hate exclamation marks.'

'I thought maybe you sent them because you were pissed off with her for killing Leah's Rebel.'

'I was. Actually, no. I wasn't pissed off, more saddened by it. She said that you weren't happy about it either.'

'So, you knew her well then? Personally, I mean?'

'We used to chat a bit. Off and on. Mostly about cats. How's Brian?'

'He's . . . You know *Brian*?'

'I don't *know* him. I know *of* him.' She paused. 'I liked your mum. And not just because of the books.'

'How did you get to know her?'

'Her publishers had sent me an ARC of *Over the Odds*, and I thought I should let them know that I wouldn't be able to write a balanced review because I feel so strongly about animals dying in books. Anyway, they must've passed it on to your mum, because she wrote to me, which was when she said how much she regretted killing Rebel off. Rebel's also the name of my cat, you see, so it felt a bit personal.'

'Oh *right*. So, the pics were of *your* Rebel.' I really should have thought of that.

GinnyRebel nodded, then reached for her own wine, which gave me a chance to see how my Leah was doing. Which wasn't great, because although she'd taken my advice and moved several metres away – presumably out of Nice Leah's line of sight – she was smoking again and staring fixedly at the book display table.

'Why didn't you just tell me who you were straight away?' GinnyRebel asked.

I chose the truth again. 'Because I've got chronic social anxiety, and I thought pretending to be someone else might help with that. And Leah is anything but anxious.' *Except at this very moment.* 'I'm so sorry for lying to you though. I'm . . . you must think I'm a total weirdo.'

'You're going through a difficult time right now. I can't even imagine how awful that must be for you.'

'Thanks.' Unable to depend on Leah's CLICK defence, I bit my lip and changed the subject. 'Can I ask you something? Why do you like Leah so much?'

'She just gets stuff done. Doesn't let anything stop her. Never gets broken down. Always says what she thinks. Doesn't take any shit.'

'You don't think she's too perfect? Too . . . wish-fulfilment-y?'

'But that's the point of her, isn't it? That she can do things we can't? And she's not perfect. She hyper-focuses too intensely and over-internalises emotions. And although she tries to hide it, and pushes people away, it's obvious that deep down inside, she's lonely.'

Lonely? That was the last word I would've used to describe her. I glanced over at my Leah, who was now staring at a wood-panelled wall. Perhaps she was. As I found out when I was having my inaugural karking episode in the cloakroom, being a lone wolf and *feeling* alone are two entirely different things.

GinnyRebel shrugged. 'I relate to those aspects of her character. I also used to wish I *was* her. In difficult situations, I mean.'

'I know. It would be so great to go for someone's throat and not worry about the consequences.'

She smiled. 'I wouldn't mind doing that to my department head. He's a bully.'

'I've got a neighbour like that.' Was this a good place to bring up the subject of Nice Leah? 'Do you ever imagine that Leah's with you? Almost like . . . I don't know, an imaginary friend?'

She gave me a funny look, which wasn't an actual 'no' but was close enough. 'What made you ask that?'

'No reason. Probably just the wine.' Oddly enough, although I could feel it burbling away in my empty stomach, I still felt relatively sober. 'By the way, I really do like your fanfic. Especially the Leah and Amara bits.'

'Really?'

'Really. I'm not blowing smoke up your arse, I promise.'

'Thanks. I haven't written any for ages.'

'The way you portray Leah in them . . . she's so different to how she is in the books.'

'I guess I was trying to imagine what she might do in her downtime. Sometimes when I read, I find that I'm more interested in what might be happening off the page.'

'That's a brilliant way of putting it.'

I knew for a fact that GinnyRebel was loosening up because my Leah sagged with relief. I'd have to watch what I said from now on.

'When is *Overlooked* coming out?' Ginny asked. 'I know they delayed the publication, but . . . sorry. That might be upsetting.'

'No. No, it isn't. Next week. Actually, I've got an advance copy back at the castle you can have. I can give it to you tomorrow if you like.'

'Don't you need it?'

'I know for a fact that my mum would've wanted you to have it. I think you'll like it too. There are no animal deaths, and Leah does a metric fuck-ton of throat-punching in it. I think it might be my mum's best book.'

We made plans to meet at the human chess board after Ginny's final panel, and my Caro task.

The hall was emptying out. GinnyRebel nodded at the dwindling queue. 'Shall we . . .?'

As we made our way over to where Fluffy was indefatigably signing and chatting and chatting and signing, I looked over my shoulder. Leah was close on my heels and was clearly feeling better because she scowled at Cupcake and Hobnob when they ran up to join us. They'd managed to get all their books signed and said that they'd meet us in the anteroom because they wanted to upload their Fluffy pics.

I was about to say to GinnyRebel that she could go first, when my alcohol intolerance belatedly kicked in, the room seemed to tip, my stomach lurched, and—

CLICKCLICKCLICK

—was the only thing that stopped me from throwing up over Fluffy and probably GinnyRebel too.

WE HAVE ALWAYS
LIVED IN THE CASTLE

CLICK.

'Ugh.'

CLICK. *You should get up.*

The light shining through the windows was hangover bright, and my mouth tasted like death. Nor did I smell very pleasant because I'd passed out fully dressed. Well, almost, because thankfully I'd taken the jacket off, although I didn't remember doing that. Quite a lot of what happened after I'd bolted out of the hall was hazy, although I did recall throwing up in a bin outside, which was better than doing it on a person, and bits and pieces of the stumble back to the castle were coming back to me. I probably wouldn't have made it at all if I hadn't been following Leah up the path like a drunken puppy. Which made me think about the bottles-in-the-bin conundrum, seeing as not being able to handle alcohol was a trait I'd inherited from Mum. Whatever she'd been trying to dull with the booze must've been particularly awful if she was prepared to put herself through this hell.

I sat up. The morning-after mortification began to creep in, and, if anything, was worse than the nausea.

The memory of fleeing like a lunatic without saying a word to GinnyRebel made my insides curl up like a dying spider.

You need to shower. And eat something.

'So do you.'

She raised an eyebrow.

'Sorry. Was I awful last night?'

No. You did some good, solid investigative work.

'Really?'

Really.

'Thanks.' The blast of dopamine was *almost* as effective as a McMuffin at soothing the hangover symptoms. 'I didn't embarrass myself?'

A shrug. *No one will care. They'll be too busy worrying about themselves.*

'Thanks. That's—'

Shower. Now.

I fired up the laptop without being asked, and then did as I was told. The shower did help, and although going down to breakfast was the last thing I felt like doing, Leah was right – I did need to eat something.

'Aren't you coming with me?'

Do you need *me to watch you eat?*

'No.' Whatever barminess was playing on the laptop was undoubtedly more entertaining than a breakfast buffet, so I didn't push her.

I could tell that the staff were itching for everyone to leave so that they could reset the tables and then go out for a vape (I'd been fired from several service industry jobs over the years, and recognised the signs), so I told them that I'd just take some coffee and croissants up to my room. I didn't feel like sitting alone anyway, because even though I knew on an intellectual level that Leah was correct and no one gave a shite, every bite or sip I took would still be poisoned with self-consciousness.

I grabbed a plate and made for the table laden with cereals and baked goods, then almost dropped it because I couldn't hold that, *and* remove the cloche covering the croissants *and* work the tongs provided. *Why does life have to be so difficult?*

'Here you go, doll.' A tall man in enormous dark glasses and a fabulous velvet suit appeared next to me and lifted the lid.

'Thanks.' I grabbed three croissants and a bun, which would probably be a more suitable confectionery item for Glenn because its currants made it look smug. It was then that I realised there was something familiar about him (the helpful stranger – not Glenn).

'Oh. You're Fluffy Carrington! I mean, A. J. Tillman. I almost didn't recognise you.'

He smiled. 'That's the point. *Love* your jacket. Is it a Westwood?'

'Thanks, and mmhmm.' I really must look at its label at some point. 'I was at your launch party last night. It was amazing.'

'Thanks, doll. Can't remember much about it. Raging hangover.'

'Me too. I almost threw up on you.'

He laughed. 'Wouldn't be the first time.' He helped himself to one of the Glenn heads.

I was about to thank him again and leave him in peace, but encouraged by the laugh, and because I was probably still a bit drunk, I hesitated. 'Can I ask you a quick question? I don't want to . . .'

'Go for it, doll.'

'I was wondering. Don't you get sick of not only writing Fluffy but *being* Fluffy? I mean, it must feel like she's taken over your entire life.' *Oops.* In came a fresh wave of mortification – as if more were needed. 'Sorry. That didn't come out the way I meant it to.'

But this borderline offensive comment didn't seem to faze him. 'You want to know the truth? I'd kill the bitch off if I could, but she's got a fucking gun to my head.' He winked. 'Stay lucky.'

He went off to join a woman who I could tell was a publicist because she was glued to her phone and her hair was fantastic. I shoved some mini butter squares and some teeny jam pots into my pocket, and then squirrelled away as if I were an interloping baked goods thief and not someone who'd shelled out an insane amount of cash to stay in a castle.

Back in the room, Leah was where I'd left her. 'I ran into Fluffy downstairs.'

Who?

'The drag-queen-slash-writer from the night before?'

A disinterested nod, then back to the action – on screen, Detective Stabler was nonchalantly interviewing a perp who identified as a vampire.

'Can't we put something else on? We've got ages until the Caro thing.' *And* the Ginny thing, although she might not pitch up, seeing as I'd lied to her several times and then fled out of a hall like a lunatic. But on the off-chance that she did, I put *Overlooked* in my backpack in case I forgot to do that later, which would be embarrassing seeing as the sole reason for meeting her was to give her my dead mother's book like a message from the grave.

And while I was doing that, my brain snagged onto something Caro had said the night before about *Overlooked*. Which led onto something Jamie had said. *Hmmm*. I took my phone, coffee, and the Glenn head over to the bed to check it out.

It took me less than thirty seconds to discover that Caro's agency had also repped Rose Parkinson, and currently represented Mimi Kim, the author who'd taken on the Carrie Ng mantle. Which again wasn't a coincidence because it specialised in thriller fiction. But. *But*. A seed of something – probably a *stupid* something – began to sprout.

I finished the pastries, swept up the crumbs, and then padded over to Leah. She barely registered my presence.

'Guess what? Rose Parkinson and Mum had another thing in common.'

This grabbed her attention. **What?**

'They're both repped by the same book agent. I'm not saying it means anything, but I'm not *not* saying that either.' I didn't think it meant anything, but I had very much enjoyed being positively reinforced earlier, and pathetically, I wanted to feel that again. And after Caro's dismissive treatment of GinnyRebel, I liked the idea of reframing her as a Machiavellian antagonist.

Explain.

'Well, we know for a fact that Mum was having issues with writer's block. We can assume that Rose probably wanted to ditch Carrie Ng because of all the online criticism. So, what if Caro decided, "gah, I've had it with these unproductive cash cows, I'll just get a ghostwriter in and turn the other writers into ghosts"? Also . . . as Caro implied last night, whenever an author dies, there tends to be a fresh surge of interest in their books.'

Hmmm. Seems far-fetched.

'Maybe. But is it more far-fetched than a fictional-cat-avenging serial killer?' *Or you?*

Leah began to pace before I could do it first.

'How *would* you feel about that, by the way? Being handed over to a ghostwriter, I mean?'

A shrug. Although, she didn't appear to *hate* the idea.

'If that did happen, would you haunt them instead of me?'

I'm not **haunting** *you.*

'You know what I mean.' But her reaction had been interesting. And hadn't she also reacted in a similar fashion when Jamie had mentioned Carrie Ng's ghost status? Could this be the answer to ousting her from my life? I put it in my back pocket. Since our truce, I found her far more palatable, but that could change at any point – I hadn't forgotten that less than a week ago she'd thrown a cigarette at my head, and made me crash a car. 'Look, I'm not saying that she *is* our perp, but professionally she's pretty cut-throat, and money *is* one of our top motivations.'

Good point.

I smiled inside.

What about means and opportunity?

'Well, we know that two days before Mum died, Caro wanted to speak to her urgently. It's possible that she'd suggested they do it in person.' Then something stupider occurred to me. 'What if she's not acting alone? What if it's a conspiracy between her and the publishers? Come on, you love a corporate conspiracy.'

You said they weren't weapon-toting mercenaries.

'Yeah . . . but they'd probably outsource the violence to an assassin who knows how to make author deaths look like accidents or suicides. You know, like in *Over and*

Above and all the other books. And – and you'll like this – what if they've got another writer in their sights, and we need to save them?' I've never had a hero complex, but Leah certainly did. 'This could be our pulse-racing ticking-time-bomb moment. I know there's the inquest coming up, but that won't be particularly action-packed, and we haven't had an exciting race-against-time moment yet.' I didn't point out that we were also missing jeopardy and a potential love interest because that was self-evident. There *had* been a lot of red herrings, though.

Hmmm. Also far-fetched.

Yeah, no shit.

How are we going to prove it?

'Um . . . I suppose the obvious way is to look at Caro's phone and see if she and the publishers were corresponding about this stuff. It's a pity we can't get hold of Amara and ask her to use her special hacking skills.' And then: 'Hang on. I suppose we could always use *my* special skill.'

A long look, eloquent with: *you have a skill?*

But I did. One that I'd honed by being my mother's plus-one at various literary events: handbag carrying.

TALK TO ME

What was I *thinking? Why* had I made such a recklessly stupid suggestion? But I knew why, of course I did: to impress Leah Rebecca Overton.

I couldn't even blame it on my alcohol consumption because the coffee, validation, and carbs had sobered me up. But I had to talk to Caro anyway, and in the unlikely event that the handbag-carrying ploy did work, I could just pretend to fiddle with Caro's phone and then say that there was no suspicious intel on it – Leah would be none the wiser.

Naturally, the event was taking place at the Hercules Hall, now the site of *two* recent embarrassments. The two women were back at their posts at the top of the stairs – the Leah Book equivalents, a pair of Kalashnikov-toting henchpeople, would probably be easier to bypass. But not today. They were too polite to say 'you again', although one of them did give me a funny look when she confirmed that my name was on the list.

The venue was filling up, but I spotted Caro knocking about in an anteroom with her fellow panellists, neither of whom fulfilled the book agent stereotype. The tall, cadaverous man to her right could have been a Victorian undertaker, and the other one had the look of a contemporary burlesque dancer.

I took a calming breath and sidled up to Caro.

She greeted me with a delighted smile, which immediately made me dislike her less and therefore regret the stupid handbag ruse even more. 'You made it, my darling.' She turned to the other two. 'This is Annie Morrissey's daughter.'

A down-turned smile of sympathy from the burlesque dancer. 'I loved your mother's writing. Are you thinking about following in her footsteps?'

'God no.' *Oops*. That came out a bit too forceful.

'Niamh is a screenwriter, aren't you, my darling?' Caro said.

Oh, Mum, I thought again. 'I just wanted to wish you luck,' I said, dodging the question. 'Not that you need it.'

'Thank you, my darling. I hate doing these things, but needs must, and I did give my word to the organisers.'

I went as if to leave, then paused. *Was I actually going to do this?* I glanced at Leah, and she gave me a nod of encouragement. 'Oh. I just thought. Would you like me to look after your things? I always used to do that for Mum and . . .' I trailed off as if this were a painful memory, which it was, so there wasn't much acting required.

'Can you watch mine, too?' asked Burlesque.

'And mine?' said the undertaker.

I ended up with six bags. *Six*. Most of which contained books and were therefore fucking heavy. I lugged my load into the hall and shuffled towards the back row.

'Go in first and take the seat at the end,' I side-whispered to Leah.

Why?

'I don't want anyone to accidentally sit on you.'

An aggrieved CLICK, but then she did as I suggested.

I was out of breath when I eventually made it to my seat. Despite this being a popular event, the chair on my other side remained empty, probably because my book luggage took up all the floor space.

I gestured at the crowd. 'Do you think all of these people have muses?'

How would I know?

There was a round of applause as the event started, and then the three agents introduced themselves.

Leah shot me a 'get on with it' look.

Doing my best to act casual, I picked up Caro's cavernous bag and placed it on my lap. I needn't have bothered with the subterfuge because all eyes were focused on the podium. Again thinking, *oh God, are you* really *doing this?* I unzipped it and felt around for the phone, which wasn't easy because it was stuffed full of notebooks, pens, some knitting, a bottle of perfume, and an enormous hairbrush, the tines of which made me wince. Nor was it pleasant – it felt almost as dirty as interrogating a grieving son about his mother's possible suicide.

But it seemed that Caro was one of those people who was permanently umbilicalled to their phone, because it wasn't in there, and nor was it in her tote of bound proofs. Which was a relief, although I pretended to be disappointed.

I was about to whisper, 'no dice' to Leah when I heard Caro saying my mother's name.

'. . . Annie Morrissey. If you haven't read the Leah Overton books, then I *must* encourage you to do so. They're a masterclass in escapism and, as Robert was just saying, are an example of a writer who really took the time to get to know her character.'

Next to me, Leah had put herself on pause. Which made me envy her because I'd begun to shake. I bent my head, shut my eyes, and clenched my fists, but the grief ambush wasn't going to be so easily dissuaded this time.

I managed to turn a kark into a cough, but there were more incoming.

In desperation, I waggled my hand at Leah, which must have looked as if I was pretending to fire a mini-gun, but she got it.

CLICKCLICKCLICK.

It didn't stop the next kark, but it toned it down.

'Thanks,' I whispered to her.

I kept my head down and attempted to wipe away the tears as surreptitiously as I could, and it was only when the event was wrapping up that I felt strong enough to look up.

I waited until the hall emptied out before I shuffled my load into the adjoining corridor. I had to hang around for ages while Caro and the other two agents chatted to various attendees. It felt a bit like the old days, albeit with two major differences – the absence of my mother and the addition of her protagonist. The undertaker came back first and handed me a business card. 'Reach out if you have anything you'd like me to look at.'

'Thanks. I will.'

Then the burlesque dancer returned to collect her belongings. She didn't hand me a card, but offered me condolences again.

And then it was just me and Caro. Well, not immediately, because Caro was a talker like Sheila, only instead of people attempting to get away from her, the chit-chat had the opposite effect (Sheila should probably become a book agent).

'I'm so sorry to keep you waiting, my darling,' Caro said. 'I hope mentioning your mother didn't upset you.'

'No. It was . . .' And then I realised that my eyes were leaking again. 'Sorry. Sorry.' I pressed the heels of my palms into my eye sockets, but the tears wouldn't stop.

CLICK.

No dice. *Shite. If only I hadn't dislodged my metaphorical bear plug.*

A couple of stragglers shot embarrassed looks my way and Leah dead-eyed them back. They were lucky she didn't exist, because their throats might otherwise have experienced some damage.

'Thanks,' I whispered, and gave her a watery smile, which set me off again.

'Oh, my darling,' Caro said eventually (she'd missed the worst of it because she'd been distracted by her phone). Then she gave me a hug, which stopped the tears immediately because the itchy fabric of her jacket set my teeth on edge. When I managed to disentangle myself, I realised that I'd left a silver snot smear on her lapel, but hopefully she'd only notice that later. She began rooting through her bag. 'I've got some tissues in here somewhere.'

I almost said, *No you don't.*

'I know how you're feeling, my darling. When my Jeremy died, it took *months* before I was even able to breathe again.'

I had no clue who Jeremy was, or how he'd died, but distracted by the tissue task, Caro lost her train of thought.

Best you start interrogating her before her phone beeps again. Come on. You've got this.

Whoa, did Leah Rebecca Overton just give me a pep talk? Either way, it worked. 'Caro . . . when I was going through my mother's emails, I saw one from you that said you needed to talk to her urgently. Um. Were you and Mum fighting about something?'

A sigh. 'Yes. I'm afraid we were.'

I tried to dredge up some anger – *maybe if you hadn't been having a barney, she wouldn't have felt the need to get pissed that night* – but my heart wasn't in it. 'Was it about . . . about . . .' It seemed I hadn't quite finished leaking. CLICK. A grateful glance at Leah. 'Um. Was it about the fact that you wanted to get a ghostwriter in?'

Caro blinked – not guiltily though, in confusion. 'Certainly not. That's not something I'd ever suggest unless the case in question was a hopeless one.'

'But Mum hadn't been writing, had she?'

'No. I'm afraid she hadn't.'

'Do you know why? I mean, did she tell you what was going on?'

Caro sighed. 'My darling, she didn't. That was the issue, you see, I had to insist that she listen to me. It's *such* a pity. I've had three authors, *three*, who've been absolutely flattened by it.'

'Flattened by what?' I was *fairly* sure she wasn't about to say *corporate murder, my darling*.

'The menopause, of course. One doesn't want to blame everything on hormones, it's *such* a cliché, but when Annie mentioned that she was suffering from excruciating joint pain and brain fog, I thought *here we go again*. One expects it to be all hot flushes and insomnia, but if it decides not to manifest like that, then honestly, it can drive one doo-lally, and so few doctors take women seriously. And, despite *sailing* through mine, I've become something of an expert on the subject because needs must. When I spoke to her about it, I encouraged her to see a menopause specialist. And of course, shortly after that, well . . . such a tragedy.'

Now *Caro* looked like she was about to tear up – perhaps her cuddly façade wasn't just a façade after all. Then she shook it off in a very Leah-esque way. 'I can see that now is not the time to discuss business, my darling. Let's chat once I get back to the office.'

She gave me another hug, which unfortunately transferred my snot-smear onto my jacket, then bustled away.

Caro might be ruthless in her business dealings, but one thing was clear: she'd been doing the opposite of harming my mother. She'd been trying to save her.

THREADS

Because we were in Wales, it began to drizzle. This didn't affect Leah – it seemed that only cigarette ash and cat hair could mar her suit – but we both took shelter in an alcove next to a giant statue of a man's head, who, I realised, was probably Hercules.

We had five minutes to kill before GinnyRebel was due to arrive, which I hoped was enough for me to recover. 'Another dead end. At least now we know why Mum wasn't writing.'

A quick Google confirmed that aching joints were one of over forty known menopause symptoms. *Poor Mum.* It also struck me that along with menstruating and going to the lavatory, this was something else that Leah would never have to endure.

She rolled her eyes and sighed. ***Don't look now.***

A familiar red anorak was weaving through the crowd, and this time, GinnyRebel appeared to be alone. Although judging by Leah's tense body language, she wasn't *alone-*alone.

'Is it with her?' I asked anyway.

Yes.

'Are you going to be okay?'

A nod. ***I'm getting used to it.***

'From what you've described, it sounds quite sweet. Like an over-enthusiastic puppy or something.'

An eye-roll followed by a look of disbelief, which cheered me up. I preferred her disparaging to shaky.

I went up to greet GinnyRebel, genuinely pleased to see her. Despite spending years loathing Leah Overton, I hadn't minded hearing that she'd given GinnyRebel some comfort. Which reminded me of something my mother used to say when I was a kid: *You're never alone if you have a book*, which in my case, and possibly GinnyRebel's, was literally the situation these days. It struck me then that I'd forgotten to assign her a piece of metaphorical confectionery. A ginger biscuit was too easy, so I decided on a Kit-Kat.

'I hope I didn't offend you last night by just running off like that,' I said without even saying hello. 'The thing was, I thought I was going to throw up.'

A slightly confused smile. 'Oh. Right. Don't worry. I wasn't offended. Shall we get out of the rain? Your jacket will get ruined.'

'It's fine. It's already covered in snot.' *Oops.* 'Sorry. I had a bit of a cry earlier.' I gestured at Hercules's alcove. 'We can go under there if you like?'

As we hurried over to it, she said, 'I've got something I wanted to show you. Your mother and I used to play this game where she'd pretend to be Brian and I'd pretend to be Rebel.' She took out her phone. 'I've kept some of the threads, and I thought you might like to see them.'

I didn't, but I couldn't say that. Most people appreciated seeing mementoes of their loved ones, and GinnyRebel wasn't to know that I wasn't one of them. She handed her phone to me, and I did my best to stay on an even keel as I scanned the screen, which wasn't easy:

You
Hi brien how r u I cawt a bebe
mice today & left bits for my
mum as a prezi

        AnnieM
        Hi rebel woz the mice delish

You
Yes but I almust choked on the
tale

        AnnieM
        Mice tails r like chewin gum
        tho

You
Cat chewin gum LOL

Wow. Also: *Jesus.* Also: I was a bit envious of their connection, even if it had been – in Brian-speak – *speshul.*

I returned the phone. 'Thanks. That was really thoughtful.'

Then I remembered to give her the book. She took it reverently, as if it meant the world to her, which almost made me sob again.

But fortunately, she couldn't hang about. 'I've got to get back. It was good to meet you.'

'You too. And thanks for not thinking I was weird.'

She didn't say, 'I didn't think you were weird,' but she thanked me for the book again. And as she walked off, I caught a glimpse of her Leah – an excessively tall and willowy figure in a black suit, with eyes the size of boiled eggs, and an unnaturally wide smile.

No wonder Leah had been so freaked out: it was fucking *terrifying*.

———

THE BAD SEED

Reading those cat messages gave me the push I needed to tackle the final task. I'd done everything else the murder quest had demanded of me, and it was time. And I wanted – no, *needed* – to do it alone.

Back at the hotel, I settled Leah on the couch with her digital muse-sitter, but for once, she didn't look that enthusiastic about it. By now, she must have watched over a hundred hours of *SVU* antics, so it was no wonder that tedium had set in. 'How about we mix it up a bit?'

Mix it up how?

It was probably too early in Leah's binge-watching career to make the leap straight to horror, and in any case, I doubted she'd enjoy the genre, seeing as I used scary films as a safe way to experience fear and adrenaline, and being a fearless adrenaline junkie anyway, she didn't need a vicarious thrill outlet. Then again, what about a crossover? The only one I could think of was *The Silence of the Lambs*. 'I've got a film you might like. Both main characters are massive over-achievers, and it also features cookery. Sort of.'

Fine.

I set it up for her, and then started edging away.

Where are you going?

291

'Just popping to the bathroom. I may be a while. The wine is still messing with me a bit.'

Leaving Leah safely ensconced with Hannibal Lecter, I sat on the lavatory seat in my upscale sanctuary, and before I could talk myself out of it, scrolled straight to the voice messages. Beginning with the oldest one first, I pressed <play>. I'd expected the 'Hiya Neevy' to slay me again, and I wasn't wrong, but I forged on. Listening for any sign of booze-related slurring in my mother's voice helped take the edge off.

'Hiya Neevy. Will you send me a text when you get this? Just want to know you're safe.'

One down. I couldn't detect any drunkenness, and that short and sweet message had only resulted in two karks and some eye leakage. And now that I'd broken the voice seal, the next one – sent two days into my glamping pod stay at Daphne's – would hopefully be easier to cope with (which it was, despite the content being more upsetting):

'Hiya Neevy. Me again. Daphne says you're doing well. She offered to have a word with you, but I told her to let you be for now. I know it must feel like I'm on your back all the time, but I just want you to be okay, you know? If glamping-life and your father get too much, just come back home. I mean it. Ta ta for now.'

Hearing her say *home* had been bittersweet, because it implied that she *hadn't* moved to the middle of nowhere to escape me. I held this close to my heart for a bit, then attacked the final one before I lost my nerve:

'Hiya Neevy. There are a few things I need to tell you. I'm done with Leah. I'm bloody sick of her if you want to know the truth. This isn't because of us or what you said. She's getting stale. The books aren't selling as well as they used to, and . . .

Look. I'm going to kill her off in the next book. I'll let you decide how to do it. Ta ta for now.'

OOF.

Talk about a bombshell. Struggling to figure out how I felt about what I'd just heard, I stood up and paced. When the pacing didn't help, I sat back down on the toilet seat.

There was a time when I would have given almost anything to hear those words. But now . . . not so much.

A tickle of something at the back of my head.

More than a tickle. This felt . . .

I'm going to kill her off in the next book.

I'm going to kill her off

I'm going to kill

And then a *whoomph,* as my consciousness did the equivalent of that disorientating dolly zoom shot in *Jaws,* only instead of being Roy Scheider sitting on a deckchair watching a shark maul a kid on a lilo, it was me, perched on a lavatory seat in a bathroom, as the metaphorical Great White of a thought ripped into me: *What if Leah was the murderer?*

No.

No.

That was *crazy.*

But.

But.

Hadn't she been uncharacteristically sympathetic when I'd told her that I wasn't ready to listen to the messages? *Was that because she knew what was on them and didn't want me to find out the truth?* After all, she could've easily overheard my mother recording them, and I knew she was into eavesdropping because she'd quoted my mother's 'House spiders are the Labradors of the insect world' homily to me.

All stories started with *what if*. There was no reason why they couldn't end that way too. My gut was telling me that *surely* I was being hyperbolic. The awful thing was, that although the crazy Caro theory and the even crazier literary felicide avenger angle had both predictably turned out to be nonsensical, this one made a sick kind of logical sense.

Okay: *Motive, means, and opportunity.*

MOTIVE: Survival. Was there a more potent motive than that?

And revenge. My mother had, after all, engineered the deaths of the two most important things in Leah's life: her mentor and her beloved cat.

Then there was Leah's befuddlement when we'd ventured to the shoppe and travelled to Luxton, etcetera. What if my mother had been treating her like some sort of prisoner-slash-muse-slave – like a semi-literal (and literary) version of the exploited blueberry farm workers in *Overlooked*? Could a longing for freedom be one of Leah's motives too?

But if Leah *was* the murderer, then why would she bully me into attempting to solve a crime that she'd committed? *Unless* . . . Was the plan all along to drag me into the quest, worm her way into my life and eventually push me towards keeping her alive, possibly by finding her a ghost-writer? But if that was her plan, then why had she been so bloody awful to me? Unless she'd been following the coercive control playbook and was being extra vile to wear me down so that I'd be even easier to manipulate.

And, *what if* her main goal was to convince *me* to be her ghost? After all, I'd helped bring her into the world, Mum had told countless people that I was some sort of hot-shit writing maven, and a million years ago, when we were interrogating Glenn, hadn't she seemed oddly subdued when I'd told him I *wasn't* a writer? Was this because she was worried that this would mess with her plans?

And, *what if* the quest was a form of 'research' for a new Leah Overton plotline?

And she lived in my bloody head all the time because I'd been so stupidly jealous of her.

It was all fitting together so neatly that I almost wanted to tell her what I'd discovered so that she'd be impressed by my investigative skills.

Moving on . . .

METHOD: I wasn't an idiot. Clearly Leah couldn't physically push my mother off the ladder. But. *But.* Anyone who's ever been gaslit, bullied, or verbally abused (on or offline) knows full well that the adage 'sticks and stones may break my bones, but words can never hurt me' is bollocks. Leah had broken me down, made me agree to this wild goose chase. My mother had been less of a pushover than me, but she'd trusted Leah. She'd spent more time with her than she had with me, until that relationship had also turned sour. If Mum *had* decided to fix the guttering that night, her stiff shoulder, possible drunkenness, and fear of heights would already have put her in a precarious position. It wasn't difficult to imagine her wobbling up there, and then Leah yelling *BOO!* in her ear. And it might not have been just a *BOO!* either. *What if* Leah had also been breaking her down like an abusive spouse or a cult leader? I knew Leah could be verbally cruel because she'd verbally stabbed me with enough force that I'd crashed the car.

OPPORTUNITY: Leah had implied that she hadn't been around Mum for a while, but I only had her word on that, and I knew from personal experience that she had the ability to hang around like a pungent fart in a lift for as long as she liked.

I happened to glance at myself in the mirror right then – my pupils were dilated, and my cheeks were flushed. I could see why people became web sleuths – it was almost as addictive as cocaine.

And . . . *what if* Leah wasn't the *only* protagonist who'd committed author-cide? Because although Jamie had been evasive about the exact cause of his mother's death, what I did know for sure was that after she'd been almost-cancelled, his mum had fallen out of love with Carrie and all things Ng. So *what if* Jamie's mum had been thinking about killing off her protagonist too, and Carrie had also got wind of her creator's plans for her? Could Carrie Ng have talked Rose into mixing up her medication? (She was a doctor after all.)

And hadn't Fluffy Carrington's author said: *I'd love to kill the bitch off, but she's got a gun to my head.* I'd assumed he'd been joking, but quite a lot of jokes were predicated on uncomfortable truths. Perhaps there was a whole underground network of characters who gave each other author-cide tips, like a metaphysical Reddit incel thread.

But now what?

I couldn't just confront Leah with my suspicions. Because if I did, that could backfire – she was already coming more into focus, to the extent that I could *smell* her. And I couldn't hide out in toilets for the rest of my life.

And it wasn't as if I could go to the police. *I'd like to report a possible murder. And when I say possible, I mean* impossible. *The name of the perp? Leah Rebecca Overton. Fictional age, twenty-nine. Real-life age, eight.*

Address?

Currently in my head.

Okay. *Think*. If she were in this situation, *What Would Leah Do?*

But she *had* been in this situation, hadn't she? With Zane, the double-crossing fake NTSB bloke. In order to gather dirt on him and his mendacious bosses, she'd had to pretend she still liked and trusted him, which of course she'd done brilliantly.

And although I was getting better at bullshitting, I was still comparatively shite at it.

But.

But.

If I was correct, and she was the perp, I'd have to fool her for long enough to write an entire book and then kill her off. Would that even work? Who knew? *Could* I fiction-ally murder my mother's killer?

DIABOLIQUE

It took me a while to gather enough gumption to exit the bathroom. I'd half-expected Leah to be waiting outside the door, ready to pounce, but when I emerged, she was where I'd left her.

I've never been great at masking what I'm thinking, and I felt like I had a giant neon sign above my head yelling: I KNOW YOU'RE THE KILLER.

I tried and failed to drift nonchalantly over to the couch.

She'd just got to the bit where Clarice Starling is visiting Hannibal the Cannibal in the cage thing in the Memphis town hall, just before he manages to escape. Was *I* Clarice in this situation, and was Leah Hannibal? (To be fair, if I was anyone in that movie, I'd probably be the person Hannibal had eaten with some fava beans and a nice Chianti.) She tore her eyes away from the screen. *You took your bloody time.*

'My stomach was still upset from the wine at the launch. Red wine always gives me diarrhoea.'

Was she buying this horrible bit of TMI? Possibly, because she did look faintly disgusted.

'Are you enjoying the movie? There's a good bit coming up.'
She shot me a suspicious glance. *What's up with you?*
'Nothing.'

A raised eyebrow.

Here goes nothing. 'Well . . . there is something I wanted to talk to you about. Only, feel free to tell me if you think it's stupid.'

An eye-roll which clearly meant, *don't worry, I bloody well will.*

'So . . . something Caro said has stuck in my head, and like I say, it might be completely crazy, but you know how I was saying that Carrie Ng has a ghostwriter?'

A frown. *So?*

'Well . . . I was thinking, what if I did that for you?' I watched her expression carefully: a blip of either shock or surprise, then back to unreadable.

'Sorry, it's a stupid idea. Forget it. I'm not a writer, and I'd only fuck it up.'

Leah fiddled with her lighter – for once without snapping its lid – and then eyed me shrewdly. *Then why did you say it?*

Good question. 'It's just . . . it doesn't even have to be a novel. Carrie's getting an adaptation, isn't she?' (I had to pause here to explain what adaptations were, even though she was currently watching one.) 'I mean, I did study screenwriting for two years, and I used to enjoy it.' That was true. Although I'd found the social aspect of student life challenging, I'd more than just *enjoyed* the studying part. I'd loved it, and hadn't felt the need to avoid doing it at all. But that had ended abruptly when I'd received my course tutor's verdict on my Spider Woman screenplay, which simply said: 'Kafka this is not.' And although that was true, his casual, trying-to-be-clever dismissal of something that I'd put out into the world – not a brilliant something, admittedly, but something that I'd cared for and nurtured all the same – had shattered something fragile and precious inside me, so much so that I practically heard it break (I can still hear it break now). After that, I went out of my way to avoid finishing anything.

But if I wanted to kill Leah off, I wouldn't just have to write something, I'd have to *finish* it too. *Talk about motivation.* Unless I just got ChatGPT to write it or killed her off in the opening scene (it was typical that even under these stressful circumstances my brain's knee-jerk response was to look for the easy options).

The seconds ticked by. Leah paced. I barely dared to breathe as she did so. Then:

I *don't* hate *the idea*.

'Really?'

A shrug. **What's the plot?**

'Um. How about we base it on this crap – I mean, this case.'

The Case of the Missing Ladder?

'I mean obviously we'll have to make it more plausible and eventful.'

Was she buying it? If this had been her plan all along, she was hiding it well, but then again, subterfuge *was* what she did for a living.

'We could call it . . . *How to Kill a Crime Writer.*' I could imagine Caro's reaction to that. *I love it, my darling – you know how much I adore a publishing trend.* I began to pace. 'So, plot-wise, I know you're a tragic orphan, but I'm thinking, what if that was just what you were *told*?'

Go on. No emotion whatsoever.

'What if – just hear me out – what if you get a message from someone who says she's your mother? She asks to meet you, but never shows up. You track her down and discover that she's a famous crime writer who's been killed off in a murder made to look like an accident. The thing is, there's an absolute fuck-ton of narratives about sons reconnecting with their fathers, and daughters reconnecting with their mothers. So, in a sense, you'd be going on your own grief quest.' Despite this being a ruse, I was getting carried away.

Sister.

'What?'

Make her a sister. Less of a cliché.

Oof. 'Okay – fine. So . . . you find out that you have a sister and start looking into her background. What shall we call her?'

Nina.

Oh God. I wasn't sure if I should feel touched by this or terrified. 'Right.'

There's a flaw in your plan.

Uh-oh.

Our case doesn't have an ending yet. Who's our perp?

I went cold. *It's you, Leah Overton – how's that for a sickeningly apt twist.* 'Um . . . we'll work that out. Maybe it is Sheila after all – we'll just have to come up with a better, non-book-related motive for her. Or we could stick with the obvious and the Wanker could be our perp.'

Hmmm.

Time to bring out the big guns. 'And I was thinking. We could get you another cat.'

INSIDIOUS

Even though Leah and I had only wrapped up our plotting session at around three a.m., I was up and in the shower before eight – a time of day that I hadn't experienced for *months*.

Bizarrely and contradictorily, I could've stayed up all night discussing storylines, and while we were doing it, I kept forgetting that the sole reason I was brainstorming with my mother's possible murderer was so I could eventually murder my mother's possible murderer. Not that I had any actual proof of my suspicions that was anything other than batshit and circumstantial. And although there was a way of potentially 'furthering the investigation', I was reluctant to do it seeing as it involved sending a message to a near stranger.

But once again, I shrugged off the avoidance, put the last part of *The Silence of the Lambs* on for Leah – she was a completionist, so she didn't find this suspicious – and scurried into the bathroom. Of course, it was only *after* I'd sent Jamie a DM asking if we could FaceTime, that I remembered I was supposed to be 'Leah' and not 'Niamh Morrissey', so I had to send a panicky follow-up one explaining why I had two different names. ('Leah is what my friends call me – it's my middle name' blah blah.)

Anyway, he didn't respond, which was just as well, because what was I thinking? Even if my batshit theory was correct, it might not apply to his mother, and even if it did, who'd want to hear that? No one. Including me.

WRONG TURN

I spent the first part of the drive home trying – and failing – to act 'normal'. Wired from a mixture of undiluted pod coffee and undiluted stress, I couldn't stop babbling – painfully aware that that annoying over-brightness had crept into my voice again.

In a desperate attempt to mask the tell-tale signs of a guilty conscience, I even resorted to playing the ABBA Gold CD, although the irony of using a grief trigger as a distraction strategy only hit me much later.

Somewhat aptly, ABBA was midway through 'SOS' when Jamie responded to my message, saying that he'd be free for a FaceTime 'in 5'. The weird rural Starbucks was coming up on the left, so I told Leah I had to make a pit stop and parked outside it.

'Aren't you coming in?' *Please say no.*

I'll wait.

Limp with relief, I wound down the window as if she were a Labrador, which was a contradictory thing to do seeing as I'd just spent an entire evening plotting to kill her, then scuttled into the Starbucks.

But just in case she did decide to tail me, I made straight for the toilets (clearly yet another pivotal quest moment was destined to take place in a lavatory). An anti-human-trafficking poster was pasted on the door of the stall, and as I stared at the photograph of a traumatised woman and the 'call now if you need help' text beneath her, instead of thinking, *God I'm bloody lucky in comparison*, in came a burst of self-pity even though our situations weren't even tangentially related.

Without bothering to shake off the nervous energy, I FaceTimed Jamie.

He'd changed his hair again and was backgrounded by a bright, arty, expensive-looking space – presumably his design studio.

'Hi,' I said. 'Thanks for messaging me back.'

He frowned and leaned towards his screen. 'Are you in a *toilet*?'

'Yes. Um. Sorry. I'm driving back from somewhere, and it's noisy outside.'

A slightly confused nod, then: 'Are you Annie Morrissey's daughter?'

Shite. It seemed that I wasn't the only person in the world who could Google an obituary and put two and two together. 'Yes.'

'Why didn't you just say that when I met you?'

Because I was going undercover for no reason and I'm an idiot. 'It was . . . look. You know when we met in the grief café? Full disclosure' – or as full as I could make it without him hanging up in horror – 'I looked you up online beforehand, so when we met, it wasn't . . . random. Which I know sounds stalkerish, because it is a bit. But as you now know, my mum was also a writer, and I suppose I just wanted to talk to someone whose mum was one too.' That didn't explain why I'd lied about who I was, but it was the best I could do at such short notice.

'But you didn't.'

'Didn't what?'

'Talk about your mother.'

To be fair, that was because he'd done most of the talking, which I'd encouraged because that was my main reason for seeing him, but I couldn't say that either. 'I know. I'm still coming to terms with it.'

'You can talk about her now if you like.'

'Thanks. It's okay. You've got enough to deal with. And better things to do.'

'I actually don't.'

I don't know why I said the next bit. Maybe it was a lack of sleep, or quest-induced delirium, or because I just wanted to air it out loud to someone else. 'The thing is . . . this is going to sound a bit mad.' He scrunched up his face at the 'mad'. 'Sorry, not mad. Unusual. Weird. The thing is . . . I thought I'd been seeing a pattern. Of authors like my mother, who had very complex relation-ships with their main characters, who . . . took on a life of their own, like muses. Which made me wonder if it was possible that the characters themselves could be responsible for causing the deaths of their creators, and—'

'Oh my *God*.'

'Sorry. I know how that must've sounded. I told you it was weird. Look, just forget it. I shouldn't have said it. I can't believe I did. Just—'

'No . . . no, you're right.'

'I am?' I almost fell off my toilet chair.

He let out a deep sigh. 'It makes sense. Because Carrie's world did consume my mother. Like, totally. Too much. It was all she thought about most of the time.'

Because he wasn't an idiot who got carried away by bullshit, he'd assumed I meant it figuratively and not liter-ally. 'I know what you mean,' I said, lamely.

306

'And thinking about Mum's work in such a literal way . . . as part of her, but also as its own separate entity? I haven't tried to frame it like that before. I think looking at it like that might be helpful. Because when she couldn't write anymore . . . that's why . . . that's why she chose to take her own life.'

'I'm so sorry. You didn't need to tell me that.'

'I know I didn't. But I also sort of did? The reason I don't like talking about it is because I kept blaming myself. Why else would she leave me like that? But you've made me see that it wasn't that she wanted to leave me, she wanted to get away from the part of herself that was *Carrie*. So . . . thanks. I'm going to take that up with my therapist.'

'Good. I hope it does help you. I really do.' I really, *really* did.

'I hope it helps you too.'

'Thanks.' I didn't say 'it won't', obviously. 'Say hi to the triad for me.'

'I will. Anyway, I'll see you at the next "Better Together" meeting.'

'Um. Like I said, I only went there to talk to you.'

'Yeah. But you never got to talk about your mum, did you? And you need to.'

Fair enough. I probably did. But that was future Niamh's problem.

After Jamie and I said our goodbyes, I stared at the poster for a bit and wondered how many people had felt the need to call that number, and how horrific it was that there even needed to be posters like that on toilet doors, and then I thought about Jamie and his poor mum and the whole thing made me feel very *very* tired. Giving a shite about things is absolutely exhausting. For once, it wasn't GinnyRebel, or Jamie or Leah who I envied, but my old self. The one whose emotions had been muted instead of turned up to full volume.

DELIVERANCE

Leah didn't say a word as I slid into the driver's seat. Nor did she glare at the almond croissant and cheeky Twix that I'd bought after I left the toilet sanctuary. Which should've alerted me to the fact that something was up.

Because there was something up, a big something too, because twenty miles or so later, when the car was in the slipstream of a pantechnicon, and I was in the far more dangerous slipstream of my own thoughts, Leah said, softly but seriously, *pull over*.

'Um . . . what?'

Pull over.

'Why?'

You know why.

Oh shite. Did she know what I was up to after all?

'I can't.' There was nowhere *to* pull over – we were driving through what was basically a mountain pass. *Oh God, please don't make me run off the road.* But then, up ahead, I spotted a 'P' sign indicating one of those makeshift lorry park areas. By the time I'd turned into it, my palms were slick with sweat, and my throat was tight. The creepy location, which had 'future crime podcast setting' written all over it, didn't help. The U-shaped layby was hidden from the main drag by a thicket of woodland, and in defiance of the outrageously beautiful surroundings, the hedgerows were garlanded with wet-wipes and a baby's discarded nappy, and the verge was a riot of squashed cider cans.

Leah CLICK-ed her lighter, then gave me a long, ambiguous look. The silence stretched. She really was excellent at suspense. I wasn't, because ten seconds later, I heard myself blurting: 'I won't tell anyone what you did.'

She baulked, then eyed me as if I were the human version of a floordrobe.

'It's not as if they'd believe me anyway, and I haven't actually got any proof, so there's no point trying to shut me up—'

You **what?**

'I said—'

I know what you bloody well **said.** *What it means is less bloody clear.*

'Um. Which bit?'

All *of it. But let's start with what you think 'I did'.*

'Um . . . I'd rather not say that out loud.'

Tough. A particularly intense Death Stare.

Oh God. 'Murdered Mum,' I mumbled.

She recoiled as if I'd slapped her. *Are you messing with me?*

'Um . . . no.'

The look of incredulity on her face was so uncharacteristic and intense that I knew, without a shadow of a doubt, that I'd got this very wrong indeed.

Method?

'Um . . . what?'

How did you think I killed her?

'I'd rather not say, because thinking about it, it is pretty stupid and—'

Do it.

'By . . . talking her to death.'

You **what?** 'Talking *her* **to** *death?*' *That's not even a thing.*

'Well . . . it sort of is. In *The Silence of the Lambs,* Multiple Miggs was talked to death by Hannibal Lecter, wasn't he?'

How would that even work?

'I think he made him swallow his tongue or something.'

A spiky, *Unbelievable.* Then: *I've never killed anyone in my bloody life.*

That was true, and something I should've factored in when I was Frankenstein-ing my stupid theory together. Even Rebel's killer had died accidentally when he'd tried and failed to do some parkour when Leah was chasing him, and although she was capable of violence, all the books' baddies – except for the billionaire oil magnet in *Over the Odds,* because he'd got off scot-free like the super-rich tended to do – ended up in prisons and not crematoriums. The mortification was now so intense it was making me feel physically sick.

Motive?

'I don't want to say that either.' I looked down at my hands.

Do it.

If *only* I hadn't got carried away. *What to do?* There were some truths that were best left unspoken, but it wouldn't be fair to keep her hanging. 'You might want to prepare yourself for this. But last night I got up the gumption to listen to Mum's voice messages. And in the final one . . . she said she was planning to kill you off in the next book.'

She didn't recoil this time, but slumped, as if all the air had left her non-body.

'I'm so sorry, Leah. And I know that must have been *awful* to hear but I think she only said it because she was seriously messed up. Not just because of the menopause – I think she was drinking heavily too. I found some old booze bottles in the recycling bin. I didn't tell you about them because . . . I suppose because I didn't want that to be the answer. And look. I truly am sorry you had to hear about the killing you stuff like that.' I genuinely was, because I knew what that felt like. Well – to a far lesser extent. Because although my mother had side-lined me a bit, as far as I know she'd never planned to kill me.

Our story, 'How to Kill a Crime Writer'. Was that a ruse?

'Yes. Sorry.'

This appeared to upset her more than the bombshell about her potential fictional death. Then she shot me a look of grudging admiration. *You did that part well.*

'It wasn't *all* fake. I enjoyed talking about it. I honestly did. But . . . Can I ask you a question?'

You just did.

For once, I didn't find this irritating. Sniping at me hopefully meant that she wasn't too broken inside. 'Why did you make me pull over?'

From the weird way you were acting, I was concerned you were having another panic attack.

'Really?'

Yes, really.

'That was really thoughtful. Thank you.' I truly was an imbecile. But this didn't stop me from asking, 'Can I ask you another one?'

A muttered, *Christ.*

'Was our murder-made-to-look-like-an-accident investigation all bullshit?'

Eh? Why would I make that up?

'When I thought you were a murderer, I assumed that you'd come up with it so that we'd go on a real-life quest for research purposes, and then you'd eventually convince me to fictionalise it.'

A long look, eloquent with *WTF?*

'Isn't that how you stay alive? By someone writing you, I mean?'

Do you need someone to write you in order to live?

For all I knew the answer was 'yes', but I've never been into philosophy because it's a major mindfuck. And in any case, no one was currently writing Leah anyway, which was something else I should've factored into my bullshit theorising.

Then she said: *And as you're always saying, you're not a writer.* Which hurt a little, even though I wasn't one.

'If my mother had . . . you know, gone through with it, would it have worked?'

You tell me.

'I'm not going to try it, I promise. I don't actually want you to die.'

A sarcastic *Ta.*

'And I really am sorry.'

I know.

'I mean it.'

I know.

'And look, the reason why Mum was going to do it wasn't because she hated you or anything like that, it was more to do with book sales. She was fond of you. More than fond. In fact, I used to be a bit jealous of you.' Well, not a *bit.* I decided not to tell Leah that on my old laptop

I'd created a file entitled 'Ways to kill Leah off' – considering the context, that would be horribly insensitive.

Give over. Why would you be envious of me?

'Well, because you're so capable and confident and brave and forthright all of the time.'

No, I'm not.

'Yes, you are.'

I don't always feel that way.

'Oh right. So, you're *not* naturally confident then?'

I didn't say that.

This made me smile. 'Anyway, in comparison to me you're basically perfect. As you found out during "The Case of the Missing Ladder", being crap is my defining trait.'

You're not crap. You pulled the wool over my eyes, didn't you? That took skill.

'Thanks.'

Just stating a fact.

'So, this thing we're doing here . . . it's definitely not a grief quest, then? A convoluted way for me to deal with Mum's death?'

It's not always about you, you know. Not all the bloody time.

Oof. I'd spent so long assuming that I was the protagonist of this story, it hadn't even occurred to me that I might be a supporting character.

And then she said, very softly: *She was my mother too.*

In came a fresh wave of guilt. I'd forgotten that on the morning after the car crash, I'd detected a crack in her carapace. A tiny crack, but a crack all the same. 'Sorry,' I said, yet again. 'I've been selfish. I've been so busy coming to terms with the fact that you're here at all, that it didn't occur to me that under your carapace thingy you were mourning Mum too. Even if she did murder Jed and Rebel.'

And then she said something that made my breath catch in my throat: *You see me much more clearly than she ever did.*

THE OMEN II

After apologising again, I'd decided it would be kinder to let Leah be. Discovering that your author was planning to kill you would be devastating for any protagonist, even one with a carapace. But despite the awful circumstances, the silence between us wasn't awkward. In fact, it was the type of silence that only happens when you know someone inside and out, and aren't worried that they'll judge you for being quiet.

When we were closer to home, I did a side-mission to a garden centre and bought two gnomes for Glenn to say thanks for fixing the guttering, and a fancy cake tin decorated with robins and brambles for Tracey, as a thank-you gift for feeding Brian. Which reminded me that I'd neglected to ask Tracey to feed the birds. *Shite*. Augustus must be furious.

Driving back along the lane felt . . . *odd*, as if Leah and I were old-school explorers returning home after an epic thirty-year adventure, only instead of kick-starting the horrors of colonialism, we'd just caused some minor embarrassment. Although the 'my-mother-was-planning-to-murder-you' bonding moment felt like the emotional denouement of *something*. And coupled with the fact that it was looking increasingly unlikely that there even was a murder to solve, I couldn't help but wonder why Leah was still here.

The Wanker's wank-mobile was parked outside the bunker, its enormous arse sticking into the lane, but by doing a seven-hundred-point turn, I managed to squeeze the Mini into the driveway.

The murder wall seemed to mock us when we went inside. Well, mock me. But other than that, it was a relief to be back in the cottage. It seemed that I really was beginning to think of it as home. Except home was where the people or – in my case – cat you loved were supposed to be, and Brian hadn't yet appeared. I couldn't hear any yapping coming from outside, so perhaps he'd taken himself off to punish me for allowing a stranger to venture inside his domain.

Leah drifted over to the fridge. It struck me then that she hadn't smoked a cigarette all day.

'Have you run out of smokes?'

She shrugged. *Lost my taste for them.*

'Then you won't need that Zippo anymore, will you?'

CLICK. And a faint wry smile.

'I'd better feed the birds.'

On the porch outside, the cake was as we'd left it – I'd probably have to nuke it from space to get rid of it. As predicted, Augustus and the gang were sulkier than usual, but that could've been because the greedy squirrel had invited a friend over for a suet-ball banquet, and they couldn't get near their McDonald's fly-thru stands.

I'd just finished topping up the feeders, when I clocked that Leah was staring intently at a patch of grass. Not only that, but she'd lost the melancholy, which was a bit quick even for someone with dark triad personality traits.

'What is it?'

Not sure. She walked towards the shed. I followed.
'Oh *fuck.*'
You got that right.
Because propped up against it was a ladder. And not just any old ladder. One of those 'fancy foldaway ones'.

RESIDENT EVIL: RETRIBUTION

Back inside, both Leah and I began to pace, which would have given Brian whiplash if he'd been here. But hopefully, greed would eventually trump his desire for revenge, and he'd pitch up when I opened his suppertime can of Sheba.

'Okay. Why would someone return what may or may not have been the murder weapon? Because that seems like a very stupid or very fiendish thing to do.'

Agreed.

'Because . . . only *we* know that we're investigating a murder, don't we? And whoever did it must have returned it while we were at the CrimeTime festival. We would have noticed if any of the weeds had been trampled before we left.' Well, Leah would've noticed.

Good point. Who knew we were going to be AWOL?

'Tracey, obviously. Glenn and Janet. And . . .' It was then that the obvious solution to the mystery dawned. 'But hang on, we were only away for two days, which means . . .' I waited for Leah to fill in the blanks, like she was prone to doing with me, but she didn't – probably because my eureka moment was tech-related. '. . . CCTV! The Weekend Wanker's cameras. The footage wouldn't have been erased yet.'

Her eyes lit up (literally as well, which was quite something to see). *Well bloody done.*

319

A quick inner purr, then I ran to the kitchen window. The Wanker's car was still parked in the lane, but it wouldn't be for long because he was climbing into the driver's seat.

Go!

She didn't need to tell me twice. I flew through the front door, ran straight up to the wank-mobile and banged on the back window. The driver's side door flew open, and out he raged.

'What the *fuck*? You again?'

Glenn came barrelling into view (judging by the bucket he was hefting, he'd been outside cleaning his already clean car again). 'Everything all right, Nina?'

'Oh great,' the Wanker muttered. 'PC Twat's come to join the party.'

'I'm fine thanks, Glenn,' I called. 'I was just . . . I just wanted to ask Mr Fiddle if he'd seen Brian.'

'Who the fuck is Brian?' the Wanker asked. 'Your fella?'

'No. I'm asexual.'

'Jesus,' he muttered.

'You sure you're all right, pet?' yelled Glenn.

'Absolutely!' I yelled back. 'Thanks, though.'

He reluctantly retreated.

I turned back to the Wanker. 'It's not actually about the cat. Although *have* you seen him, by the way?'

'Are you fucking joking?'

'No. But . . . I'm sorry to ask this. And I'm sorry I called you all those horrible things the other day, but I need to look at the last three days of your CCTV footage.'

'Not this again.' He went to get back into the car.

Blackmail. Now.

Fuck it. 'What do you think your CEO aka wife would say if I asked her if the hot tub's been fixed yet?'

He froze.

'Shall we find out? I've got her number right here.' I didn't, but it was probably on her website.

He turned to face me. '*What* did you just say?'

Tell him he heard you.

'You heard you. I mean me. You've got two choices. You can give me the last three days of footage, or I'm going to see if your wife knows what you get up to in her investment properties.'

'Are you *threatening* me?'

'I am, actually.' I was. And I was fine with that.

His eyes hardened and he took a step towards me.

Hold your ground.

I did, and the aggression seemed to seep out of him. Glenn was right. The Wanker *was* all mouth and no trousers. 'Fuck's sake. How do I know you won't tell her anyway?'

Tell him he doesn't.

'You don't.'

'So why should I help you then?'

Tell him that if he plays fair with you, you'll play fair with him.

I did as Leah suggested.

'Three days, you said?'

'Yes. From Friday morning till now.'

Another muttered, 'fuck's sake.' Then he gave me a curt nod of acquiescence.

'Really?'

'Do you want it or not?'

'Yes please.'

Tell him we need it now.

'I need it now, though.'

He swore under his breath. 'What's your email? I'll send you the file.'

I gave it to him, and he fiddled with his phone for what felt like three years, his sausage fingers tappity-tapping clumsily. 'Done.'

I checked my inbox. The email was indeed there, although he hadn't bothered to add a subject line.

'Happy?' he sneered. He tapped his forehead. 'You're not right in the head, are you?'

I smiled dryly, wryly, *and* cynically at him. 'You *literally* don't know the half of it, mate.'

Leah snorted. *Let's go.*

It was then that I remembered the phone. 'By any chance, did you lose a phone a while ago?'

He recoiled. 'How did you know about that?'

'I found it.'

'Where?'

'Behind your hot tub. It's completely fucked, by the way.'

Leaving him dumbfounded, we hurried back to the cottage.

THE OMEN III

Coffee. Computer. No cake this time, but two out of three wasn't bad. Behind me, Leah paced and CLICKed, CLICKed and paced, which wasn't as irritating as it sounds.

The cameras were motion-capture, and the Wanker hadn't been bullshitting about the resolution. And the angle was equally as fortuitous, seeing as it was wide enough to take in the entirety of the cottage, the garage and – most notably – the gate that led into the area formerly known as the Death Zone.

I began with 10.33 a.m. on Friday. There was me, backing out of the driveway, and doing a poor job of it. Unsurprisingly, the passenger seat appeared to be empty (if Leah *did* exist outside my head, then she clearly inhabited a metaphysical plane that was only visible to chronic introverts, ailing nonagenarians, cats, and a random smattering of wildlife).

10.53 a.m. The postie's van trundled across the screen. She didn't pause at the cottage, so presumably she was off to do a drive-by at Sheila's.

11.27 a.m. The postal drove back again. And judging by the length of time in between trips, Sheila was feeling much better.

11.55 a.m. Tracey strolled past with Petticoat.

12.16 p.m. Tracey and Petticoat strolled back home.

12.45 p.m. Glenn appeared, hefting a ladder – a normal one, not one of those 'fancy foldaway ones' – went through the cottage's side gate and disappeared from view. Presumably he was about to make good on his promise to fix the guttering.

1.02 p.m. Janet came into shot, wrapping her cardigan around her. She paused to eye Mum's recycling bin – I couldn't see her expression, but she was probably stunned that it was accessible to the refuse workers for once – then she peered over the side gate. After a second or two, she scurried back home.

1.20 p.m. Glenn re-emerged.

2.35 p.m. A stray sheep wandered along the lane, blissfully unaware that it was destined to be the subject of a long and tedious WhatsApp discussion.

2.45 p.m. A trio of bewildered ramblers rambled past (they were clearly lost). And, in the background, I spied Brian sitting on the cottage's gate. Aww: Was he doing a feline Greyfriars Bobby and waiting poignantly for me to return?

3.05 p.m. It seemed so, because when the same trio of (now bickering) ramblers returned, he was still there.

5.45 p.m. The Wanker's wank-mobile cruised into shot – *no, no, no, don't block my sightline!* – but then he reversed and thankfully parked selfishly, so I still had a relatively unrestricted view of the gate. The Wanker – who was alone this time – disappeared into his bunker. The gate was cat-free – hopefully Brian had given up and taken himself off to bed.

8.01 p.m. A fox padded nonchalantly along the lane, making for the woodland at the end.

9.02 p.m. Another fox followed suit.

9.20 p.m. *Another* fox! Perhaps there was a fox night-club in the woods.

Saturday:

2 a.m. I let out a yip of delight as a badger waddled into shot and snuffled at the cottage's overgrown fence line (clearly the Countryside Alliance wasn't active in this area).

3.01 a.m. Another yip of delight as a large doe, her eyes rendered silver by the infrared, picked her way confidently across the Wanker's driveway (I resisted the urge to smile smugly at Leah). The doe looked straight into shot – *why yes, I am ready for my close-up, Mr Wanker* – then went on her way.

4.34 a.m. Two of the foxes came padding back along the lane. There was no sign of the third one – perhaps it had passed out in the club.

7.45 a.m. The Wanker exited the bunker, went to chuck something into his wheelie bin, shook his head, and then disappeared off screen. And in the background, Brian was back on his waiting post, which really made me feel guilty for abandoning him.

8.01 a.m. Tracey arrived at the cottage to give Brian his breakfast. Curiously, instead of fleeing at the sight of a stranger, Brian – still on his post – allowed her to stroke his head, and then followed her inside (perhaps he knew she was a cat person).

8.15 a.m. Tracey reappeared.

9.20 a.m. Another rogue sheep trip-trapped past. I hoped it was off to join the other one – I liked the idea of the escapees banding together and starting a free community where they'd be safe from getting eaten.

*

And then:

'Holy *shite*.'

What is it?

I was so shocked at what was unfolding on my laptop screen that all I could do was flap a hand at it. Because at 10.35 a.m. Tracey had returned to the cottage. Only, this time, she was carrying a ladder, and it definitely *was* one of those 'fancy foldaway ones'.

SHADOW OF THE CAT

Leah was the first to find her voice. *I knew she was too good to be true.*

'Well, yes, but the fact that she brought the ladder back doesn't *necessarily* prove that she's a murderer. There could be a reasonable explanation for it.'

Like what?

'Well . . . what if she found it in the woods when she was walking Petticoat? The Phantom Child Thieves could've fly-tipped it there after they nicked it. And she knew I was looking for it, so perhaps she simply brought it back to be kind.'

Then why did she look so guilty when she was returning it?

Good point. There *had* been something furtive about the way Tracey had glanced around before she'd carried it through the gate. 'Okay. So say she is our perp, what possible motive would she have to murder Mum? There's the gazumping thing of course, but we discarded that earlier, because it was too stupid. Unless . . .'

Unless what?

'Well, for argument's sake, *what if* Tracey was so desperate to live here that she offed Mum so that the cottage would come back on the market? Only, when I moved in, this messed with her plans, and because it would look weird if both Mum and I died under semi-suspicious circumstances, instead of killing me off, she decided to murder Sheila instead so that she could live in the area?' I glanced at Leah, then answered my own question. 'But that seems a bit far-fetched, doesn't it? The hamlet's not bad, but it isn't the sort of place you'd *literally* kill to live in.'

Agreed. Other possible motives?

'Well, there's the *Overlooked* connection, but that one's even stupider. Maybe I should watch the footage again. See if there's something we're missing.'

Go for it.

As I replayed it, and let it run right through to when Leah and I had arrived home, my brain automatically clicked into roguelike puzzle-game mode. I was concentrating so hard that I didn't even yip at the sight of an unusually large hedgehog.

And then I got it. There *was* something missing. And that something was Brian.

Because after Tracey had done her ladder fly-by, there was no sign of Brian at all – his Greyfriars Bobby post remained disturbingly cat-free. This could just be because he'd taken himself off to punish me for abandoning him, but what if he hadn't?

I went completely cold. Had I inadvertently invited a cat-killer into my life? It was far too easy to imagine Tracey poisoning Brian's Sheba and then shoving his corpse into a wheelie bin (not Glenn and Janet's, obviously). This horrible twist would, after all, fit our 'dead cat' red herring of a side-plot.

I turned to Leah. 'What if *Brian* is Tracey's motive? I mean, it wouldn't take a rocket scientist to figure out that the reason Petticoat barks is because Brian winds him up. We know that Mum's car wasn't in the driveway like it always was when she was at home. So, Tracey might've assumed that Mum was out that night and nipped over to murder Brian. And *what if*, as she was creeping through the side gate, Mum had confronted her, and they'd had an altercation?'

Leah frowned. **What about opportunity? She doesn't live in the hamlet.**

'Well, she said she'd met Mum once or twice, so she could've been staying with Sheila four months ago, I suppose. But even if that *were* the case, why would Tracey nick the ladder? I suppose the obvious explanation is that she was worried she might've left her DNA on it or something. Although that would only be an issue if the cops decided to reinvestigate Mum's accident.'

Or bothered to investigate it properly in the first bloody place.

We shared a look of self-pity.

And why bring the ladder back?

'Um . . . to throw us off the scent, maybe? No. That doesn't make sense because only we know that we're even conducting a murder investigation. Although . . . she would've seen the murder wall! I mean, I know it's rubbish, but the drawings of the ladder and Brian are fairly recognisable, and if she was feeling any guilt or paranoia about her crime, then she could've put two and two together.'

My brain hadn't done this much work for years and I was beginning to get a headache.

'So.'

So.

'Our only course of action is to go over there and

confront her, or at least try and get a bit more evidence to back this up.'

Agreed.

I glanced at the time. Unbelievably, considering that so far today I'd driven back from Wales, consoled a grieving fashion designer while sitting on a toilet, had an emotional breakthrough in a layby, discovered a vital piece of evidence next to a shed, blackmailed a wanker, *and* done some digital forensic work, it was only three p.m. That was the problem with being active – instead of time blurring together into one amorphous forgettable mass, it slowed right down and created memories.

But. Having spent the equivalent of probably decades consuming true-crime content, I knew far more than Leah about the implications of real-life baddie confrontation.

'Let's go over to Glenn's first and mention that we're going to Sheila's. That way, if Tracey does kidnap me or whatever, there'll be a timeline. I mean, he *is* an ex-cop.'

Leah rolled her eyes.

'Look, I'm not suggesting that we tell him what we're up to. I couldn't do that anyway – it would take days just to give him the context.'

Fine.

'Great.'

I collected the 'thank-you' gnomes from the Mini's boot – God knows why anyone would want to nick them; to me they looked like mini sex offenders – and trotted next door.

The blare of the telly was so loud that I could hear it from the driveway – presumably Janet had a headache again – and I had to ring the bell twice before Glenn came to the door.

'Sorry to disturb you,' I said, brandishing the gnomes. 'I bought you these. To say thanks for fixing the guttering.'

He appeared to be genuinely touched. 'You didn't need to do that, pet. Janet will be chuffed, though.' He took them from me and placed them on the patch of nothingness where the old ones had once spent their miserable existence. (I now felt a bit guilty for supplying Glenn and Janet with fresh victims, even if the gnomes' fixed smiles were objectively disturbing.)

'How was your trip, pet?'

'Good, thanks.'

'Grand. Fancy a cuppa?'

'I can't. Thanks, though. I have to pop over to Sheila's. That's where I'm going now. To Sheila's. To see her. And Tracey too, probably.'

Glenn nodded in confusion. 'Right.'

I was about to turn away, when he said, 'I couldn't ask you a favour, could I pet? We've got a couple of house viewings next week, and Janet's getting anxious about it.'

'Is she? I'm sorry to hear that.' I began to back away. Carrying on talking while the person you're talking at was clearly trying to escape was more of a Sheila thing to do. *Read the room, Glenn.* 'I'd better . . .'

'Would you mind if I popped over and strimmered your lawn? You can see it from the bedroom windows, like, and . . .' he trailed off, unable to bring himself to say: *and we don't want potential buyers to think that a massive slob lives next door.*

Desperate to get away, I said: 'Sure. Course. Go for it.'

He sagged with relief. 'Thanks pet. I'll pop over in the morning, like.'

'Great.' *Hopefully I'll still be alive then.* 'Well . . . I'd best go to Sheila's now.'

'All right pet.'

'Bye.' In case he attempted to conversationally lasso me again, I turned and legged it, which probably looked a bit odd, but considering that my next chore was confronting my mother's potential murderer – for real this time – that was the least of my concerns.

I KNOW WHAT YOU
DID LAST SUMMER

We were almost at Sheila's door when I realised that I'd left the new cake tin behind, and because it gave us a plausible undercover-style excuse for our visit, I ran back to get it (I didn't bother scratching off the price sticker, though).

Pulse racing from this tiny bit of exercise, I glanced at Leah. 'God, I'm nervous.'

You'll be fine.

'I hope you're right.'

So. Remember when you were interrogating GinnyRebel in that fancy hall and you drank too much wine, and instead of vomiting on a queue of people you managed to run outside and do it in a bin instead?

'Are you saying that if I'm capable of not throwing up on a drag queen, then I can do anything?'

No. I'm saying that there's no way this can be worse than that. A beat, then, *For me, anyway.*

I laughed, and the tension loosened its grip. 'Thanks – I think.' Then I rang the bell.

Tracey beamed at me when she came to the front door, which threw me off a bit. 'Lovely to see, you, bab. How was your trip?'

'Um. It was great thanks.' I brandished the tin. 'We – I mean *I* – bought you this to say thanks for feeding Brian.'

'Bless you. We can always do with extras.'

'I hope he wasn't any trouble?' This sounded excessively pointed to my ears, but Tracey didn't seem to pick up on it.

'No trouble at all. Come on in. Auntie would love to see you. She's just having her tea in the conservatory.' Tracey certainly didn't have the demeanour of someone who'd recently snuck into a neighbour's garden to return a vital piece of evidence in a non-traditional murder investigation, and Leah looked as nonplussed by this as I felt. Either Tracey was a sociopath with the acting skills of Kate Winslet, or we'd got this very wrong (*again*).

'How is Sheila?'

'Much better ta, bab. Still a bit frail, but that's to be expected.'

An enormous lemon drizzle cake took pride of place on the counter. Considering the circumstances, I shouldn't have eyed it greedily, but the stomach wants what the stomach wants. Was there a way to segue into 'Did you kill my mother?' via small talk and cake?

Jump straight in. It'll catch her off guard.

'Tracey . . . um. Did you return my mum's ladder, by any chance?'

Her shoulders slumped. 'I did, yes.'

Antagonists weren't supposed to admit things unless they were under duress. And yes, okay, I had been looking forward to showing her the Wanker's footage in a 'gotcha' moment. 'Why did you take it in the first place?'

Tracey sighed. 'I didn't, bab. Auntie did.'

Leah and I exchanged *whoa* glances. Was Sheila the murderer after all? Seeing as she was one of our first suspects, that would be more in keeping with a Leah book. 'Why would Sheila have done that?'

'It'll be the booze, no doubt.'

'Booze?'

'She falls off the wagon every so often, bless her. She's been struggling with it on and off for years. I keep telling her that it won't help with the UTIs she's always getting, but she doesn't always listen to reason. I thought you knew about that, bab. Haven't you noticed that she puts her empties in your bin?'

Oh. I side-eyed Leah. So Mum hadn't been a secret drinker after all. Which was something I would've known all along if I'd bloody well bothered to do the recycling.

'She does it so that the bin men don't judge her,' Tracey continued. 'That's why Mr Misery chains his up. Your lovely mum turned a blind eye to it though, bless her. Not that I blame Auntie for having a tipple, she can do what she likes at her age, and a broken heart will do that to you, won't it?'

'Her husband you mean?'

'Not him, bab. Like I said, he was a bit of a one. Thelma. Used to live in your cottage. Died ten years ago.'

'Thelma the free spirit? The one who's buried in the graveyard?'

'That's right. Auntie came up with that epitaph. Lovely, isn't it? Thelma was an artist, you see.' She nodded at the painting of the sleeping woman. 'She did that. You'd never know it was Auntie, would you?'

No, you wouldn't. Mainly because she wasn't talking in it. 'It's a beautiful picture.' It was. There was something intimate about it, too.

'I've always liked it.'

'I was going to take Thelma some gin instead of flowers.'

Tracey chuckled. 'She'd like that. Auntie would too. Thick as thieves, she and Auntie were. Lived in each other's pockets. When Thelma went, it almost killed her. Doesn't like to talk about it, though.'

Poor Sheila. No wonder she hadn't shared her Death Stories. As I'd learned the hard way, you can only verbalise those when you're able to do it without karking.

'Come to think of it, that could be why Auntie was being so strange about the tin she lent you. Reckon it must've been one of Thelma's.'

Uh-oh. A sob came burbling up.

CLICK.

Phew.

'I didn't realise Auntie had been taking things, though,' Tracey said, pausing to hand me a ginormous piece of lemon drizzle cake, which, for once, Leah didn't glare at (possibly because it had a bit of vitamin C in it). 'Found them when I was clearing out the spare room. The ladder was under the bed, and I knew it was the one you'd mentioned on account of the delivery sticker on it. There were also some gnomes, half a hosepipe, and some other bits and bobs. Oh. And a flamingo. God knows who they belong to, or why she does it.'

'Well . . . the gnomes belong to Glenn and Janet, and the flamingo is from Warren Cottage, and . . .'

Then something dawned. I glanced at Leah, and we said in unison:

'Revenge!' *Revenge!*

Tracey gave me a funny look. 'What was that, bab?'

'I think Sheila took things to punish people who were being arseholes. As you know, Glenn kept having a go at her about Petticoat barking, and I know she doesn't like the way he treats his garden because I remember her telling me that loads, and a while ago, she mentioned that someone in the hamlet had dumped grass cuttings on one of the footpaths, and I'm pretty sure the flamingo belongs to him.' I had to restrain myself from monologuing like a baddie doing exposition. *But why take the ladder?*

Appeasement confectionery!

Of course. 'And I think she took the ladder to punish me for forgetting to return the cake tin.'

Had we finally solved 'The Case of the Missing Ladder?' It seemed so, and as was tradition, the answer wasn't only mundane, but also utterly bonkers.

Tracey sighed. 'I'm sorry about that, bab. I would have told you. It didn't seem right not to return it because you'd said it was important to you, and I popped it over when Auntie was napping so that I wouldn't embarrass her. Mind you, I'm not sure she remembers doing it. Auntie's not usually vindictive, but if something's bothering her, then she's like a dog with a bone.' Another sigh. 'I suppose I'll have to give the gnomes back to Mr Misery too. He'll bloody love that.'

'Don't worry. I gave him some new ones.'

This caused some confusion.

Phone.

'Good thinking,' I accidentally said out loud.

'What was that, bab?'

'Sorry, Tracey. The thing is, my mum's phone is also missing. I don't suppose Sheila accidentally took that too, did she?' Well, not *accidentally*, seeing as she was obviously a binge-drinking compulsive thief with a side-line in weird revenge activities, but anyway.

'I haven't seen it. But if it turns up, I'll let you know.'

'Thanks.'

'Would you mind not mentioning the ladder to Auntie? Like I said, she won't remember it, and she'll be mortified.'

'Course I won't. It was my fault for not returning the tin earlier. Specially because it meant so much to her.'

'That's no excuse, but bless you for saying that.' She nodded at the conservatory. 'Go on through and say hello to her if you like.'

There *was* something I wanted to ask Sheila, but I glanced at Leah first. Sheila had, after all, been solely responsible for one of our most tedious red herrings. Taking her shrug as assent, I went on through.

Sheila was sitting in a rattan chair, a blanket on her knees, and although she still looked frail, she'd lost that haunted, glassy look. Now I knew more of her backstory and what made her tick, she'd come more into focus for me.

'Hi Sheila.'

She gave me what appeared to be a genuine smile. 'Hello, dear. Tracey says you've been *marvellous* with Petticoat.'

I sat in the chair next to her. 'I'm glad you're feeling better.'

'Thank you dear. So am I.'

'Sheila . . . can I ask you a question?'

'Please do.'

'Before my mum died, did you suggest that she do something? It's just . . . when I came over to see you when you were ill, you mentioned that you'd told her to do something, and it sounded important.'

'Did I? What could that be, I wonder?' Then she nodded. 'Ah yes. She'd offered to water my roses for me when my hip was acting up. And I said to her, "Annie, you don't have to do it every day, but roses like a good long drink, not a splash and . . ."'

Sensing I was in for the long haul, I tuned out. *Another minor mystery solved.* Leah and I exchanged 'oh for fuck's sake' glances, then she wandered over to the glass doors that led out into the garden. Judging by the vast variety of shrubs and trees that fringed the overgrown lawn, coming up with low-stakes revenge tactics and talking weren't Sheila's only skills. It was a pity I'd never be able to get a word in edgewise to ask her for some gardening tips.

'. . . new book for me.'

This grabbed my attention. 'I'm sorry, Sheila, I missed that.'

'I was saying that Tracey has ordered Annie's new book for me. I'm sorry to say I haven't read your mother's writing before, she was so unassuming about that part of her life, wasn't she? I'm not much of a reader these days because of my eyes, but Tracey says that she'll lend me her tablet and she tells me that you can make the print large enough to . . .'

I tuned out again while I wrestled with an unexpected moral dilemma, which was whether I should warn her that Mum had 'repurposed' her husband's hunting accident and turned it into a murder scenario in *Overlooked*. It would be a bit weird if I didn't, and even if her husband had been a bit of a one, Sheila might still find it triggering. I waited until she drew breath (it was a long wait), then jumped in with: 'Actually, there's something you should know about Mum's book, Sheila. Tracey told me how your husband died – I'm sorry for your loss, by the way – and I think my mother might've used his hunting accident as inspiration for one of her plots.'

Sheila blinked. 'Goodness. How interesting. Are you sure, dear?'

'Well, it *might* just be a coincidence, but I thought I should tell you so that when you read it, you don't get triggered. It is very different though, in lots of ways. For a start, Mum turned it into a murder.'

Sheila laughed (it was the first time I'd ever heard her do this, and it was quite a nice laugh). 'Well, well. Naughty Annie.'

'*Did* you tell her about it?'

'I did indeed.' Sheila paused (it was the first time I'd ever heard her do this too), and then said, 'Not the *whole* story of course.' And then she winked. A subtle wink, but a wink all the same.

Tracey bustled in with a tray of delicious carbs. 'You look cheerful, Auntie.'

Sheila smiled innocently at me. 'We've been having a lovely chat, haven't we dear?'

Still discombobulated by Sheila's ambiguous wink, all I could manage was an equally ambiguous, 'Mmhmm.'

Leah turned to face me. **You'll want to see this.**

Oh God, what now? 'Do you mind if I have a look at your wonderful garden, Sheila?'

'Please do.'

I stood up and joined Leah. She gestured at a patch of grass beneath the overhanging maple branch.

'Oh wow!' I forgot to murmur, and then laughed. There was Petticoat, lying on his back, paws in the air, and next to him, washing himself nonchalantly, was Brian.

It seemed Leah had been wrong about Brian being the only one in the hamlet who wasn't hiding something. Perhaps Petticoat had a case of Stockholm syndrome, or maybe the yapping was the equivalent of a *Romeo and Juliet*-style serenade (to be fair, this story *had* been lacking a romance sub-plot, and it made sense that this would also be batshit).

'Sweet, isn't it?' Tracey said from behind me. 'Auntie says they started doing that off and on after your mother had her accident, didn't you Auntie?'

Accident. Because that really was what it had been, all along. And, as I glanced at Leah, and took in her defeated body language, it was clear that she'd come to that conclusion too.

DEAD END

'Shite.'

Fuck, *more like.*

Which was fair enough because she was allowed one F-word per book and sadly, this was the perfect time to deploy it.

We gravitated to the couch in the snug because there was nothing else to do. What other unfinished business could there be?

I'd confronted the Trigger Zones.

'Got off my arse and out of the bloody house' for more than just a bit.

Had various interactions with various neighbours with varying results.

Told a complete bastard that he was a meat condom, and then blackmailed him.

Lied to a grieving polyamorous entrepreneur I actually liked.

Lied to a Leah Overton super-fan I actually liked.

Come very close to throwing up on a drag queen.

Rooted through a top literary agent's handbag.

Solved several minor mysteries, including 'The Case of the Missing Ladder'.

Listened to my mother's voice messages.

Accused a fictional character of committing matricide.

Had an emotional breakthrough in a layby.

Discovered that my cat was in love with a Bedlington Terrier.

Cried more in the last two weeks than in the entirety of my (semi) grown-up life.

And . . . discovered that this wasn't a true-crime murder mystery after all. Well, not unless Sheila *had* actually offed her husband, and if that was the case, then there was *some* unfinished business, but not *the* unfinished business.

I didn't ask Leah why she was still here. Instead, I fired up the laptop, and we sat in silence and watched Detective Stabler extracting a false confession out of a pyrophiliac by suggestively lighting matches and then blowing them out.

THE LAWNMOWER MAN

DUN-DUN.

CLICK.

We've got company.

I lurched awake. I'd fallen asleep on the couch again, and mindful of my aching neck, I sat up carefully, letting out a yip of surprise-slash-horror when Glenn's head suddenly appeared at the window.

Shite. I'd forgotten he was coming over to commit bramble genocide.

I jumped up to open the front door, trying and failing to pretend that I'd been awake for hours. 'Hi Glenn!'

'Morning, pet. No need to put the kettle on.' He held up a thermos.

'Oh right.'

'Thought I'd get an early start. Any idea where I can plug my extension cord in?'

No was the obvious answer to that, but we eventually decided that the boot room was the best option for plugging-in purposes. I held the back door open for him as he unreeled the cable, and the birds scattered as he backed out onto the porch.

He paused and eyed the cake with confusion. 'You'll want to watch that doesn't attract rats, pet.'

'Yeah. I don't think it will.' It was more likely to drive them away.

'Surprised you don't get them anyway, what with having so many bird feeders.'

I hadn't noticed any rodents. Perhaps Brian scared them away (he certainly didn't hunt them). His tree balcony had shed most of its leaves, and despite it being pre-brunch, he was already lounging on his favourite branch waiting for his cross-species Romeo to pitch up.

I left Glenn to it, did a pit stop in the cloakroom, and then headed into the kitchen to put the coffee on. This time, I *had* fallen asleep in the jacket, and I made a mental note to send it to the dry cleaners at some point. It was then that I clocked that although *SVU* was still *DUN-DUN*-ing on the laptop, Leah wasn't on the couch. But instead of a *maybe she's gone for good this time!* hope-blip, in came a wave of anxiety. I eventually found her standing on the back porch, glaring at Glenn. He and his industrial-sized strimmer had already felled several ranks of the weed army, and the roar it made was more intrusive than the collective yaps of fifty Petticoats. How come he and Janet could handle that and not a bit of barking?

The Mum-robin appeared and hopped onto the cake. Considering what my mother had been planning to do to Leah, I was grateful I hadn't told her about my dead-mother's-soul-in-a-bird concept, but in any case, her attention was focused elsewhere. I was about to head back in to decant Brian's brunch, when she flinched and then paced at speed towards the chestnut tree.

Thanks to Glenn's efforts, the stone bench underneath it was now partially visible, and Leah dropped to her haunches next to it. Then she looked over her shoulder and called: *Neevy!*

The shock that she'd called me by my name at all, and *Neevy*, not Niamh, was so great that it took me a second to recalibrate. Then I ran over to join her. 'What is it?'

She nodded at a tangle of decapitated foliage, and as I crouched down next to her, my eyes snagged on the flash of pink nestled within it. 'Oh my *God.*'

We'd finally found Mum's phone, which – fortunately – *was* still in the fuchsia waterproof case that I'd given to her.

I disentangled it and wiped it on my sleeve. Hopefully the case and the weed army had done enough to protect it from the elements. I must've looked as shocked as I felt, because Glenn turned off his weapon and called, 'Everything all right over there, Nina?'

'All good thanks, Glenn.'

'What you got there, pet?'

'My mum's phone. I've been looking everywhere for it.'

'You're lucky I didn't catch it with the strimmer.' Then he rolled his shoulders and got back to business.

PREDATOR

Fortunately, I hadn't bothered to tidy away the charger that I'd used on the Wanker's macaroni phone, and despite the tsunami of adrenaline, it only took me two tries to insert it into the iPhone's port (I also realised that it was a far older model than the one we'd found next to the hot tub – once again, my lack of attention to detail had been responsible for sending us chasing after another red herring).

'This might not work. It's been lying out there for ages.'

We won't know till we try.

I waited for it to juice up for a bit, and then said, 'Here goes nothing.'

It blinked into life, but the relief was short-lived. 'Shite. The passcode.' But I took a punt and tried '1234', which worked. FFS.

I scrolled through the contents – it seemed my mother had also been in the habit of clearing out her phone regularly too, and there was very little on it apart from some spam, a 'Brian-speak' message to GinnyRebel's 'Rebel', which I skipped over hastily because I'd done enough vomiting for one week, and . . .

'Oh.' In drafts was a single unsent voice note meant for me. And according to the timestamp, it had been recorded

347

ten minutes after Mum had sent the pivotal protagonist-murder message. 'I'm not sure we should listen to this. I mean, what if it's worse than the murdering-you one?'

Do it.

Without bothering to steel myself for a kark-fest, I did it:

"'Hiya Neevy. Look. Just ignore what I said about killing Leah off. I didn't mean it. I was just venting. Fact is—'"

I pressed pause. 'She wasn't going to kill you after all!'

Keep going.

'Don't you need a minute?' *I* did. In fact, my first thought when I'd heard those words was, *oh thank God,* which was such a U-turn from where Leah and I had started out, I'd almost laughed.

No. Keep going. But I didn't miss the hint of relief in her voice.

I pressed 'play' again:

"'—I've been a bit down. More than down. Caro gave me a right talking-to about seeing a menopause specialist. I thought that might be what was going on, but I didn't think it'd be as bad as this. Funnily enough, it's given me more of a perspective on how you must feel some of the time. Sorry to load this on you and to . . .'"

Mum's words trailed off. Then she gasped.

The sound of a fist knocking on glass . . .

Faint footsteps on wood . . .

The creak of the back door opening . . .

Then Mum shouting: 'Oi! What the hell are you doing?'

In the background, a faint male voice: 'I thought you were away.'

I knew that voice. Leah did too.

Mum yelling: 'Get down from there!'

The sound of exertion, a grunt, and then the phone went dead.

From behind me came: 'It was an accident, pet.'

Both Leah and I jumped, and I whirled around. Without Leah noticing that we had company for once, Glenn had snuck into the cottage and was standing in the doorway that led into the boot room.

A glimmer of what looked very much like fear came into Leah's eyes. ***You need to get out of here, Neevy.***

She was right of course, but the shock of discovering that Mum's accident really hadn't been an accident after all, and the horror of being just metres away from her murderer, were both so intense that I could barely breathe, never mind move. Yet, despite this, my brain decided to latch onto a relatively unimportant consideration: *No wonder Leah always treated Glenn with exaggerated suspicion – her gut must've told her that he was the perp all along.*

God knows how long I would've stood there like a hobbit-sized mannequin if Leah hadn't then CLICKed as if her life depended on it, which it didn't, although mine did because Glenn was now in the kitchen. I sparked into life, grabbed the trusty wooden spoon from the butcher's block and brandished it at him. 'Stay back.'

'Calm down, pet. Let me explain.'

He's stalling. Run!

'That chestnut tree. It was messing with the satellite signal, see. I'd just popped over to trim a couple of branches, like.'

'Hang on . . . weren't you at the theatre?'

'We were. It was a matinee, but . . .'

He's stalling. Get out of here!

I knew Leah was right, but I needed to hear what he had to say.

'She went up the ladder after me, but things got out of hand. She fell, hit her head on that bench. I could see it was bad. I'd asked her to cut the tree back, see, but she said the birds were nesting in it. I'd asked her loads of times.'

A burst of anger so pure, it eradicated the fear and shock. 'Are you trying to blame *Mum* for this?'

Glenn took a step towards me and held up his hands. 'Now, now. There's no need to get heated.'

'Why didn't you just say it was an accident? You were in the *police*.'

You know why he didn't.

Then I went cold. No. Freezing. 'She wasn't dead, was she? But instead of calling an ambulance and running the risk that she'd survive and then do you for assault, you moved her and made it look like a—'

RUN! It was this that snapped me out of it. Leah *never* shouted. Remaining calm in stressful situations was another one of her traits.

But before I could do that, Glenn darted forward to grab the phone and I threw the wooden spoon at his head. It made a satisfying meaty *thwack!* as it hit his forehead, and he flailed back.

I skirted around him, bolted into the boot room, and made for the back door.

I fled out onto the porch, which was when I tripped over Sheila's cake, and then—

FINAL DESTINATION

Dead. Dead. Dead.

No. Can't be. I can smell something. Blood. Not just blood: the acrid stench of vomit too.

Then: *Boom* – a sickening throb deep inside my head, as if my brain was too large to fit inside my skull.

I opened my eyes, but all I could see were vague, shadowy shapes that could've been anything.

Breathe.

Can't. There was something pressing against my mouth. *Can't breathe, can't breathe, can't breathe.* A surge of panic, and another wave of that poisonous throbbing. Then a little voice whispered: *you're breathing through your nose. That's why you're not dead yet.*

'Leah,' I tried to say, but nothing came out because my lips couldn't move. *Leah. I need you.*

No Leah.

I tried to lift my head, but it felt as heavy as Sheila's cake, and doing it brought on a surge of nausea. Despite this, in came: *there is* literally *no way that when you've hurt your head this badly you can just carry on like normal.*

I blinked, blinked again, and gradually my vison cleared. I appeared to be sitting in the passenger seat of a car.

Why am I in a car?

No. Not just any car. The Mini. *Why am I in Mum's Mini?*

Through the windscreen I could make out the outline of what looked to be shelves. I tried to bring my hands up to my face to wipe my eyes, but they didn't seem to want to move, and my fingers felt tingly and useless. I blinked again. Now I could discern a huge pack of green and yellow washing-up sponges, and tubs of bird food. *I'm in the garage. Why am I in Mum's Mini in the garage? I never park it in the garage.*

I tried lifting my arms again and this time I managed to heft them high enough to see why they felt weird – my wrists were bound together with a zip-tie.

In came another surge of fear-fuelled adrenaline, but fortunately, this time it had the side effect of banishing some of the woolliness.

A clunk came from outside the car.

Leah. Leah!

Another CLUNK. Then the scuff of footsteps.

Oh God oh God oh God. LEAH!

You're on your own. She can't help you.

But no. Even if she couldn't be here, she *could* help me because: *What Would Leah Do?*

What *would* she do in this situation?

She'd—

Play dead.

That's right. She'd play dead and bide her time. She always gathered *valuable intel* before she made a move.

The footsteps were coming closer.

Don't panic. Play dead. Just like Leah did in the prologue of Overlooked *when she was in that shallow grave.*

The driver's door opened, and I could sense someone sliding in next to me. 'Won't be long now, pet.'

The molecules around me shifted. Glenn was very close to me – probably double-checking that I was still out cold. *Play dead play dead play dead.*

The air around me seemed to empty.

Then the engine fired into life, along with Abba's 'Take a Chance on Me'.

Was he planning to drive me somewhere?

The crump of the car door closing.

More footsteps, although it was harder to hear them over the music and grumble of the engine.

Another smell wafted my way: acrid, bitter smoke, undercut with the stench of petrol. *Exhaust fumes.*

Oh *shite*.

The creak of the garage's main door opening, a few seconds of brighter light, then SLAM.

I sniffed in a shallow nose breath, held it, and turned my head to the right – the end of a hosepipe was peeking through the top of the driver's side window, sealed in with gaffer tape.

And then I got it: Glenn was trying to murder me and make it look like a suicide. *OH, COME ON.*

'Take a Chance on Me' drifted into 'Mamma Mia', and despite everything, I couldn't help thinking, *that's a bit on the nose, isn't it?*

Now what? Should I crawl across and turn off the engine?

No!

No is right. Glenn wouldn't be able to stay in the garage to check on my death progress, but he'd be lurking close by to make sure that I didn't come to and squirrel out of the car, and if the engine died, then I'd alert him.

So.

So.

Now what?

You know what to do.

I did. I actually *did*.

Because there were two things about me that were so far out of the realms of normalcy that they wouldn't have occurred to Glenn (or anyone). Thanks to Mum, I knew how to break out of zip-ties – we'd spent hours and hours researching how to do it, after all – and my lady jacket had an unusually practical inside pocket, in which I kept my phone. Was it still in there? My fingers were now almost completely numb, but by pressing my forearms against my chest, I could just about make out its hard, blocky shape.

Okay. So:

Stay calm.

Exit the car.

Break free of restraints.

Retrieve the phone.

Call the police.

Exit the garage.

The only exits were the main garage door or the one that led into the boot room. He could be waiting outside either, but I decided to pick the little one. If I made it through there, then I knew exactly where to go.

I waited for the 'Mamma Mia, here I go again' chorus, then batted at the door latch with my floppy hands. The feel of the metal brought enough life back into them to allow me to grip it. But it just flapped ineffectually. *Oh god, oh god oh god, if this were a horror film, this is exactly what would happen and—*

Don't panic. You're not in a horror film. You're in a true-crime story.

Then:

There are no child locks on the driver's side.

Right. Of course there weren't. Children didn't drive, and if they did, they shouldn't.

The fumes were now so potent that my nostrils were burning, but I shuffle-crept across to the driver's side, thunking my poor old cake-brain against the headrest in the process.

I gripped the handle – *here goes nothing* – and pulled, hearing the *riiiiiip* of the tape as the door opened. I stumbled out, reeling like a drunkard. I sucked in air, then the fumes began to leak into the garage too.

I went to close the car door, then:

No! He might hear that.

Good point.

Next: Break free of restraints.

To get out of the zip-tie and call the police, I needed my teeth *and* my voice. I managed to get my fingertips to latch onto the end of the tape covering my mouth and yanked it off – my brain side-thinking: *Jesus, waxing hurts like shit, why do people do it?* I accidentally breathed in deeply then, the world tipped and began to drift out of focus, and in desperation I imagined a furious *CLICKCLICKCLICK*.

It helped.

What now? *Come on, come on, come on . . .*

Tighten the zip-tie's locking mechanism as tight as you can.

Of course – I remembered thinking, *that seems like a counterintuitive thing to do* when Mum and I were doing our zip-tie research. What next?

Raise your hands above your head and spread your elbows as far as they'll go.

Easier said than done – my balance was off-kilter. But somehow, I did it without falling over.

Now thrust down as hard as you can.

I did that too. But all that happened was that I wobbled into one of the shelves. I didn't have the strength to do it with enough force. But I'd have to – I couldn't feel my fingers at all now, and I needed them to extract the phone from my pocket.

Don't panic. You've got this. Try again.

Then the music suddenly cut out, and a few seconds later, the car sputtered and died – it had run out of petrol. Neither Glenn nor I had factored in that being crap was another of my special skills.

Behind me, I heard a creak as the big door began to open. I'd only have seconds now, not minutes.

Try again. Pretend you're going for Glenn's throat.

Okay, one, two, three: I brought my hands down . . . and *snap!*

GO!

I lurched for the connecting door, and somehow managed to open it. A few metres away was my cloakroom sanctuary. And even though I knew that Glenn was just moments behind me, before I threw myself in there, I hesitated: it was the one place that Leah – even the Leah who was just in my head – couldn't follow.

A TALE OF TWO SISTERS

According to Daphne, the first thing I said when I came to was, 'where's Leah?' Because *Daphne* was there, *my father* was there – well, not literally, he was getting a latte from the hospital's café at that exact moment – but Leah wasn't. And according to my father, after that I'd sobbed for quite a long time, which everyone assumed was caused by the trauma of tripping over a cake, sustaining a nasty concussion, and narrowly avoiding being murdered by a neighbour.

My father and Daphne had to fill in the blanks because not being a fictional character, I couldn't get knocked out and then breathe in fuck-tons of carbon monoxide without my memory taking a serious beating. Apparently, shortly after locking myself in my sanctuary and calling 999, I'd passed out again, and I was so out of it that the police had to kick the door in (before I was discharged Daphne asked Ivan the handyman to fix it – fortunately, he's in remission and his prognosis is positive).

Apart from that, life, it turns out, sometimes *is* stranger than fiction. As if by design, well, not *design*, because you couldn't make this shite up, the perp had been right there, all along, in the first third of the story. The rest had been one giant red herring. Or loads of smaller, uneventful but preposterous ones.

It even had a twist, seeing as it hadn't just been a grief quest after all. Although it had been one of those too, even if all I'd learned was that the pain doesn't go away, you just get better at dealing with it, and you can't get better at that if you avoid it (which is something I could have found out by reading the first lines of one of Jamie's grief blogs).

Leah's gut had been right *and* wrong about the murder element in Mum's case. Well, sort of, because second-degree murder was still murder (it wasn't first-degree because although Glenn had been intent on murdering the chestnut tree that night, he hadn't intended to murder my mother – that had come later). But she'd been right about my mother's death not being an accident, and right about the feud element. Because it had all kicked off when Mum had refused to trim the branches that were interfering with both Janet's reality telly addiction and Glenn's obsession with keeping his garden free of current and future leaf debris. Which, if you think about it, was all Augustus and his gang's fault because according to Glenn's confession, the reason Mum had refused to mutilate the tree was because the birds were nesting in it. Not that I blamed the birds obviously, because, like the weeds, why shouldn't they come first?

Clearly, I couldn't tell Daphne, my father, and the police the whole truth because as far as they were concerned, I'd just stumbled across my mother's phone in the garden, listened to an unsent voice message and fallen foul of a panicking, corrupt ex-police officer (unsurprisingly, Glenn had been a crooked cop as well as a crap one). In any case, Daphne was already beside herself with worry that I'd be permanently traumatised, and bringing Leah into the picture wouldn't exactly help with that.

According to my family liaison officer, who I quite liked because he reminded of Jed, my mother's inquest would have to be postponed until the police had finished with all their bureaucracy, which I might've been relieved about if I hadn't been forced to stop my campaign of grief-avoidance. Nor would there be a trial in my case because the evidence against Glenn was so overwhelming that he had no choice but to plead guilty. Not only had his attempt at making a murder look like suicide been caught on the Wanker's cameras, but Janet – who it turned out didn't suffer from headaches but severe depression caused by being married to Glenn – had refused to provide him with an alibi for either of his crimes. According to the postie, Pam and Elaine from the shoppe, and the man who delivered the heating oil, after being cleared by the police Janet immediately moved back to Newcastle to live with her sister, who hopefully has a home with very large windows and unlimited broadband.

After I was discharged from hospital, Daphne and Dad stayed with me for several days. Daphne tried to convince me to move in with her and Dad in Cornwall, which I absolutely wasn't going to do – not because that was where I'd been when I heard the news about my mother or because the wifi there was shite, but because I now thought of the cottage as home. In any case, Tracey was planning to move into the manor to keep an eye on Sheila's drinking, and she promised Daphne that she'd keep an eye on me too. And the day after I'd been discharged, a box containing a ring camera system appeared outside the kitchen door. There was no note with it, but it could only have come from one person (I still thought he was a wanker, though).

Spending time with my father gave me the opportunity to solve yet another minor mystery, although he was initially confused when I asked him to explain the intended meaning behind the cloakroom's painting.

'Meaning? What do you mean by "meaning"?'

'Well, I was wondering if the women's husband-slash-father is supposed to be on that ship in the distance.'

'Ah, I see. Yes. Yes, he is.'

'So, they're basically about to watch him drown, then?'

'Drown? *Drown*? The ship's not sinking. They're watching him sail away on a great adventure.'

'Oh right.' *Should have known.* I moved it into the kitchen anyway – I needed something to cover the stain now that the murder wall was in the recycling bin.

Just before they returned to Cornwall, I gave Daphne and Dad a hug, which surprised all three of us, thanked Daphne for having my back, and told her that although I didn't think grief journeys ever ended, grief quests did (I *almost* asked her what she saw in my father, but decided against it – not every mystery could be wrapped up, and in any case, I now felt a lot warmer towards him and his art).

The first thing I did when they left was get out the Henry Hoover. *Come on, you old pervert.* And although it was upsetting, the memory of my mother's vacuum-related banter was comforting too, because people can live on in our minds even if they're not here physically. Which, if I was sentimental, would be another good place to end this story.

But because I'm not, and because this is real life, instead of the shitshow resulting in me 'experiencing personal growth', 'opting back into normal society', and 'doing something with my life', Brian and I slid back into our old ways. Well, mostly. As well as our usual time-sucking activities, I spent quite a lot of time sitting on the porch watching the birds, attempting to extract gardening tips from Sheila (I was understandably keen to stay on her good side), and visiting Thelma with Petticoat. And the following month, when Saturday rolled around, I drove to Luxton, got stoned in a graveyard with Jamie, and we both talked about our mothers.

All of which would've been *fine* if it weren't for the fact that Leah had also been right about what would happen when the unfinished business was finished.

Relationships are complicated and contradictory and painful and irritating and exhausting. And Leah was all those things, as well as patronising, but I *missed* her. Not as much as I missed Mum, but there was a finality to that which felt different somehow. Well, either I missed Leah, or like Petticoat, I had a chronic case of Stockholm syndrome. Nor did I care if she was a muse, an unusually detailed hallucination, or a fictional character who'd stepped off the page and into the parts of a story that – as GinnyRebel had pointed out – you don't usually get to read about. Because she'd been real to me. *Was* real to me.

But anyway, there was only one thing I could do about that.

How to Kill a Crime Writer

A PI Leah Rebecca Overton adaptation

by

N. Morrissey & L. Overton

EXT. LEAH'S FANCY LOFT APARTMENT BUILDING
– NIGHT/EST
The sort of stillness you only get when
the world is sleeping. A Twix wrapper
tumbleweeds along an empty pavement. A

BLACK CAT WITH ONE WHITE PAW hops down
from his perch on top of a recycling bin
and bats at it.

INT. LEAH'S FANCY LOFT APARTMENT - NIGHT
The moonlight shining through the window
bathes the space in a bluish light. A
single uncomfortable couch. No flatscreen.
A kitchen that resembles a morgue.

The front door opens and LEAH (late
twenties, wearing a suit that urgently
needs dry-cleaning) enters cautiously. She
flicks the light switch. Nothing. *Someone
must've tripped the breaker.*

                    LEAH
      If someone's here, show
      yourself.
      I'm warning you. I've got a
      Zippo in my pocket and I'm not
      afraid to use it.

Moving like a cat - not a domestic one -
Leah paces along the corridor . . .

INT. LEAH'S FANCY LOFT APARTMENT/BEDROOM -
NIGHT
Leah enters this room cautiously too.
Frowns. *Hang on* . . . there's a strange
door that she hasn't noticed before. She
creeps towards it. Takes a breath. Yanks
it open. Inside it is a GLEAMING LAVATORY

(one of those expensive Japanese ones).
She gasps and

CLICK.

Then: *Hilarious.*

I whirled around in Mum's chair. No: *My* chair. There she was: arms folded; eyebrow cocked. A kark slipped out, followed by a laugh of relief. 'Where have you been?'

In the protagonists' holding cell, course.

'Give over.'

Leah smiled, without needing an adverb for once. I noticed then that although her hair was freshly trimmed, and her suit was ash-free, under her jacket she was wearing a T-shirt with a 'Hold on, I've Just Seen a Cat' slogan on it.

'So.'

So.

'If we're going to do this – properly, I mean – we should probably put some ground rules in place *before* we begin.'

Fine by me.

'One: If you *do* decide you want to hook up with Amara, then I'm bringing GinnyRebel in as a romance consultant. Online only though, so that we don't have to deal with Nice Leah.'

An eye-roll, although she did look a bit chuffed about the romance part.

'Two: You can't be around me twenty-four-seven like before. I'll need some downtime so that I don't burn out.'

You're not the only one.

'Three: you should probably teach me to fight in case I ever run into someone like Glenn again, even though I'll be crap at it.'

This *really* seemed to please her. *You won't be crap at throat-punching when I'm finished with you.*

'And then there's the most serious and urgent issue of all.'

A hint of anxiety. She was *definitely* becoming more like me. *Go on.*

I let a few seconds tick by – I was *definitely* becoming more like her, too: 'What the fuck are we going to name your new cat?'

And then, for the first time in this story and possibly ever, Leah Rebecca Overton laughed.

AUTHOR'S NOTE AND ACKNOWLEDGEMENTS

First, an apology. I don't usually do what I'm about to do, but this book was born out of a very particular set of circumstances, and for some reason I feel the need to explain why I wrote it, so here goes:

In 2022 I published a novel called *Impossible* (or *The Impossible Us* if you're stateside), and at the end of the acknowledgements, I wrote this:

To Savannah Lotz and Charlie Martins: Thank you for being there. In this world and others, it's impossible to imagine a life without you.

Just before the book went to print, my publishers asked me if I wanted to change that sentence. The reason being that in October 2021, my husband Charlie died suddenly and unexpectedly. He was 54.

I said no, because I meant every word of it and the sentiment still stood (it still stands).

Charlie had a quirky and sometimes obscure sense of humour. Did hardcore motorbike enduro racing for fun. Could spend hours sitting on the porch watching the birds in the garden. Was once known as the 'worst dressed lawyer in Cape Town'. Loathed Donald Trump and George W. Bush with a passion. Spent years trying to get a class action suit together against the UK and US governments for atrocities committed during the Iraq War. Could be grumpy as fuck but always for a good reason. Loved sweets, especially liquorice. Fell asleep on the couch every Sunday while watching the Grand Prix. Swore like a trooper. Adored the landscapes of Namibia and Botswana. Couldn't get enough of David Bowie, Queen, and Pink Floyd. Could endlessly re-watch *Better Call Saul*, *The Big Lebowski*, and *Withnail and I*. Didn't suffer fools. Was a tough-but-fair father and stepfather who showed love with actions, not words. And he *never* backed down from a fight. There's a lot more I could say about who Charlie was and what he stood for, but the following sums it up: after he died, I received countless emails from mutual friends, strangers and clients who, without any fanfare and without my knowledge, he'd helped with various legal issues pro bono.

Integrity and kindness were everything to him, and he was everything to me.

Charlie wasn't just my husband; he was my best friend, confidant, partner in crime, and the person who 'got' me (and I'm a fucking weirdo, so when we met, I couldn't believe my luck – I still can't). This is not the place to go into what it feels like to lose your person, except to say that I am no longer cynical about the term 'soul mate' and I now believe that it's possible to die from a broken heart. The other day I told my fabulous, stalwart friend Alan that I feel like a swan who's lost its mate, and after a perfectly timed pause, he said, very softly, 'I think you mean a penguin' (thank *fuck* for friends with wonderful senses of humour).

Charlie didn't just recognise that writing fiction was the thing I loved doing above all else, he clocked that it was something I *had* to do, and without his encouragement, I wouldn't have had the courage or confidence to pursue it as a career. He dragged me out of my writing shed at one a.m., listened patiently as I bored on about plot points, and was always up for a batshit research trip. These included sneaking around the underbelly of a particularly grim cruise ship; a hastily planned excursion to China, Nepal, Tibet, and Everest base camp; and a hardcore caving expedition in South Wales (there's a clip of this one on YouTube – in it you'll see Charlie effortlessly scaling a sheer, underground cliff-face and loving every second of it, and me being winched down it while sobbing like a terrified child and begging for Haribos).

Charlie was also the first person who read the first draft of a manuscript. He would do this on our bed, propped up with pillows, red pen in hand, and I would hide in the stairwell and spy on him, popping up every so often to ask him which bit had just made him laugh – or tut. He was never afraid to tell me when something I'd written was shite, and I trusted his opinion unreservedly.

Impossible is a speculative romcom, and because I had a two-book deal and a lot of rescue dogs to feed, I had to write a follow-up. Another romcom was out of the question for obvious reasons, and although my comfort zone is the horror genre, that felt too on the nose. I spent over two years starting book after book – 167,000 words of non-books to be precise – discarding each one at around the 40K mark. I write every day whether I feel like it or not, it's what I've felt compelled to do since I was seven years old, and I've never had a problem finishing anything before. Part of it was caused by the terror of that empty space on the bed: *if you finish a book, he won't be there to read it*. Part of it was because a voice at the back of my head kept insisting, *you've just been through something cataclysmic, and you need to write about it.* But I couldn't write about losing Charlie – too soon, too raw, and in any case, I didn't have the words or talent to do it justice. A subject as complex and universal as grief and loss is best left to poets and writers far above my pay grade (my recommendations are the unparalleled Patrick Ness and Max Porter).

I live in a cottage very like Niamh's with my daughter Savannah and stepdaughter S. J. (although to me, she isn't a 'step' anything), and my endless book angst was driving the girls and the dogs round the twist. And it was while I was pacing annoyingly around the cottage at three a.m. that the seed of an idea began to sprout. Because I've spent most of my life living alongside people who don't exist in this reality, I've always had a thing for the 'fictional characters coming to life' trope, and one night, I mentioned this to Sav. Was there a way of tying this trope into a non-maudlin grief narrative of sorts? To give me enough distance to tackle the subject, Sav suggested that I funnel the story via the POV of a millennial who'd lost a parent. As she pointed out, it's a loss that most of us will face at some stage, even though we'd much rather not. Although my mind is as wonky-wheeled as Niamh's, I'm her mother's age, so Sav and S. J. kindly offered to act as my 'Millennial Consultants' (how's that for life imitating art or vice versa?). Being far more insightful than me, Sav had also recognised that writing about the death of an author who leaves a daughter behind might also help me work through my fear and anxiety about accidentally pegging it and leaving the girls with no back-up and a giant mess to clean up (that's the other thing about unexpected loss, it can make you hypervigilant and an absolute pain in the arse to be around). It did help a bit, although I won't be fixing the guttering anytime soon (ironically, it does need fixing; our cottage is basically held together with dog hair and hope). And because black humour is how our family copes with anything and everything, this distance would give me the licence to play with that too.

It also gave me the opportunity to write a love letter of sorts to crime fiction and horror films, both of which kept me company during countless sleepless nights. Using a murder mystery as the vehicle for a grief narrative isn't unique, but it was challenging and fun – something in short supply at the time. And because I've always used horror as a cathartic way of experiencing 'safe fear' and processing trauma responses, every chapter starts with the title of a horror film or series, all of which I watched or rewatched after Charlie died.

At the risk of boring on, exacerbating the mental fuckery was the onset of perimenopause. Despite this being something that will affect over half of the world's population at some stage, I had no idea that it can have over forty symptoms (nor, unfortunately, did my doctors). Everyone knows about hot flashes and night sweats, but like Niamh's mother Annie, my symptoms were relatively lesser known and manifested as anxiety, insomnia, disassociation, suicidal ideation, aching joints, and debilitating brain fog (which, for any gamers out there, feels a bit like being plunged into the disorientating, gloopy realm of the *Silent Hill* remake, with the added horror of not being able to remember why you went in there in the first place). The doctors I consulted brushed me off with *no hot flashes? Then it can't be menopause, love. Here, have some SSRIs and STFU.* My friends Helen and Kate staged an intervention and told me to get some HRT *stat*. Within 48 hours of slapping on an oestrogen

Sarah Lotz

patch, the back, shoulder, and neck pain that had been plaguing me for five years disappeared. Then the gloop dissipated, and the lights began to come back on. I'm mentioning this here in case anyone reading this is currently in the same disconcerting boat. Fortunately, there are now more online resources available, so whether HRT is an option for you or not, if you are taking strain, please don't feel you have to 'muddle through' alone – we all know that if men suffered from menopause, there'd be vending machines dispensing free hormones on every fucking corner. (Incidentally, I found Reddit's r/menopause sub to be particularly helpful – the group's members are supportive, kind, brutally honest, unjudgemental, and often hilarious.)

If you managed to get through that, thank you for letting me be self-indulgent. Here's the acknowledgement part.

Multiple shedloads of gratitude go to:

Kate Sinclair, who, despite tragically losing her own 'best beloved' three months after Charlie died, somehow still managed to be a tireless book cheerleader and a fiercely kind and protective friend. This is a woman who read the first draft of the book while trying to make sense of her own smashed heart *and* while doing the Camino, and who had the generosity of spirit to let me know which bits she found funny along the route. The Thelma bits are for you, Kate – you know why.

Helen Moffett, who, despite spinning more life and work plates than a three-ring circus, read countless non-book drafts, and had the kindness and bravery to 'do a Charlie' and tell me that I'd fucked up this novel's rewrites (she didn't actually use the term 'fucked up' – unlike me, Helen is pure class). Then, she swept in like a one-woman SAS-style editing rescue squad and helped me fix it. This is a woman who, without being asked, took on the mammoth task of checking the *Impossible* proofs because she knew that doing so would finish me off. The Brian bits are for you, Helen – you know why.

Paige Nick, who, despite also being bereaved, busy writing her own (superb) novel, and running a business, also read countless non-book drafts, generously gave me Mr C's secret recipe for Napolitana sauce, *and* hopped on a plane from Cape Town to mop up me, the girls, and the cottage. This is a woman who doesn't just notice that a fucked-up friend's fridge light is broken, but quietly replaces it (I don't think there's an act of love and kindness more eloquent than that). The pasta-making men-in-underpants bits are for you – you know why.

My brilliant mum, Carol Walters, who read one of the fucked-up rewrite drafts and yet amazingly, is still talking to me. I hope you like this version better, Mum. The hamlet bits are for you – you know why.

My brilliant brother Si, who had my back and made me laugh when I needed it most. The Hannibal Lecter bits are for you – you know why.

My brilliant brother Nige and sister-in-law Gemma, both of whom are human equivalents of back-up hard drives. The Petticoat bits are for you – you'll be able to guess why.

My brilliant agent Oli Munson, who over the years (and it's been a lot of years) has put up with a lot of shite with grace, kindness, and good humour. The Caro bits *aren't* for you, Oli – you deserve far better than that.

My editors Charlotte Brabbin (HarperCollins UK) and Sareer Khader (Berkeley, Penguin Random House US). I know this isn't the book you wanted me to write, and it might not be the book anyone wants to read, but thank you for letting me do it and for being so kind and endlessly patient.

Everyone at HarperCollins, A. M. Heath and Berkeley.

And to my Grey Gardens housemates, Savannah and S. J., who I hope will always be the Leah to each other's Niamh (and vice versa). Thank you for 'bringing me back to life' (I'm just sorry it took longer than 23 seconds), and remember that if all else fails, we can always become a family of travelling acrobats. The entirety of this book is for you – you know why. And you also know what I'm going to say next: Thank you for being there. In this world and others, it's impossible to imagine a life without you.